034016190

D0280108

*LONG ACRE*
*BOOK VI OF*
*THE PERFORMERS*

*Long Acre* is the sixth novel in Claire Rayner's
sequence *The Performers* in which she will
follow the fortunes of two families through
succeeding generations from the beginning of
the nineteenth century into the twentieth. It
tells the story of Amy and Fenton Lucas,
grandchildren of the famous star of the theatre
Lilith Lucas.

Amy and her brother Fenton were born in
Boston, Massachusetts, after Lilith's son had
emigrated to America more than twenty years
before this tale begins. They arrive as orphans
in the London of the 1860s determined to find
fame and fortune on the stage. But for Amy
there is another deeper quest which is destined
to set ablaze the embers of a family feud
which has flared and smouldered through forty
years. Her search for her forebears and her
present relations inevitably brings her into a
family conflict which she cannot understand
and refuses to accept. But it brings her, also, a
passionate attachment to a young man whose
connections with both families lie in faraway
places.

Also in Arrow by Claire Rayner

THE RUNNING YEARS
FAMILY CHORUS

## THE PERFORMERS

# Long Acre

## Book VI of

## The Performers

Claire Rayner

ARROW BOOKS

Arrow Books Limited
62-65 Chandos Place, London WC2N 4NW

An imprint of Century Hutchinson Limited

London Melbourne Sydney Auckland
Johannesburg and agencies throughout
the world

First published in Great Britain
by Cassell & Co. Ltd 1978
Reprinted 1979
Corgi edition 1980
Weidenfeld & Nicolson edition 1982
Arrow edition 1986

© Claire Rayner 1978

Printed and bound in Great Britain by
Anchor Brendon Limited, Tiptree, Essex

ISBN 0 09 944400 3    034016190

For Joan Chapman
with gratitude for her ever-patient rusty shoulder

# FAMILY TREE I

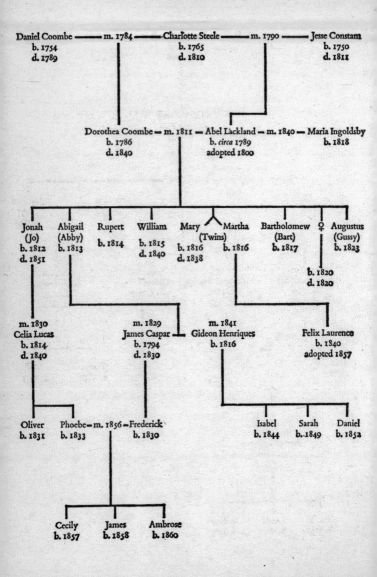

# FAMILY TREE II

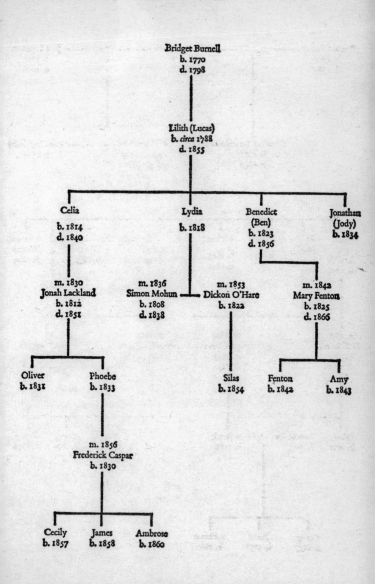

# CHAPTER ONE

The mist lay low on the river, melting the hulls of the tangled shipping that cluttered the banks on both sides to a gentle shifting greyness. Above it rose the masts, aloof and slender and festooned with rigging, some of them with a badly furled sail or two flapping mournfully in the occasional breath of wind that moved across from the northern bank to the southern. From away down river came the distant bleat of foghorns, and in the intervals of their melancholy cries could be heard the shrieking of the gulls, swooping low over the fish market at Billingsgate, searching for fish guts and scrapings. The air smelled of rotting wood, dead fish, mud and oil and smoke.

'Altogether,' thought Amy, shivering and pulling her cloak more tightly about her, 'it looks very dismal. I ought to feel dismal too—'

But she did not. She was cold, she was more than a little hungry, and she was very tired, for all night there had been noise and scrapings and swayings as the steam tugs had been made fast to the *Daniel Boone* at Gravesend, and brought her slowly chugging up the river to St. Katherine's Dock. So, there had been little sleep for the steerage passengers. But despite all that and despite the gloom of the morning, Amy Lucas did not feel dismal. She was filled with an excitement so vast, was consumed with an anticipation so huge that she could almost forget the emptiness of her belly. After four weeks of bucketing across the Atlantic in a tiny creaking cargo ship smelling powerfully of cocoa butter and pepper, a particularly sickening combination, even St. Katherine's Dock in a mist seemed like Elysium.

She felt rather than heard Fenton behind her, and turned her head to peer up at him, and said breathlessly, 'Oh, Fenton, is it not *incredible*? We are here—we are actually *here*. I almost cannot believe it!'

'Keep your voice down,' Fenton said in a soft growl and came to stand beside her, and set down at her feet the two valises with which they had crept out of Boston all those weeks ago. 'Look here, Amy, you must do exactly as I say, do you hear me? When I give you the sign, pick up the two bags, and hide them under your cloak. Then I will follow you down the gangplank and keep curious eyes off you from behind. And when we reach the bottom, you must take a sharp turn to the left—there, can you see? Between those piles of sacks there seems to be a way through. I will take the valises from you as soon as we are out of sight of the ship, I promise you—'

She frowned at that. 'But, Fenton—my breakfast! I am very hungry—'

'Then you must stay hungry. Until we are ashore, that is. Come on, girl—don't be so stupid! We have little enough money, God knows. I see no sense in handing seventy dollars over to that captain to drink himself pie-eyed with when I have much better use to make of 'em!'

'But Fenton, we have travelled quite comfortable, you know. And it is always possible we may wish to go home again, and if we have mulcted this captain, will he not tell all the other shipping people here? It has happened to us before, that sort of thing—'

'I am not going home again. Not ever!' Fenton said shortly, and leaned on the rail beside her, his narrow green eyes never leaving the dock side below them. 'And I have no intention of paying him, whatever you say. So you may as well bite your tongue.'

And with the practice born of a lifetime as Fenton's sister, Amy bit her tongue. On that theme at least. Had she been asked to speak the total truth, she would have had to admit that she saw no real sin in attempting to deprive the captain of the remainder of the passage money due to him; her honesty as regarding material things was as hazy as her brother's. How could it be otherwise, when she adored him so, and looked up to him so, and admired his acumen so? If Fenton regarded such behaviour as right then she supposed she must too. But she was worried, a little, about the possibility of being apprehended in the act of so depriving the captain, for he had shown himself a formidable man in many ways during the long crossing, and, she shrewdly suspected, would not think twice about throwing not only their luggage but Fenton and herself head first into the greasy water now slapping the sides of the *Daniel Boone* far below them. But, with her usual sunny optimism she pushed her doubts away, and leaned on the rail beside Fenton, happily watching the bustle below them, and edging up close to him to feel the warmth of his body.

There was more to see now, as the late October sunshine at last struggled through the morning clouds of the eastern sky and began to shred the mist to nothingness. Now Amy could see upriver a good deal further, to the spread of chimneys and roofs and spires lifting above the river's traffic, and she clutched Fenton's arm suddenly and cried excitedly, 'Fenton! Look over there! Is that not St. Paul's Cathedral of which Papa used to speak? There—that dome there? It looks for all the world like a bubble that will float away—'

He looked and grimaced. 'Oh, Amy, there is no need to be so boring! You sound like all those dumb old cats that Mama used to sit and talk with who prosed on and on about their travels in Europe and seemed to have done nothing but visit cathedrals and ruins. We have not come to London for that! As for what Papa used to say—' he grinned suddenly, 'it was what he used to say about the theatres that I recall, not what he used to say about *cathedrals*.'

'Do you really think we shall find anyone who knew Papa?' Amy said, and now her face was suddenly sad and a little pinched and her eyes wide and imploring as she stared up at Fenton, and he laughed at her.

'Oh, don't look so woebegone, you silly creature!' he said. 'Papa has been dead these ten years, and still you come the tragedy queen when you speak of him! Save your acting for

11

the stage, when you have a job, my girl—don't waste it on me.'

She pouted then and laughed, her face at once lighting up. 'I cannot help it!' she protested. 'I have always had a very *speaking* countenance. My speach teacher Miss Farraday always said that I—'

'Oh, to the devil with Miss Farraday, and to the devil with everyone we ever knew in dreary old Boston and to the devil with dreary old Boston!' He picked her up in one muscular arm and swung her round, so that her feet left the deck and her head swirled, and she squealed with laughter, and looked up at him with the usual adoring expression now investing her wide grey eyes and pointed face. And he grinned back, so that his own face creased, and his narrow green eyes glittered, showing he was as filled with excitement and anticipation as she was. '*He's so handsome*,' Amy thought, filling with pride, '*so handsome everyone in London must surely be crazy about him*!' And she threw her arms about him and kissed his cheek, and he, as he so often did, changed his mood abruptly and put her down and pushed her away and told her not to be so mawkish.

The noise from the docks below began to build up as more and more men came to lounge about and stare at the new arrival, and Fenton glanced back over his shoulder at the hatch openings that led down to the bowels of the ship.

'They are opening up, Amy,' he said softly. 'And that means they are nearly ready to unload cargo. I cannot see easily from here—is there a clear way to the head of the gangplank? Walk along and look—but be careful, for Pete's sake. We don't want anyone smelling a rat.'

Obediently she turned, and pulling her cloak warmly about her strolled with great nonchalance up the deck towards the waist of the ship. One or two of the crewmen she passed leered at her, but she ignored that; they had been behaving so ever since they had left Boston Harbour, though it had gained them nothing. At the far side of the deck she could see the Captain, talking animatedly to one of the tugboat crewmen, and after a moment they both turned, still talking and waving their arms about, and went down the companionway that led to the captain's quarters.

12

Amy hurried back to the rail where Fenton was waiting. 'It's clear,' she said dropping her voice conspiratorially. 'I just saw the captain go down with one of those tugboat people to his cabin. They'll be drinking and shouting there for long enough, I reckon, if you're really *sure* you want to welch on him—though I do wish you would not. It could be—'

'Shut your trap, and come and take these—' He picked up the two heavy valises. 'Now, hold each one, so, and I'll tie your cloak across the front, so—there! Your cloak hides all—I knew it would. Now, you go ahead, and walk quietly down the gangplank, and remember—turn to the left at the bottom. I shall be close behind you.'

Once again she put on her insouciant expression, and once again turned to walk across the deck past the sweating deckhands, now beginning to manhandle malodorous barrels of cocoa butter up from the bowels of the ship. The valises were heavy, and slowed her down, and made it difficult to give an air of being just a casual stroller, and she turned her head to look appealingly at Fenton strolling along behind with his hat on the back of his head and his hands thrust deep in his trouser pockets so that his topcoat bunched out behind, but he scowled at her and jerked his head in the direction of the gangplank, and with a tiny sigh she went on.

But now, she used the trick she always used when faced with a disagreeable task: she pretended she was acting. In her mind's eye she set a proscenium arch around the ship, and a huge adoring audience in front of it, and conjured up within her the tension and excitement and the fear and the faint nausea that a performance always created in her. And then she could do it. She strolled across the deck, the valises feeling almost weightless, so unimportant were they now, swaying a little to give an impression of lightness and ease, and smiled bewitchingly at the deckhands and went smoothly on to the top of the gangplank.

Here her imagination strengthened, and it was as though she were treading a catwalk down, down, down, into the heart of her worshipping audience, and she looked from side to side with gentle inclinations of her head, almost as though she were bowing to them, and her smile widened and her eyes became even more lustrous, so that several of the stevedores waiting on the dock below stared at her with their mouths open. She was something very much worth staring at.

She remembered to turn left at the bottom—had she ever forgotten a stage move? Not Amy Lucas, not she!—and then she was between the towering piles of sacks, surrounded by the heavy reek of coffee, and Fenton was behind her and taking the valises from her hands.

'Good girl—you carried that off famously! Now come on—we'd best move fast—'

She blinked up at him, still lost in her fantasy, and he said impatiently, 'Come on, I said! Are you asleep? We may be ashore, but they could still catch up with us!' and he pushed her to one side far from gently, and led the way past the sacks of coffee, and another great stack of barrels, this time smelling of malt, and she went after him as fast as she could, stumbling and slipping occasionally on the wet wooden slats.

It was as though he had been living and working in these smelly shadowy docks for all his life. On all sides were heaps of barrels and bales and sacks and between them only the narrowest of passageways; yet he moved forwards unerringly, seeming to know precisely where he was going, and, breathless at his speed, she followed as best she might. Not once did he look back to see if she was there but then, she did not expect he would.

At last the heaps of cargo began to diminish, and the wood underfoot became cobblestones as he turned sharply right and began to climb a narrow roadway that ran up between tall dark warehouses. By now too breathless to pay much attention to anything but her own feelings, Amy toiled after him, her head down and her cloak and gown held high in each hand in an attempt to keep the hems out of the mud that plentifully streaked the cobbles. And at last arrived at the top to find they were in a fairly wide thoroughfare, teeming with people and traffic and noise.

'Well, what a fuss to make!' Fenton said coolly, as she leaned against the wall and gasped, and rubbed her damp red face with both hands. 'You're as much use as a baby, you are, making such heavy weather! It's small thanks to you we're seventy dollars richer than we would have been!'

She fired up at that. 'And *who* carried the luggage off the ship? *Who* got us off with never a whimper? Don't you speak to me so, or I'll—I'll—anyway—I am very tired, and very very hungry! Last night, when we ate dinner, you did not leave much for me, and—'

'Oh, let's not start that again! You should have come to your dinner sooner! Anyway, that is all done now. We've arrived!'

He lifted his head and looked around him, his chin up, and his hat set rakishly on the side of his head so that it showed his crisp dark curling hair to great advantage. 'No more of that miserable scrimping we've had to put up with for so long! We must settle ourselves in an hotel as soon as we can, and then we shall go and have a great blowout, and you will feel splendid! Trust me! First we must find ourselves a growler—that is what they call a four-wheeled cab in London, you know, and the drivers always know the best places to go—'

Amy, who had heard as many of their father's stories of London life as had Fenton, and had remembered just as much as he had, shook her head and grinned to herself, her good temper quite restored. She was never one to sulk, and she was amused by Fenton's little lecture on London ways. So she merely smiled at him, and pushed the hood of her cloak back on to her shoulders and followed him along the street, looking from side to side with great interest. And enjoyed not only what she saw but the reactions of passers-by who looked at them.

Used as they had both been all their lives at home in Boston to obvious admiration being paid to their good looks, she had not been quite sure that here in London, which was a bigger metropolis, they would be at all remarkable, and it gratified her a good deal to note that they were. Passing women looked with sudden interest at her brother's elegant profile—and Amy was the first to agree it was one of quite stunning male beauty—while the men tipped up their chins and narrowed their eyes in obvious approval of her own pert face and bobbing curls. '*It's going to be all right*,' she told herself. '*It's going to be all right*.' They would surely have big parts in a good production in no time, and be all set upon their new career. And she tucked her hand under Fenton's arm, despite the fact that he was still burdened with the two valises, and smiled up at him with pure delight.

He, concentrating on the matter in hand, ignored her in favour of a cab plying for hire across the crowded way and he shouted at the top of his voice, 'Hi! You there—c'mon over here!'

People within earshot turned and stared, and grinned, and now Amy was not pleased at all with the effect they were having. 'Be quiet, Fenton,' she hissed and pulled his sleeve. 'You are making a cake of yourself—perhaps they do not behave so in London—'

But he shook her off and waved, and now the cabman whipped up his horse and brought it wheeling across the traffic, to the accompaniment of much cursing from other drivers, to pull up beside them.

He looked down at them, and then sniffed and hawked and spat luxuriously over the side of his perch.

'An' where does you two fine Yankee birds want to go then?' he said and leered at Amy, who stared up at him in amazement.

'How did you know we come from Massachusetts?' she said wonderingly and the cabman stared at her and laughed. 'I ain't never 'eard o' no 'Chusetts, lady, but I knows a Yankee when I 'ears one. Especially when I 'ears one yellin' like that! Where're yer goin'?'

'The Albion Hotel in Great Russell Street!' Fenton said grandly. 'And put our luggage aloft, my man, at once!' And he dropped the two valises on the kerb and opened the door of the cab and handed Amy in with great style.

'How did you know where to ask for?' she whispered, as they sat side by side and listened to the grunts and snorts of the jarvey as he climbed down from his perch and loaded their bags on to the roof, and Fenton laughed and leaned back against the dusty squabs.

'Oh, I made inquiries, you know—around and about at home, before we left!' he said airily, 'and was told this was a good enough place, and would not cost us too much and was in a very good part of London for those seeking to be among actors. So, that is where we go!'

16

The jarvey at last whipped up his horses and the growler lurched and then gathered speed and Amy leaned forwards to stare eagerly out of the greasy window, her fatigue and hunger quite forgotten again.

The streets through which they were passing did not look very grand, she thought. And the people—she let her gaze travel across the mass of humanity thronging the sides of the road; men in the flat caps and short dark woollen coats of seamen; frailer, more bent men in neater but undoubtedly threadbare coats that denoted a life spent in clerkly affairs in dingy sooty offices, women in dull stuff gowns with shabby shawls about their heads, children in rags—these people did not look as she had imagined London people would look. In her many daydreams of how life would be in London she had seen it as elegant, if not positively wrapped in grandeur. She had imagined the men as handsome as her brother, the women as well endowed with beauty as herself. But these grey-faced creatures—these were not at all what she had expected.

But then the cab turned north, into another wider street, and now gradually, as it went at a spanking pace across the cobbles so that the two passengers were thrown up and down like balls in a basket and Amy had to hold on tightly to the loop of worn strap beside the window, the character of the area changed. The men she saw were more prosperous-looking, in dark rich coats and glossy top hats and with an air of importance about their bustling that was familiar to her. They looked, she thought, for all the world like her Mamma's brothers and cousins, those tedious Cabot and Fenton uncles who had tried so hard to stop the two young Lucases from living their lives in their own way—

Her lips curved reminiscently as she thought of it all, how she and Fenton had smiled so limpidly upon their careful cautious leathery old uncles and promised them with innocent smiles that yes, they would settle to a quiet life at home in Boston, after poor Mamma's funeral, and of course they would invest all their money as the uncles thought fit, of course they would. And how they—or rather Fenton—had gone about secretly selling the old house and converting the few poor stocks Mamma had left them into gold and eventually got them both a passage on a cargo ship making its first

17

landfall in Boston, after leaving Valparaiso on its way ultimately to London. The uncles must be beside themselves with rage, she thought gleefully, and stared again at the busy, important, clearly very pompous men bustling along on the pavements, and laughed aloud.

'This is the City, Amy,' Fenton said, staring out from his side of the cab as eagerly as she was. 'It is where the money men are—my Uncle Tobias has connections here and he is rich enough for ninety. One day—' he turned his head and grinned at Amy in the dimness of the dusty cab. 'One day, Amy, when I have made my packet, such men as those will bow and scrape to me as I drive past them in a carriage of such style as'll blind 'em. I'll show Uncle Tobias and the rest of those dried up twigs at home what Fenton Lucas can do!'

'Indeed you will, Fenton,' Amy said warmly. 'I know you will, and so shall I. I shall be the greatest actress the town ever saw, and I shall—'

'Yes,' Fenton said absently, staring again out of the window. 'My, Amy, but there's a lot going on here! Everywhere you look they're building something new! Oh, indeed and indeedy there's money to be made in this town!'

And Amy too stared and marvelled, for still the growler moved rapidly through street after street, each of which was clearly more genteel than the one before and each of which, as Fenton had said, showed evidence of vigorous rebuilding and lavish spending of money. London might turn out, she thought, to be much more bewildering than she had expected, and she yawned suddenly, and her belly rumbled and contracted, and she remembered just how tired and hungry she was.

At which point the cab stopped and Fenton jumped out, and stood on the pavement staring up at the building before which they stood. 'Albion Hotel' announced the facade, in well polished brass letters. 'Family Accommodation. Coffee Rooms. Smokers' Divan.'

Amy, climbing out of the cab behind him, looked up too, and the final flicker of her excited anticipation flared and then settled down, for this, at last, after the long weeks of scheming and cheating the uncles, the long weeks of travelling and dreaming and wondering, was the reality.

18

It was 20 October 1866, and they had arrived at their first home in London. And she bowed her head imperiously at the jarvey and then lifted her chin and swept up the pair of steps and in through the big mahogany doors.

## CHAPTER TWO

They sat side by side at the scrubbed wooden table, contemplating their empty dishes. They had put on a very creditable show of being languidly bored by the need to eat, ordering only a little crimped cod for the lady, and a rather heartier mutton chop for the gentleman, denying any desire for soup or bread or vegetables; but now it was eaten, Amy felt even hungrier than she had been when they had come in here.

Fenton, now leaning back and picking his teeth with the elegant silver toothpick he had been given by Mamma for his twenty-first birthday, seemed less famished, but then, he had been having the lion's share of all the food they had bought in the last month, for after all he was a man, and therefore more in need of sustenance. Amy did not grudge him his extra rations, but she was hungry; the cod had been the first food she had eaten since this time yesterday, and then they had only a meat pie bought in one of the little streets nearby to the Gaiety theatre and taken back to their hotel room to be gobbled to the last crumb.

She sighed a little, and looked round at the rest of the chop-house's customers in an attempt to take her mind off her stomach. They looked a solid enough lot, mostly business men, she opined, very like those top-hatted ones their cab had passed on the way from the docks. She sighed again as she remembered that. Could it really be a full month ago that they had arrived? It had seemed to be much longer. A full month of trailing from theatre to theatre, seeking managements ready and willing to employ them.

To start with they had been quite gay, not to say a little arrogant, both of them quite determined they would accept only roles as principals. Not for the Lucases mere supers' walk-ons.

They had sailed with great aplomb into the first theatre they had found, the Theatre Royal, New Adelphi, going to the front of the house and addressing the first person they saw in lofty tones, asking to speak with the manager.

The slattern leaning on her broom had stared at them and sniffed and then said harshly, 'Mr. Terrance don't see no one no'ow wivaht e's got an appointed time, an' anyway, 'e's always rahnd backstage. Yer gotta go to the stage door. Yer never finds *managers* front o' the 'ouse of a morning—'

So they had gone to the stage door, and been sent smartly packing by its formidably large custodian who told them with some force that Mr. Terrance was certainly not interested in auditioning anyone at the moment, were they Kemble and Siddons reincarnated, and to be about their business; to which Fenton had retorted with even greater force, pointing out that the custodian's overbearing behaviour was depriving his manager of the most exciting new talent that had come into the country in years.

'Tell him,' he had said sumptuously, 'that we are Mr. and Miss Lucas from Boston in Massachusettes in the United States of America. I think he will know the value of adding interesting Americans to his company, even if his lackeys do not!'

At which the large man had laughed loudly, and not without some genuine sympathy.

'Well, well, my young cock-sparrer,' he said when his spluttering had ceased. 'Is that the shape of it, then? Thinks yer special on account of bein' from foreign parts, eh? Never think it, my lad, never think it! Why, there's a dunnamany Americans floatin' around London this very moment. We don't find the likes o' you remarkable in the very least, and that's about the shape of it! You take a tip from an old trouper, my friend, one as was one o' the most successful tumblers in burlesques as 'ad ever bin, until I broke me leg fallin' into the pit. You go aht into the small places fust, my cockalorum! Get yerself a bit o' *real* experience somewhere's on the road, working at the public fairs an' that, afore you comes demanding London auditions.'

At which Fenton had bridled and lost his temper and sworn mightily, and the man had sworn even harder and they had squared up to each other for a fight, and would no doubt have beaten each other severely had not Amy managed to drag the fuming Fenton away.

'Never mind,' she had said as soothingly as she could, standing outside on the dirty pavement. 'It is only the first theatre we have been to, and possibly we chose a very bad one to start! For all we know, we have had a most fortunate escape! Come, we will go and seek elsewhere. I have no doubt we will have found a good management with the sense to take us before nightfall!'

But they had not found such a management that day, nor the next, nor the one after that. They had gone at first jauntily and then with deepening depression, from the Royal Italian ('Actors? No ducks. We wants singers and ballet dancers. You oughter 'a known that!') to Drury Lane ('Experience? Where? In *Boston*? Oh, dear me, no! What we want is people with experience *here*. You go get some good work out of town and then come back and we'll think again.') to Terry's, to the Royalty, to the Globe, to everywhere they could find.

And everywhere it was the same. Coolness at best, downright insults at worst. There had been the man who had ogled Amy and offered her 'good money' for some unspecified but clearly highly dubious activity that mainly seemed to involve wearing hardly any clothes at all, to reward which suggestion Fenton hit him hard and had the satisfaction of making his nose spurt blood; there had been the man who had told them that he knew of an out-of-town company that might take them both on and train 'em well for the London stage for a premium of just a few pounds apiece, to which he would gladly introduce them in exchange for a reasonable commission for himself; there had been the sneering ones, the tired ones, the bored ones and the angry ones, and with each passing day

Amy had become more and more dispirited and Fenton more and more irritable and quixotic, so that Amy was hard put to it to keep him reasonably happy.

And although she did not realize it, her very real acting ability spoke against her in their present circumstances. As her speech teacher Miss Farraday had so accurately said, Amy Lucas had a very speaking countenance; her depression, her anxiety and her hunger and fatigue showed clearly in her face, so that much of her charm and sparkle, which could be so captivating, was quite missing. So, when they presented themselves at stage doors, all too often all that those they sought to impress saw was a passably pretty but not particularly engaging little scrap of an American girl who might have been considered for some sort of walk-on, had she not been attended by so belligerent and occasionally pugnacious a gentleman.

For this was Fenton's problem, had he but known it. His good looks were in no way dimmed by his emotional state; indeed, his anger added a glint to his eye which could be very fetching to a certain type of female audience, but managements in theatres were careful, canny people, and knew better than to risk backstage fights and problems by deliberately taking on a bruiser. It happened by accident often enough, God knew; many were the meek and apparently biddable young actors who had seemed so eager and grateful for the job at audition who had turned out to be hell raisers and thorough trouble-makers with their truculence. So no manager in his right mind would consider Fenton as long as he approached would-be employers with the arrogance he did.

And this very morning his rage had been enormous, as he realized that they had but three shillings left between them. He had marched about his room stamping and kicking at the furniture with such abandon that Amy, dressing in her room next door, had come running to see what ailed him and had needed close on fifteen minutes to calm him down so that he could tell her.

And when she had realized that not only had they only three shillings left, but no money with which to pay their by now very large hotel account—for Fenton had managed to persuade the management, she knew not how, to wait until

22

the end of the first month of their stay for their settlement—
then she was very frightened.

'Oh, Fenton!' she had said, her eyes wide and dark with
anxiety. 'What shall we do? We know of no one here who can
help us—no one! And we have no money to go home—oh, I
wish you had listened to me and agreed to search for Papa's
family as soon as we arrived here! Then we would perhaps
have had someone upon whom we could throw ourselves!'

'Well, complaining at me now is no answer!' he had
shouted. 'And you can't be sure we would have found them
so easily, anyway! How would you do it, hey? How would
you do it? Stop people in the street and simper at them and
say, "Did you know my Papa? He used to live here in London
when he was a boy. Mind you, he's been dead these ten years,
and lived in Boston for ten years before that, but never
mind—I'm *sure* you know him!" Is *that* what you would do?
If you've nothing better to say than that, then keep quiet, you
fool! I've enough to worry about without such—'

This time she had burst into tears, and since this was
something she very rarely did, and only under extreme prov-
ocation, he was first nonplussed and then angry and finally,
as her sobs grew louder and her distress even more painful,
contrite, and he had hugged and kissed her and told her
stoutly that it was all a nonsense anyway—he had been giving
in to his megrims and should know better.

'For we can get out of here as right as ninepence without
fretting over the bills, for have you not a little balcony outside your room? I can hand the luggage down to you, late
tonight, and we'll be on our way, and no one the wiser! And
then we'll find another hotel and start again—come, don't
weep, Sugar-Amy, please don't weep, for it makes me feel
very put about—'

And at the use of her childhood nickname and with his
dear arms about her she was able to stop weeping, and feel
that perhaps after all they would manage. They always had,
after all. All through the ten years of their mother's bewildered widowhood—for she had never really recovered from
the loss of her dear but feckless husband (who had died so
saddled with debts that even the lawyers had been in awe of
the total)—they had managed.

They had lied and cheated their way into and out of all sorts of agreeable escapades, while at the same time convincing their poor, dear, oh-so-upright and oh-so-proper Mamma that she was succeeding in bringing them up to be respectable members of her own clan, the Fentons and the Cabots. To the day of her death she had not known how many scrapes they had been in, and wriggled out of, how near to the wind Fenton had sailed on so many occasions, gambling both with the money and feelings of tender and very rich young ladies who allowed themselves to be captivated by his Apollo Belvedere appearance. Surely, surely, they could manage again!

So Amy had returned to her room to complete her dressing and wash away her tear-stains with cold water and sally out with her dear Fenton to spend their precious three shillings on the day's food.

She had thought they would do better to go to a cookshop and purchase as much as they could get for their cash there, but Fenton had said grandly, 'You must behave always as you wish matters to be! To go again to one of those cookshops is not to be considered. They are vulgar and low, and not fit for you, my dear sister. We shall eat in decent style, even if frugally. Come!'

And he had taken her through the bewildering network of streets among which their hotel lay, to Maiden Lane, to Mr. Rule's chophouse, and ordered the cheapest fare he could; and if, in ordering his mutton chop because he could not abide fish he had deprived Amy of some of her share of the nourishment that was available for three shillings, well, she was not the sort to complain.

She stirred now and sighed. The chophouse was beginning to empty, as it was now close on three o'clock, and those who dined unfashionably early were making way for those who would come shortly to dine elegantly late.

'I suppose we must be on our way, Fenton,' she said timidly, for he seemed abstracted to a degree, and was sitting staring unseeingly at the yellow painted walls with their new gaslight sconces. 'Though quite *where* we are to go, I do not know—'

His eyes shifted then, and he nodded, a trifle heavily. 'I was wondering if we could leave here without paying, but we ate so little, it hardly seems worth the effort of trying.' He threw up three shillings on the table and stood up. 'Well, come on. We shall go.'

'Where?' she said again, hurrying along beside him as they came out of the warm sawdusty rooms into the chill November blowiness of Maiden Lane.

'I think I saw in the Strand a jeweller's shop,' Fenton said. 'One that is a pawnbroker's as well. They had the three balls of the Medici on display, anyway. We shall see what my toothpick will fetch—'

'Oh, no—Mamma gave you that!'

He shrugged. 'She gave me an appetite too, and I daresay she would as lief I pawned her present as starved for want of something to use my teeth upon. Anyway, I shall but *pawn* it. It will be possible to redeem it as soon as we have earned some money—'

And she hadn't the heart to point out to him that it was their inability to find anyone who would let them earn money that had brought them to the present pass, so she kept silent, and trotted along beside him, down Maiden Lane to the Strand.

The Strand was very, very busy. Already the winter afternoon was dwindling to a close and shop fronts were ablaze with lights which spilt out onto the pavements and made the bleak light coming from the sky seem even more limited than it was. They stood for a moment staring at the crowds, the fashionable women in their huge crinolines sailing along like galleons, their bell-like skirts dipping and swaying. They made Amy feel very unfashionable, for her skirts, while quite wide and well petticoated, did not surmount a wire crinoline cage, and could not until she had a chance to earn the money to buy one. These passers-by wore fur-trimmed pelisses, too, and delightful chip bonnets with ribbons trailing half-way down their backs, and she had none of those refinements in her dress, and her gloom deepened. And Fenton too looked at the men and glowered, for where was his fur-trimmed short coat, where were his elegant narrow trousers and high-lapelled waistcoat? Above all, where was his silver-headed cane? Every man in this busy glittering thoroughfare had such a one and he felt very deprived. And said as much to Amy.

'I know, my love, I do know! I yearn, I truly yearn for such a gown as that one there. You see? The lady standing there waiting for the crossing sweeper to make way for her—'

She brightened then. 'We could be much more distressed, you know. Suppose we were crossing sweepers! Then indeed we would be bereft!'

They both watched the scrawny little boy who looked to be no more than twelve, going by his height, though he had the wizened and resigned face of a man five times his years, at his bruised and blood-spattered legs—for clearly the wagon and cart drivers saw no harm in whipping out at the little creatures who dodged among the traffic trying to clear a clean way for the gentry to pass—and at the few pitiful rags that clung to his bony frame. And then Fenton said sharply, 'You can be real dumb, Amy! How can you compare us with that sort of creature? They are not *people*—it is these others we have to look at. The ones with rich houses and so much money that these goddam shopkeepers come crawling out on their bellies to get 'em into their shops to spend it. There has to be a way to part some of 'em from enough cash to set me up— there just has to be. I'm sure as hell not going to go on as we are much longer—'

Amy tucked her hand into his arm. 'No, love, of course not,' she said soothingly again, and suddenly felt very old and tired and lonely, for her voice had sounded in her own ears the way her mother's voice had been used to sound when she spoke to Fenton. All the years of worrying about Fenton, of deferring to Fenton, of putting Fenton in the first—where had they led her poor mother, after all? She had died barely three years after her fortieth birthday, exhausted and frightened for her beloved son's future welfare, thinking only of him. And what care had Fenton given to her death? Hardly any.

Amy remembered suddenly, standing there in the middle of the pavement in the Strand in London, how she had sat beside her dead mother's bed in the old frame house in Boston with tears blotching her face, and how Fenton had come creeping in and stared down at the face on the pillow, so still and grey, and had said softly, 'Amy—what is happening?'

'Oh, Fenton,' she had said huskily, 'dear Fenton, you must

be strong—poor Mamma—she has died, my dear one, she has left us—'

And he had lifted his head and stared at her with his eyes bright and sparkling, yet quite blank, and said in a tight hard voice, 'We are on our own, then! We are on our own. And must take care of ourselves—'

She shook herself a little. It had been long time since she had allowed herself to remember that afternoon, how for the first time in all her life she had looked at her adored brother and found him wanting. She had managed to persuade herself she had imagined it, that exultant note she had thought that she had heard, that he had in fact been expressing the same grief that she had felt, and had closed her mind to the memory of his glittering eyes with a firm determination never to think of it again. And yet, now, three thousand miles away from Boston and many many months away from that time, it had all come back to her—

Perhaps it was because she was so abstracted that it happened; perhaps it was because she was tired—for worrying and fretting always made one weary—or perhaps it was because she had been weakened by her hunger. Whatever the cause, she obeyed Fenton's irritable twitch on her arm and stepped forwards to the pavement edge to set out on the crossing to the other side where lay the jeweller who displayed the three brass balls of promise outside his establishment.

And instead of doing as she had learned to do on her first day in London, and looking to the right to see what traffic was bearing down upon her, she behaved as she had always behaved at home, and looked to the left. And seeing nothing approaching, had stepped out confidently.

Quite what happened then she was never able to remember with any clarity. She heard shrieks and shouting and a terrifying clatter and rattling of hooves and wheels coming at her from her other side, and turned her head and saw with a sudden intense clarity a horse rearing high above her. Its hooves were flailing in the air, its great leather-strapped belly seemed to be about to come down to crush her, while its teeth, hugely yellow in its wide open mouth, looked as vast and as menacing as gravestones.

She screamed and tried to pull back, but then she felt her-

27

self pushed forwards with enormous strength and had to go that way, almost falling as her feet scrabbled against the cobbles, and finally losing her balance so that she went sprawling in the middle of the roadway.

The screams and shouts went on, and she turned her head, stunned and bewildered by it all, and managed to scramble to her feet and stand with her eyes closed, swaying as she tried to regain her equilibrium. And then she opened them and looked, and her eyes widened and she heard a scream coming from somewhere very near.

There, lying on the ground almost under the wheels of the wagon to which the horse was harnessed, lay Fenton. His face was white, with one cheek incongruously streaked with mud, and his eyes were half open and quite, quite blank, so that he seemed to be staring into depths unknown. One leg was stretched out awkwardly to one side and the other—the other was bent in a most unnatural way, and the fabric of his trousers was so ripped away that the strong muscular curve of the outer side of his thigh could be seen—but it was the lower part of his leg upon which her gaze was fixed. Bent horribly in the middle of the shin and with a great wound stretching almost from ankle to knee, it was pouring blood, and already a little pool had formed on the cobble stones, making them gleam redly in the reflected light from the shops.

It was then that she realized that the screaming she could hear was coming from her own throat.

# CHAPTER THREE

'You are very kind, sir. You are very kind,' she said again, and sat back on her haunches, and rubbed her face with one hand, unaware of the streak of mud she left upon one pale cheek. And the young man kneeling beside her looked at her and in spite of his anxiety about his patient, lying there on the cobblestones before him, felt a twinge of admiration. This was a handsome young woman, by gad, he told himself. Quite remarkable handsome.

'It is my pleasure, ma'am,' he said formally, and looked down again at Fenton. 'Indeed it is. I think, you know, that we have stopped the bleeding. It was that which most alarmed me. He has not lost more than is reasonable, thanks be—there, you see? He regains his senses—'

He leaned forwards and set his hand on Fenton's forehead and said softly, 'There, there, old man—take it easy, will you? You are safe enough now, I promise you—'

Fenton's head turned a little restlessly on the fabric of the coat someone had bunched up and set under his head and he blinked as his gaze cleared, and he saw Amy, leaning over him with her face white with anxiety and shock. 'You dumb cluck—damn near killed yourself—' he murmured, and Amy's face crumpled and she burst into tears.

'Oh, Fenton, my dear, dearest one, you saved my life, you truly did, and your poor leg—your leg is all cut, and it is all my fault—'

'No, do not fret yourself, ma'am,' the young man beside her said, and looked up at the crowd of people standing staring with great interest at the little group in the middle of the road. 'Is someone fetching a shutter? Good—there, you see, ma'am?' He turned back to Amy. 'There is help coming to transport your—er—this gentleman to the hospital, where I can promise you—'

Her eyes darkened with fear, and she turned to stare at him. 'The hospital? Oh, no—surely not! Why, if he goes to a hospital he will never—oh, no—please not, sir. He needs much care and—'

The young man shook his head and ventured to put out his hand to pat one of hers reassuringly. 'Please do not distress yourself, ma'am. The hospital to which I wish to take you is Queen Eleanor's. It is an excellent establishment, and—'

'That's right, missie!' A voice came out of the crowd of eager starers, who were pressing so close they threatened to quite overwhelm the three of them, down there on the cobble-

29

stones. 'There ain't nowhere as good as Nellie's—you'll be all right there, you and yer 'usban'—don't you fret—'

'Fenton is my brother,' she said absently, still staring at the young man, whose countenance lifted unaccountably at her words. 'Is it true, sir? Is this a good place? I know so little of such matters. Except that at home, hospitals—' she shivered.

'Indeed, it is true,' the young man said. 'No one likes to be ill and in hospital, of course, but Nellie's—Queen Eleanor's—is indeed a suitable place for a gentleman like your brother to be—I can promise you that.'

'You know it well?' Her anxiety was still piteous, and she looked down again at Fenton, who had slipped into a half faint, half sleep, and she put out her hand to touch his forehead, to reassure herself that he was all right, and was comforted when he turned his head away fretfully and muttered.

'I am a surgeon of Queen Eleanor's,' the young man said, and his voice took on a note of importance. 'My name is Foster, ma'am. Graham Foster, at your service.'

'Oh, Dr. Foster, how glad I am to make your acquaintance!' She put out a hand towards him in a touchingly formal gesture. 'You have indeed been a good Samaritan to us—I am deeply indebted to you, sir, for your friendship—'

'Er—thank you, ma'am—er—I am Mr. Foster, in point of fact, ma'am, since I am a surgeon and not a physician, you know. Or to be quite precise, will be. I am still in the last year of my studies, you must understand, but confidently expect to be admitted to the Royal College at the end of the year—I am a pupil of Mr. Abel Lackland, you see, and—'

'Well, you are a very remarkable surgeon, sir, whether you have completed your studies or not, so to have saved my brother from bleeding to death, as I am sure he must have done but for you—I thank you most *gratefully*—'

'My pleasure, ma'am,' Foster said gruffly and got to his feet as the crowd surrounding them shifted, and then separated to allow two men carrying a shop shutter between them to come to the side of the little group in the road. 'Now, we must take great care—if someone will perhaps lend me his shoulders—aye, you'll do—'

There was a little bustle as two of the gawpers came forward and, with Foster carefully instructing them, helped the

30

shutter bearers to lift Fenton, who woke and swore and then seemed to faint again as his leg was moved, on to the rigid slatted board.

Amy, her face whiter than ever, clung to one of Foster's arms, at which he made no demur whatever, and then as the man slowly lifted the shutter with Fenton on it she ran forwards, and pulling her cloak from her back laid it tenderly across him. And then, walking as close beside the shutter as she could, and with Foster on its other side, they made their way to the side of the road, and the starers, the spectacle over, drifted away, and the traffic once more began to rumble over the patch of bloodstreaked cobbles where Fenton had lain.

Amy gazed back over the road and saw the clock over the jeweller's shop to which they had been making their way, and marvelled, for barely ten minutes had passed since she had looked the wrong way and set her foot into the roadway, and now here they were, she shivering and mud spattered, and Fenton lying on a shutter with one leg heavily bandaged. And she shook her head, and tried to speak but all that came out of her lips was a silly giggling sound.

She turned her head and looked at Foster who seemed to understand, for at once he came round the shutter to stand beside her and set his arm about her shoulders, and she turned her head and laid her face against the rough fabric of his coat and wept hugely and bitterly.

'Come along now, come along, my dear Miss—er—please to come along,' he murmured, and jerking his head at the two men carrying Fenton, set out towards the streets behind the Strand where the hospital lay, and Amy, almost unaware of what was happening, so deep in her distress was she, allowed herself to be led along with Mr. Foster's arm firmly holding her against his swelling chest.

The next hour was a nightmare. The journey through the narrow streets with passers-by staring and jostling them, the climb up the steps that led to the hospital, and the noise and smell of the place as they made their way through echoing stone-floored corridors was bad enough; but the hubbub and horror of the casualty ward was even worse.

They had lifted Fenton from his shutter, a manoeuvre which made him cry out in agony as his leg was awkwardly moved by one of the bearers, and set him down on a table in the middle of a big room vividly lighted with big gas flares and so full of people and noise and movement that Amy felt almost dizzy at it all. There were rows of benches upon which sat grey-faced men and women and haggard children, and there were young men in heavy black frock coats who bustled about and looked important, and women in sober print gowns and unbleached calico. aprons, their hair tied up in severe mob caps, hustling the people on the benches, shouting instructions at each other, and generally adding to the hubbub. Threading through it all were the moans and groans and shouts that came from the people who lay on the tables similar to the one upon which Fenton had been put, and who were being attended by the men in frock coats; and overlying all that was the smell—of unwashed humanity, the reek of beer and gin, of mud, and a thick sweetish cloying odour that she knew instinctively was blood. And she closed her eyes and felt her throat tighten with nausea and wished she could sink into the same oblivion in which Fenton lay.

But then there was a sudden hush and the babble of voices became subdued and she opened her eyes and looked up and saw that standing beside Fenton was a tall old man wearing a very stained frock coat. He had a face that seemed to have been cut out of solid wood, so deep were the crevasses that divided his cheeks, and so sharp were the lines between his narrow green eyes. He had very white hair that swept back from his forehead in a thick springing mane, and his expression was tight and watchful. Looking at him, Amy was aware suddenly of a feeling of authority, the sort of feeling she had been used to experience when she was in the presence of her Cabot and Fenton uncles. When she had been with them this had made her irritable and truculent, for it had always seemed to hem her in, to make her a smaller and lesser person. But this man's authority conveyed to her only comfort, a secure sensation, a feeling that here was someone who knew all the secrets of the world and could make her feel happy again. And she sighed tremulously and let her shoulders slump a little.

A man standing beside the tall white-haired one looked up, almost as though her small movement had called his attention to her, and glanced at her sharply. He was a stocky man, clearly much younger than the man he accompanied, being perhaps in his later thirties, and his head was crowned with as thick a crop of red hair as the white thatch beside him, and suddenly she wanted to giggle, and bit her lip hard. She was not going to give in again to the great wave of hysteria that had swept over her earlier, and which had left her shaking and ashamed.

The old man was bending over Fenton now, and with very tender fingers was unwrapping the bloody bandage which covered his leg; Fenton whimpered suddenly, and like a flash Amy left the bench where Foster had set her, and ran to stand at Fenton's head.

The old man looked up and stared at her from under his heavy white brows. 'Who might she be, then?' he said gruffly, and his voice seemed to match his face, so hard and dark in tone was it.

'Er—she is the sister of the patient, sir.' Foster spoke timidly but with some resolve from his place on the other side of the table, and looking at him Amy realized suddenly just how young and unsure of himself he was. But he stood now with his eyes bright and determined and a rather mulish expression on his face. It was almost as though she could read his mind; she knew that he was thinking that this was *his* patient, and no one, not even this clearly very important man, was going to take him away.

'I was walking in the Strand and saw the whole affair, sir. This young lady, who is clearly a newcomer to London, stepped into the road under the hooves of a carrier's horse, and her brother, sir, was very gallant and pushed her out of danger and thus sustained his own injury.'

He lifted his chin as the old man stared at him, his eyebrows raised, and shakily but with some resolution, Foster went on. 'I recalled your teaching, sir, about the importance of preventing too great a loss of blood, and set a tourniquet to the injured leg, and—'

'Humph! Did you so!' the old man said, and bent his head again, quite ignoring Amy. 'I hope you thought to take it off

33

again, then. For if you did not he's lost his leg as sure as eggs—'

Amy's hand flew to her mouth and she cried out in horror, and the old man looked up at her and said harshly, 'If you are going to stand there and squeak, madam, then you can go elsewhere to do it, for I will have no truck with screaming women.'

'I am not screaming!' she retorted sharply, her distress receding under a wave of anger, and she lifted her chin at him and he smiled, a thin sardonic little flicker of a smile, and said, 'Aye, I thought you'd more meat on your bones than was to be seen at first sight. You are from America, I collect?'

'And what is wrong with that?' Amy said, sharply. The sense of security had gone now, and she felt once again that she was faced with a dry-as-dust authoritarian old broomstick of just the same sort as her uncles, and was not going to tolerate from this one what she had always had to put up with from her mother's relations.

'Nothing at all, except as it makes you unable to walk safely in our busy thoroughfares, ma'am, and so allows you to make work for surgeons that ain't in any need of additions to their burdens.'

He was once again working on Fenton's leg, slowly removing the last of the bandages Foster had fashioned out of kerchiefs begged from the passers-by in the Strand.

'Hmmph. Good man, Foster. You did remove the tourniquet.'

'Of course I did, sir!' Foster said indignantly. 'You taught me so—'

'What I teach and what students do are two very different matters, usually,' the old man said. 'But you've done well enough—now, Freddy—' and he turned to the man at his side.

'If it is too much trouble to you to take care of my injured brother, sir, then we shall take ourselves elsewhere!' Amy burst out, and pushed her way past Foster to stand in front of the old man with her fists on her hips, and her elbows akimbo. 'I wish no favours from—'

'What does the woman go on about?' the old man said, and stared at her once more.

'You said we made work for busy surgeons, being Americans and strangers as we are. So, if it is too much trouble—'

'Oh, pish, woman, and hold your noise!' the old man said. 'You make a fuss over nothing, when I am more concerned over more important matters. Like your brother's injury. Now, Freddy—' and he turned again to the hitherto silent man at his side. 'What do you think?'

Still silent, the red-haired man also bent over Fenton's leg, and Amy watched him, still smarting from the old man's sharpness, but realizing that he was right, and Fenton's care must come before her offended feelings. And she watched with shrinking horror as the younger man, with fingers steady and very gentle, explored the horrid wound in Fenton's leg.

Fenton moaned a little and rolled his head, and she put out her hand, and set it gently on his forehead, and he settled again, his eyes tight closed, and Amy realized that he was neither asleep nor fainting, but found it easier to deal with all that was happening by literally closing his eyes to it.

He had always done so as a child when he was thwarted in any way, lying with his eyes tight shut and refusing to communicate with anyone, clearly showing his dislike for what was happening around him. In those long ago days such an action had been able to drive his mother to distraction, and she had always given in to his demands. Anything was better than to look at her beloved boy lying on his bed, his eyes tight shut and refusing to say a word or show any sign of understanding of what was said to him or done to him.

Well, such a trick would not help now, Amy thought mournfully, and stroked his forehead, and felt the guilt well up in her, for was it not her fault that he lay here in such pain, and was so unhappy?

She turned her head again, feeling her gaze pulled back to the ugly oozing wound and was glad to see that the red-haired man had stopped his probing and was gently covering the leg with a clean piece of old linen.

'Well, now,' he said slowly. 'This is not so fearful as it looks at first sight.'

'Hmmph. Looks nasty enough to me. I think the fracture is a simple one—I felt no bone fragments—but the question is, can the bone heal under so extensive a flesh wound, and not putrefy? It is my belief it cannot. I would say immediate amputation is the answer. He sustained the injury in mud and horse manure and dirt—the putrefaction is like to be excessive—'

'No!' Amy heard the word come cracking out of her. 'No—you cannot!'

But the old man ignored her, his eyes still fixed on his younger companion. 'Well, Freddy, what say you? Will you operate? Or shall I? I have time this afternoon and could manage well enough, I think—'

'Well, sir, I am not so sure he needs such heroic surgery, truth to tell,' Freddy said and looked at the old man, and smiled fleetingly, and for a moment it seemed to Amy that he looked very like him; but then she thought confusedly, it's because he too is like the uncles, a man of authority, one who knows—

And knew better than the old man. It had to be so, and she turned her head and said urgently, 'Sir—Freddy—I do not know your proper name—'

'I am Frederick Caspar, ma'am, at your service,' the red-haired man said, and smiled.

'Mr. Casper, then—you say my brother's leg need not be lost? Please sir, *you* must take care of him and see that it is not—he is an actor, sir, and to lose his leg—oh, sir, Mr. Caspar, I insist, indeed I do, that *you* look after him, and—'

'No one who comes to Nellie's *insists* upon anything, madam,' the old man said harshly. 'All the insisting is done by us, the surgeons. And I do not hesitate to tell you that if we believe the best way to save your brother's life is to chop off his leg, then off it shall be chopped! Unless you want his death upon your conscience—'

Amy felt Fenton's muscles tighten under her fingers as he clenched his jaw, and a fleeting glance showed her that his eyes were now so tightly closed that they seemed like mere slits in his face, and she patted his forehead with as comforting a touch as she could and turned back to Mr. Caspar.

'I speak, sir, to *you*,' she said very loudly. 'I ask you to treat my brother so that he shall not—not be so mutilated as your friend here insists—'

'I do not insist, dammit, woman! You are too full of your-

36

self by half, indeed you are. Are all your compatriots so noisy? Will you listen, and mind your manners—'

'Now, let us be a little cool, if you please! This gains us nothing but headaches.' Mr. Caspar spoke soothingly, and put his hand on the older man's arm. 'You will recall all I have told you sir, of Mr. Lister's method? I saw him operate on several occasions during my recent visit to Glasgow, and it was impressive—most impressive. Now let me explain, sir, why I spoke as I did. The bone is not at all exposed in this wound. Were it a compound fracture, I would be less sanguine and share your opinion as to the need for immediate amputation, although Lister's case was of compound fracture and he succeeded very well with it. But that's all one—in this case, with a bone protected by the tissues, and only tissue injury to heal as well as a simple fracture I will be happy to try using Mr. Lister's method. I believe that by so doing I can provide this patient with a clean and serviceable limb and no putrefaction at all—'

'Mr. Lister, sir?' Young Foster was staring open-mouthed at Caspar. 'He uses a spray for the air, does he not? We have been hearing about it all. It sounds very—well—strange—'

'Not at all,' Mr. Caspar said. 'Not strange in the least. It is but an extension of the method Mr. Lackland here has been teaching you these many years, young man! He insists, does he not, that you operate always with clean hands, in a clean well scrubbed operating theatre? Quite so! Well, Mr. Lister maintains that even scrubbing does not quite remove all the dirt and the hazards that dirt can bring, and that there is in the air some—shall we say *substance*—that is involved in putrefaction of wounds. This is an opinion he has obtained from a Frenchman, one Pasteur, who maintains the air contains in it little animacules which cause putrefaction. To speak the truth, I care little for the theory of it all. It is too much for a poor simple surgeon! But I am most taken by the technique, and I have waited all this month for a case upon which I could attempt it. I have brought back from Glasgow one of Mr. Lister's carbolic sprays and I think, sir—' he turned back to the old man, 'I think, sir, that with your permission, I will take this case and operate today, and clean his wound, and repair the torn muscles and fascia and set the bone in a splint.

If putrefaction commences and he shows undue fever with rigors, why then, sir, we still have time to amputate. But it seems absurd when we have such a patient not to try the new method, when we have the materials ready to hand.'

There was a short silence between them and suddenly Amy was very aware of the other sounds around them, of the shouting of the nurses and the moaning of the patients, and the clatter of bowls and instruments, and she shivered and tried to imagine Fenton on crutches, Fenton with one trouser leg pinned up behind him, Fenton on stage—

She shook her head almost violently and said loudly, 'I speak not only for myself, but for my brother. He would, if he felt able to speak to us at all—and he suffers greatly from his state, I know—he would refuse, even at risk—' she swallowed and then went on, 'even at risk of his life, he would refuse to allow his leg to be—to be lost. Please, Mr. Caspar, will you do what you think needs doing? I would not have this—gentleman—' and she made the word as scathing as she could, 'I would not have this gentleman set so much as a finger upon him, regarding us as he does, and being so eager as he is to mutilate my brother!'

The old man gave a crack of laughter and suddenly and to her amazement grinned down at her. 'Well, you're a woman of spirit! There's not many as willing to stand up to me as you did—but I still tell you you're a fool!'

He looked at his red-headed colleague then and said sardonically, 'Well, Freddy, you can have your way. Here's the patient's sister gladly giving you permission to use her brother to do your experiments upon. I never seek permission from patients for aught, since I always know better than they do, but you are more tender in such matters so you should be happy! I wash my hands of the whole matter—the patient is yours! And you may make what cat's meat of him you may. I have others to tend who will value me and my skill and advice more highly!'

He turned away from the table and shouted over his shoulder and one of the aproned nurses came hurrying up with two of the frock-coated young men in her wake.

'Well, woman, what else have you waiting for me here this afternoon? I have no more time to waste on wilful screaming

38

women!' and he went stamping away and Mr. Caspar bent over Fenton's leg and examined it once more.

'You must not mind him, ma'am,' he said in a low voice, not looking up, 'He and I have many such arguments, but you know, he is a very wise, not to say wily, surgeon, with great experience. He agrees with me, in fact, and believes that I *can* repair your brother's injury. He would not have left me in command otherwise, I do promise you.'

Amy was trembling now, and she felt her eyes fill with tears. It had been easy to keep calm while the old man had been there, stirring her to a courage she did not know she had. But now she felt shaky and frightened and said piteously, 'Are you sure, sir? I know I said it would be dreadful for Fenton to lose his leg, but oh, sir, it would be much worse to—to lose Fenton. He is my very dear brother and—'

Caspar looked up and smiled, his face once more cracking into a faintly familiar shape, so that again he looked like the old man who was now dealing with an injured child on the other side of the big noisy room.

'Of course he is, and you must not fear. We can make no promises, of course, but I believe I can do a good piece of surgery here. And so does my grandfather, or he would not, I promise you, he would not have allowed me to have my way. He may be gruff and he may seem harsh, but he is indeed a great and experienced operator. We are agreed on your brother's care, and you will see—all of us here at Nellie's will do the best we can to ensure a swift recovery for him.'

'Your grandfather?' Amy said, staring at the old man's back across the room. So, the two master surgeons had a reason to look alike. 'Well, sir, so he may be, but I do not scruple to tell you that I think he is hateful, plumb *hateful*. And I am glad, indeed I am, that you will take care of my Fenton.' And she looked at Freddy Caspar and suddenly produced a smile of such brilliance that he blinked. 'I trust you, indeed I do, to do all that is needful.'

'And so shall I, Miss—er, ma'am,' Foster said behind her. 'So shall I, I promise you. I shall take a *very* special interest and care in your brother. He shall have only the best—'

Caspar's lips quirked as he looked at the young student and then at Amy, now bending over Fenton and whispering softly

39

into his ear. Clearly the young man was set upon his ears by this pretty and spirited young American. And equally clearly, this patient would not want for a moment of attention if Mr. Foster had his way.

Nor, he thought then, from me. The chance to use Mr. Lister's antiseptic system was one for which he had been waiting eagerly for some time. Now it had presented itself, there was not a moment to waste. And he lifted his head and called imperiously to one of the nurses, and began to give her instructions about the operation he would perform in a couple of hours' time.

# CHAPTER FOUR

Below her she could see the table in the middle of the room looking foreshortened and somehow lonely and she stared at it almost ferociously, trying to force her gaze to remain fixed upon it. That was the only way she could prevent herself from looking at all the other horrible and menacing objects in the room.

But it was no good; she could not prevent her gaze shifting and she looked about at the whitewashed walls with their gas sconces, flaring with a yellow blaze, and at the big table upon which was spread a white cloth, itself covered with an array of instruments that made her face blanch as she looked at them.

There were saws and chisels and hammers all as clearly recognizable as the implements that their old gardener, who had dabbled in a little carpentry about the place, had kept in the outhouse of their Boston home. There were knives and forceps and strangely-shaped pieces of gleaming metal and tortoise-shell whose function she could not imagine, but which looked capable of inflicting sickening injuries. There were even, she saw, as one of the frock-coated men moved to come up to the table, a row of outsize needles and heavy thread, and she closed her eyes, trying not to visualize them being pushed through Fenton's flesh—

'Are you all right, Miss Lucas?' Foster hissed softly in her ear, and she opened her eyes and looked at him and he went on worriedly, 'I should never have agreed to bring you here— it is not fitting for you to see such things—it was wrong of me—'

'Indeed, it was very right of you, and I would have been dreadfully upset if you had not brought me!' she said stoutly, and conjured up her most brilliant smile for him, at which he visibly softened, and relaxed and smiled back. Amy, who had been able since her childhood to judge to a nicety the degree to which she had enslaved an admirer, patted his hand and returned her attention to the room below. She knew she had an ally in this young man who would do anything she asked of him, and could be trusted slavishly to satisfy her every whim, and she was glad of the fact, although in time, no doubt, it would be tedious to fend off his amorous declarations. But let tomorrow and its problems take care of themselves; at present she was here, waiting for Fenton to be made well by the red-headed Mr. Caspar, determined to watch every step of the way.

Her determination was based mainly on guilt; she would have much preferred to remain in the casualty ward, huge and malodorous and noisy though it was, but it was her fault that Fenton had been so dreadfully injured, and this was the only recompense she could make. She could not be beside him while he underwent his agony; not even the adoring Mr. Foster could arrange that. But she could sit up here in the students' observation gallery and see what happened. And so she had determined she would. And she settled herself grimly in her place, and fixed her eyes on the empty table in the brightly lit area below her, and waited.

She did not have long to wait. The little group of young men in the room below suddenly became more alert and turned away from their desultory conversation as from just below Amy's vantage point there was a sound of arrivals. Then, as she leaned forwards, craning her neck, he appeared; the red-headed man.

He was now without his coat and appeared in his shirt-sleeves, with the cuffs rolled up above his elbows, and she could see his strong forearms with their dusting of sandy freckles, and the power of the muscles beneath the cambric over his shoulders, and shivered a little. Such strength seemed frightening suddenly, and she drew a deep breath and tried to concentrate entirely on what she could actually see and hear, so that her mind did not run away with itself, conjuring up horrible visions of Fenton lying in a blood-boltered bed, or with only one leg—

Below her, Mr. Caspar turned and looked up to the gallery, and she shrank back to get out of his sight.

'Gentlemen,' he said loudly, 'I am glad to see so many of you have presented yourself for instruction this afternoon. I am about to perform a repairing operation upon the leg of a young man who suffered an injury under the wheels of a cart this afternoon in the Strand. He has several deep lacerations, involving mainly the muscles of the extensor digitorum longus. There is some injury to the gastrocnemius, but less than I had feared. There appear to be simple fractures of both the tibia and fibula, which I hope to be able to reduce adequately following the repair of the muscalature. You may be a little surprised that we are attempting such a repair since, as you will see, the injured area is extensive and the risk of putrefaction high. However, I shall be using Mr. Lister of Glasgow's method, and operating under the protection of this—'

He turned and lifted his hand and one of the young men came forward, pushing a small round table. Upon it stood a brass object some twelve inches high, and egg-shaped, on the top of which was the handle of a plunger. From one side of the brass egg came a tube and from the other a bell-shaped extrusion. Altogether it looked very strange, and Amy stared at it, puzzled, as did all the other occupants of the gallery, who leaned forwards eagerly to stare down at all that was happening.

'This will be used to spray the air above the patient with a fine carbolic mist. Carbolic, I must tell you, is a substance devised from coal tar and developed in Manchester by one Calvert, who used it to disinfect sewage in Carlisle—'

There was a snort of laughter from somewhere at the back of the gallery and one of the students made a ribald remark at which Caspar raised one eyebrow.

'Some of you, gentlemen, may find it amusing that we use the same material for the prevention of wound putrefaction as we use for the problems of sewage putrefaction. Both are equally disagreeable, as Mr. Kent, whose voice I believe I recognized, will discover when he acts as night soil man for the whole of hospital for the rest of this week. You will see then, Mr. Kent, as you deal with those slop buckets, just how severe a problem putrefaction can be, whether it is to be found in a chamber pot or in an injured man's body. So be it, Mr. Kent?'

'So be it, sir,' the voice came dolefully from the back of the gallery, and a faint ripple of laughter moved through the ranks of the young men, and for one brief moment Amy felt and shared in their camaraderie and wondered what it must be like to be one of such a band of students, to learn and observe and become a surgeon. And then almost smiled at her own absurdity, for who had ever heard of a woman being a surgeon? And returned her attention to Caspar, still lecturing below.

'The muscles will be repaired with Lister's own suture material, an absorbable organic substance he calls catgut, and which is prepared for use by prolonged soaking in carbolic. These sutures, once placed, need no removal nor are they extruded through sinuses of the sort with which we are all too familiar. Finally, the wound will be packed with a lac plaster also containing carbolic and the whole area will be enclosed in a firm splint, to allow the bone to heal. If we find signs of putrefaction appearing in spite of our use of carbolic, then we will know that the system is not all that Lister claims for it, and we will have to amputate the limb with great expedition. However, I shall be exceedingly surprised if that should be needful. I found Mr. Lister and his work most impressive— ah, here is our patient—'

And now Amy could not, would not, look. She leaned back against Mr. Foster and he, nothing loath, set his arm about her shoulders and held on, while several of his student friends

43

made expressive faces at him. But he ignored them; they too in their time had been known to smuggle their friends in to watch operations, for it was considered a most fashionable (if somewhat fast) form of entertainment in some sections of young London society. And *his* lady friend had every right to be here, for after all, was not the patient her own and only brother? And was she not alone and frightened in a strange country, far from friends and relations to care for her? But now she had *him*, and his arm tightened about her, and his fair round face glowed, for there was little doubt that Miss Amy Lucas was quite the prettiest and most captivating illicit guest the students' gallery at Nellie's had ever harboured.

The scent of carbolic, pungent and acrid yet pleasantly fresh to the nostrils, came drifting up and she lifted her head and made herself look down again at the scene below. At first she could see little but the bent heads of the men clustered about the table but then one of them moved and she could see Fenton lying there, a sheet across his upper body, and his eyes closed above a pad of white gauze that was held to his nose and mouth by one of the young assistants. Even as she looked, the young man picked up a dark green bottle and with great care dripped some of its contents on to the gauze pad, and she jumped as Fenton began to cough and writhe.

'Do not worry, Miss Lucas,' Graham Foster whispered. 'That is the chloroform, you know. It is to ensure that he feels no pain, and he will be quite insensible throughout the operation. There, you see? He is quite still, and quite out of pain—'

She looked and saw two of the other assistants carefully unwrapping the dressings on Fenton's leg, and moving it quite freely, but he made not a sound, apart from a faint snoring as he breathed, which noise she found comforting. So she sat up a little more and watched, her mouth half open and her eyes opaque with concentration.

Somehow it was not Fenton down there now. He was asleep, quite free of pain and just was not there. So, she could watch with interest and no hint of guilt or fear at all, just as she had been used to watch with fascination when old Lewis at home had killed a chicken for the table and the cook had pulled its feathers and drawn its guts before cooking it. She

44

had never found that caused any squeamishness in her—much to Cook's disapproval—and now she felt just the same; quite entranced with all the newness of it, and the strange beauty of the exposed flesh.

As one of the assistants pumped vigorously, sending a fine but quite visible spray of carbolic from the brass egg all over the table and Fenton, Caspar set about treating the wound.

Using forceps and a long-handled tortoise-shell knife that he took from the table beside him, he rearranged the torn muscles, cutting away at the tattered edges of the wound to leave a clean line. It was as matter of fact and as ordinary as though he were a butcher cutting meat for a rich man's table; the flesh beneath his implements looked as red, as fibrous and as commonplace as steak. To Amy it was so impossible a sight that all thoughts of Fenton, teasing, selfish, sometimes remorseful, usually thoughtless, but always lovable Fenton, were quite banished. The work being done in the bright circle of light below her had nothing to do with him at all. She could watch it all and feel no hint of anxiety or distress of any kind.

Caspar threw the knife and forceps onto the table behind him, so that they clattered against a dish and made Amy jump and he picked up and threaded a curved needle with a length of greyish-coloured material he took from a glass dish, and Amy wanted to giggle. He looked so womanish and yet so heavily male that the contrast was comical. But then he turned back to the table and the exposed wound and her laughter vanished. Now he was all man again, even though he was sewing with stitches set with great delicacy. Any watched, her eyes wide and unblinking as first one and then another of the torn edges were brought together and carefully sewn into place.

Slowly, the hideous bloody mess that had been Fenton's leg began to take a new form, began to be more shapely as, without one false move and with great dispatch, Caspar's needlework went on.

An assistant cleaned away any blood that dared to appear—and it really seemed to Amy in her gallery that Mr. Caspar was so much in control of all that was happening that even blood obeyed him—until at last the muscles were all back in position, and all that remained to be set in place were the edges of the skin.

'You will have observed, gentlemen,' Mr. Caspar said, breaking his silence at last, 'that I have performed a cleansing and debridement of the wound, and removed all visible traces of foreign bodies. Some pieces of gravel that were there have now been taken out. Now, we wash the wound once more with carbolic—I am using it in a dilution of one part to twenty parts of water, for it is a powerful antiseptic. Lister has found that in its concentrated form it can cause damage to the skin that delays healing, but it is effective against putrefaction in this dilution—and now I shall suture the skin. I make the stitches as fine as I may, for this young man is, I am told, an actor, and as such one who cares much for the appearance of his body. It would be tragic, would it not, to sew his leg so awkwardly that he did not present a pretty picture when in tights.'

The students above laughed at this sally, and looked sideways at Amy, but she stared on, not one whit put out by Mr. Caspar's jest; as far as she could see he had spoken no more than the truth, for it was indeed important that Fenton's beauty, even of a part of his body usually undisplayed, should be preserved.

'So, small stitches. When I started my career, gentlemen, we could not enjoy the luxury of seeking to confer a handsome result with our sutures, for the use of chloroform came when I was but a student, and we had already been taught to operate with great speed for fear of the patient's pain. Indeed, medicine and surgery have made such remarkable progress in these past few years that I find myself wondering what is left to conquer! Just as the city we live in is being changed beyond recognition by all the building and reconstruction that is going on, so is our profession undergoing extraordinary changes. Ah well, I wax philosophical—there we are! As neat a bit of sewing as ever my wife performed, I am sure you will agree! Now, the splint—you two, set yourselves to the ankle, I will take this side, so, and Jennings, lie upon the hip—aye, that is the way. Now, have you the splint ready? Excellent, excellent! So, Jennings, hold tight, and you two—pull. Come now, harder than that—pull! You're like school-

46

room misses, you are so feeble! That's better—pull—good lads! I think—yes, the fracture seems reduced. Let me see the other leg—uncover it! Aye that's it. Hold it straight—yes, there is no shortening I believe—so, the splint—splendid—hold it close—aye, now the bandages—firmly, mind—splendid, splendid! We will, I am sure, get a good union there, as long as Mr. Lister's pump has not let us down! You may stop your efforts now, young man—the stuff is making my face and hands feel quite numb—'

It was all over. Amy sat and stared down at Fenton, now snoring in good earnest, his legs lying neatly side by side, one splinted, and one bare and elegant in the gaslight. As she watched, two burly men came forward with a stretcher and lifted him on to it, and throwing a blanket over him, bore him away, and suddenly, it seemed to Amy, the world had gone silent. As soon as the splint was in position the other students in the gallery had gone clattering boisterously away, leaving Foster and herself in sole possession, and now that Fenton was gone, so were the assistants and Mr. Caspar from the theatre below. There remained only one of the nurses desultorily cleaning up the bloody towels.

She opened her mouth to speak, and then closed it again, and tried to stand up, and felt her knees buckle beneath her, and Foster gasped and once more put his arm about her and caught her as she sagged helplessly against him, her head thrown back and her eyes open but quite blank.

'Oh dear, oh dear, oh dear, oh dear—' he gabbled, and looked about him desperately for help, but still she lay against his arm, a dead weight, and there was no one to help at all. So, tenderly, and as carefully as he could, he laid her down on the bench upon which they had been sitting and began to chafe her hands and fan her face, still muttering, 'Oh dear, oh dear, oh dear,' beneath his breath. However effective a man of action he might be when faced with a traffic accident in the Strand, when faced with a faint in a lady for whom he had developed the most tender of feelings he was as helpless as an errand boy.

She moaned softly and opened her eyes, to his intense relief, and he looked at her anxiously and said, 'I am so sorry, Miss Lucas! I should never have let you—it is something that happens often, I am afraid, fainting in the operating theatre. Many of the students do—I *knew* I should have never let you come, but you were so set upon it that you would—would—oh, dear, I am so sorry—let me take you home, at once. Your brother will not be fit for conversation for some hours, indeed not until tomorrow, and I am sure you need your rest. I will take you home and then return here and remain with your brother constantly to be sure he is in good care and—'

She shook her head dolefully against the hard wood of the bench, and tears pushed themselves out of each eye and overflowed onto her cheeks.

'I have nowhere to go, Mr. Foster,' she said piteously. 'The hotel—the place where we are staying I cannot return to, for we have used all our money and owe them so much for our account, and I—oh, Mr. Foster, I am so hungry and so tired and I have nowhere to go at all! Can I not stay here? You seem to be a most *important* man here, and I am sure you can arrange it for me! Please, Mr. Foster, will you? I cannot leave Fenton, for he is my own dear brother, but even if I could, where could I go? Until he is well I must stay here, I am afraid—there is nothing else I can do—'

And now she wept in earnest, and Mr. Foster, his young face creased with anxiety, took his handkerchief from his pocket and did all he could to dry her tears and comfort her.

It took Amy more than half an hour to persuade him that to arrange for her somehow to remain in Queen Eleanor's would not only be permissible but possible. Half an hour of tears—most of them quite genuine, for she was indeed exhausted, and frightened for Fenton, as well as exceedingly hungry—and tremulous smiles and sweet words, but at last he agreed, though unwillingly, to do what he could.

'You must understand that it will be very difficult, Miss Lucas! I can see to it that you receive food—I live at home with my Mamma, you see, and I daresay I can bring victuals from our kitchen, and no one at home will know—I mean, that will be better than the food they give here. It is not *bad*, you must understand, but not very agreeable either, and anyway, Nellie's is always worrying about money, and the rations for the patients are very carefully doled out. It is somewhere for you to sleep that is the problem and—well, there *is* that small cubbyhole that lies beside the ward where I know your brother is to be lain to recover. It used to be the office of the bursar, before the ward was made out of the offices there— oh dear, you are making me babble like a goat! I am so put about—but, well—we shall see—come along, Miss Lucas. Please to lean on my arm, so—yes—there now! We will go slowly and you will be very well—'

The ward, when they reached it, was busy, with several of the medical students bustling about as well as two or three of the calico-aproned nurses. Amy wanted to stop, to see Fenton, but Foster was adamant; he would still be under the effect of his chloroform, and Caspar would be most put out were she to arrive at his patient's bedside at such a time. 'Indeed,' he assured her earnestly, 'we must pass through very quickly, or we will be stopped and then there is no hope of doing as you wish.' And unwillingly, Amy had to agree to move swiftly but with self-assured nonchalance across the expanse of wooden floor between the beds and through into the corridor that ran from one corner. At the end of the corridor was another door, and he opened it, turning a key that lay in the lock, and pushed it open.

Once inside, she looked about her and smiled, still holding very firmly onto Foster's arm, for her legs still felt very shaky, and she was far from her usual buoyant self.

'Oh, you are so clever, Mr. Foster, to think of this! Look— there is even a pile of mattresses I can sleep upon—are you sure they will not seek me here?'

'I hope not, indeed,' Foster said gloomily. 'But there is this key to the door, you see? And if you make sure you slip in here when none can see you, and lock yourself in, you should do well enough. It is all wrong, you know, quite improper—'

'I know,' she said, and smiled at him sweetly. 'Of course it is, dear Graham—may I call you Graham? But what can I do, alone and bereft in London as I am? I have no home, and no money—'

'You could stay at my house, perhaps,' Mr. Foster said, a thought which clearly cast him down from the heights to which her use of his given name had lifted him. He thought of his formidable widowed mother, and paled as he imagined bringing this beautiful and captivating but undoubtedly far from elegantly dressed young American to her, and asking for shelter. He could imagine her response and her basilisk eye all too easily.

'I would not hear of it!' Amy said stoutly, and much to his relief, 'for I must remain close to my Fenton. You, I am persuaded, will understand? Have you a brother, dear Graham?'

'Only—only a sister, Miss Lucas,' Foster stammered, his face once more scarlet with pleasure.

'Is she at all of my sort of size, Graham? And if she is do you think she would loan me a gown?' Amy asked artlessly. 'For you see how bedraggled I am, and there is no opportunity for me to obtain my luggage until Fenton is well, and we have the money to pay the hotel. They will insist on holding our possessions as a surety till then, I know. It is all very difficult—'

'Yes—yes, of course. She is a little larger than you, perhaps, but—yes—of course.' The infatuated Foster beamed at her, and then with one final grip of her wrist said, 'I must go and leave you here now. I regret it very much, But I must see to my patients, for it is getting very late. I will bring you some food and—and a gown if I can as soon as may be, but it cannot be until after seven, when the nurses of the daytime leave the wards. At night there is but one nurse between two wards, and it will be easier to come and see you then, and settle matters—I will scratch on the door, so do not unlock it for any sound but this—listen—' and he ran his nails down the panels of the small door.

She nodded and smiled at him again, and he smiled back, and then suddenly, with an awkward bob of his head, said breathlessly, 'Miss Lucas, this morning I did not know of your existence. Now, I believe—I believe you to be the most remarkable as well as the most beautiful person in—in all the world. I—I am privileged to know you—'

And then, his face flaming red, he bobbed his head again, and slid out through the door and closed it softly behind him and she stood in the middle of the dusty little room, looking about at the stack of old chairs that stood in one corner, the battered table with one leg missing that leaned drunkenly against another, and the pile of old, but apparently clean, mattresses that stood against one wall.

She looked down at her dress, which had started the day looking so sprightly and fresh with its lemon sprigged ruffles and its darker yellow trimming but now sadly crushed and muddied, and grimaced and yawned and almost fell onto the mattresses.

She was dreadfully tired and felt absurdly weak, but of one thing she was sure. Dreadful as Fenton's accident had been and painful though his recovery would be, she knew he was going to get well, and still be able to use his leg. That man, Mr. Caspar, had been so careful, so neat, and so concerned that it *had* to be, and when Fenton woke up from his chloroformed sleep, she would go out into the ward and tell him so, so that he need not worry any more. That, she told herself sleepily, is what I shall do. I shall go and tell him as soon as he wakes up—

And she fell asleep herself with the suddenness of an exhausted baby, curled up on her pile of mattresses with her hair tumbling its rough curls round her sleeping face and her gown rumpled about her. Had Mr. Foster been able to see her at that moment there is little doubt his already stricken heart would have broken completely in two.

# CHAPTER FIVE

It proved to be a great deal easier than either of them would have imagined possible to keep Amy's presence in the hospital a secret.

Each day, very early in the morning before the hospital was awake, she slipped out of her little cubbyhole to pad silently down to the huge kitchens below, easily dodging the night nurse who made her rounds in a most desultory fashion. In the dark stone-flagged kitchens deep in the basement and inhabited mainly by cockroaches and one very old and very deaf nightwatchwoman who slept soundly beside the banked-up fire, she would wash herself in ice-cold water from the pump, and tidy her gown, and then, as the cooks and scrubbers and porters came clattering down the area steps from the street outside, coming in to work from their hovel homes in the tangle of streets outside, she would slip back upstairs to the main hall of the hospital.

She learned very quickly how to time her movements so that she appeared there just as the night porter handed over to the day porter, and there she would stand, fresh and beaming, to greet the yawning day man with a cheerful 'Good morning!' that made him sure she had just arrived.

And then she would go tripping up to the ward to sit beside Fenton and chatter to him and cajole him and deal with his crotchets—for he was a most impatient patient—and generally be the most devoted sister anyone could imagine.

At first the nurses had made attempts to bar her from spending such long hours in their domain. They were not used to such prolonged visits to their patients, for most of them were poor men who, if they had relations at all, certainly did not have any who enjoyed sufficient leisure to permit them to sit all day at a bedside. Their wives and sisters, if they had them, might appear for a little while at the end of their own long working day, coming grey-faced and exhausted to sit in anxious silence beside their men, peering at them worriedly and trying to understand what they were told about their sickness and its progress. But all day? It was unheard of.

But as Amy put herself to some trouble to ingratiate herself with the nurses, regularly offering to help them by sitting at Fenton's bedside with a pile of grey charpie on her lap, teasing out the threads to make the soft dressings they used, a task the nurses much hated and for which they were responsible, they were mollified.

The other patients liked her presence too, finding her pretty face and cheerful chatter very restorative, while the medical students quite adored her, managing to find remarkably frequent and pressing reasons to come to the men's ward

52

where the operation cases were cared for. Which made Graham Foster both furious and immensely proud.

It was he who made it possible for her to remain there in the hospital, for each day he brought her food, bread and cheese or cold mutton, and occasionally apples or cake wrapped in a neat white kerchief, coming ostensibly to see his patient, Fenton, but quietly slipping his gift into Amy's hands as she sat there smiling up at him. And for him, those smiles were more than enough payment for all his efforts (which were considerable; stealing food from his mother's kitchens, ruled as they were with a rod of iron by that formidable lady, was no easy feat). And he would look at Fenton's splinted leg, and check that he could move his toes, and then bob his head at Amy, scarlet-faced and adoring, and go away to sit over his books and dream about her thickly lashed grey eyes and her curly hair and the way her mouth moved when she smiled.

Fenton was very scathing about him, considering him to be the flattest flat he had ever seen in all his life, but Amy was vigorous in his defence.

'How could we manage if he did not help us, Fenton? I have to eat and sleep *somewhere*. You are here and they are glad enough to treat you for no charge, since you were injured in the street and they have benefactors who pay for such cases—but what of me? You must realize we would be in a sorry state if it were not for Mr. Foster.' She giggled then. 'Though really, he is very tedious, is he not? If only he would not *bob* at me so! He looks just like a jackrabbit, the way he bobs and gawps—'

'And if he has his way he'll behave like a jackrabbit too, if you give him half the chance—' Fenton said, and moved his leg awkwardly in his bed and swore as a twinge of pain shot down his calf.

'You must not be coarse, Fenton,' Amy said reprovingly. 'A coarse mind is very damaging to the countenance. It sets ugly lines upon it, Miss Farraday told me—'

'To hell and damnation with Miss Farraday! If she'd taught you right, you'd have found a part to play and we shouldn't have been in such straits that we have to pawn our things, and wouldn't have had to cross that damned road, and I wouldn't be here—'

And once more, Amy set about coaxing him back into a good humour, stricken as she always was with a huge guilt whenever he showed any distress about his discomfort.

Not that it was a very great discomfort. Mr. Caspar, who came to see his prize patient every afternoon at six o'clock, was, for so self-contained a man, quite obviously cock-a-hoop over the success of his operation. There had been no fever to signal underlying putrefaction, no general malaise in Fenton that could not be accounted for by the tedium of being incarcerated in a hospital bed, and clearly he was making a steady recovery. Within two weeks he was able to move about the ward with the aid of a pair of crutches, and after three was begging Mr. Caspar at every visit to remove the splint, which he found irksome in the extreme.

'Four weeks and no sooner, Mr. Lucas,' Mr. Caspar said firmly. 'Four weeks, or I will take no responsibility. By then it is my belief your bone will have knitted well, and we may remove the splint and examine the state of your wound. If we do it too soon, why then, all would have been wasted. And you might even lose your leg yet—'

Which threat sufficed to silence Fenton when Mr. Caspar was about, though it did not halt his constant grumbling to Amy.

It was perhaps because she was more tired than she realized by her devotion to Fenton's care, and more debilitated than she knew by the long hours cooped up inside the fetid hospital ward without adequate exercise, or because her alertness had been dulled by the ease with which she regularly emerged from her cubbyhole each morning and disappeared into it each evening; whatever the reason, she *did* allow herself to be discovered.

It was about a quarter to six on a cold Wednesday evening. The ward, in spite of the big coal fires burning at each end, felt chilly, and the men lay hunched and quiet beneath their blankets. There was none of the usual buzz of conversation which followed the modest supper of hot soup and bread and ale that the men had at five o'clock. Outside it was snowing, the lowering December sky having been threatening it all day, and now the thick white flakes were drifting against the big uncurtained windows in a way that made Amy feel very mournful.

She had had a very miserable day; Fenton had been crotchety and unkind from the moment he woke; Graham had brought the most disagreeable of cold mutton pies for the third day running, apologizing profusely for providing such short commons but finding himself unable to offer her anything better; his mother had just dismissed her cook for pilfering, and the new cook had not yet succumbed to Graham's wiles. And Amy had the headache too, a dull throbbing pain that settled itself over her eyebrows and made her feel very dolorous.

And now the snow—that added deeply to her distress, for it suddenly made her remember Christmas and the way it had been at home when she was a small child and funny, indolent, indulgent, lovely Papa had been alive. The way she had been used to walk with him through the snow in the streets of Boston, and how he never minded when she made balls of it and, squealing with delight, had thrust them down his collar, to reach which she had to stand on tiptoe. The way he would bring her the most absurd and delicious of Christmas gifts, sugar plums strung together into dolls, bought from the little Dutch grocery shops she loved so dearly, or French dragees in silver papered boxes or oranges wrapped in the shiniest of blue and green paper. And now Papa was dead, long dead, and so was Mamma who, for all her dull seriousness and constant tiresome nagging about decorum and proper behaviour, had loved her dearly, and done all a mother could be expected to do for so wilful and headstrong a daughter.

Sitting there in the dreariness of the big quiet malodorous ward, Amy felt her eyes fill with tears, and knowing how Fenton hated to see her cry she turned her head away from him and said huskily, 'Fenton—I am very tired and have a headache. If you will forgive me, I think I will not sit with you any longer tonight but go away and go to sleep. I am sure I will feel better in the morning and be better company for you—'

Fenton, who was reading a five-day-old newspaper with some difficulty, for the gaslight was turned low above his bed, did not look up.

'If you like. I do not *ask* you to sit here all the time, so do not blame me for your megrims—'

Which piece of injustice made her eyes smart even more, but she felt too wretched to give the spirited retort she would usually have offered, and merely bent and brushed his forehead with her lips, and turned to go.

Usually she was much more circumspect. She would stroll with well limned nonchalance down the ward, stopping occasionally to speak a friendly word to another patient so that no one could possibly guess she was actually making her way towards the corner where the little corridor led to her hiding-place. But tonight, with her eyes blurred with tears and her head throbbing so nastily, she simply walked across the ward, making a beeline for the corner.

All might still have been well if she had remembered the fact that Mr. Caspar was so precise a man in all his actions that a clock could be set by him. At five minutes to six each evening he appeared at the door of the men's operation ward, possibly with a student or two to accompany him, and after some colloquy with the nurse in charge, who at this time was usually hovering by the door awaiting him, would make his solemn round of all his patients.

But she did not remember, and Mr. Caspar, arriving at the door of his ward, was startled to see the figure of Miss Lucas crossing the floor in a very direct way, and disappearing into the little corridor that ran off the far corner.

He stood for a moment, watching and waiting to see her come out. Perhaps she had torn a ruffle on her gown, or one of her stay bones was pressing into some tender part of herself, and needed attention? Such dilemmas were very much a part of his wife's experience, and many were the occasions when the patient Mr. Caspar had been left standing waiting in a ballroom or in a warehouse while his Phoebe disappeared to deal with such private feminine affairs.

But Miss Lucas did not reappear with a sweet smile of comfort upon her face, and Mr. Caspar was puzzled. It seemed such an *odd* place for Miss Lucas to go; he knew quite well that there was nothing beyond that corridor but one dusty little storeroom; why was she there?

He performed his rounds in a slightly distrait manner, examining his patients with as great care as ever, and being as punctilious as he always was with his treatment and decisions, but still, his mind was exercised by the strange little puzzle of the disappearing Miss Lucas.

When he stopped beside Fenton's bed he looked down on him and said casually, 'Your sister, Mr. Lucas—she is not with you tonight?'

Fenton looked up and smiled limpidly, his eyes crinkling very charmingly.

'Why no, Mr. Caspar. She had the headache, you know, and I told her it would be better for her to go to bed. So she has gone. It is kind of you to inquire, and I shall tell her you did.'

'Hmm. Yes, indeed, please to give her my good wishes. Now—your leg. You are feeling comfortable tonight, I trust?'

He finished his round in a thoughtful mood, very aware of the fact that Miss Lucas did not reappear from the corridor, and stopped on his way out, after he had seen his last patient, at the foot of Fenton's bed. He opened his mouth to speak to him, to ask him more about his sister's whereabouts, but Fenton looked up again from his newspaper, and gave him his usual sunny smile, and the question died on Mr. Caspar's lips.

But when he reached the door of the ward, his curiosity was too much for him. He sent his students away about their business and told the nurse he had no further need of her, and with a firm step, crossed the floor and marched into the corridor beyond.

It was dark and silent, and after a puzzled moment, he moved forwards and set his hand on the knob of the storage room door. It should be locked, of course; it usually was. But there was no harm in trying, so he turned the knob and pushed, and was so startled when the door opened that he almost fell through it, and then stopped short and stood staring.

Amy was sitting on the pile of mattresses, in her petticoats, and with a heavy blanket thrown across her shoulders. Her gown had been laid carefully across a couple of broken chairs, and her shoes lay neatly side by side on the floor beside it.

The mattresses were covered with a rough sheet—Mr. Foster had 'borrowed' this for her—and on the floor at her feet stood a little penny dip candle throwing its fitful light across the dusty floor and making a small pool of illumination in which she sat, her shoulders hunched, and her head bent.

She sat up and stared at him as he burst in, greatly startled, and he looked at her and felt a sharp twinge of emotion. He could not quite put a name to the feeling; perhaps it was admiration for her pretty face, for the line of the cheek as it merged softly into the chin and then into the long slender throat was very lovely, or perhaps it was pity, for those cheeks for all their beauty were sadly tearstained. Or—and this thought he found very embarrassing—perhaps it was sheer animal desire, for her shoulders were naked and the shape of her breasts could be clearly seen under her chemise.

He gave himself a mental shake; that he, the husband of a woman acknowledged to be among the most beautiful in London, should feel so was quite shameful, and his awareness of his self-disapproval hardened his face and made his voice sound harsh even in his own ears.

'What on earth are you doing here in such a state, Miss Lucas? You amaze me!'

She stared at him for a long moment, her grey eyes seeming almost black, so dark and huge were the pupils in the dim light, and her face a white blur against the dirty wall behind her. And then she shook her head, and tried to speak and couldn't and burst into tears, cradling her head on her arms and rocking to and fro like a frightened child.

'My dear child,' Freddy was horrified at the effect his words had created, and he almost ran across the room to squat down in front of her, and set his hands upon her shoulders and tried to peer into her face. 'My poor dear child, you must not so distress yourself! I did not mean to alarm you, but I was so surprised to see you! What are you doing here? I do not understand!'

She snorted softly and shook her head, and then extricated one hand from her blanket to rub the back of it across her nose in a very childlike gesture which he found most touching. It reminded him forcibly of his eleven-year-old daughter, Cecily, who never could find her handkerchief when she needed it; and almost without thinking he put his hand in his pocket and pulled out a big square of white cambric and used it to mop away her tears, and even held it to her nose so that she could blow, just as though she were in fact eleven years old, rather than just looking it.

'There, there,' he almost crooned it. 'There, you really must compose yourself—there is not need for such weeping.' He wiped her nose quite firmly and then thrust the handkerchief into her hand and she grasped it tightly and sniffed and looked up at him with swimming eyes.

'I am so sorry, truly I am! I did not mean to be so—to behave so badly, and I know Mamma would have been so dreadfully—though Papa, he would have laughed, I daresay and—well, it was not my fault, nor Mr. Foster's either, for I nagged and nagged at him, and the poor boy could not—for after all where else could I go? Poor Fenton so set about and all my fault too, and the hotel bill and everything—but I am so wretched, and so *cold* and I do have such a headache—' and she mopped her eyes again and sniffed and looked at him with a face so woebegone that he could not help but laugh.

'I am not sure that I fully understand what it is all about, but of this much I am certain. I shall never understand sitting here in this dust hole, and freezing half to death! Put on your gown and shoes now and then come with me to my office, where I believe there is a fire, and possibly some small sustenance for you. Come along—'

Obediently she came along. He turned his back prudently as she struggled into her gown, and then in the most fatherly manner possible helped her to fasten her bodice at the back and then, when her shoes were on, led her quietly out of the door. He stopped in the dark corridor outside and held out his hand and she cocked her head and looked at him inquiringly.

'The key,' he said gently. 'I cannot believe that you do not have it?'

She reddened and thrust her hand deep into the bodice of her chemise and drew it out. 'If I had done as Graham said, you'd never have found me. I should have locked it every time I went in, but tonight, my head was so aching and I felt so blue-devilled I did not think about it—'

He said nothing, locking the door and pocketing the key, and led her out to the ward and she looked fearfully across to Fenton's bed, but he was fast asleep. He would be angry with her in the morning, and what would she do? Where would she go? She could not help allowing another sniff to escape her and Mr. Casper patted her shoulder and said gruffly, 'Come—no need for whimpers! We shall set it all to rights, I daresay, one way or another!'

Childlike, she followed him from the ward and down the stairs. It was very comforting to be told what to do. Very agreeable, however miserable she might be underneath, to know that she was no longer alone except for Graham and Fenton. Graham had done his best and a very good best it had been, but all the time when she was with him she was aware of being in charge, the controlling influence. With Mr. Casper she felt anything but in charge, and very much controlled, and it was a great deal more pleasant to feel so than she would have thought possible. As for Fenton—well, what could he do to help her, tied as he was by his splint? But this Mr. Casper would help her, if she tried to explain to him what was amiss. Wouldn't he? Had he not had that familiar look in his eyes, just for a moment, when he had stared at her there in her hateful little cubbyhole?

By the time she reached his office she felt a good deal better, though her head still ached and she still displayed a most dolorous countenance. Surely she could manage to sort things out with this man. Surely she could!

# CHAPTER SIX

In fact, it was rather more difficult than she had expected. First of all, he refused to speak of anything until she had eaten and drunk, sending a surprised-looking nurse hotfoot to the kitchens to bring her bread and cold beef and a mug of hot ale spiced with cinnamon. He ensconced her beside the fire in his neat little office, stirring the embers in the grate to dancing flames, and then sat and watched her as she ate the food with great eagerness and drank her ale with equal relish. By the time she had finished it all, putting down the empty mug with a sigh, her headache had receded to become little more than a dull memory of itself behind her brows, and she was relaxed and comfortable and much less woebegone.

And, she realized, had therefore lost some of her advantage. To persuade him of her need for help and to convince him that she was not deserving of some sort of reprimand for hiding away in the hospital for all this time would have been much easier if she had remained as she had been when she came into the office, white-cheeked and tearstained. But now, warm and rosy from the combined effects of ale and firelight and with her gown a trifle stretched over her comfortably full stomach she felt and therefore knew she looked far less appealing.

She sat up straighter and looked at him on the other side of the fire, sitting leaning back in his chair with his legs outstretched and his hands in his trouser pockets, and tried to think herself back into the state of sadness in which she had been when he had found her and been so charmed by her helplessness, rearranging her face into a suitable expression;

and suddenly he laughed, throwing back his head and opening his mouth wide to show strong white teeth.

'Oh, Miss Lucas, you remind me very much indeed of my wife, you know, and of my young daughter! I recollect that your brother is an actor—are you of the same profession? I think you must be, for my wife has just the same gift that you have of making her face speak for her, and she was always of the theatre—and now my Cecily bids fair to follow her—'

She stared at him, her embarrassing situation quite forgotten for a moment. 'Your wife, sir, is of the theatre? Does she—could she—oh, sir, could she help us find a part, do you think? Not for Fenton yet, of course, but for me—for of *course* I am an actress—and then for Fenton when he is quite well again? We are so sorely in need of—'

He shook his head. 'My wife, Miss Lucas, is my *wife*! She does not occupy herself upon the stage any more, of course! Although she is often engaged upon producing drawing-room tableaux for her friends and for charitable purposes, you know—' He frowned for a moment. 'Now, we must speak of you! I did not bring you here to speak of my family affairs!'

He was suddenly annoyed with himself; this young woman who could at one moment fill him with the pity owing to a sad child, the next with sheer sensual feeling of the sort due only to a wife—or a courtesan of some skill—and then make him as prosy as an old woman sitting in a chimney corner, was very irritating; and he was tired, and had worked hard all day. This matter must be settled forthwith. His voice took on a harder edge as he sat up and looked at her very directly.

'Now, Miss Lucas! We must get down to cases. *Why* were you skulking in that room in your petticoats? And have you been using it all the time your brother has been here? And with whose connivance has it all been possible? I have a shrewd idea of the answer to the last question, but I wish to hear it from your lips, so that the matter may be sorted out. I must tell you that Nellie's—Queen Eleanor's hospital—is a well-run institution and does not permit some of the excesses that occur at other establishments.'

She looked at him for a long moment, her lower lip caught between her teeth and thinking hard. Should she try to beguile him? Should she play the captivating lady of the world, the helpless child of misfortune, the—almost imperceptibly she shook her head, and with the unerring instinct of the born performer made the right decision. She would be direct, telling him the plain unvarnished truth, and asking his help, rather than his mercy, and his appreciation of her as a fellow human being rather than as an object of pity.

So, sitting very upright with her hands crossed primly on the lap of her crumpled gown, she did just that. She started at the beginning, with her mother's death. She told him of her English Papa and his many stories of life in London and the theatre, and how she and Fenton, who had done his best to take care of her, she assured him, had decided to come to London to seek both their fortunes and their theatrical forebears.

'For, it seemed to us, sir, a great likelihood that there would be *some* that would recollect our father, for although it is more than twenty years since he left here to go to Boston, people do remember, do they not? My Cabot uncles are always talking of matters that occurred *forty* years ago, as though it were but last quarter day! Well—we came—'

She wondered for a moment whether to admit that they had mulcted the captain of the *Daniel Boone* of his just payment and discarded the idea. There was no need to be *excessively* direct, and she went smoothly on, but Freddy Caspar noticed the faint change in her tone and rhythm of speech and wondered what she had left out. But he was so interested in all she was saying that he let her run on, and dismissed the moment of doubt that split second of hesitation had aroused in him.

And she was well worth listening to, for she sketched in very graphic words the picture of their first weeks in London, the high hopes with which they had started, the slow loss of their spirits, and the moments of despair which almost overwhelmed them. And then, as she told of the day upon which Fenton had so swiftly leaped to save her life and Graham Foster had come to their rescue her account became even more vivid and he almost felt the fear and guilt with which she had been so consumed.

Her eyes were dark as she stared at him, her mouth drooping. 'I know my brother can be a little difficult sometimes, sir,' she said. 'I know there are some who think him—well, a little selfish and—and shallow, you know. But he is not. He is very absorbed in the matter of building his career, I grant you, and that can make even the best of persons seem antipathetic to others. But at bottom he is a good and loving brother, and the dearest boy! He did not hesitate for a moment when I was so foolish as to walk under those hooves. And a man who can risk so much for his sister—well, he is a *worthy* person, is he not?'

Freddy nodded, any shreds of doubt about her veracity melting away in the warmth of the response she had aroused in him. All his life he had been a person who much valued family ties; a true friend to those to whom he gave his regard freely, to his relations, towards whom he knew he had a duty as well as great affection, he was as a rock. There were none in his family who would not turn to Freddy in times of anxiety, and he had become for all of them—his mother and stepfather and their children, his wife's brother as well as his grandfather and aunt—a bulwark. Looking after all of them as well as his own wife and children was what Freddy believed himself to exist for, and to find that this patient of his, who had undoubtedly seemed to him at times to be shallow and ungrateful was in fact a young man of genuine family feeling, was all he needed to forgive all. Fenton's alternating sharpness and smooth sweetness, all his sulks and his megrims could be laid at the door of his anxiety for his sister's welfare while he was cooped up in pain in a hospital bed. Whatever plans had been made to protect Miss Lucas during this difficult time were, however underhanded they might seem, made for the best of reasons, Freddy told himself, and even young Foster's complicity would have to be forgiven under the circumstances.

And so he smiled at the girl in the chair opposite him, a smile that lifted his face into a much younger expression, and raised her hopes vastly.

'Well, I think I can see what the situation has been. And why you did as you did. It was of course highly irregular, but we will say no more—'

She dimpled at him, her eyes sparkling and her hands slipping into a supplicating posture. 'And you will not punish poor Mr. Foster, sir?'

'None of your beguiling tricks with me, ma'am!' Freddy stood up and looked down at her. 'Recall, if you please, that I am the husband of one who once used the self-same pretty behaviours you are using now! I know them all! No, I will not punish Mr. Foster, not because you asked me not to, but because I can quite see that the poor wretch had little choice in what he did. To one as inexperienced as he, your stage wiles must have acted like laudanum upon anxiety! He will be told, of course, in no uncertain terms, of my displeasure. But my grandfather will not be told, so there will be no need for Mr. Foster to have any fears! The question now, of course, is what we do with you? You cannot remain here, that much is sure!'

'No—I suppose not.' She looked up at him trustfully and he grimaced and turned away. Take her home to Phoebe? No, that was not the solution, he told himself, and could not quite decide why. Phoebe would welcome the girl, he was sure; they had room and to spare in their handsome house in Tavistock Square and her presence there would discommode nobody. But, all the same, he thought not. Concerned as he was for the welfare of his patient—and he was a special patient, after all, having responded so well to the use of Mr. Lister's technique—and for his patient's sister, he could not extend his care too far. But a solution must be found.

It was in thinking of Fenton as a patient that he found his solution, and he turned back to her smiling with some relief.

'I have the very answer! There is another patient of mine— a lady who has suffered considerable attention at my hands and professes herself exceedingly grateful, and is always asking me to make use of her services in any way I wish. Now, she and her daughter reside very near here, in a most comfortable little house, and they have rooms to let. I daresay— indeed, I am quite certain—that I can prevail upon them to accept you and your brother, who progresses well and will, I think, shortly be ready to join you, as lodgers. That will do capitally! And then—'

She shook her head, almost impaiently. 'But you do not seem to understand! If we had the money to pay our shot *anywhere* we would not have any difficulties! We would stay where we are, at the hotel—where our luggage is. It is because—'

He brushed that aside. 'You need not worry about that matter. Your account at the hotel will be paid and your luggage reclaimed. Also, Mrs. Miller and her daughter will be settled with your first month's rent which will, I am certain, be much less than that for the hotel. Then—'

'You are very kind, sir!' she said, and jumped up and ran towards him, her hands outstretched, and at once. he shook his head and said sharply, 'You must not regard this money as a gift nor me as a financial benefactor, Miss Lucas! That would not be proper at all! I can arrange to loan you the necessary funds from the Nellie's Bursar's supply—he always has some moneys to hand, from the various charitable bodies which support us—but we will expect it repaid as soon as you may!'

Her face crumpled again. 'But *how*? How are we to repay when we have no work, and no—'

'I have thought of that as well!' He smiled again, and the moment of tension dissolved. 'My brother-in-law owns and manages an establishment in King Street; near by Mrs. Miller's lodgings. It is a Supper Rooms where respectable people may eat a meal and enjoy some agreeable entertainment. He, I am sure, will find for you, and your brother in due course, some work that you may do, using your talents. I have not of course seen you perform, and must trust to it that you *are* a capable entertainer, but he will be able to assess your value, I am sure. And then, when you are earning, well, you will be able to pay back what you owe to Nellie's and then in due course set about repairing your own fortunes. It really seems to me that there can be no better plan—'

'I am deeply grateful to you, sir,' she said, but there was a note of dubiety in her voice that he found a little irritating. Had he not come up with a most splendid and suitable plan, and offered to put himself to much inconvenience to settle her affairs? To cavil now was to be most ungrateful.

She seemed to recognize his feeling and went on hastily, 'I am much indebted to you for your plan, and for your offer of help in obtaining both respectable accommodation and employment, and above all for the loan of such as we need to get back our luggage—but it is the *work* you suggest about which

I am concerned. You see, Fenton and I—we are *actors*, and—'

'Oh, as to that, have no fears!' Freddy said. 'I know that the bill Oliver—Mr. Lackland, my brother-in-law—presents at his Supper Rooms is very varied. I daresay he will find something that is suitable to your talents. So, it is agreed! I trust you are content, for it grows late and I am expected at home. I would like to put the matter in hand and see you settled tonight, and then be on my way.'

She was all contrition. 'Indeed, sir, it is settled. We will worry about the work that your brother-in-law offers when he has offered it, shall we? Then if—well, we shall see what follows!'

She was tired again now. The effects of the ale, which had been strong as well as hot and spicy, were receding and her headache was returning, and she rubbed her eyes suddenly, as a child does, and he nodded and went to his desk to unlock and take out a large iron box.

'Well, you shall tell me which hotel you are at, and I shall send the porter to pay your account, and collect your luggage. Then, we shall make our way to Mrs. Miller in Long Acre and see you comfortable.'

'I hope she will be there and able to take me at such short notice,' Amy said and yawned, and he smiled at that.

'She will be there! Mrs. Miller is a most respectable lady, and spends all her time at her own establishment when she is not here with me seeking relief for her many aches and pains and assorted tribulations. She will be there!'

Amy sat and dozed by the fire while the porter, grumbling mightily but not daring to refuse Mr. Caspar's request to take himself to the Albion Hotel in Great Russell Street, went to collect their luggage. Then, when he returned, she was roused by Freddy, bundled into a shawl he had obtained from she knew not where, and taken out to the four-wheeler cab which waited outside. Her luggage was piled on top, a sight which made her eyes light up in delight. The thought of being able to dress properly again in her own clothes instead of that dreary gown that Mr. Foster had filched from his sister lifted her spirits in a way nothing else could have done, and she climbed into the cab, with Mr. Caspar assisting her, with a will.

'I shall tell your brother in the morning all that has transpired,' he promised her when she suddenly remembered that dear Fenton knew nothing of what was afoot, and tried to climb out again to run up to the ward and wake him and tell him. 'You need not fear. I doubt he will object to all we have arranged!'

'No, I am sure he will be very grateful,' she said and put her hand on his arm and peered up at him in the darkness of the cab as it rocked its way across the old cobbles towards Long Acre, a few streets away. 'As indeed I am. If I had but known how kindly and—and *sensible* a person you are, I would not have prevailed upon poor Mr. Foster to do as he did—'

She paused then and added reflectively, 'I think perhaps I will have much to explain to him. For he—well, I think perhaps he has a small tendre for me, and *that* will never do!'

'I am sure he has,' Freddy said and his voice was amused in the darkness. 'Since I have not the least doubt that you made sure he would, in order to aid you in your nefarious doings!'

'Well, perhaps I did,' she said, and giggled. 'But you know, it was not difficult! He's a very—very *new* young man! No town polish at all! I was amazed when he said he had lived always in London, for he seems to me just like the boys who come to Boston after living all their lives on the farmsteads. Rather tedious, you know and—'

'Tedious or not, he risked much for you,' Freddy's voice sharpened. 'You must not forget that!'

'Of course I shall not! I am most appreciative of all he did! But—well, he is not a *man*, is he? As you are!'

'This part of town is much known for its coach manufactories,' Freddy said in a repressive voice. 'No doubt you are aware of the odours that are reaching us. Turpentine, and of course timber, and paint—'

'I had wondered,' she said demurely, and sat beside him in the darkness, careful not to touch him and wickedly aware of the way she could disturb even a man as glossy with town polish as Freddy Caspar. Her spirits began to lift, and she breathed deeply, absorbing the pleasant woody smells which indeed filled the musty air of the cab, and thought happily, if a little sleepily, about the morrow.

As ever, the young Lucases had fallen on their feet; Fenton was nearly well, they had had their debts paid and their possessions restored to them; been given a place to stay, which no doubt would be pleasant enough, and even the promise of work of a sort. From now on, surely, she told herself, yawning yet again, everything would surely be quite splendid.

# CHAPTER SEVEN

It was, if not precisely splendid, certainly comfortable. Mrs. Miller, a round lady of diminutive stature who made even the slight Amy feel positively carthorse-ish, had greeted the knock on her door, a red-painted and brass-knobbed door set flush with the street, by peering out with great suspicion through the curtains which tastefully draped the window set in the brick wall beside it. But then, as she had recognized Freddy Caspar, she had rushed to unbolt and unlock it, accompanying every action with much twittering and gasping and Bless My Souls and Dearie, Dearie Mes, and sundry other breathless comments.

Her house was, Amy decided after her first rather doubtful glance, a charming one. Tall and narrow, it boasted on each floor, of which there were four, only a narrow passageway and a staircase and two small square rooms set neatly one behind the other. Mrs. Miller led Freddy and Amy and the grunting porter bearing the luggage up the first flight of stairs, talking and gasping all the way.

'Oh, bless my soul, bless my poor old soul, but you amazed

me, Mr. Caspar, that you did, seeing you standing there! Whoever'd've thought of it! A quiet evenin' by my fire sitting there minding my own business, and then who should bob up but the kindest and best surgeon as ever set hand to a poor woman's aching legs and back! It's no wonder I'm all set about—now, never you say another word—'

This in answer to Freddy's attempts to stem her flow of words in order to explain why he was accompanied by a young rather shabbily dressed but very pretty lady, and a man bearing her luggage.

'Whatever it is, it don't make no never mind, and never you think it, Mr. Caspar, sir, never you think it! If you wants to bring the whole Brigade o' Guards here for reasons of your own, why, my duck, then you bring 'em and never a question asked on account of I owes my very life to you, never mind my happiness and peace of mind and comfort and here's my Emma, as took aback with the surprise of seein' you as I am, I have not the least doubt!'

By this time they had reached the next floor and been led into a very cosy little room which was, Amy decided, the reddest and warmest she had ever seen. The walls were papered with a ferociously plushed and crimsoned paper which was patterned with festoons of feathers. The floor was covered with a heavy red turkey carpet. The furniture was draped wherever there was a drapable portion with thick scarlet chenille. The fireplace in which burned a large fire, the flames seeming to be the brightest hottest red possible, was surmounted by a mantel which was trimmed with rose-coloured tassels and fringing. In the candlesticks on each side of the tall oil lamps stood thick twisted red candles, each burning with a tall flame. And on all sides there were crimson upholstered little chairs and tables all of which bore ornaments and framed pictures and pieces of china and mounted needlework, in a glad hugger-mugger that winked cheerfully back at Amy's dazzled gaze.

In the middle of all this stood a girl as tall and thin as her mother was short and round. Her pallid rather thin hair was pulled into tight ringlets on each side of her narrow face, and each cheek bore a round red patch which seemed to match the room, and she was wearing a gown so determinedly girlish that Amy would have regarded it as unsuitable for her own twenty-three years, yet this girl was in truth no girl, being at least, Amy decided with one demure upward glance, three and thirty if she was a day.

She stood there smiling and nodding but saying nothing as her mother rattled on.

'There now, Mr. Caspar, you remember my little Emma, I'll be bound! As good a girl as ever drew breath and so kind to her old mother, staying at home with me to bear me company when all the other young giddy ones is running about the balls and parties as selfish as you please!'

Emma blinked and produced a little self-deprecatory grimace and smiled even more widely as the accolade went on. '—the best teacher of singing and music, on the pianoforte and the violin, you know, as there is in the whole of Covent Garden *and* beyond and could do much to better herself, had she the mind, but not my Emma. Here she is, she tells me, and here she stays, don't you, my duck?' And she beamed fondly at the silent Emma who still stood there in the middle of the room in her white gown with its pink sash, smiling broadly.

Freddy managed to silence the breathless Mrs. Miller at last, by urging her to sit down, from which position it appeared she was almost unable to speak at all, and with a few succinct words told her of Amy's and her brother Fenton's plight (at which Mrs. Miller, threatening to haul herself to her feet again, immediately responded with clucks of sympathy) and gave her a sovereign 'to last them as long as it is possible, Mrs. Miller, after which time, I am sure they will be able to pay you themselves. But if they cannot, then do not fear—we will seek a way to manage matters so that you will not be incommoded. I am grateful to you indeed, and now you must all forgive me, for it is time I was at home. My wife will fear I have been locked up for ever in the hospital, if I do not get to her soon! Tomorrow, Miss Lucas, if you will attend me at the hospital, we will see what can be done about your brother's removal from the wards, and then, why, we will be ready to introduce you to my brother-in-law! Then you will be able to work, and get upon your feet. But tomorrow we shall talk more.'

And away down the narrow stairs to the cab, the porter

following him noisily, he went, leaving the now almost exhausted Amy to the ministrations of Mrs. Miller which, though voluble, were nonetheless comforting. She provided a bath for her in a warm lamplit bedroom at the very top of the house, sitting her in the high-backed tin tub before the fire and pouring great quantities of hot water into it, which the totally uncomplaining Emma brought up the stairs with the help of a lugubrious and equally silent maidservant. Then she had tucked Amy into the soft comfort of a linen-sheeted bed (which after weeks on the rough blankets and old mattresses of the ward cubbyhole felt like total bliss to Amy's weary body) and then unpacked her luggage, exclaiming delightedly over her pretty gowns and chemises, and stowing all away neatly in a tall chest of mahogany drawers, before doing the same for all of Fenton's clothes, using the room behind Amy's for him.

So that Amy fell asleep to the sound of the clatter of her breathless little voice to slumber more soundly than she had since she had arrived in England all those weeks ago.

After two weeks in the Miller household, both Fenton and Amy felt they had lived there for ever. Freddy had decided that Fenton could leave the hospital forthwith, and could return a week later to have his splint removed, and his wound dressed, since both of them pleaded with him to permit it. Amy because she was sure that Mrs. Miller would take superb care of him, and Fenton because he was heartily bored with life in the wards at Nellie's.

They had settled down in the tall thin house with its ill-assorted occupants and within a matter of days were virtually lording it there.

Mrs. Miller had become twice as breathless and twice as voluble at the sight of Fenton, his face pale after his weeks in hospital and his hair, sorely in need of cutting, flopping romantically over his brow, and set about nursing him with such gusto that even he felt himself overwhelmed with attention. As for Miss Emma Miller—she had opened her eyes wide when she was first introduced to Fenton, and for the first time in Amy's hearing had spoken, saying 'Good morning,' with great intensity in a surprisingly deep and resonant voice.

And from then on, all was indeed splendid for the Lucases. Mrs. Miller, who worked hard as an artist's colourman, selling powdered pigments and oils and charcoal pencils from the crammed shelves in the front downstairs room, would come bustling up to her parlour on the first floor where the young Lucases spent much of their time to make sure they had all they wanted, while Emma, who taught her music to a procession of depressed-looking young ladies who came toiling up the stairs at hourly intervals from nine in the morning till seven at night, found many excuses to slip shyly into the front parlour while a pupil trilled uneven scales or thumped the unfortunate pianoforte unmercifully, ostensibly to find a mislaid sheet of music or her reticule, but never failing to smile tremulously at Fenton and ask him in her strange deep voice if he needed aught.

Fenton, well aware of the havoc he was wreaking in poor Miss Emma's heart, wickedly fed her passion for him with smiles and even, on occasion, little winks, which made Amy remonstrate with him.

'For,' she said, 'you are a very beguiling young man, as well you know, and we do not wish another episode like poor Sophie Varden, do we?'

At which Fenton, who remembered all too well Miss Varden and her histrionics, including her rather inept attempt to take poison for love of him, agreed, and tried to be remote. But failed, for Miss Emma's adoration was balm to his soul, so long had he been without agreeable feminine company (for who could count Amy?) and was soon smiling and winking as much as ever. So that by the end of the first week it was arranged that he should enjoy a daily singing and pianoforte lesson, totally without fee, of course, from the besotted Miss Emma.

He found in fact, that her skill was considerable, and under her devoted eye learned a great deal, and his pleasant tenor voice would fill the little house in a very agreeable way, and Mrs. Miller downstairs amid her sacks of powdered gamboge and sepia, madder and burnt umber would cock her head and smile delightedly, and Amy too would listen and admire her brother's new talent, and long to start seeking work again.

It had been decided, after much discussion over Fenton's leg on the day the splint was removed, to wait another week before arranging for an audition with Oliver Lackland.

'I spoke to him of you,' Freddy said in the big casualty room one afternoon as he tenderly examined the scar left in Fenton's leg, 'and he will gladly see you, but advises waiting until he is ready to set his new programme afoot. It is now but two days to Christmas, and the present show will end on New Year's Day, I am told, and a new one will be put in hand shortly after. He says it is better to clear his mind of all that is happening now and then he will be able to offer you more guidance on what are his needs. Meanwhile, I have spoken to the Bursar and it is agreed that the funds will bear you a little longer—no, do not puzzle yourself over it, Miss Lucas. To tell you the truth, I would be loth to lose so interesting a patient!'

He smiled at Fenton, who was frowning heavily as he stared at his leg with its livid puckered scar stretching down the side of the calf.

'I am very proud of your progress! You have done excellent well, and your leg is as good as new—I will wish to show it, with your consent, to some of my colleagues and students. That will be some recompense for our—ah—help—regarding the Bursar's fund—'

'Done well, you say?' Fenton burst out. 'Can you look at that, and tell me I have done well? When it's so ugly and—'

'Hush, Fenton!' Amy said, and reddened. She knew better than anyone that but for Freddy's insistence and skill, Fenton would have had no leg at all to complain about, might not even have had his life, but he went on furiously, 'I do not care! You shall not hush me, Amy! It is *hideous* and—'

Freddy, to Amy's surprise, took it well. 'I understand your concern, my boy,' he said gently. 'I was aware of the importance of your appearance the day I operated and sewed you as neat as I could! You must not be distressed at the look of the scar now. It will take time, but I assure you the livid colour will fade, and the shape of your leg will greatly improve, as you exercise it. Now your bone is knit well, and what you must do is walk a great deal. Yes, do not look so surprised! Each day, walk at least from one end of Long Acre to the other—so that you strengthen your muscles and set your leg back on the road to its former handsomeness! The muscles have healed very well. The rest is now in your hands, or, rather feet! The sooner you start with exercise, why, the sooner you will be back on a stage! So—another week, and then Christmas and New Year will be over. And I will send a message to you to come to Nellie's once more for an examination of your leg, and then we will arrange for the meeting with my brother-in-law.'

In the event it was less than a week later when the message came to 56 Long Acre bidding the Lucases to come to 11 Tavistock Square.

'I have not yet had the pleasure of making your acquaintance, Miss Lucas,' Mrs. Caspar wrote, 'but I look forward to doing so with much pleasure. My husband has spoken to me of your dilemma and your brother's sad accident, and that he intends that you should meet my brother in order to place before him your abilities as performers for his show, and it seems to me that no better opportunity will present itself than the little soiree I have planned to welcome the New Year. I hope we may see you at seven o'clock in the evening, to dine, and trust you will remain and share our festivities until 1867!'

'She seems very charming!' Amy said, folding the heavy writing paper carefully, and tucking it away in her reticule. 'Inviting total strangers to what is clearly a family party! Do you not find that agreeable, Fenton?'

Fenton stretched his legs to the fire, and began once again the foot exercises he had developed to improve the rate at which his leg regained its power—which it was fast doing, since he spent so much of his time now walking up and down Long Acre—and said lazily, 'Oh, I don't know! I guess she wants something a bit out of the ordinary to entertain 'em all with, and thinks a couple of Yankees will make good table talk! Women are the same all over the world, and you know how the Cabot aunts would snaffle any visitor to town and feed 'em and lionize 'em! This one's the same, depend upon it!'

'Well, I don't care if we are being lionized!' Amy said

stoutly. 'It will be such a joy to visit a really elegant house, and to have something worth dressing up for!' She dropped her voice a little then. 'Mrs. Miller and Miss Emma are very pleasant, of course, but—well, they are very—'

'Cheapjack!' Fenton said loudly. Amy reddened and turned her head to look apprehensively at the door of the parlour and said, 'Hush!'

'Oh, they won't hear! They're down in the kitchen, the pair of them, cooking up something special for our dinner!' He laughed then, and leaned over and kissed Amy soundly on one cheek. 'Oh, but we fell on our feet here, Sugar-Amy! And you did it all on your own! I couldn't have found a better berth myself, and I don't mind saying so!'

'It wasn't all my own doing. It was Mr. Caspar—he meant very kindly, and still does. And now this invitation! It really is very splendid. It's my guess these Caspars are very rich, for Mrs. Miller tells me he is a very highly thought of surgeon and that his mother is married to a very rich man, who owns half London—or so she says—and that Tavistock Square is a very elegant place to live! It could be, Fenton, that we are about to be launched into just the sort of society we need! And as soon as we can manage it I must have some new gowns. Mrs. Miller says that Emma is a pretty needlewoman and if we can but afford the stuff, she will make for me—'

The door rattled behind them and Mrs. Miller came in, breathless and talking even before the door was fully opened.

'—I told him as you'd been resting, Master Fenton, and that you was still resting too, Miss Amy, just as you said I should, but he's that determined that it takes more than me and my Emma put together to get rid of him, so I said as I'd come and ask again, that I knew as you were resting, as I said, and I had my instructions—'

She pushed the door closed behind her and leaned on the panels, beaming at them both and puffing from the exertions of her climb up the stairs. 'Not, Miss Amy, that it doesn't go to my heart to see the poor boy's face when he asks for you! Every day this week he's been here and said as he needs to have words with you, and do what I may to think of a new reason each day to send him away, he still comes back, so he really does have a determination about him that makes itself felt! You'll have to see him sooner or later, Miss Amy, of that much I'm certain, and if you don't see him today, he'll only be back tomorrow—'

'Mrs. Miller is right, Amy,' Fenton said and smiled brilliantly at Mrs. Miller. 'You can't keep sending him away! Why not agree to talk to him? What harm can it do?'

'He's—oh, he's—oh, you know perfectly well why!' Amy hissed at him, and Fenton laughed.

'Oh, come, Amy, we don't want another Sophia Varden episode, do we? Sauce for geese and ganders, Amy, sauce and geese and ganders!'

'I am not encouraging him, you fool!' Amy was scarlet with mortification. 'It is quite different! I'm doing the very opposite of what you are doing with—'

'Send him up, Mrs. Miller, send him up!' Fenton said loudly, and laughed aloud at the expression on his sister's face, and then stood up.

'Really, Amy, you're behaving like a real baby. Well, I shall take my exercise, I think, before the weather makes it insupportable to be out of doors!' He limped to the window and peered out between the crimson curtains at the heavy lowering sky outside. 'It would never do to miss my exercise, but I don't want to be snowed to a standstill, either!'

'Fenton!' Amy said wrathfully, and jumped to her feet, sending the sewing which had been upon her lap flying in all directions. 'Fenton, don't you *dare* go out and leave me alone with him! If you do, I shall never—'

'Speak to me again?' Fenton said sweetly, and turned towards the door as it began to open. 'Oh, I doubt I shall ever enjoy anything as good as that, Amy! You couldn't stop speaking to save your bacon! Good afternoon to you, Foster! Good of you to call! Forgive me if I leave you to my sister—I have to take my daily exercise you know, as advised by your good master, Caspar! I shall be back by and by!'

And he went, leaving Amy staring furiously after him and young Mr. Foster standing with his hat turning awkwardly between his hands, and his face drawn and tense.

'Good—good afternoon, Miss Lucas,' he said stiffly. 'I am

glad to see you again. When—when you would not see me, I began to fear you were ill, for I could think of no harm I had done you that you should forbid me your company!'

She blinked and looked at him properly for the first time, and at the sight of his white face and the lines that had appeared between his brows was quite stricken with compunction. He looked so miserable that she felt her own eyes prickle for a moment, and held out both her hands to him impulsively.

'Oh, I am glad to see you! Please do not be angry with me for denying you when you have called all this week—it was Fenton, you know!' And she took a sharp pleasure in maligning her brother behind his back. 'He has been *so* captious, and would not let me leave his side, and refused to speak to anyone at all! I have been very miserable, I do promise you!'

The effect of these words on Mr. Foster was quite remarkable. The lines between his eyes seemed to melt away, his cheeks rounded and lifted and the pallor which had invested them receded beneath a tide of pink. He stammered and stopped and took a deep breath and then cracked his face into a smile of sheer relief and came forward to seize her hands in his, dropping his hat and almost treading on it in his eagerness.

'Oh, I am so *glad* to hear you say so, Miss Lucas! I have been much exercised in my mind, to see if I could fathom how I had offended you! I knew you had no other friends in London, and I just could not understand when Mrs. Miller kept barring my way—well, how *are* you? Are you well? I know from Mr. Caspar that your brother is doing splendidly—'

'Oh, he is, he is,' Amy said, and sat down, indicating the chair on the other side of the fireplace to her guest. 'And I—well—' her face slipped into lines of sadness and she allowed her shoulders to slump a little. 'I have been, I cannot deny, very weary. I am more than grateful to Mrs. Miller for her care, but you know, looking after a captious invalid—and Fenton is *very* captious—can be so wearing!'

At once he was all concern, and she realized that he was about to sweep forwards to kneel before her and offer his undying care and total responsibility for captious Fenton and any other rub that should even appear in her way, and hastily changed her performance to become the Brave Little Fighter Against Adversity. '—but no need to fear—I am able to manage! I always have managed, and I shall now! So—tell me of your own affairs, Mr. Foster! What has passed with you since we last met?'

'Well—' he looked at her a trifle sternly. 'Well, I cannot hide from you the fact that Mr. Caspar was—well, to say the truth, his rage was monumental! He spoke to me most sharply of the way I had aided you and hidden you there at Nellie's, and for a day or two I feared I was to be sent about my business, with my studies uncompleted, and I could not imagine what my Mamma would say, for it has taken much of her slender resources to see me as far as this on a surgeon's career—'

Amy stopped acting, all at once, and sat and stared at him with her eyes wide and her lower lip caught between her teeth as he went on.

'—and I was most set about for that time, and came to see you twice in the hope you would intercede for me, for I knew Mr. Caspar held you and your brother in some regard, for had he not arranged to help you, and set you up in lodgings here? All the hospital knew of it. But you would not see me, so—' he shrugged, and looked down at his hands on his knees.

'Oh, I am sorry, Graham! I have been so selfish and unkind, thinking only of myself—'

'No, I understand now—it was your brother's fault, not yours.' He looked at her with his eyes glittering with emotion. 'You could not be unkind or selfish if you tried, Miss Amy—Miss Lucas. I know you could not, for you are as sweet as any angel—'

'Oh, please, do stop!' Her discomfort made her face flame crimson, and on Mr. Foster the effect was electrifying and once again he moved as though to hurl himself at her feet to pour out all his feelings, his devotion and his plans for a shared future, and with the readiness born of many similar experiences with lovesick young men she jumped to her feet and moved away to stand beside the window.

'Oh dear, it is getting very dark and it is snowing again—I do so hope Fenton will be safe, and not slip on the icy ground! It would be dreadful were he to damage his leg again,' she murmured and then turned back to him with a brilliant but somehow remote smile on her face.

'But tell me, Mr. Foster, is all well now? I am sure Mr. Caspar, who has been so kind to us, could not punish you for being equally kind—'

'No, you are right, Miss Lucas.' Mr. Foster seemed to have gathered his control together and was now able to speak with some dignity. 'Indeed, you are right. He is a most kind and thoughtful man. He has assured me that I shall not be punished further and that Mr. Lackland, the senior surgeon, you know, will not hear of—of what happened with you. And that I am able to complete my studies and take the examinations set by the College. So, I have no more fears in *that* direction. He has gone further, however. He tells me you and your brother have been invited to spend the thirty-first of December evening at his house, and has asked me if I will arrange to bear you both there. He—he—'

He suddenly went very red, as he wondered whether to tell his beloved, standing there with her head on one side and waiting for him to finish what he was saying, the truth of the matter; that Mr. Caspar had said to him 'That young lady is very charming, Mr. Foster, very amusing and quite a little heartbreaker, I believe! If you are a fool, you will allow her to break your heart. If you have any sense, you will enjoy her company, and keep your feelings well under control.' But he decided not to. Instead he went on, 'Mr. Caspar told me that his wife has bidden you to be her guests but had given no thought to the matter of your transport. So, I am here to offer my services, if you should wish them.'

'Oh, are you going to the party too, then, Mr. Foster?'

'I? Dear me, no! Of course not! I am but a medical student, Miss Lucas. Mrs. Caspar would never dream of inviting *me* to her house! No, it was just that—well—' He reddened even more, if that were possible. 'Well, I asked Mr. Caspar if there was aught I could do to help you—er—and your brother of course—and he told me of this. So, if you wish, I shall come here on that day at half past six, with a carriage, and convey you both to Tavistock Square. And I will wait for you, if you wish, to bear you back again.'

'But—Mr. Foster—you are not a coachman! I could not allow you to so—so demean yourself as to—'

'It would not be demeaning in any way, Miss Lucas,' Mr. Foster spoke with great earnestness. 'It would give me much pleasure. At half past six, then, I shall be below with my equipage. I have arranged the hire of a coach from a nearby manufactory—it will be my pleasure to take you to your party, indeed it will.'

# CHAPTER EIGHT

Even before they left the house the snow was lying thickly in Long Acre and covering the roofs and chimneys with a layer of whiteness that transformed the normal sootiness of London into a fairytale beauty. Amy, standing poised on the doorstep, peered out from beneath her cloak hood and would have clapped her hands in delight, had they not been securely muffed.

'Oh, it is quite, quite beautiful! And just like home! I do love snow so much, don't you, Mr. Foster?'

Mr. Foster, his hat brim weighted down with slush and blinking as the icy drips ran down his forehead to paint his nose as red as Mrs. Miller's sitting-room, said earnestly, 'Indeed, yes, Miss Amy. It is delightful!'

'You're mad, man!' Fenton said gruffly from behind Amy. 'The stuff is wet and cold and very disagreeable! For Pete's sake, Amy, do make a move and don't stand there mopping and mowing. It's freezing out here!'

So Amy, stepping out as prettily as she could, moved forwards and then stood hesitating on the edge of the pavement, for the snow was thick and would clearly go well over her dancing pumps if she ventured further. Mr. Foster came to-wards her, and with only a momentary hesitation set one arm round her shoulders and the other round her hips and, lifting her clear, carried her to the waiting carriage, much to the admiration of Mrs. Miller and Miss Emma who were watching the young Lucases' departure from the parlour window above.

He settled her with much fussing of carriage rugs and hot bricks, and Fenton followed her in, making some play of his limp. In fact his leg was coming on very well indeed, his daily exercise and basic good health and strength having combined to ensure a rapid recovery, but he felt a limp added an air of romance to his posture and was quite enjoying cultivating it. Certainly Miss Emma was most touched at the sight of him, almost falling out of the window in her efforts to catch one last glimpse as he disappeared.

Mr. Foster, with equal reluctance to leave Amy's side, at last could fuss no longer and closed the carriage door upon his precious charge and climbed up into the box to pick up the reins, heavy and slippery and difficult to control because of their coating of ice, and stamping his feet against the step, shouted at his horses. They, moving slowly because of the heavy calico bandages around their fetlocks as well as the depth of the snow, tossed their heads and with much jingling of harness, the equipage set off.

Amy peered out of the window with great joy, watching the snowflakes tumbling wildly against it, and snuggled deeply into her rug, curling her toes against the warmth of the brick Mr. Foster had set so solicitously beneath her feet. 'He really is the *kindest* young man, is he not?' she said. 'I cannot imagine how we would ever have got there tonight without him, for Mrs. Miller says all the jarveys put their cabs away in such weather, and no one stirs abroad who has not his own carriage. I am so grateful to him—he is a little tiresome with his lovesickness, I know, but such a good friend to us—'

'Good friend he may be—but he's like to prove a consider-able nuisance if you don't watch it,' Fenton said, and rubbed his window to clear the haze and peer out. 'Every time you so much as look at him he falls half into a swoon—he's a damned good driver, mind you. The roads are hardly fit to pass and he's going great guns! We're almost at Oxford Street, so far as I can tell—'

They were, and now they could see that already snow was drifting up against the shop fronts in great piles, as the wind blew steadily and sculpted the thick flakes into valleys and dales that made London look almost like a remote country village. To Amy and Fenton, well used to the heavy snows of their native Massachusetts, it was not particularly surprising, but to Londoners, few of whom could ever remember seeing so severe a winter, it was a source of much amazement.

As Amy and Fenton found when they arrived, only ten minutes later than they had hoped, at Tavistock Square. Mr. Foster, much emboldened by his previous efforts to carry his beloved (the memory of which had made the hazardous journey from Long Acre a dreamy delight), seized her again and bore her over the wide snow-choked pavement to the flight of carefully swept steps that led up to the house, leaving Fenton to struggle after him as best he might, and set her down reluctantly, his face glowing with effort and with cold and with emotion.

'I shall return to collect you at one o'clock, Miss Amy,' he said a little breathlessly, 'but do not hurry yourself to leave if you do not wish to. I shall be happy to wait.'

She peered up at him in the dim light that was thrown from the house windows behind them. 'But where shall you go? You cannot stand about all these hours! You will need some food—and the horses, too. They will die of cold if you keep them waiting so—'

'It is most kind of you to care, Miss Amy, but I have made arrangements, I do assure you. There is a livery stable across the square where I and the animals will be warm and comfortable. I have some studying I can do while I wait, so it will not be wasted. And it is, as ever, my pleasure to take care of you—'

'Are you quite sure?' she said anxiously, and turned to Fenton, now shaking snow off his hat. 'Fenton, should we not perhaps ask our hostess if she will—'

'I am sure Mr. Foster will take excellent care of himself, Amy. Hey, Foster? The way these women fuss! Why, you'd think you were some sort of milksop, wouldn't you, to listen to her?'

Mr. Foster, whose spirits had lifted sharply at the thought that Amy might ask for hospitality on his behalf, nodded at once.

'Of course, I shall be perfectly well!' he said earnestly. 'You are kind to be concerned, but do not, please. I shall be in excellent comfort, I do assure you—' and he turned and went clumping down the steps, already covering again with a layer of snow, as the big door opened and a butler appeared to bow them in and imperiously call up a maid from the area below the steps to come up and sweep again.

Amy, once inside, sighed with sheer pleasure as she looked about her. A handsome house, with its marbled floor in polished black and white squares, its heavy mahogany staircase, its panelled walls covered in gilt-framed and heavily varnished paintings, it breathed of comfort and money and success, and she warmed to it. The only aspect of contact with her Boston uncles that she missed was life in houses such as this. Their homes had been as richly comfortable, as secure and as arrogant in their awareness of the status of riches as was this establishment and for Amy it felt very like home.

Her sense of the familiar affected her more than she realized, making her seem very relaxed and self-assured, and she turned as a door opened on the far side of the hall, and stood looking inquiringly, her head on one side, and her hands clasped lightly in front of her.

The woman who came through the door stopped and stared at the girl standing there so comfortably. At her dark curly hair, simply dressed in a very beguiling way so that her wide brow bore a few pretty tendrils, at the elegantly long waist and curving back in its plain but well cut deep blue gown, and above all at the face, with its wide heavily lashed grey eyes and pointed chin. She was quite extraordinarily pretty, and also had something more than mere prettiness; there was an invitingness about her, a potential for sensuousness that even another woman could recognize. And envy a little, even a woman who herself had always been regarded as exceedingly pretty and was now considered to be one of the most beautiful women in her social circle.

Amy, for her part, saw a handsome women of below middle height—perhaps an inch or so shorter than herself and of between thirty and thirty-five years, wearing a gown of a deep amber colour that perfectly set off her creamy shoulders and the rich curves of her breasts. She wore her hair, which was as dark as Amy's own, dressed sleekly above her wide grey eyes, and pulled back into a heavy knot at the nape of the neck, and bound with fillets of gold lace. On the bodice of her gown she wore a diamond brooch of great splendour and her waist was encircled with a gold lace girdle on which was a smaller but no less beautiful diamond buckle. She looked very expensive, very assured and very very beautiful, and Amy felt some of her own self-assurance drain away as she stared at her.

Not so Fenton. He too looked at the woman standing in the doorway and assessed her very quickly indeed, and with a tiny jerk of his head that sent the errant lock of hair that had flopped over his brow back into place limped forwards with an inquiring smile on his face.

'Mrs. Caspar?' he said. His voice was low, and even to his sister's ears seemed to sound very American. At home in Boston he never used quite so marked a twang in his speech, much preferring the English sound that was customary among his mother's family, but now—she smiled a little. He had been scathing enough about the Boston hostesses who lionized visitors, and here he was making sure that his London hostess would be given value for her efforts to do the same.

'It is most good of you to invite us both, strangers as we are. We can't pretend we weren't rather lonely, so far from home at this festive season of the year. We much appreciate your husband's kindness to us in both taking care of me in my need, and in thinking of our general welfare as he has.'

He was by her side now, and after a moment she smiled and held out her hand. 'You are very welcome, Mr. Lucas,' she said. 'I have looked forward to meeting you both—' and then reddened. Fenton, with only a hint of theatricality, had bent and kissed her fingers.

'Miss Lucas—how kind of you to come out on so disagreeable an evening!' She turned to Amy as Fenton relinquished her hand. 'It must have been a most unpleasant journey for you—'

'I'm charmed to be here, Mrs. Caspar, and the journey was far from disagreeable. We had the help, you see, of—'

'I trust your other guests have not suffered from the journey, ma'am?' Fenton said and she turned back to him and smiled up into his face.

'Why, I cannot say as yet! Hardly anyone has managed to arrive at all! We must wait and see how—ah! There, I think are some arrivals. Well, I think we shall not stay here in the hall, but leave Tansett to deal with them. Come up to the drawing-room, and tell me about yourselves. Once everyone is here, we will have little time to talk, I think.'

Fenton held out his arm and she took it, and then turned to his sister, crooking the other elbow, and she too accepted his offer, and they went up the stairs, the two gowns, one amber and one blue, bobbing on each side of their limping escort.

Felix, standing in the hall below and kicking snow off his shoes with one gloved hand looked up and saw the blue-gowned figure and wondered who she was. Phoebe, of course, he knew well, even when she was wearing a new gown as she was tonight. He would know the curve of that neck anywhere; but this other one—

She turned her head and looked down and he saw wide eyes, a trifle worried, he thought, in expression, and curly dark hair which lay over a broad brow in a very charming way, and involuntarily he smiled, and the girl in blue allowed her lips to tremble into a slight smile in return.

And then the trio disappeared at the bend of the stairs, and Aunt Martha behind him said, laughing. 'Dear boy! I think I shall fall over, my shoes are so coated with snow! Will you—ah, that's better!' as Felix bent and used his glove to remove the last traces of snow from her foot, much to the butler's disapproval.

'My dear boy, what a night! I said we were mad even to think of coming!'

He shook his head and smiled down at her as he relinquished his coat to Tansett. 'Now we are here, I agree! We would have been much wiser to remain safe and snug at home in Bedford Row. But I am glad we came. And it was not so far, after all. Come, aren't you happy to be here?'

She looked up at him and laughed again. 'Yes, I suppose I

am! Though to make such efforts to see one's relations, when one sees them as often as we do—it is quite absurd. Well, let's go up to the drawing room, and drink some of Freddy's excellent punch and find out what the family gossip is—and here are more arrivals! We are not the only mad ones tonight! Good evening to you, Abby, my love! And Gideon! And dear Isabel. You look charming, quite charming, doesn't she, Felix? As always! We are going upstairs at once to warm our icy bones with punch. Be quick, now, all of you—'

And they went upstairs leaving Tansett dealing with the Henriques, and also Oliver Lackland, who arrived hard on their heels. The New Year's evening party at the Caspars' had begun.

'Thank you,' Amy said a little tremulously, 'but you know, I have already had one cupful, and if I have any more, I am very afraid that I shall not behave as properly as I should.'

'Oh, it is innocuous enough,' Felix said, and put the glass firmly into her hand. 'A great deal of fruit and cinnamon and mace, and only a modicum of brandy, I do promise you. Freddy sets great store by the wines he gives with his dinners, and would not spoil his guests' palates with excessive drinking of such stuff as this, not for anything. It is only because it is New Year's evening that he offers punch at all! But Phoebe insisted. Now, I am determined. You shall tell me all about yourself. On these occasions it is rare indeed to see any here but members of the family, and I had no notion we were to be so fortunate as to enjoy the company of strangers tonight! And I am determined you will not be a stranger for very much longer. So, tell me all about yourself. Who are you? And how come you to be here?'

She peeped up at him over the rim of her glass, and took her time sipping at it. It really was quite extraordinary how she felt. She, who was well used to having a devastating effect on young men, and having them make a beeline for her and talk to her and try to flirt a little, even on a first acquaintance, was quite thrown out of gear by this young man's reaction to her. He was naturally friendly and kind, she knew, for she had stood to one side as the new arrivals came surging into the big drawing-room in what seemed to her to be a great flurry of sound, and their hostess greeted them with cries of delight and much kissing and exclaiming from them all at once. And this young man had come over to her and murmured some pleasantry about the weather—which subject was now totally absorbing the chattering group about Mrs. Caspar—and insisted on bringing her another glass of punch.

She had watched him as he had walked away and been quite startled at the effect his appearance had on her. She was used to good looks; she who had been Fenton's sister all her life could hardly be otherwise. But this young man was not goodlooking at all; or not in that sense. He was square and stocky, not a great deal taller than she was, being perhaps some five feet and eight inches, with a wide almost ugly face set in lines that showed his broad mobile mouth was very used to smiling. He had dark hair cut very short and not particularly glossy in appearance, grey eyes which were pleasant but nondescript, and a heavy chin. Nothing to make Amy look twice at any man, in all truth, and yet, the combination of his features, and the air of good humour and kindness about him made her feel positively glowing towards him. It was very odd.

And as he had turned from the table to come back to her, holding the punch glass carefully in front of him, he had looked up and caught her eye and smiled at her with such a cheerful glint and warmth that she felt her face redden, and had to drop her gaze. It was truly *very* odd.

Now, looking up at him above the rim of her glass she found herself wondering, as she always did in such circumstances, how to behave. And once again caught his eye and felt the little tide of redness in her cheeks and said hurriedly, and without any artifice at all, 'Well, as to me—there is not much to tell. I would much prefer, if you would, if you could tell me who everyone here might be. I know only Mr. Caspar, you see. I have discovered who his wife is, of course—but I know no one else. Will you tell me?'

'Well, of course!' he said heartily. 'With whom shall I start?'

'You,' she said, baldly, and again reddened and bent to sip more of the hot punch to cover her confusion.

'Oh, I am not very interesting, but I shall, of course, obey you! I am Felix Laurence, ma'am, at your service. A physician of the Middlesex Hospital, and still learning my craft, though long since completing my studies, and taking a special interest in disorders of the heart.'

'And all these are your family, then?'

'My adopted family,' he said calmly and drank some of his own punch.

'Adopted? That sounds very romantic.'

'Oh, not particularly,' he said, in a very matter-of-fact voice. 'It was more a matter of convenience.'

'Will you tell me of it?' She was genuinely concerned, truly wanting to know, and stared up at him, her eyes fixed on his face, although usually when she was amid strangers she allowed her gaze to dart from one to another, assessing, observing and seeking for evidence of the effect she herself was having on others. Altogether she was behaving very strangely tonight, she thought briefly, and wondered if it were, after all, the punch. But still stared up at Felix Laurence's face with her lips parted.

'If you wish,' he said. 'My father died in the Crimean War, when I was but a boy. Some eleven years ago now. I was sixteen, and could have fended for myself well enough, I daresay. But—well, Aunt Martha—as I learned to call her—was working with my father in the hospital at Scutari, and was—they became attached, you know. But he died before they could be wed, and when she returned to England she proposed to take care of me for his sake. An arrangement which I found very agreeable, for she is the kindest and most sensible of ladies.'

'Is she here? Which is she?'

He nodded his head slightly in the direction of the fireplace where a rather plain-faced but friendly looking lady wearing a dark brown gown was sitting talking animatedly to another who was plump, indeed almost stout, and very elegant in green.

'The one with grey hair? She seems very pleasant,' Amy said, studying the woman in brown, who looked to her to be a little older than her mother had been when she had died, being perhaps about fifty.

'Oh, she is, she is. A very delightful and trustworthy lady. I bear a great affection for her.'

'You live in her house?'

'Indeed. Well, not precisely her house, though she holds it in trust. She is a lady much given to charitable works, and is greatly interested in the affairs of a refuge for poor women and their children which is situated in Bedford Row. There are many of these women living there as well, but we enjoy the comfort of the top part of the house, where we have our own apartments.'

She looked up at him again and opened her mouth to ask him more about himself, but then without quite knowing why, changed her mind and said instead, 'And to whom is she talking.'

'Ah, that is Aunt Abby! A most remarkable lady. She is a woman of business, is Aunt Abby! She was a widow, with one son—Freddy. Your host, you know! She had her own apothecary business, inherited from her first husband. And then she married Gideon—over there, you see? The tall thin man, with his hair almost white? He is no older than Aunt Martha but contrives to look very much older and wiser than anyone I know! He is very rich, being a business man himself and involved with banking and the like. What with that and the apothecary affairs, which grow apace, they are very well bestowed! The family is most proud of them, I do assure you!'

'And the exceedingly handsome girl there—talking to my brother Fenton? I collect she is a daughter of theirs? She looks very like Mr. Henriques, except she is so dark—'

'Indeed, the lovely Isabel is the oldest of the Henriques three. There is also Sarah, over there, you see? Just out of the schoolroom, she is. And they have a son, Daniel, who is too young, I think, to be brought to such a late-night party—'

'And the man talking to Mrs. Caspar? The one with—wearing spectacles—'

He laughed at that, his wide mouth curling agreeably. 'You are polite, indeed you are! Not to mention that his pate is as bald as any billiard ball! That is Mrs. Caspar's brother Oliver—he owns—'

'Oh!' She looked again at the round man with the shining head fringed with a little sandy hair with a new interest. 'He is the one who is to give us some work, then, at his Supper Rooms. It is because of him that we are here! Are you sure he is Mr. Lackland? He seems to look quite unlike his sister.'

'Oh, I am sure! He looks like none of the family—yet he is related to all of them, more than I am! Freddy and Phoebe are first cousins, you see, as well as man and wife.'

'Oh! Then the unpleasant old man at the hospital—I beg your pardon—I mean—'

He laughed again. 'You mean the unpleasant old man at the hospital! I know quite well how terrifying he can be. So, you have met him, have you? Yes, he is grandfather to Freddy—Mr. Caspar, and to his wife, and to Oliver as well, and to all of Abby's children—and though the matter is never discussed, he stands so to me, I suppose, as well, for Martha is his daughter too, of course!'

'But he is not here?'

'No, not he! He remains always in his own house at Gower Street with Maria. She is not related to us, you will be glad to hear, being a second wife. In fact, I wish she were closer. She is very pleasant, but he is not at all given to putting himself out. The family visit him from time to time but never all together. He cannot abide it! And now, you must tell me about you! I have poured at your feet all this information, and still do not even know your name!'

'Miss Lucas!'

Amy turned and found Phoebe Caspar standing behind her. 'My dear Miss Lucas, it is high time we stopped gossiping as we have all evening, and brought you to meet my brother. And then, when we have dined, you shall talk to him of what it is you wish to do and he shall see whether it will be possible for him to help you! Come along, my dear—and Felix, when dinner is announced, be so good as to take in Isabel, will you? I have placed her next to you—'

And Phoebe bore Amy away, who, interested as she was to meet Mr. Lackland, could not forbear to look back over her shoulder at Felix Laurence. To find to her chagrin that far from standing there smiling back at her, he had already turned away and was talking to the tall and very beautiful Miss Isabel Henriques, and Fenton. And was most startled at the surge of feeling that this circumstance aroused in her.

# CHAPTER NINE

Dinner was exceedingly good, and she ate heartily, greatly enjoying the splendour of it all, for there were a great many servants, and a great many beautifully presented dishes. It was all very unlike the way they took their meals at Mrs. Miller's; there the food was plentiful and flavoury, being made up largely of stews and hot meat pies and vegetable broths, but undoubtedly humdrum. No roast baby quail or exotic eastern olives were proffered in Long Acre, that was certain.

She felt a moment of compunction when the table conversation came back yet again to the remarkable weather, remembering poor Mr. Foster, but then caught Fenton's eye across the table and was a little worried. He looked quite splendid tonight; his eyes were glittering magnificently, his hair was curling even more wildly and romantically than usual and his colour was high. From the laughter each of his sallies brought from his two table companions—the Misses Henriques—it was also clear that he was being at his most witty and urbane, and with sisterly practicality she wondered for a moment if he were a trifle overfilled with Freddy's excellent champagne.

And then was annoyed with herself, for whatever Fenton's character faults might be, drinking heavily was not one of them. Their father had done that often enough in young Fenton's sight to give him a horror of the way men who were drunk could look, all loose-lipped and blotchy and very far from beautiful. No, Fenton was elevated tonight by the splendour of the house, the elegance of the company and most particularly by the admiration that was clearly being paid to him by Miss Isabel Henriques.

She leaned forwards slightly to see if she could see her more clearly and Felix, sitting on Isabel's other side, caught her eye and smiled at her in his friendly way, and at once she leaned back, a little confused, and turned her attention to her neighbour, Mr. Oliver Lackland, who had been prosing away happily to Martha on his other side.

Politely he turned to her now and began to talk of her past theatrical experience, making it quite clear that he was well aware of why she had been bidden to this family party, and making no effort to engage her in any general conversation.

She did not mind this in the least; indeed, it quite comforted her, helping her to feel that she was being of some real service to Fenton, for whatever pleasure he might find here tonight, the harsh fact was that they were present but on sufferance. Tomorrow would start a new year, and with it a renewal of the urgent need to earn their livings. So she told Mr. Lackland all she could about their theatrical past, while uneasily watching Fenton turning from one pretty neighbour to another and generally drawing attention to himself, and wishing that he would not enjoy himself quite so much. He would find the return to Long Acre much more painful if he went on as he was.

Because of her abstraction she made less effort than she might have done to impress Mr. Lackland, and told him no more than the bare facts of their previous acting experience, failing to garnish it with any of the detail she would normally use to make a good impression. So that by the time dinner was over, and Phoebe collected the ladies together to leave the men with the port decanter a little longer, he had a very clear and accurate idea of what the Lucases had done in the past and what they might be able to offer him.

It was close on ten o'clock before the men rejoined the company in the drawing-room, by which time Amy felt quite exhausted, and was longing for some male company. Especially *easy* male company, like that of Mr. Laurence. The Misses Henriques both quizzed her busily about her brother and his activities—about which she boasted shamelessly—while the older ladies sat and talked comfortably about children and people and places that meant nothing to her but clearly fascinated them. She was grateful to Miss Martha

Lackland, however, who, recognizing her boredom with the two sisters—for beautiful though they were, neither seemed particularly interesting—drew her into conversation, asking her about her plans for the future.

She sat beside her on a low hassock with her gown spread wide about her, explaining about how important it was for them both to start earning for themselves, and was also about to explain to her the plan she had made to seek for her dead father's relations, when the door opened and the men returned, and she looked up.

Freddy returned first, as host, with Oliver beside him, and as they came through the drawing-room door, the first person Oliver saw was his young dinner companion. She was looking up, her lips a little parted and her eyes sparkling with reflected firelight, and her hair was curling, rather more profusely on her brow than it had done before. He blinked and looked again, and was almost surprised that he had not noticed before how agreeable a young woman she was. At dinner he had been much occupied in talking to Martha of her charity's financial affairs, for he was her adviser on many fiscal problems, and had also been much occupied with his food, for he was a moderately greedy man who enjoyed exercising his appetite. So, he had hardly been aware of anyone else, except in the most cursory way. Even when he had talked to his neighbour he had been more concerned to hear of her experience than to look at her, so that he could decide whether he could find work for her.

He had in fact been very doubtful on that score and had said as much very quietly to his brother-in-law, who had looked somewhat put out at his words.

'How can you say?' he had said sharply. 'When you have neither seen nor heard them perform? Come, Oliver, it is rare indeed I seek such help from you—and this patient is of great interest to me. I would be very loth to lose him, as I must if he does not obtain work, for surely he will return to his home!'

'Well, I will listen to them sing, perhaps. She said nothing of singing, only of her acting ability, for which, as you know, I have but small use! However, we shall see—'

And now, back in the drawing-room, he did indeed see. He

saw her in a very new way, and was startled at the emotion his vision created in him. He spent much of his working life looking at handsome women and pretty girls; they were in a sense his stock in trade, and always he had been most matter-of-fact about those feminine charms that were displayed for his approval. So matter-of-fact, indeed, that his affectionate sister and female cousins had long since given up hope of finding him a suitable wife.

But now he stood and looked at a girl sitting on a hassock staring up at him with wide eyes and slightly parted lips, and felt emotions which were very strange to him. So strange that he did not recognize the stirrings for what they were; but he did know that it was imperative he find some way in which this child could work in his Supper Rooms.

What he did not know was that immediately behind him in the procession of men returning from the dining-room was Felix Laurence, accompanied by Fenton Lucas, and it was at Felix that Miss Lucas was looking with such wide-eyed eagerness on her speaking countenance.

Phoebe surged to her feet. 'Thank you, Freddy, for not staying in the dining-room any longer! It would be a pity to miss the excellent entertainment I am sure we are about to enjoy! I thought, my dears—' she turned to her cousins, still sitting side by side on a sofa and looking very delightful '—that you young ones would entertain us all! Your duet would be charming, and I daresay we can prevail upon Felix to let us hear again that very amusing comic song to which he treated us at Christmas. And then perhaps, Miss Lucas—'

Amy stood up, opening her mouth to say at once that she would prefer not to, since she lacked any pianoforte or singing ability at all, but she could not say a word, for Isabel and Sarah were both speaking at once. It was Isabel who won the day.

'We shall sing, dear Cousin Phoebe, only if you will! You know that you are better than any of us, and it would be cruel indeed to deprive us! Come along, do! You first and then we shall see about the rest of us!'

Demurring prettily, Phoebe allowed herself to be led to the large and very handsome grand pianoforte in the corner and sat down as the company settled itself about the room, putting on a suitable listening face. Amy, feeling a very real anxiety, tried to catch Fenton's eye; this wretched woman, she wanted to warn him, this wretched Mrs. Caspar has devised this just so that we can be auditioned for her brother, in front of all of them! We cannot do it, we cannot—and anyway I can't sing—

But he was totally unaware of her, limping elegantly over to the Misses Henriques' sofa to sit between them, much to their obvious delight, and she sat down on her hassock again, feeling quite wretched.

She felt rather than saw someone bring another hassock to sit beside her, and turned her head, as the first notes trilled from the piano under Phoebe's fingers, hoping it might be Felix. His friendly company would be very comforting at this moment, she thought.

But it was Mr. Oliver Lackland, and she smiled at him politely, if a shade mechanically, and returned her attention to the pianoforte, her head spinning. How would she evade having to perform and make a fool of herself? She would perhaps recite the 'Quality of Mercy' speech from *The Merchant of Venice*, she thought suddenly. Perhaps that would satisfy them? And it would show this boring man beside her, who was looking at her steadily and making no attempt even to pretend to be interested in what his sister was singing, that she had a real talent.

Phoebe had started singing, a rather old-fashioned melody, Amy thought, about a Girl in a Garden whose lover, it appeared, had gone to war as a soldier. It was a mawkish song, Amy decided, and her lips curled a little as she listened. She was glad indeed that she could not sing, if it meant having to produce such foolish songs as this—

The sound trickled away, as Phoebe's voice died to silence, and Amy came out of her brown study to the sound of clapping, to see Freddy Caspar standing beside the piano holding his wife's hand in his and looking down at her as though they were sweethearts rather than respectable man and wife, and she stared at them, slightly puzzled.

'That song has a great meaning for them, you know,' a voice said in her ear, and she jumped and turned her head the other way to find Felix beside her.

'Indeed? I must say, I thought the song a trifle—' she shrugged, and he smiled at that and she reddened, for it seemed to her that he was aware of the cause of her petulance and was amused by it.

'Well, it *is* a silly old song, no doubt, but you see, Freddy was in the Crimean war, as my father was, and she—Phoebe, you know—she went out there as well, and sang that song, among others, to the soldiers there—'

She could not answer him, for now Phoebe was on her feet and saying loudly, 'There! You insisted, so I have sung! Now it is the turn of you young ones—Isabel? Sarah? That charming duet of yours—'

Amid some fluttering of music and rearranging of pianoforte stools the sisters settled themselves at the keyboard, and Amy had to admit that they made a delightful picture, their dark heads together, their elegant long necks and sloping shoulders outlined against the lamplight, and clearly she was not alone in her approval; for suddenly Fenton rose to his feet, and limped across the room to stand behind them, ready to turn the pages of their music, and Isabel looked up at him over her shoulder and smiled, and he smiled back and for a second Amy felt a stab of surprised anger. Fenton, to look so at a girl? He had often looked at girls and simulated admiration—she knew his repertoire of charming mannerisms as well as he did. But she had never seen him behave with quite such sincerity before, and she felt a sudden little chill in her belly as she stared at the three young people at the piano. Tonight was altogether turning out to be most disturbing.

The duet was tinkling and pretty, and when it ended to a spatter of warm family applause, with Abby and Gideon both beaming widely with parental pride, Isabel turned her head and whispered to Fenton who after a moment nodded, and Sarah stood up and returned to the sofa, while Isabel moved across and Fenton stood closely behind her.

'Oh, no—' Amy said involuntarily under her breath as a small buzz of approval rose in the room, and Felix leaned forwards and said softly, 'What is the matter?'

'He cannot sing!' she whispered. 'He must be mad to try it! He has never studied or—'

But she had forgotten besotted Miss Emma of Long Acre.

In two short weeks she had taught Fenton more than his sister had realized and she sat there with her eyes wide, watching and listening in some amazement.

He chose a song that was very popular, being whistled and sung by every errand boy in Covent Garden, but yet which was perfectly respectable and suitable even in as elegant a drawing-room as this, being comic without being offensive in any way. He stood with one hand lightly resting on Isabel's shoulder—a circumstance of which they both appeared to be totally unaware, although Isabel's mother was not—and warbled pleasantly in his easy tenor '—then love your neighbour as yourself, as the world you go travelling through. And never sit down with a tear or a frown, but Paddle your own Canoe!'

The applause he received was warm and genuine and he stood there flushed and smiling, refusing an encore (and Amy guessed shrewdly that he had learned no other suitable songs from Miss Emma) and then apparently on an impulse he turned to Amy.

'Amy, my dear, you are being much too quiet there!' he said, and his voice was rallying. 'Come here, now, and Miss Isabel and I will play a duet for you, and you shall do your charming dance! Then both of us will have made our small effort! Do, now, dear, please do!'

She stared at him in horror, her eyes wider than ever, and at once Oliver Lackland beside her got to his feet, and held out one hand.

'Indeed, it would give us all much pleasure if you would, Miss Lucas,' he said, his glasses winking as he looked at her with great earnestness. 'Your brother sings very well, but I have no doubt your dancing will excel him.'

Martha and Phoebe began to applaud, and the clapping was taken up by the others, and Amy, knowing herself defeated, walked across to the piano, as Oliver busily removed a small table or two from its immediate vicinity, and pushed back a sofa to make more room.

'Which dance, Fenton dear?' she said in a sweet low voice, looking up at him, and her eyes were glittering with rage as he grinned down at her with great insouciance and said airily,

'Oh, you know, my love! The charming divertissement that you learned from Miss Farraday—?'

Since the only dance she had ever done while being taught by Miss Farraday had been a cruel mimicry of her teacher's attempts to be stylish and move well, Amy's rage increased, but there was nothing she could do. Fenton and Isabel were now seated side by side on the piano stool looking up at her expectantly, and Fenton said, 'A waltz rhythm, as I recall, Amy? Yes? Then Miss Isabel, shall we about it? *One*, two, three,' and they began to tinkle out a melody in a rhythmic three-four time.

She turned and stood poised in front of them all, her hands hanging loosely at her sides and her mind filled with rage and hurt that Fenton should treat her so and sheer embarrassment at being forced to make, as she was sure, a fool of herself, and feeling very close to tears. And caught the encouraging expression on Felix Laurence's face.

He was looking at her with his head on one side, and his mouth curled into a smile and she stared at him and it was almost as though he spoke; she seemed to hear him say, 'You can do anything you wish! Go on—you know you can!'

And suddenly she did know she could, and she waited for a moment until the music reached a suitable point and then, lifting her arms, began to dance.

She had never been taught to dance, just as she had never been taught to sing. Her mother had preferred to have her taught what she regarded as quiet accomplishments such as water-colour drawing and the speaking of French, having a deep distrust of all the performing arts. She had only agreed to allow the speech lessons because Amy had told her that Miss Farraday would improve her French accent, and help her to speak in the sort of low voice her mother much admired. Yet, despite her lack of teaching, Amy did have the theatre running in her blood, given to her by her father, and whoever had gone before him. Just as Fenton had been able to learn how to sing a song and make it sound agreeable in just two short weeks with an indifferent teacher, so she could put on a semblance of dancing that would satisfy these people. For what did they know of such matters, after all?

99

So she told herself as she allowed the rhythm of the music to enter her muscles, and her body to take what direction it would in response. These people would not know, and could easily be persuaded that she was a superb dancer—if she *acted* the part of a dancer.

And so she did, dipping and swaying and turning and making little leaps with all the aplomb of one who has spent half her life in the corps de ballet, drifting lightly and delicately about the small space available to her as easily as any one of the snowflakes still falling into the silent square outside.

She danced with her chin thrown up, and moved her head as well as her body and her limbs, knowing that the swirl of a curl against a long neck could beguile attention away from any faults in her footwork, and that an expression of beatitude on her face could persuade even the most unresponsive of individuals that she was really dancing well, instead of merely going through a sketch of it.

To Oliver watching her, bemused, she was almost painfully perfect. He looked at the curve of her narrow back and the way her hands fluttered and shaped themselves as her slender fingers stretched and then curled, watched the turn of her head against her neck and was totally bewitched. He found his heart beating thickly in his chest, and was startled. He found his hands damp with perspiration, and was even more surprised. And when she had finished and stood there with her head flung back and her arms spread wide he was amazed to hear his own voice crying out, 'Bravo, bravo! Splendid performance, quite splendid!'

Freddy was delighted and called out above the sound of the applause, which was considerable, 'Well, Oliver? Are my proteges to join your company, then?'

The sound of applause drifted away and Phoebe turned her head to look at her brother, her eyebrows raised. Not as susceptible to Amy's charms as he was, she had clearly seen the flaws in her extempore performance, and with all her own experience of stage work doubted very much whether this girl, with all her charm, could translate what she had done into any sort of appearance of which paying customers would approve. But, seeing his flushed face and eager expression, she

100

said nothing, being too surprised to do so. That *Oliver* should look at a girl like that—she turned her attention back to Amy and looked at her with new eyes.

'Well, Mr. Lackland, am I to understand that we have given a successful audition?'

It was Fenton's voice which was raised now, and he stood looking challengingly at the bald man, who nodded and smiled widely and said simply, 'Of course! We shall design our new show in such a way that both you and your sister will appear to advantage. I have no doubt that between you you will give me one of my most successful seasons!'

'No!' Amy stood and stared at Fenton with horror all over her face. 'Fenton, are you quite mad? We are not singers and dancers! We are *actors*, you and I! I said at the start that this would be—oh, Mr. Caspar, did I not say to you that we were actors! That I could not imagine what we should do in such a show as you said was performed at your brother's establishment and that—' She turned back to Fenton. 'Truly, Fenton, I did say it! We cannot work as *singers* and *dancers*.'

Her voice seemed to drip with scorn as she said the words, and even Fenton, usually well able to keep her in control, stepped back in some surprise.

She turned to Oliver, moving so swiftly that her gown belled and lifted, showing her ankles and creating a waft of air that made the candles on the piano dip and flutter. 'I'm sorry indeed that you have been misled, sir, truly I am. But we are *legitimate* actors! We do not—we don't cavort and dance about the stage! We are better than *that*, I do promise you!'

There was a short and uncomfortable silence and then Phoebe, without moving from her place on her sofa, said in a low but very clear voice, 'Miss Lucas! I spent my girlhood *cavorting* on the selfsame stage upon which you are being offered an opportunity not merely to earn your keep—which I understand is a matter of some urgency for you—but also to enjoy a very respectable acclaim. *Legitimate* or not, the stage of the Celia Supper Rooms is not to be scorned! I think you should reconsider your hasty rejection of the very splendid offer my brother has made to you, and accept it, if he is still willing to stand by it—and I do not hesitate to tell you that I would not be so meek!—and perhaps, apologize to him? Your response to his generous approval of your—er—performance is I feel, a little less than appreciative!'

'I—I did not mean to be—to seem ungrateful or—or—' Amy stared at Phoebe for a long moment, at the cold gleam of dislike in her eyes, and then at Oliver who looked merely blank with amazement and then shook her head and tried to speak, and to her horror found tears rising in her throat, choking her with a needle sharpness more painful than any she had felt even when her tears had been shed for her dead mother. Indeed, not since Papa had died had she felt so bereft, so lost for understanding and love. And the thought of Papa was more than she could bear and she shook her head wildly again and, to her eternal shame, burst into tears.

The result was electric. Oliver after one horrified moment hurried across to her, his hands held out in an almost comical gesture of supplication, and Fenton jumped up and began to move towards her. But it was Felix, moving with a deceptive easiness, who reached her first and said comfortably above the little hubbub of conversation that had broken out, 'I think she is a little over-excited by her exertions—strange people, you know, at a party, and then dancing—I will soon see her settled. No, Freddy, all is well, I do assure you. I will just take her up to the morning room, if Aunt Martha will accompany us? Thank you, Aunt Martha. Some sal volatile to settle the nerves and I am sure all will be perfectly comfortable with her. Thank you, Aunt Martha—that's the way, Miss Lucas—just come with me—'

And he led her out of the drawing-room with one protective arm about her shoulders while Miss Martha Lackland hurried ahead to open the morning-room door and make sure there was a sofa ready for her to collapse upon, and hide her mortified face.

# CHAPTER TEN

She was in fact recovered long before she was prepared to admit it. Aunt Martha had mixed the sal volatile and insisted she swallowed it, though it had made her cough and caused her tears to run even faster, and then after a few words with Felix had gone rustling away, back to the drawing-room. And Amy had lain there on the sofa with one arm flung up to hide her face trying to regain her self-control, but, above all, trying to plan how she would behave to get herself out of this silly, highly shameful situation into which she had fallen.

No ideas came to her at all. Dignified silence? Not very effective, since she would have to break it sooner or later. Lip-trembling shyness? That was possible but difficult to maintain, and anyway, her behaviour in the drawing-room had been the very reverse of shy. Icy rejection of them all? That would hardly be practical. The Lackland man had, after all, offered them both work, and heaven knew they needed it. Perhaps if they agreed to work for him she could persuade him that a much better idea would be for her to do the 'Mercy' speech from *The Merchant of Venice* than to leap around the stage like some sort of burlesque queen? Which she was not nor ever would be—

She turned her head on the cushion sharply, trying somehow to see a way out of it all, and Felix's voice came equably through her self-absorption.

'Will you stay so all evening? We have barely half an hour to go to midnight, and they will all expect us to be with them to welcome the New Year. Do you think you have recovered yet?'

She lay very still, her arm still up, her thoughts rushing around like mice. Throw herself on this young man's care? He has been so friendly and kind, though not, to be honest, showing any signs of being at all enamoured of her; she thought momentarily of Mr. Foster, out there in the snow somewhere, and wished he were with her; he could not do much to help, perhaps, but his care of her, and his willingness to do anything she asked, was very comforting. This young man would never be so biddable, that she knew. Yet perhaps he would help her, talk to his relations, make them forget what a cake she had made of herself—

'Well, if you are not going to talk to me, I might as well return to the drawing-room. To sit here with a totally silent female is no sort of entertainment, I can assure you—'

Still she lay there remote and quiet and after a moment she heard the scrape of a chair being pushed back and footsteps crossing the floor and at once she sat up and said breathlessly, 'No—do not leave me, please!'

'I will stay with pleasure, if you will talk to me, and stop lying there like a tragedy queen. You are not so badly put about, after all!'

'Not put about? How can you say that—how *can* you? Fenton—I could kill Fenton! He made me dance, knowing full well I could not and—'

'You still managed very well,' he said calmly and came back to sit down in the chair beside her again. 'I am no expert but to my eyes, you looked charming. As well you know.'

She shook her head impatiently. 'Oh, it is easy enough to look tolerable! But to have to do it always, when I am an *actress* and not a dancer—'

'Miss Lucas, will you permit me to advise you? I am somewhat your senior, after all, and although I am but a physician with little personal knowledge of the ways of the stage, I belong to this family which is much involved with theatre matters. And I think you should stop insisting so much upon your status as an actress. If you say it too often, when none have seen you act, you will harden their lack of interest in ever seeing you do so. I am sure you understand me! If you were able to entertain here tonight—as you did, more than tolerably well—why, then you may do so upon a stage. Cousin

Oliver may not seem to you to be the thespian ideal, but I have to tell you he is a very shrewd man, who has built himself an excellent reputation and a comfortable fortune from his Supper Rooms. You will lose nothing and gain much by accepting, indeed you will.'

She stared at him for a moment, and then shook her head. 'I daresay you are right. I hate the idea of working as a dancer—but work we must. And anyway, I daresay I could persuade him to let me do other things—but, Mr. Laurence, how can I now? I have upset your family shockingly, and behaved very badly. How can I go to them and—and oh, it is not to be borne!'

'Nonsense!' His voice was very bracing. 'You have but to go downstairs and say prettily that you were sorry you allowed yourself to be so overcome by emotion and—'

The door behind him opened, and Fenton's head appeared in the crack and at once she was on her feet.

'Fenton! You are beyond any shadow of a doubt the most hateful, unbelievable, *nasty* creature it has ever been any female's lot to have to deal with, and if you think—'

'I shall go away again if you don't stop that noise! And I shall go back to the drawing-room and undo all the good I have done on your behalf—and anyway, what did I do that was so terrible?'

He came into the room and grinned cheerfully at Felix. 'I'd sure hate to be a female, hey, Laurence? Going off into such fusses for no reason!'

'No reason? When you know perfectly well I can't dance? How *could* you—'

'Oh, pooh! Can't dance? I thought you danced very well, didn't you, Laurence!'

'Very well,' Felix said. 'There is no doubt that with a little advice and practice she could give a most creditable display.'

She whirled at that and looked at him very hard. 'So you *don't* think I was any good, then!'

'I did not say that. I said that you could give a creditable performance, with teaching and practice.'

'Then how can you advise me to accept Mr. Lackland's offer? If you think I am not up to scratch—' her voice was tinged with a note of tragedy.

'Oh, come, Miss Lucas, you're doing it up rather too brown, you know! One minute you tell me that you know you are no dancer, and then take umbrage because I agree that you need some practice! Do be reasonable—I have not said you lack talent! Indeed, I think you have a good deal. But it is senseless to get up into your high trees because I do not lie to you, and tell you you are Terpsichore come again!'

Fenton gave a great crack of laughter. 'How very well you read my sister's character, Laurence! She is a shocking little—'

'I've had enough of *you* to last me all evening, Fenton.' Her voice was low and very cold and he stopped and looked at her and she said menacingly, 'I mean it. It is rare that I set my face against you, but tonight you have behaved appallingly and led me into a very unpleasant situation. I will have no more of it, and so I tell you. Do you understand?'

He looked at her consideringly for a moment and then nodded, and smiled. 'Well, you are right, I daresay. I should not have thrown you in deep water as I did, but you acquitted yourself very well, and the upshot of it is all is well worthwhile! I have made all smooth and no more will be said about any of it. Your stamping about, I mean, and so forth.'

'Then we may return to the drawing-room in peace, and welcome the New Year?' Felix stood up. 'We have been away quite long enough, I feel.'

'I am sorry if being with me *bores* you!' Amy flashed at him and he smiled that curling wide-lipped smile she was beginning to feel was very familiar.

'Oh, come, Miss Lucas! You should know better than to try such missish tricks as that! You know quite well what I mean. Which is simply that we have been away long enough. You say, Lucas, that you have made all well with the family?'

'Indeed I have. I told them that my sister is suffering from an excitement of the nerves following on my injury and all that has happened to us since our arrival in England—which I am sure you will agree is very likely—and that she will be happy to accept the kind offer of employment made by Mr. Lackland, as I am, so that we may repay the many loans we have had, and also start to put ourselves in some sort of order. Mr. Lackland has asked that we attend at his Supper Rooms tomorrow afternoon, Amy, and I have said we shall. Mrs. Caspar has been most understanding about it all—so you may come back with your head up. All is forgiven—if you forgive me, that is?'

She looked at him, her mouth set in a hard line, and tried to hold on to the anger with which his behaviour had filled her, but he cocked his head to one side and smiled at her, and all his usual magic began to work on her, no matter how hard she tried to prevent it. Despite herself her lips quirked and then she was smiling and shaking her head in mock despair.

'How any female can cope with you, Fenton, when even your sister is so easily cajoled, I cannot imagine,' she said. 'I should scold you all night and half the morning for your behaviour, but—'

'But you won't,' he grinned widely and turned back to the door. 'Well, Mr. Caspar has sent for some more punch with which to welcome 1867, and I must be there to join in! I would not miss it for the world, for I am quite convinced that this is to be our year. Amy! The annus mirabilis for the Lucases! I'll tell them you're coming—'

Felix crooked his arm for her, as Fenton went hurriedly through the door, his limp less in evidence than it had been earlier, and after a moment she took it and walking sedately beside him went down the stairs to the next floor.

At the drawing-room's double doors she stopped, and looked sideways at him. 'I don't think I can,' she said, her voice rather tremulous. 'I really don't think I can. No—I am not acting now, truly I'm not.' She looked at him imploringly. 'I do act a great deal of the time, as I think you have recognized. I daresay physicians are extra smart about such things. But—'

He shook his head at that, smiling a little. 'It's nothing to do with being a physician, Miss Lucas. It's to do with being—well, never mind. I am glad you realize that you are acting as much as you are. It would be sad if you were one of those people who were so busy putting on different faces that they did not know what the real one was like.'

She looked up at him in the dim light of the hallway, very conscious suddenly of the rich carpet beneath her feet, the heavy pictures on the walls and the glossy double doors before

107

which they were standing, hearing the muffled voices of the rest of the party coming from the other side.

'Perhaps I am like that,' she said slowly. 'I don't really know sometimes—'

He shook his head, and his hand came down on hers in the crook of his arm. 'Well, I would not worry about it. If you can be aware, as I say, that is a large part of the battle.'

'Battle?'

'Well, perhaps that is a bad word at that! Search might be better. The search for sincerity. It is rare, and many people never find it. Especially those who never look.'

'You are a very unusual person, Mr. Laurence, aren't you?'

'Do you think so? I have never considered myself much different from my fellows.'

'Oh, but you are—you are! If you only knew some of the men I have talked to—all—all gawping, you know, and making sheep's-eyes, and being very *boring* you would know how different you are.'

He smiled more widely at that. 'Perhaps it is not their fault they make boring sheep's-eyes, when it is what you demand of them.'

She drew away from him a little, but his hand remained warmly over hers and she could not move far away. 'How do you mean?'

'I mean that you have perhaps a special performance for susceptible young men. Is it not possible that you show them a picture of a girl who is so pretty and charming and witty that they cannot fail but be dazzled and lose their commonsense? If they behave so, is it not you who make them do it? It is quite easy for some people to make others dance to their piping. And if that dancing does not appeal as much as was hoped—well, you must not blame the dancers for it! Nor must you object to the way some listeners fail to dance at all—'

Her face suddenly became exceedingly red. 'I am sorry if you have seen me as a—as some sort of heartless flirt, Mr. Laurence. I may act a great deal, since that is my chosen avocation. But it does not mean that I am a—that I behave to men so that—as you have suggested—'

'I am sure it does not.' He was still smiling that curly easy smile but now she found it far from attractive. It seemed to have mockery in its curves and it was not a kind chiding mockery, but one in which there was too much sharp knowingness.

'I'm glad to hear you say so,' she said stiffly. 'Now—'

'Yes. Now. Shall we go in?'

'I—' She swallowed. 'I have already told you that I feel I cannot. I am grateful to you for your concern, Mr. Laurence, but I think I will go home now. If you will forgive me. I would be further grateful if you would make my apologies to the company, and thank your cousin for her kind hospitality. I will call upon her in the future to tender my thanks in person, of course. Goodnight, Mr. Laurence.'

And she pulled her hand from his elbow and turned and went down the wide flight of stairs to the quiet hall below with what dignity she could muster, stepping out as delicately as behoved a young lady, although every part of her wanted to run headlong down the stairs and out into the street, and back to the cosy little house in Long Acre.

She heard the drawing-room doors open, and an upsurge of the sound of chattering voices, and then they closed again, and tears prickled her eyelids. He might think her a flirt, he might be quite untouched by her charms; but surely he could have behaved like a gentleman and escorted her to her home? To leave her to go alone, and on such a night like this—

By this time she was at the door and the imperturbable butler appeared from the back of the house and picked up her cloak and muff from the marble table upon which they lay, and she put them on, averting her face so that he should not see the tears which were now edging her lashes. That *hateful* Mr. Laurence! And she had thought him so kind and gentle and—

The butler bent his head. 'Shall I send out for your coachman, Miss? If you are leaving early, perhaps he is not ready? I will certainly send a footman to find him, however, if you wish it—'

'Never mind, Tansett.'

She turned sharply, to see Felix coming quietly down the stairs.

'I shall see to it that Miss Lucas returns home safely. You

go to the servants' hall now—I'm sure you want to see the New Year in, and it wants but a few moments—go along now—'

The butler went with alacrity and she stood there in some uncertainty. A large part of her was crying out to throw a great scene with much foot-stamping and ringing announcements that she would *not* accept his care for her. But another and more sensible part was warning her that he would only stand there quietly and smile that crooked smile and wait for her to finish. And anyway, the weather—

She turned and with some effort pulled the heavy door open and peered out, as Felix, behind her, struggled into his coat. It had stopped snowing now, and the Square lay before her white-shrouded and luminous and very quiet.

The sound started gently at first with a remote chime and then seemed to grow like a bubble as nearby chimes took it up, and increased until it seemed to her that all the air was filled with it; clocks and bells shouting a melancholy farewell to a dying year, a hopeful greeting to the newborn one.

She stepped forwards out on to the top step and stood there looking up at the sky scudding with clouds and with a few stars appearing fitfully and let the melancholy fill her. She thought of faraway home, of long ago New Year evenings spent with familiar faces, in familiar places, and enjoyed the luxury of letting the tears on her lashes increase and then tumble down her cheeks, making no attempt to wipe them away.

'A happy and prosperous New Year, Miss Lucas,' Felix Laurence said quietly and she turned her head and looked at him standing in the shadow of the doorway behind her, her eyes huge and mournful, and he put out one hand and with the edge of his little finger swept the tears from her cheeks.

'Shall we forget all about last year? Last year we seemed to start a hopeful friendship, and then spoiled it. I think we should forget that, and meet as strangers again, now that 1866 is dead and gone. May I introduce myself? Felix Laurence, at your service. I have never met you before. How do you do, ma'am!'

She looked at him for a long moment and then blinked and

110

sniffed and tried to smile a little. 'Yes, I think that—how do you do, Mr. Laurence—'

'Miss Amy!—Oh, Miss Amy, I had so hoped that—A Happy New Year!'

She turned again, and stared down the steps and saw Graham Foster on the pavement below her. His hat was in his hand and his upturned face looked pale and drawn in the feeble light thrown from the half open door.

'I know I said I would not return until one o'clock, but as the time drew near, I felt I so much wanted to be near you. And now you are here!' He ran up the steps to stand very close to her, and she could smell the faint hint of brandy on his breath and thought confusedly, 'He did more than just study while he was waiting,' and turned her head to look for Felix. But he had drawn further back into the doorway and only his shadow could be seen.

'I—Mr. Foster! I have been worried about you. Have you been well bestowed all this time? I would have asked Mrs. Caspar if you could—'

But he was not listening, just standing there staring at her with his eyes very wide open, and a look of quite ludicrous adoration on his face and she broke off and shook her head and said sharply, 'Mr. Foster, please, do not look at me in that stupid fashion!'

'I cannot help it—I cannot help it!' His voice was thick, and it was clear that he had been sipping his brandy at a pretty steady rate all evening. 'Ever since I held you in my arms this evening I have been able to think of nothing but the softness of you, and the sweet scent of you, and the touch of you and, oh Miss Amy, I do love you so much. I would die for you, I really would, I would dig up roads for you, if you asked me! I can think of nothing else but you and—'

'Oh—you, you—' She was so acutely aware of Felix there in the shadows behind her that she lost all her common sense and all her intrinsic kindness. Although Mr. Foster's behaviour was not the sort to which she was usually exposed, still, she had always been able to stop such lovesick declarations painlessly, even in full flood, as long as she kept her head. But tonight she did not. She just stamped her foot and shouted, 'You *stu-*

*pid* man! You stupid, stupid creature, be quiet! I do not want to know of—be *quiet*!'

So violent were her tones that even in the depths of his brandy haze Graham Foster heard her and stopped his flood of words and stood there blinking at her. There was a long pause and then uncertainly he lifted his hand and rubbed one cold cheek and said, 'I—I beg your pardon, Miss Amy. I had no right—you are quite right, of course. I have been *very* stupid, I am but a foolish medical student, and you are—well— please to forgive me. I think—it was cold, and the stable men offered me some brandy and—I am sorry.'

'Oh—you—you have spoiled everything!' she said, and put out her hand to him. 'I did not mean to be so unkind, truly I did not. But you were being so very foolish, I had to stop you and—'

'Oh, it doesn't matter,' he said, and his voice was quieter now, and a little more blurred. 'I—'

From behind her came the click of the door, and she turned her head and looked, and realized that he had gone. Felix Laurence had gone back into the house, and left her out there in the snow with a silly half-drunk fool, and she did not know who she hated most in consequence, Felix Laurence, the half-drunk fool, or herself.

## CHAPTER ELEVEN

Amy sat in the broad marble-floored hall, her head down and contemplating her gloves held crushed between her hands which were on her lap. That she had managed to come this far had amazed her. That she, who had never in her life followed any young man anywhere, who had never apologized, had never attempted to explain, should go to the trouble she had to track him down and actually come after him was a source not only of surprise but also some shame. Not until she had actually found herself passing under the elegant gateway and into the busy courtyard that led to the hospital proper had the embarrassment of it hit her. But then, as she had made her way under the lamp in the portico and into the building and actually seen the people inside—the same sort of frock-coated young men and calico-aproned nurses who populated Nellie's—it had come over her like a great wave beating on a seashore. What *was* she doing here?

She thought again about the past week; and the horrid interview with a sick and sorry Graham Foster who had blushed and stammered and then told her icy countenance that he was desperately sorry, that he would never ever again behave so; about Fenton's unusual sympathy for her in her distress—for she had indeed made a dreadful fool of herself that New Year's evening—and the way his unwonted kindness had made her feel worse than ever; and she let her head droop even further.

It had been a most disagreeable week, and the misery of it had made her feel positively bewildered. She had always been a sunny-tempered individual, and well able to shake off any attacks of the bluedevils, and to be upset for more than a day, for whatever reason, was exceedingly unlike her. Yet now, because she had been made a fool of in front of a young man with a square friendly face and a square stocky body she was thrown into total disarray.

It had been yesterday, waking once again with a heavy feeling of misery and a dull ache in the middle, that had hardened her resolve. Clearly she would have to find Mr. Felix Laurence and explain to him. He would have to be *told*. That thought had warmed her considerably and she had eaten her breakfast with almost her old appetite (making Mrs. Miller beam in relief, for she had been most upset by Miss's moping, as she had told her silent daughter) and set off for Mr. Lackland with quite a spring in her step. He would tell her how to find Mr. Laurence. After all, he was his cousin, in a sort of a way, was he not?

So, during a day of rehearsals for the new show Mr. Lackland was preparing and which would strongly feature Mister and Miss Lucas, Newly Come to Town from Boston, Massachusetts, she had watched for her opportunity, and during the luncheon break, had prattled artlessly to the bedazzled Mr. Lackland about his family, and most especially his adopted cousin. (And, incidentally had thereby made him feel much happier. The rehearsals for the new show had been going very badly, with Miss Lucas drooping sadly and showing no verve at all in her dancing, despite his most careful coaching. And now for the first time she was displaying some of the animation and magic that had affected him so deeply at his sister's house. He began to feel much better—).

It was as a result of this chatter that she now found herself here. Oliver had reminded her that Felix was a physician working at the Middlesex Hospital, and had told her without undue prompting—or any suspicion that she had a special interest in the knowledge—precisely where the hospital was. So that this morning she had been able to tell Fenton she had the headache, and send him off to rehearsal alone, leaving her to sally forth, wearing her rather daring cherry-red mantle over a deep blue gown and her brand new fur-trimmed, flat-crowned hat with its elegantly curly brim, feeling every inch the lady of fashion.

All of which had sustained her until she had arrived in the courtyard of the hospital and realized just how shamefully she was behaving. And how foolishly. She had decided that Mr. Felix Laurence was to receive an explanation, that he was to be told. But told *what*? And how could she frame any explanation of how she had been feeling this past week? And why should she? It was all too discouraging and now almost in tears, as her spirits slithered down from the heights in which she had been able to maintain them all morning, she stood up and began to thrust her hands back into their soft kid gloves. She would go and she would rehearse and she would tell herself that Mr. Felix Laurence was a totally unimportant person, and one in whom she had no further interest.

'Why, Miss Lucas!' The voice came from behind her and she stood very still, feeling her face suffuse to a rich crimson. 'It *is* Miss Lucas, is it not?' the voice said insistently. 'I do not think I am mistaken.'

114

She took a deep breath and turned, doing her best to put on an insouciant smile. 'Indeed it is, Mr. Laurence. Good morning.'

He stood there looking at her with his head a little to one side and his face as friendly as she had remembered it. His eyes were slightly narrowed as he smiled, and the cheerful glint she remembered most was very much in evidence. Perhaps, she told herself, with a sudden lift of spirits, perhaps he has quite forgotten how it was, and is not at all disgusted with me? a thought which cheered her so that she smiled now without any effort at all, and poured every atom of charm she had into it.

'I am surprised to see you here, of all places,' he said, still as pleasant as ever, and then looked round at the busy hall. 'I collect you are here with Mr.—ah—your friend from Nellie's? Your coachman friend?'

At once her mercurial spirits sank again. He had remembered! That hateful, shameful scene on the snowy steps in Tavistock Square was as vivid to him as it was to her. She was plunged back into the misery that had plagued her all week, and as he turned back to look at her his expression changed for the first time and he said in some alarm, 'Miss Lucas! Are you well? What has happened? You look quite—quite desolated!'

She swallowed and opened her lips to speak, and closed them again and bent her head, presenting a picture of confusion and distress that would have touched any heart, and he put out one hand and said quietly, 'I think perhaps you had better sit down—come along. There is a quiet place just round the corner here—'

She let him lead her, not looking where she was going, and trying to collect her emotions. It was not easy. His hand on her arm made her feel quite extraordinarily excited and yet shy at the same time, and although her embarrassment and confusion were undoubtedly real, deep underneath these emotions lay others; pleasure at being with this young man and hope that she would be with him a great deal more and sheer lifting exhilaration. All of which were feelings she could not quite understand; and why should she? For all that she had excited these same emotions in a great many male breasts in her time, Miss Amy Lucas herself had never experienced them.

'Now!' He pushed her firmly but not ungently down onto a bench, and then sat down beside her, turning his body so that he could look at her. 'Just what is the matter? Why did you look so distressed in the hall? Is there anything I can do to help you or your friends?'

'I—I came to see you,' she said in a low voice and bent her head to look again at her gloved hands, clasped on her lap and with the fingers twining and untwining restlessly. But she could not forbear to peep up at him from beneath her lashes, and as she caught his glance reddened yet again, and looked away.

'To see me? That is very kind in you, but is this not a—well, a strange way in which to make a morning call? I am working here, you know! I do not enjoy the luxury of time in which to make and accept mere social calls!'

Stung, she lifted her chin. 'Neither do I!' she snapped. 'I am far from being a lady of leisure, Mr. Laurence! I am in fact working as an actress now, and should be at rehearsal this very instant!'

'Ah, yes. The rehearsal for my cousin's show—I am told he has devised a very pretty dance for you! You are acting as well, you say? Now, that I had not been told—'

'Oh, you—you *wretched* man! So suppose my part *is* all dancing! It is not such a terrible thing, after all, and—'

He raised his eyebrows a little. 'But I agree, totally! I never said it was. It was you, as I recall, who felt it was such a dreadful thing for an actress to dance for her living. Ah, well, let us not quarrel over that. Tell me instead why you are here, if you are not paying social calls which I wouldn't be able to accept in any case. Are you seeking some medical advice? I would have expected you to go to Nellie's for such help as that—'

'No, I am not seeking medical advice! I told you, I came to see you—'

'Alone? That is even more strange! Or is your friend, Mr.—ah—I am afraid I forget his name. Indeed, I seem to recall we were not precisely introduced—'

Once more she felt distress rise in her, overcoming the spark

116

of irritation as well as the pleasure in his company she had been feeling and her face reddened yet again.

'It is—it is in part because of—because of that evening that I am here.'

'Indeed?' His face was as friendly as ever, his smile as relaxed, but she no longer found this comforting; instead it seemed to her that he was hiding from her behind a mask and she wanted to tear it from his face and see what he was really thinking of her. This sense of isolation made her feel cold suddenly and she drew herself away from him and said as carefully as she could, 'I think—it seems to me that I should tell you that I am sorry about it.'

'Sorry? But why should you be sorry?'

'As I recall, you had been very kind to me, Mr. Laurence.' The chill in him sharpened her own voice a little. 'You had supported me when I had behaved quite disgracefully—for which I also wish to apologize, and now do—and then you were good enough to concern yourself with my safe return home—and—' She stopped and swallowed and with some courage—for his face remained as inscrutably friendly as ever, quite unchanging in its expression—went on, 'And then, you were good enough to give me the opportunity to mend my new-made and new-spoiled friendship with you. I recall it if you do not. However, at that point, Mr. Foster—well—'

'Ah. Yes. Mr. Foster. Our coachman friend—' he murmured.

'He is not a coachman!' She flared up at the flatness in his voice. Had he been at all scornful, put any hint of disparagement in his tone, she would have found it easier to understand, but his quiet flatness gave away nothing. 'He is a medical student and very—very kind, and caring of my welfare, if somewhat—well, that night he behaved very foolishly, and I wished to apologize to you for it and to explain that—oh—it does not matter! I am sorry to have bothered you—' and she stood up and glowered down at him, still sitting there on the bench.

'Now, why should you apologize to me because of him?' he said. 'I would have thought that he owes you an apology if anyone does—or is it that you perhaps have—shall we say,

117

treated him in such a way that his behaviour that evening becomes fully understandable and therefore forgivable?'

'You are unsupportably rude, Mr. Laurence! How dare you say such a thing? How dare you—I have never been so—'

'Oh, now, do come down out of your high trees, Miss Lucas! I meant no insult, and you are foolish if you find one in my words! If we are to be friends, you must accept that I am a very direct man. I have no use for the twirlings and moppings and mowings of what is called polite society. I believe that I should say what I feel needs to be said. You came to me to apologize for another man's behaviour—a man who, after all, means nothing to me. I do not even know him! I tried merely to suggest a reason why he might feel constrained to behave as he did. Is that something to be so agitated about?'

'You accuse me of—of playing games with a man's feelings, Mr. Laurence! Or as good as did so! I say as I believe, and I believe that is something a lady is fully entitled to find offensive!'

He laughed aloud, with real amusement in his voice, leaning back on his bench and smiling at her in such a friendly way that they might have been discussing the latest theatrical comedy rather than exchanging angry words.

'But my dear Miss Lucas, I have not the least doubt that you did play with his feelings! That you have bedazzled that poor young man and confused him, and made him your slave for ever! That you try to do so with almost every man you meet, and always succeed. Or almost always! That is not so wicked a thing, after all, of which to accuse you! From my own observations of polite society, it is something young ladies are constantly trying to do. The difference between you and others is that you seem to succeed more often than most.'

'How—how dare you suggest that I—' She was mortified, and once again she felt her face filled with that surging tide of colour and could almost have wept with rage because of it.

'You are right if what you are about to say is that I hardly know you well enough to count your conquests for you. But, I saw you at my cousin's party and saw you dance and, do you know, I feel I am able to make this much of a judgment of you on the basis of that short acquaintance. You are a heartbreaker, Miss Lucas, and well you know it! You cannot really be offended because I am aware of the fact.'

And again he laughed up at her, and this time it seemed to her that the chill was quite gone, and he was the same friendly genuinely interested person he had been the night she had met him and was, in fact, paying her a genuine if sharp-edged compliment.

She looked at him uncertainly for a moment, and then looked down at her hands, and then again peeped up at him and said with a pretty hesitation, 'I do not know quite what to say, Mr. Laurence—'

He threw his head back and positively shouted with laughter this time. 'There! You see? You are trying your tricks with me now! You are unable to behave otherwise! No wonder your poor Mr. Foster was so—'

Now she could not find any answer at all and after one furious glare at him turned and marched away down the corridor that lay ahead, pulling her cherry-red mantle about her with what shreds of dignity she could. He was insufferable, she hated him, she could not imagine why she had wasted her time or her consideration on him and she was going to rehearsal. Immediately.

'You are going the wrong way, Miss Lucas!' he called after her. 'Unless, that is, you wish to find yourself in the hospital lecture room. If you seek the street, then you must return this way!'

She stopped, and hesitated, and turned after a moment and came marching back, her chin up and her eyes staring resolutely ahead, but as she reached his bench he came easily to his feet and put out his hand and gently took her hand, and with one smooth movement turned to face the same direction and tuck her hand into the crook of his elbow.

'Now, let us have no more of this! I am indeed very pleased you should have bothered to come and see me, and tell me about poor Mr. Foster—'

'Stop calling him *poor* Mr. Foster! You make him sound like a—like a—puppy-dog!'

'Well, that is perhaps not so false an idea at that—however, no more. He is forthwith plain Mr. Foster, and no longer poor in my eyes. Let me say again, I am pleased you should have come. I think we could be good friends, and I would be happy if we were, as long as you realize that I am not a man who is interested in the pretty tricks of the stage, or the drawing-room, come to that. I am a *direct* person, Miss Lucas, and I tell you in my direct way that I like you. I think you have some wit and not a little good sense in you, if one can but find it. I hope we can continue to know each other without quarrelling. There now! Is that not what you came to arrange with me?'

Indeed it was, but she was far too mortified to say so, and walked on beside him in silence as he led her across the crowded hallway, toward the hospital's main door.

'I am shortly to attend in the wards, Miss Lucas,' he said, 'and so cannot make time to find you a hackney to see you safe home. And the streets are still very snowy, are they not? I would not wish to see your elegant toilette spoiled by the weather for want of a little care on my part, however, so I must see if I can find someone else who will—ah!'

He stopped suddenly, and she, perforce, stopped too, and tried to draw her hand away from the crook of his elbow, determined to show not only him but all those about them that she was aloof and unconcerned about him; but he, with no apparent effort, maintained his hold on her hand, and she could not, without an unseemly struggle, extricate herself. So she stood still, and looked across at the man at whom Felix was now beckoning with his other hand.

'Charles!' he called, and above the chatter that surrounded them the other man heard him and turned his head, and after a moment smiled broadly and made his way through the groups of people to their side.

'Why, hello, Felix! How are you? It's good to see you—'

'I am well, I thank you, Charles. But my young friend here is in need of your aid. Miss Lucas, may I present Mr. Charles Wyndham, a physician of this hospital at present, and but lately returned home from your own country. Charles, this is Miss Amy Lucas, of Boston, who is visiting England and shortly to appear in my cousin Oliver's show at the Supper Rooms in King Street.'

Amy bent her head with some regality; she was still simmering with anger at Felix Laurence's behaviour and was hardly aware of the man standing before her and bowing with some theatricality.

'I am enchanted to make your acquaintance, Miss Lucas! Particularly so as I have not only visited your country—indeed, I was involved in my own small way with your late hostilities, and happy indeed that I was able to contribute in some measure to the success of the Union—but because I am very interested in the theatre.'

'Indeed, Mr. Wyndham? How interesting.' She tried again to pull her hand from Felix's elbow, but he merely smiled down at her and held on, and she glared at him and turned to Charles Wyndham to bestow upon him the sweetest smile she could. 'How extremely interesting! I have never before met a physician who sometimes acts.'

'Ah, Miss Lucas, it is quite the other way about! I am an actor who sometimes physics!' He smiled widely at her, and his full-lipped mouth was very mobile, and yet very studied in its movements. 'At present, I do not scruple to tell you, I am here at the hospital only because I cannot find a good management to offer me work more suited to me. But as soon as may be, I shall be back on the boards, that is quite certain!'

She looked at him with real interest now, noting his sleek dark hair and very lustrous dark brown eyes. He looked about thirty, self-assured and relaxed.

'I too, Mr. Wyndham, I too. My present engagement is far from being as—as *satisfactory* as it should be. Supper Rooms, you know—singing and dancing—*far* from my usual interest, I do assure you!' And she threw a sideways glance at Felix to see how he had taken this gibe at the activities of a member of his family. But he merely smiled agreeably back at her.

'I am sure you will have much to talk about with Charles, Miss Lucas. But at present, as I say, I must make my way about my business. Charles, will you be so good as to find Miss Lucas a hackney carriage? She is on her way to the Supper Rooms, dislike them though she may! And needs some conveyance.'

'At once. With the greatest of pleasure, Miss Lucas.' Charles turned to go.

'One moment, Charles—I have a thought—as I say, you and Miss Lucas have much in common. Perhaps you will join us at a small dinner party at Bedford Row? Nothing very special, you know—Miss Lucas and her brother, also an actor, yourself, and perhaps my cousins. You remember the Misses Henriques? I introduced you at a tea party my Aunt Martha gave, I recollect.'

'Of course I recall them. Charming ladies, both—but not, may I venture to say, as charming as your present companion, Laurence! Indeed it will be my pleasure to accept. Dinner, you say? Upon which evening?'

Felix turned to Amy, his eyebrows cocked inquiringly. 'The day, Miss Lucas! You have but to choose. I am sure that everyone else will fit in easily. Yourself and your brother are free—when?'

'I really cannot speak for my brother, Mr. Laurence,' Amy said stiffly. 'He is a busy person, you know, and—'

'Well, perhaps I shall seek him out myself and arrange matters with him, then. I noticed that he found Miss Isabel Henriques' company agreeable, and I am sure he will make efforts to find time for us—'

Knowing full well what Fenton's reaction would be should he discover that such an invitation on his behalf had been extended to her and not seized forthwith, Amy capitulated. She knew when she was defeated; and anyway, accepting it would mean she would see this tiresome, infuriating, altogether hateful Felix Laurence again. Which, she told herself stoutly, she wished to do entirely in order to put him firmly in his place.

'I daresay I can speak for him this Friday night,' she said after a moment. 'Yes, I believe I can.'

'Splendid. That is possible for you, Charles? Excellent. Then, if you will both forgive me I must be on my way. I relinquish Miss Lucas to your care, Charles, and I will look forward to seeing you both this Friday at 27 Bedford Row to dine. Good morning, Miss Lucas!'

And this time, he let her hand go, and bent his head and went quickly away, walking with a smooth easy lope, and she stared after him and bit her lip and wanted to weep with rage, while at the same time feeling her chest thicken with excitement at the thought of this Friday. Very confusing feelings indeed, and quite incomprehensible. But then, Amy Lucas had never been in love before.

## CHAPTER TWELVE

Dinner had been over for some time, and they were sitting about the drawing-room comfortably, talking desultorily and all seeming to be very relaxed. But in fact there were undercurrents pulling in different directions, and Martha, sitting upright and with her embroidery on her brown silk lap, as befitted a lady of her years, watched her guests above the flash of her needle and pondered.

There was Oliver, for a start. He had been invited especially to entertain her, and so was sitting fairly near her, ostensibly sharing conversation with her, but in so abstracted a manner that Martha had long since given up attempting to make any sense of his occasional utterances. He was staring dolorously at Amy Lucas on the other side of the drawing-room and making no attempt whatsoever to hide his feelings. Martha sighed softly. After all these years of apparently happy bachelorhood, it was little short of tragic, she told herself, that he should let himself be so captivated bu such a flighty madam as that one.

She looked casually across at Amy Lucas, exquisite in flounced sea-green taffeta, and tried to be objective about her; but it was difficult. She had taken a sudden dislike to the girl this evening, which had quite surprised her, for she was polite enough; indeed her manners had been charming, and perfectly punctilious, as were those of her excessively handsome brother.

Martha looked at him now, and once again felt that stab of irritation that the sight of his sister aroused in her, and set her needle down for a moment to give some thought to her own reactions. As an intelligent woman, she was not one usually given to making harsh sudden judgements on people; why had she done so with these two apparently delightful people?

She thought carefully. Was it the foolish manner in which Miss Amy Lucas had behaved at her niece Phoebe's house? No, it was not that. Martha had found that little display quite touching at the time, and far from a cause for dislike. At most it might have made her impatient, for she had little use for the flutterings in which so many modern misses indulged themselves. But what she felt now was not impatience but plain dislike.

So, what was the cause? She looked again at the brother and sister, and then after a moment picked up her sewing again, and bent her head to it. Poor Oliver, she thought. He will have no joy at all from this one.

For she felt now that she knew what it was that had sparked her dislike. On one side of the room sat Miss Lucas flanked by Mr. Charles Wyndham and her own much-loved Felix, while well away from them was the other little group—this time Fenton, with the two Henriques sisters sitting one on each side of him. Each Lucas, in his and her own way, had taken the centre of the stage, and it was this that Martha found unpleasant and so dislikable.

She pondered further. Was the real problem that she objected to Felix's interest in the Lucas girl? That was a painful thought, but one that had to be faced. Ever since the death of Felix's father, Alex, far away in Scutari, there had been no room in her life for anyone but Felix. She had returned from the Crimea sick, exhausted and emaciated by her experience, to find the sixteen-year-old Felix waiting for her at the docks. And he had taken one look at her, and without a word tucked her hand into the crook of his arm and led her to a waiting carriage. He had returned with her to Bedford Row and the care of the now dead Miss Carrie Garling, who had been her friend and her predecessor as the Secretary of the London Ladies' Committee for the Rescue of the Profligate Poor who owned and ran the Bedford Row house as a hostel, and in the ensuing weeks of her slow recovery had remained firmly by her side. They had, in those long-ago days, built and then cemented a relationship which though it owed its inception to the love they had both borne the dead Alex had developed from their mutual respect and growing affection for each other.

And throughout the succeeding years it had grown, this closeness. They were friends in a way that no blood related people could ever be. And although the situation had been regularized when legal adoption proceedings were taken and she became his mother in the eyes of the law, it had never changed from being a deep and satisfying friendship between equals in intelligence and in respect for each other, despite the disparity in their ages.

But now, for the first time, he was sitting beside a girl of near enough his own age and showing an interest in her that hurt Martha. And Martha looked at him again, and bit her lip, remembering. She had only once before in her life suffered such sharp stabs of the emotion she was now experiencing, and hated the feelings when she had had them then. It had been when Alex was alive, and she had found herself jealous of the boy Felix, for whom Alex felt so much love and concern. And now, it was Felix himself who was creating the pain of jealousy. She bent her head once more to her sewing. The undercurrents here tonight were indeed powerful ones.


'So, tell me, Miss Lucas, can you be happy performing in this show? I can quite understand the *need* to do so, for no one knows better than I how one must, in the theatre, accept disagreeable engagements occasionally in order to live, but I wonder, can you be *happy* as a dancer?'

Charles Wyndham set his head on one side and beamed at her in a self-satisfied way and she stifled a moment of irritation. It was odd, really, because he was just such a man as she would once have regarded as extremely interesting and indeed exciting. He had told her with only a hint of mock modesty of his history, from his birth in Liverpool via his schooldays in France and his medical training in Dublin to his military adventures in the American Civil War. He had told her of his attempts to build a theatrical career, first as an amateur and now as a professional, and had made several witty and edged remarks about the people he had met and had to deal with. Altogether he was amusing and attentive and pleasant to look upon. So why was she not more interested in him?

She slid a look sideways at Felix, only to find he was sitting back comfortably in his chair and looking at her, and he quirked one eyebrow as he caught her glance and grinned, and she primmed her lips and turned back to Charles Wyndham with a somewhat exaggerated display of interest in what he was saying.

'—so, tell me of yourself, Miss Lucas. You are quite the mystery lady, you know, as far as I am concerned! I daresay our host here knows a great deal about you—but I am woefully ignorant. Will you tell me all?'

'All, Mr. Wyndham?' she said and dimpled up at him, and then heard a dry little cough from Felix and looked at him again, and once more his eyebrows quirked, and she said hastily, 'There is not a great deal to tell. My brother and I are orphaned—'

Usually she would have made much of such a statement, giving it all the pathos she could and engaging her audience's sympathies at once, but with Felix sitting there beside her, silent and a great deal too aware of her, that was impossible. So she went on in a matter-of-fact tone, 'After my mother's death we decided to come to England to seek theatrical success. There is really little more to say.'

'But why England, Miss Lucas?' Wyndham seemed genuinely interested. 'I know, for I have worked there—though with no marked success, I must confess!—that there are excellent theatres in your own country. I would have thought that the London stage had little more to offer than say, New York—'

'I have—had—well, perhaps still have—connections in London,' Amy said. 'My father—well, he was English. From London.'

'Indeed? So you have relations here?'

'That is what I would very much like to know.' She kindled now, and sat up a little straighter. 'I have always thought there must be someone here who will remember my

Papa. He was such a—such—oh, such a lovely man! Funny, you know, and kind and so—well, I know he was what my Fenton and Cabot uncles called feckless—'

She stopped at the puzzlement of his face. 'Oh, dear, I am rattling on. Well, you see, my Papa came to Boston from England, and married my Mamma, who was Mary Fenton and was one of such a *proper* family! Her mother's family were Cabots, you see, and in Boston that is a very important thing to be, a Cabot. So I think the uncles were not kind to Papa. And I always thought, well—I am sure that my Lucas uncles, if I have any, are as Papa was. Kind and funny. And if I could find them—'

'Well, now, Miss Lucas—' Wyndham began, but suddenly Felix was on his feet, and holding out a hand to her.

'Miss Lucas, will you allow me to tear you away from Charles's beguiling company to come and talk to Aunt Martha? I feel we have neglected her sorely this evening. You will forgive me, Wyndham? I am sure you will—look, there is Miss Sarah, with an empty chair beside her—'

Charles's brow furrowed as he stood up and politely obeyed his host. A pleasant enough evening so far, he thought. But some strange undercurrents. If the man wants to keep the delectable Miss Lucas to himself, why did he so cheerfully consign her to my care t'other morning? Indeed very strange.

'Well, to tell you the truth, Miss Henriques, I am frightened when I contemplate the future.'

Fenton looked lugubriously at Isabel Henriques, who, much touched, put out her hand to pat his, lying so negligently but conveniently close between them, and at once pulled it away, her cheeks warm and her eyes very bright. Looking at her, Fenton thought she was really quite a delightful sight. Especially adorned as she was in pretty earrings and a charming necklace, both of which bore the unmistakable watery gleam of diamonds. Her liquid eyes shone no less, and he looked deeply into them and dropped his voice a little lower.

'You see, I am fit only for a stage career. I have no talents other than myself, my voice, my care for the great words of the great writers of our noble language, and of course my body. And my late injury—'

He sighed and shook his head and then straightened his shoulders.

'Well, I must not repine, I am indeed fortunate to have the use of my limb, let alone my life. Had it not been for Mr. Caspar—' he shook his head again. 'Well, I dread to think of what the future might hold.'

'You must not worry yourself, please, Mr. Lucas,' Isabel said, urgently, and with some daring again put out her hand and rested it with equal negligence near his own, so that with just the smallest movement on his part, they could inadvertently touch.

'I have heard my brother—he is my half-brother you understand—speak of you to Mamma and Papa. And he is most concerned that all should go well with you. He cares deeply for all his patients, my brother Freddy, but I feel he has a special concern for you—as indeed we all have—you really must not worry—'

Obligingly Fenton allowed his hand to make the necessary move so that his little finger almost overlapped hers, an occasion which made Miss Isabel feel almost swooningly happy, and made her lustrous eyes more liquid than ever.

'Do *you* have concern for me, Miss Isabel—I beg your pardon—Miss Henriques?' he said softly.

'Please, do call me Isabel—there is no need for greater formality—and yes, yes, indeed we all do. For you and your sister, of course—that is why we were all so pleased when Cousin Oliver was able to find some acting for you both—well, I know it is not precisely *acting*, is it, but I am told by Cousin Phoebe that you sing divinely in rehearsal and look forward with great eagerness to hearing you when the show starts—and well, I am sure one day the people who arrange plays will come to hear of you and see you and make you a great actor—'

'You are too kind—' he smiled deeply into her eyes and quite deliberately closed his hand over hers. No accident now. 'I am so glad Mr. Wyndham took your sister away—but you will not tell her so, will you? She is a dear sweet girl, and I hope will always be my friend. But I am glad he took her away. Are you?'

All Isabel could do was lower her thick lashes over her shining eyes and sit modestly saying nothing. But she did not pull her hand away from his. The undercurrents in this corner of the room were running close enough to the surface to be almost a full flowing tide.

'I am sure you make too much of my small talents, Mr. Lackland,' Amy said, and smiled at Martha, trying to engage her attention. She was interested in the older woman, partly because she mattered so much to Felix Laurence (a fact which Amy knew should not matter to her, but did, all the same) and partly because she had been kind to her on New Year's evening in Tavistock Square. But tonight, Martha seemed cool and remote, so Amy, a little puzzled, returned her attention to Mr. Lackland.

He was looking at her with his eyes seeming blank behind his round spectacles and with his bald head shining in the gaslight and she smiled at him almost absently, very aware of Felix sitting comfortably on Oliver's other side. Why was it that this young man could make her feel so uneasy? Ever since she had been very small she had been at ease in company, well able to sparkle at will, well able to make other people dance to the tunes she piped—and suddenly she remembered the way Felix had talked scathingly of girls who made others dance to their piping and lost the thread of what Oliver was saying. She shook her head almost imperceptibly to recover herself and concentrated.

'—that you would succeed in such an entertainment was never in any real doubt. Indeed, I am delighted, truly delighted, that all is going so well now with rehearsals. At first, I cannot deny, I was most concerned, for you were so unlike the way you had been at my sister's party. But this past few days—why—'

He beamed suddenly, one of his rare smiles that seemed to lift his face into much younger lines.

'—why, you have been quite quite delightful! And your brother's singing is pleasant, very pleasant. We shall have an excellent show, I am certain. I hope to be able to—well, no details now—' Again that young smile lit his face. '—but, I daresay we can adjust the rates on the pay list in a manner that will not meet with your disapproval!'

129

'Will Miss Lucas be performing every night once the show opens, Cousin Oliver?' Felix asked abruptly.

'Eh? Oh—well, now, I am not perfectly sure at present—why do you ask? Are you wishing to book your tickets in advance?' Oliver laughed heartily at this. 'It will be a good idea, for I shall be using handbills, you know, and some of the more costly methods of putting the news of the show abroad. I confidently expect we shall be hard put to it to find places for all those who wish to attend!'

'Of course I shall come to the show, cousin. But I asked not for myself but for Miss Lucas. She tells me she has some—ah—business of her own she wishes to conduct in London, and if she is occupied each night, then she will be in some straits to prosecute it. And usually, I seem to recall, you run some different programmes on different nights?'

'Well, yes, sometimes I do—' Oliver said somewhat unwillingly, and removed his glasses and began to polish them busily on his large white handkerchief. He looked very naked, Amy thought, without them. A little lost and rather touching, like a worried baby, and she smiled at him, a very bright and direct smile and he caught it and flushed brick red and hastily hooked his spectacles back round his ears and settled them fussily on the bridge of his nose. '—and I would not for the world wish to prevent Miss Lucas from any other matter that is of importance—is it anything in which I can be of help, Miss Lucas?'

She blinked and looked at Felix and opened her mouth and he shook his head and said easily, 'Oh, it is a matter to do with her family, Cousin Oliver. I thought I might be of some guidance in it—there is no need to concern yourself. You have ample to do with preparing the show. So, when will the performances be?'

'Well, I thought—let me see now—' Oliver took a small booklet from his pocket and began to turn the pages over with some flurry. 'I suppose we can say—yes, I think perhaps we could run the other programmes, without Miss Lucas, on Monday, and your brother, Miss Lucas, can then have his free evening on Thursdays. I trust that will be suitable for him? Monday is never much of a day, and I doubt we will miss you so much as we would on Thursdays—yes, Mondays for you—

130

I hope that will be enough time for you to deal with whatever the matter is? If not, we could perhaps—'

'Oh, ample, cousin, ample—' Felix got to his feet and crooked his arm at Amy.

'Well, now, Miss Lucas, I feel we must go and talk to my cousins Isabel and Sarah. Delightful girls both, and we have all monopolized you so all evening you have had no time for any of the girlish chatter that I am convinced young ladies much prefer to wasting time on dull male topics—'

As she allowed him to lead her across the broad expanse of the drawing-room she hissed, 'I thought you were a *direct* man, Mr. Laurence? That gibe about girlish chatter was extremely devious, I would say! And what about this family business you were speaking of? If that isn't devious, I do not know what is! What were you talking about?'

He stopped in the middle of the drawing-room and at a point at which they were just out of earshot of all the rest of the room's occupants, and stood there looking down at her.

'Devious, you say? I think not. I was simply using the common drawing-room device—of speaking to you in terms that you would understand but which others would not. I have heard my cousins and their husbands and wives do it many times.'

'We are not a husband and wife,' she said tartly and once more felt her face suddenly react with what was becoming a hateful redness; it was quite ridiculous that this man could make her behave so! 'And what is this family—'

'Ah, yes—as to that—well, now it seemed to me, when you were speaking to Charles of your father, that you were expressing some very real and very important feelings.'

She looked up at him, a little puzzled. 'But of course!'

'There is no of course about it,' he said, and his voice was suddenly gentle. 'Miss Lucas, let me explain something to you. I believe you to be at heart a lady as capable of sincerity and—and directness in your dealings as any other person. But all the years you have spent steeped in theatricality have made you to an extent artificial—and the artifice has become so much a part of you that you do not even know when you display it! I daresay it is an impertinence in me, but I have set myself the goal of—shall we say, of helping you to recognize your artifices and use them only when it is right and proper that you should. This is why I torment you as I do. And I daresay you do regard it as some sort of unkindness in me.'

She blinked and looked away, frowning. 'I suppose you are right. Not that you torment me—precisely—you make me angry, I admit, but torment—that is a very different matter. I know what you mean, of course. That I act a great deal, but it is what I am *for*—' and she looked up at him appealingly. 'I cannot change that.'

He smiled. 'I am sure I do not wish you to change in any real way, Miss Lucas. But I would wish to teach you—no, shall we say, help you to learn—how to control your artifices. As I think you will—but as I was saying, in the matter of your father—'

'Well?'

'When you spoke of him, you did so with such feeling that it seemed to me that you really care deeply about finding any of his family.'

'I told you I did! Could you not believe me?'

'Yes, I believe you. In this, I really believe you. And, so did Wyndham. He was about to offer to help you make a search for these relations, you know.'

She whirled and looked about the room for him, but he was in the far corner with Miss Sarah, playing a rather noisy game of cards at which both were laughing quite immoderately.

'He was? Then I shall speak to him of it immediately! Because—'

He put out his hand to restrain her. 'There is no need. That is why I was speaking so to Cousin Oliver. *I* shall help you seek your family. On each and every Monday evening, if you will permit, we shall make such inquiries as we may. If you would like that, of course.'

'Like it? I would like it above all things!' She was staring up at him with great delight, and his own eyes narrowed appreciatively as he smiled back at her pleasure.

'Then, next Monday, I suggest that I call for you at your lodgings in Long Acre, and we sally forth upon our search. Perhaps you and your brother will dine with me first at an hotel? There are several excellent and respectable establishments where a lady may safely be seen—'

'I shall ask him—right now—'

'Oh, I think I would not disturb him.' He turned his head towards the far corner of the room where Fenton and Isabel were seated side by side at the piano with their heads close together, picking out a pretty little Mozart duet, and Amy nodded and smiled and turned back to Felix.

'Well, yes, I daresay, it would spoil their concentration on the music—but I shall tell him tonight, as soon as we may, how kind you are being—and—and—' she stopped and bit her lip.

'Well?'

'I was so angry with you the other day, I quite *hated* you. And from what I have seen of you already, I daresay there will be times when I will hate you again. Most heartily! But at present, Mr. Laurence, I will be as *direct* as even you could wish, and tell you I like you very much!'

'You mean you are grateful at the moment, Miss Lucas! But never mind—you are indeed speaking just as you feel, and I find that most refreshing! And now, I think, we should join the card-players, don't you? Drawing-room manners may be tedious, but they needs must be adhered to!'

Martha, watching still from behind her embroidery, sighed again. The undercurrents were now running very smoothly, it seemed. And she wished she could have been happier about it.

## CHAPTER THIRTEEN

January snowed and then thawed in to a blustery February which blew itself with gusto into a crisp pale March, and Amy was as happy as she could ever remember being.

Each Monday morning she spent in dealing with her wardrobe, an activity she much enjoyed, with Miss Emma Miller to help her (and she turned out to be as pretty a needlewoman as she was a teacher of the pianoforte) while Fenton slept the morning hours away and left them in peace. He would then join them, yawning hugely, for one of Mrs. Miller's 'scratch luncheons' as she called them, to eat vast quantities of boiled ham and mutton pasties and apple and currant pies before taking himself off to meet his cronies at the Wrekin coffee house, just round the corner in Broad Court. Here he spent his afternoons until it was time to go to King Street for the evening performances, sitting and drinking and gossiping with other actors and singers—for the Wrekin was an acknowledged meeting-place for the profession—leaving his sister alone to occupy herself as best she might.

Not that she had any difficulty in finding occupation. Arrayed in whatever new item she had devised with Miss Miller's aid—were it a hat, or a newly trimmed muff, or occasionally a completely new gown—she would sally forth to walk about the handsome shopping streets of London admiring the goods spread on the counters of the richest establishments in the richest city in the richest country in the world. Her lack of money with which to buy the splendid creations offered to the eager gaze of passers-by bothered her little; it was enough at present to admire. The deep-down discontent which had been so much a feature of her life since she had grown up and which had expressed itself hitherto in a hungry longing for anything and everything she saw or could imagine was damped down, and it was some time—well into March—before she realized just why it was she was so serene.

The reason was, of course, Monday evenings. They had devised a ritual quite early in their acquaintanceship and followed it as regularly as clockwork, a patterning which in itself gave Amy a most agreeable sense of security. The suggestion that Fenton should join them to dine soon shrivelled away, for after one evening which Fenton spent with them and clearly found exceedingly boring—for Felix was an abstemious man, and ordered only one bottle of wine to their dinner, which Fenton clearly found inadequate—he made excuses not to accompany them. So, just the two of them would meet each Monday at about five o'clock, when Felix left the hospital, and would stroll even in the most inclement of weather—for as Amy stoutly told him, they had *much* worse winters in Boston—to one of the pleasant if rather dull little hotel dining-rooms or respectable family restaurants in the district, there to eat a comfortable meal.

And they would talk.

Sometimes of patients he had seen that day, sometimes of episodes she had experienced at the Supper Rooms, sometimes of Fenton's doings (though that was rare) occasionally of books he had read or music he had heard, and wished to introduce to her. Gradually he taught her, even though she did not realize she was learning anything, to be relaxed and comfortable with him. The pretty little tricks of behaviour that she had used when with men for as long as she could remember—the sidelong glances, the sweeping of her thick lashes, the little pouts that so delightfully displayed the errant dimples at the corners of her mouth—were all abandoned with him. She would still use them at the Supper Rooms, both as part of her performance and when talking to the customers after each show, but with him, never.

She did not know that this was the reason he did not come to watch her, even when she put a new dance in her repertoire. He told her simply that he had seen her first performances, and remembered them well enough; he had no need to see more. And though that at first had made her angry, and indeed quite hurt, she had been mollified by the obvious pleasure he took in their Monday evenings, when he would sit across the table from her and talk, and encourage her to talk, listening with his face bearing its usual friendly expression, yet with a grave interest that was very warming.

For him it was a comfort that she had accepted his calm refusal to attend the Supper Rooms to see her and he was grateful for it, for he had suffered a good deal of distress about his feelings when he had seen her there. Indeed, Felix was going through what was for him a most difficult time. Although he was a mature man of some twenty-seven years he had never yet been at all touched in any way by any young woman. He had grieved long and sorely for his beloved father, and found much comfort in the easy close relationship he had built with Martha, and that had been enough for him.

135

Over the years of his arduous medical training and early struggling years as a qualified physician, he had held himself aloof from females, hiding his most tender feelings behind a mask of friendliness that had maddened many a hopeful young lady on the lookout for a husband. And Martha's friends had long since given up hope of snaffling him for one of their daughters.

So that when he had been caught unawares by the sight of a girl in a blue gown going up the stairs of his cousin Phoebe's house, he had been extremely startled by the effect. When, that same evening, he had heard young Foster's declaration he had been positively amazed at the stab of rage and disappointment he had felt; and when she had come to see him at the hospital he had to admit he was captive. Every turn of her head, every tone of her voice, was as dear to him as life itself.

Not that he had not tried to fight what he regarded as a weakness in himself. That he should be captivated by one who was, in a sense, a professional captivator hurt his self-esteem keenly. He had tried hard to provoke her into behaviour of the sort that would free him of the thrall into which she had cast him. But that did not help. In a very short time he realized that for all the guile there was in her, there was no malice. Indeed, at bottom she was a good honest girl, he discovered; a little too biddable perhaps by her brother (and he, Felix shrewdly suspected, was far from good at bottom) rather too easily swayed by the opinions of others, but a dear good girl for all that.

In other words, Felix was head over heels in love, although none, seeing his calm exterior and hearing his easy quiet speech, would ever have thought it.

It was that which made it impossible for him to sit and watch Amy perform at his cousin's establishment. All the falsity which he so disliked appeared in her there with such glitter and cleverness that the girl he so deeply loved seemed to disappear altogether to be replaced by a grinning posturing painted creature he positively despised. And in addition, he realized full well just how besotted Oliver had become with his new performer, and the sight of him standing in the shadows of the wings, staring at her with a fatuous beaming glow upon his face and his eyes shining almost with lasciviousness as

136

he watched Amy's pirouettes and swaying movements across the small stage, was agony for Felix. Better, by far, he told himself, to stay away. He could see no other way in which to battle against the ignoble jealousy which so filled him when he went there.

But, fortunately, she came to terms with that and as winter gave way to spring enjoyed their Mondays more and more. With him she felt safe and comfortable and deeply happy; and yet at the same time greatly excited. She did not analyse her feelings, made no attempt to put a name to her relationship with him, and would have been amazed if someone had told her she was in love. That was something that happened to young men for her sake, or to foolish young girls who fell into a trance at the sight of Fenton's handsome face. It was not conceivable to Amy that *she* should ever be such a one, so she did not conceive of it. She was just content to be as she was.

Graham Foster was no longer a problem to her, for he had passed his final examinations and taken himself and his broken heart off to work in a hospital in Southampton (where, if he missed Amy quite agonizingly, he was at least free of his masterful mother's attentions); she was working in a reasonably agreeable occupation which had the great virtue of allowing the Lucases not only to pay their way (for Oliver was providing most generous salaries) but to pay back their debts and even to save a little, and was being looked after with great cosiness in the little house in Long Acre. With all that *and* a Monday evening in every week, life seemed to be offering her all it could as the months pleated themselves contentedly into each other.

They did not forget the reason they had started their ritual of meeting each Monday. Amy was genuinely eager to make a search for any connections of her father's who might be found, and Felix was genuinely eager to help her. He, who had loved his own father so dearly, could enter closely into her feelings for her dead Papa. He too could remember the delight of spending childhood time with a man who had made him laugh and made him feel safe and happy. He too could feel the pangs of guilt which sometimes Amy felt; she would talk with remorse of the way she had been captious or noisy or shrill and had spoiled outings by fighting with her brother, or stamp-

137

ing and balking at her mother, and he would remember his own great guilt about his father's death. How he had to learn to live with the fact that it had been his own impulsive schoolboy desire to 'fight in the Crimea' which had forced his father to make the long and tedious journey to follow him; how his father had stayed behind in Scutari because there was only one passage available on the ship going home to England, a passage which he had insisted the boy Felix should take. And how his father had died there. These were matters upon which he had thought many times over the years and which had given him much pain. But now, in a curious way, he felt he was to an extent expiating his own guilt in helping Amy to make her search for her father's family.

They covered much the same ground that Amy and Fenton had covered in their early days in England, when seeking work as actors. They went to the Theatre Royal in the new Adelphi, to the Royal Italian, to Drury Lane, to Terry's, to the Royalty, to the Globe.

They would see the performance in the theatre each time, whatever play was being done. It seemed reasonable to both of them to assume that any connection of her father's would be involved with the theatre still, and so might well appear in a playbill, so they would sit in the comfortable stalls and eagerly peruse the list of players in search of Lucases; until Felix pointed out that the assumption that her father would have had only male relations of his own name was absurd; could he not have had sisters who had married and produced offspring with quite different surnames? Which obvious fact quite cast Amy in the dumps for a little while—until he pointed out that they could look at the actors for family likenesses to herself and Fenton, both of whom had been very like Papa.

Which they did, conversing in soft whispers about whether or not that actor had a nose like Fenton's or a head shaped like her own. And came to the conclusion at last that this was not really the way to make their searches, but at present could not devise another. Not that they thought about it very hard; for both of them it was the sharing of the evening that mattered. There seemed to be plenty of time yet in which to carry out their plans.

It was late in March, when the flower-sellers at the street corners were offering bunches of violets and primroses and occasionally even daffodils and the roads were noisy with the chatter of sparrows who made themselves heard even above the clatter and roar of the traffic that they accidentally bumped into Charles Wyndham as they entered the restaurant they had chosen for their dinner that night.

Amy had almost forgotten him and greeted him with real pleasure, and he glinted at her as he bent over her hand and said in a voice which sounded richer and rounder than ever: 'My dear Miss Lucas! How good to see you! Indeed today is full of such coincidences! Here I have not set eyes upon you since that delightful dinner—' and here he bowed at Felix, '—was it as long ago as last January? And now I see both you and your brother on the same day!'

'Oh?' Amy smiled up at him. 'Indeed? How very curious! I imagine you went to the early performance at the Supper Rooms, then?'

'Oh, no, nothing so mundane! I have seen your show, of course, and quite delightful it was, quite delightful! I am not surprised to hear your cousin is doing such good business, Felix, indeed I am not! No, my dear Miss Lucas, I saw him in the Burlington Arcade, with Miss Henriques, you know, quite girdled about with her packages! They seemed to be on very happy terms—so happy, indeed, that I forbade to speak to them. It would have been quite an intrusion, I fear, to have interrupted their colloquy!'

Felix looked at him with a hint of dislike in his eyes. He had not remembered the fellow as being quite such a coxcomb, with posturings and posings, and he wanted to send him away as fast as he could, fearing that his precious evening alone with Amy was about to be spoiled. But she responded to his words with some surprise, and was talking eagerly.

'My brother? In Burlington Arcade? With Miss Henriques? Oh no, I am sure you were mistaken, Mr. Wyndham! My brother went to the Supper Rooms early today. He told me he was going there directly from Long Acre, instead of spending his usual couple of hours with his friends at the Wrekin. He is there most afternoons, you know, except on days when there is an early performance.'

139

'Oh, I am sure it was he, my dear Miss Lucas! I was almost as close to him as I am to you—yet still he was so absorbed in his fair companion he did not see me. The Wrekin, did you say? I am often there—most afternoons when I am not occupied at the hospital, and certainly almost always at luncheon time, you know, and I have never seen him there—yet as I say, I see both of you on the same day! Is it not strange?'

'Not very strange, I am sure,' Felix said a little sharply. 'Large as London is, the parts in which people work and shop are not so widespread. I am never surprised at anyone I may meet—'

'Well, I am indeed delighted to see you both! Will you take a little wine with me, perhaps? It would be agreeable to share a little talk with you, Miss Lucas, on matters theatrical—'

Felix opened his mouth to demur, but at once Amy said eagerly, 'Indeed, it would be pleasant to talk, would it not, Felix? And I must say I am very puzzled that Mr. Wyndham should have seen Fenton as he says he did—I had no idea he was—well—let us sit down, shall we?'

Felix, philosophically accepting the inevitable, led the way to the table he had reserved and beckoned the waiter to set another chair, and Wyndham settled himself with a pleasant if rather theatrical flurry, chattering busily meanwhile.

'I do trust, Miss Lucas, that I have not set any cats among any pigeons! I would not for the world reveal any secrets a young man may have to his sister, however charming that sister may be. But it did not occur to me at all that there could be any wrong in speaking of such an observation. Miss Henriques is, of course, a most charming young lady—charming—and most respectable, is that not so, Felix? A cousin of yours after all—'

'Yes,' Felix said repressively. 'Amy—Miss Lucas—I think we had best order our dinner, or we will, I fear, be late at the theatre. I imagine you will take a chop with us, Wyndham?'

'You are very kind,' Wyndham said with alacrity and pulled his chair closer to the table. 'I insist that I should order the wine, however—'

'Not at all,' Felix said crisply. 'This is my table, I believe. You must allow me to play host—waiter—the table d'hote, if you please, and fast about it. We go to the theatre—'

With careful talk of the play they were to see that evening and some firmness from Felix, the conversation was led away from Wyndham's sighting of Fenton squiring Isabel Henriques, but both Amy and Felix pondered over the matter as the chatter flowed over them. Amy wondered why Fenton should have been secretive with her on such a matter. He had never been one to hide his doings from her, unless they were in some way nefarious, and there could be nothing nefarious in any dealings he had with the very proper and rich Miss Henriques. Could it be, she wondered, much struck by the idea, that Fenton was serious in his feelings for a girl? A strange idea indeed, and one that would need much cogitation. She decided to talk to Fenton about it all that very evening, when he returned from the Supper Rooms, and now turned her attention back to Wyndham and his fascinating theatrical gossip. He seemed to know everybody and everything that was happening on or around the stages of London and she plunged into it all with great relish.

Felix, meanwhile, was uneasy. Fenton and Isabel? He thought of his cousins Abby and Gideon, and tried to imagine them reacting with any pleasure at the news that their precious older daughter was involved with a penniless actor; and could not. They were both so very proper, so very aware of their station in life and of their riches; he knew quite well that they had ambitious plans for the lovely Isabel and that such plans could in no way ever encompass a Fenton Lucas.

He sighed softly. There could be trouble brewing there, he felt. Perhaps he should speak to Fenton, and try to warn him in some way, before his affections were completely engaged. At which thought he stole a glance at Amy, her face alight with laughter as she listened to Wyndham telling some droll story of a recent attempt to audition for a part in a play at the Haymarket Theatre, and sighed again. How would he feel if someone came to him and told him he must not squire Amy about? Very angry indeed, he thought. Exceedingly so. It would not be easy to deal with Fenton if he was as captured by Felix's cousin as Felix was captured by Fenton's sister . . .

'Oh, we have been searching, you know!' Amy was saying, as Felix wrenched his thoughts back to the conversation. 'I recollect I told you of my Papa? And that he was English?

Well, Dr. Laurence has been so kind and helpful, and we are seeking out theatres, you know, in the hope that at one of them we may see an actor—or actress of course!—who is like enough to Fenton or to me to make it seem possible that we are connections—'

'It seems a rather—well, not a very *thorough* way to search,' Wyndham said carefully, and looked at Felix. Perhaps Laurence had his own reasons for making such a desultory attempt to help Miss Lucas? But Felix's face seemed smooth enough, and Wyndham went on, 'You would do much better to talk to the stage-door keepers, you know. In London it is quite customary for such servants of the theatre to remain at the same post for many many years—quite unlike America, dear Miss Lucas, where they all change their employment with quite bewildering regularity! Have you spoken to any of them?'

'Why, no—' Amy was much struck. 'We have not. But of course, you must be right! I daresay there will be some of the back-stage people who would be old enough to have been in the theatre when my Papa was! Shall we do that, Felix—Dr. Laurence?' She blushed charmingly and tried not to look at Wyndham; to so display their intimacy was rather fast, and she might anger Felix. But Felix seemed unmoved and said merely, 'Indeed, it sounds an excellent idea. I am afraid my knowledge of theatre ways is sketchy in the extreme. No doubt we should have tried talking to people inside the theatre much sooner than this. I daresay we would have thought of it eventually, however—'

She smiled at him, and her dimples showed fleetingly in the old manner. 'Well, we have enjoyed some delightful evenings at the play, so there is no loss,' she murmured. 'But after this, we shall indeed talk to stage doormen. Thank you for the idea, Mr. Wyndham. And if I find my relations in this manner—why, you shall be the first to be told!'

# CHAPTER FOURTEEN

Abby was eating cucumber sandwiches in a contemplative sort of way, watching Daniel on the far side of the drawing-room showing his small cousin Ambrose a particularly complex form of cat's-cradle. The room was buzzing agreeably with noise, as was usual on Martha's Sundays, but it did not feel as comfortable as it usually did, and Abby turned to look for Gideon to discuss the matter with him. He was not too far away but was very occupied with talking to Cecily and James and she watched them fondly, her plump face creasing gently. It seemed so absurd, looking at her elegant spare Gideon, who despite his white hair looked so very young, to think of him as a grandfather, albeit a step-grandfather. It was even more absurd to think of herself as a grandmother; after all, she was only fifty-three—no age. Yet there was Cecily, already at almost eleven showing signs of her incipient womanhood in her tight-bodiced gown, and sturdy James with his red hair, and funny, bouncy little Ambrose.

She looked at James again and sighed softly, trying for a moment to remember the grandfather after whom he had been named, and who had been so long dead; James, her first husband whom she had loved so dearly and lost so young. So much to have happened in such a short time; after all, fifty-three is no age—

Gideon looked up and caught her eye and stood up, sending his young listeners off to talk to their Aunt Martha, and came to sit beside her, reaching for a cucumber sandwich from the dish beside her.

'Why is it that the comestibles Martha arranges for tea on

Sundays always have a special taste of their own? I find it very strange—'

'No stranger than the fact that you may eat as much as you like, my love, and gain not so much as an inch, and I have but to look at cucumber sandwiches or anything else, come to that, and I am immediately afflicted with even more *embonpoint*. There is no justice . . . Gideon, I am puzzled. It is almost five o'clock, and we have been here for at least two hours, and there is no sign of Felix. Now, that is very unusual, is it not? Where do you suppose he is?'

'It is no more unusual than the absence of our own Isabel, my love,' Gideon said, and his voice was fretful. 'I am still most put out—she has had a great deal of freedom for one of her age and I do feel she could have bent her will to us a little today. I much prefer her to spend her Sundays with us, as a family. All week, when I am at the counting house, she can gad about with her friends. Why choose my one free afternoon to—'

'Now, Gideon, do not, I pray you, start that again,' Abby said, trying to be soothing but contriving only to sound tetchy. 'I told you—this picnic was planned by the Canterburys—oh, months ago. And after all, it is rather boring for a young girl to spend a whole afternoon prosing with her relations—'

'That's as may be,' Gideon said sharply. 'And the party before that? Last week? I know you tell me it is wrong of me to think so, Abby, but I tell you again—I fear she is deceiving me with some admirer of whom she knows we will not approve—'

There was a short and rather painful little silence between them. It was not until Isabel had started to grow up that there had been any real rifts between them on the subject of their children, but as Isabel reached maturity and showed herself to be a girl of considerable beauty as well as an heiress Gideon had reverted to type, and become as possessive and anxious as his own father had been. Abby and he had talked about it in depth only once, and it had left much pain behind it, that discussion. Gideon had been driven to tell his wife flatly that it was his dearest wish that his daughter should marry within the faith into which her father had been born.

'I know that in marrying you as I did, Abby, I seemed to show disregard of the customs of my people,' he said earnestly, 'but that does not mean I do not care about them. It would in a sense give me back my faith were Isabel and Sarah, and of course Daniel, to embrace the synagogue and its laws—'

'I could not, in all honesty, support you in any disagreement on such a matter,' Abby had said quietly, trying not to let the pain his words had inflicted show on her face. Had she deprived him of his religion in allowing him to marry her, all those years ago? Remembering the way she had fought her own desires, the efforts she had made to prevent their marriage, she knew she had not. His choice had been his own, freely made. Yet now, after all these happy years, still he felt in some way guilty about it. Perhaps because his father had died unreconciled to his son's marriage; perhaps because his mother too had gone to her death still suffering silent distress about her son's lapse. Whatever the cause, the guilt was there, and showed itself as this concern that his own children should marry Jews like their father. It was a subject they talked of rarely and then only obliquely, but when they did, it always left, as it did this afternoon, faint traces of distress in the air between them.

'I do not agree,' she said now a little stiffly and turned to look across the room again, this time catching Martha's eye. She got to her feet and came to join them, settling herself easily as Abby made space on the sofa beside her, and the moment of unease passed.

'Well, my dear, that is an elegant gown—yet another new one?' Martha said comfortably. 'I think that shade of brown is excellent on you. So warm—'

'Martha, where is Felix?' Abby said, and looked directly at her sister. 'I cannot remember there ever being a Sunday here when Felix was not with you. We seem to be so thin of company without him—'

There was a little silence and then Martha said lightly, 'Oh, he will be here shortly. He is out with Miss Lucas, you know.'

'Oh.'

There was a brief pause and then Martha said almost defiantly, 'He is seeing a great deal of her these days. Indeed, there has not been a week in which he has not taken her to some theatre or other since the start of the year.'

'Really? That is—ah—' Abby hesitated. 'Do you mind?'

'Mind? What is there in that for me to mind? He is not my possession, you know, Abby! He is a young man of sense and ability and—indeed, it would be most improper in me to attempt to place any controls upon him! I may have adopted him, but he achieved his majority more than six years ago, you must recall, and—'

'Indeed, I do recall,' Abby said hastily. 'And that was a splendid party you gave to mark it, was it not? Well, I am sure he is a sensible boy—'

'Man. A sensible *man*,' Martha said flatly, and again a small silence fell, and Gideon reached for another cucumber sandwich and said nothing.

'To tell you the truth, Abby,' Martha burst out suddenly, 'I am not entirely happy in my mind about it all. I look at Oliver and I think—oh, I do not know what to think!'

Abby too looked at her nephew, sitting on the far side of the room in the window seat ostensibly staring abstractedly out of the window but quite clearly watching with some eagerness for new arrivals.

'He has been so the entire afternoon, waiting for her!' Martha said. 'It is so *sad*! I cannot pretend I do not find her a little tiresome, with her airs and graces and that drawly way she speaks—not that she can help that, I suppose, seeing she is an American, but when you are irritated by a person you tend to be irritated by everything including things they cannot help and which do not matter—you know how it is!—but I could tolerate all that if only she would be kinder to poor Oliver instead of hanging out after Felix!'

'I think perhaps you are a little unfair, my dear,' Abby said gently. 'Do you not agree, Gideon? After all, she gave Oliver no encouragement that I could see. It is indeed sad that the dear boy should wait so long to find a girl he could love and then choose one who is only too patently not interested in him. But you can hardly blame the girl for that—'

'Oh, I know,' Martha said fretfully. 'I know it is not the girl's fault—and that Oliver is behaving very silly for a man his age. He is hardly a boy—why, he must be—'

'Thirty-five,' Gideon said glumly. 'And I agree with Martha. It is inelegant in a young lady to behave so—she should be aware of the effect she has on gentlemen—on people, and be *retiring*—'

Abby could not forbear to smile at the thought of the ebullient Miss Lucas being retiring and said comfortably to Martha, 'Well, I daresay you are worrying unnecessarily. I am sure Felix is a sensible young man, and will come to no harm. He has never shown signs of being unduly susceptible, and I am sure will see through any artifice. Fortunately he is not precisely rich, is he? It is not as though she will be dangling after him for his money.'

'He is not precisely poor, either,' Martha said tartly. 'And I agree—he is sensible enough to take care of himself. But for all that, I—well,' she smiled a little sheepishly, 'I do think it wise to welcome her here often. So much more sensible, I feel, than setting my face against her. Do you not agree?'

'Oh, indeed I do,' Abby said and looked at Gideon. 'It is always wiser to try to go along with one's young people. To set out to guide them too forcefully—it can lead to so many problems.'

Freddy had come over to them and was standing with his cup and saucer in his hand looking down at them with a fond grin across his pleasant face.

'I do enjoy watching you two chattering, Mamma, Aunt Martha,' he said. 'For all the world like a pair of pussies lapping up the cream and licking their whiskers. I take it you are busily tearing a reputation to shreds?'

'That is most unjust, Freddy,' Abby said with some dignity. 'We were speaking of Felix —how could we possibly tear him to shreds? Apologize at once!'

'I apologize!' Freddy said promptly. 'Aunt Martha, you are a very dear, good aunt, and we all love you, but I promise you that the next time you present young Ambrose with yet another toy book, I shall insist that he will not accept it. All this giving—it is bad for his character, indeed it is! He will be ruined—'

'I am sure he will not. Not with you and Phoebe as his Papa and Mamma.'

'You do not make it easy—tell her, Mamma.'

147

'Oh, do not ask *me*—I spoil Cecily outrageously, as well you know! And Gideon sees to it that young James gets his share—and there are no signs that any one of the three are anything but a credit to you, my dear Freddy—ah! Here he is, at last!'

There was a little flurry as the door opened and Amy came in, her face flushed with the sharpness of the April air and her eyes sparkling with excitement.

She stood there untying her exceedingly pretty straw bonnet, her soft yellow gown billowing as she swayed, and almost without their realizing it everyone in the room turned to look at her, so that she became the focal point of the whole party; Oliver standing in his window embrasure with his mouth slightly open, and his eyes filled with adoration; Freddy, frankly admiring; the three women, Abby, Martha and Phoebe, watchful and the children, including Sarah, quite bedazzled. Felix, standing behind Amy, looked at them all and felt a surge of mixed emotions. Pride and embarrassment—she was so very *noticeable*—and deep down a little cold fear. He was filled with a sort of premonition and tried to dismiss it; such a fanciful notion was not like him at all. Yet still it was there.

'Well, so you are here! I had quite given up hope of seeing you this afternoon,' Martha said smoothly and rustled to her feet. 'Freddy, my dear, will you just set your hand upon the bell? We need fresh tea for these two travellers, I think—'

'Good afternoon, everybody!' Amy said, and her voice seemed to bubble with some hidden delight. 'How agreeable to see you all! Sarah, how well you look—I do like your gown!'

'Thank you!' Sarah said eagerly, and then, gauchely, 'Is—is your brother not with you?'

Amy shot a quick glance from beneath her brows at Abby and then said, as she smoothed the gold-coloured ribbons of her bonnet. 'Why, no. He—he has another engagement. But I—well, I have such *interesting* news! You cannot imagine— oh, thank you. No, no cream. Just a little lemon—that is delightful—well, may I tell you my news?'

'I think we would be hard put to it to stop you,' Freddy said dryly, and went to sit down beside Phoebe, who said not a word. She just watched the sparkling girl, now sitting on the sofa in the middle of the room, with an apparently blank gaze in her grey eyes but still a very watchful one.

'Well, you may recall I mentioned that my Papa was English? And that it was my hope that I should be able to find his relations here? That was one of the reasons we came to England at all—well, do you know, we may be on the track!'

'I did not know you were looking,' Martha said in a tight voice, and her gaze slid across the room to Abby who frowned suddenly.

'Oh, did you not? Why, yes, that has been our occupation these many weeks—every Monday, you know!' Amy said airily. 'And it is *so* exciting—now we believe we have found some news!'

'Oh? That sounds very clever of you! Explain yourself, my dear, do!' Freddy seemed genuinely interested and leaned forwards.

'Well! We went to the Haymarket Theatre—the stage door, you know, for Felix's—Dr. Laurence's friend, Mr. Wyndham, who knows a lot about the theatre here said that is what we should do—well, anyway, we did. We told him—the stage doorkeeper, of my Papa and that he was named Lucas and did he know of any actor named Lucas? And he said—well! It was so *interesting*, was it not, Felix?' And she looked up at him and smiled so trustingly and so happily that Martha felt her chest lurch with resentment as well as an underlying fear about what Amy was about to say.

'Indeed, he was most interesting. It appeared he had been the stage doorkeeper there for close on fifty years, and before that his Uncle was. It is, you might say, a family occupation—' Felix said.

'Like the slicing up of patients is with us,' Freddy murmured.

'Oh, *Papa*—' Cecily shrilled, and the two smalls boys laughed loudly and fell to pretending to slice each other up with great ferocity, an occupation from which they were separated by their forceful grandmother.

When order had been restored Amy went on with the story. 'He told us that he knew of no actor called Lucas, and then he said it was as though the name had some meaning for him, but he could not quite collect what it was. And then we had to go away, for the play was about to start and he had work to do. But he said to come back today, for he often works there on Sunday afternoons, and he would see what he could recall. Felix was very wise and gave him some money, and today we went back—and he gave us more news! He was so interesting—real fascinating, all the things he told us! He remembered so much of the old days—even when they used limelights, you know, for the wings! It sounded very romantic!'

'Did he remember your father?' Freddy asked, deeply interested, and seemingly unaware of the tension in his mother and aunt.

'No—but he remembered another Lucas!' Amy said triumphantly and drank some of her tea, enjoying stretching out her story for as long as possible. She did not see Abby suddenly stiffen and her eyes glaze, nor Martha's very still face.

'You must tell us, at once!' Sarah said, and came rustling across the room to sit eagerly beside Amy. 'This is beginning to sound most exciting!'

'Oh, it is! He told us that fifty years ago—imagine, fifty years!—there had come to London from the provinces an actress who was so splendid and so charming that everyone adored her. That she was the best actress in London for many years, and then—oh, such a story as he told us!—that she had just disappeared! Overnight!'

'Disappeared? How do you mean?'

'It seems she suffered some injury or other.' Felix's voice came coolly, bringing down considerably the tension Amy had so carefully created. He was far from enjoying the relish with which she was telling her story. 'He was rather vague about it—despite a considerable amount of greasing of his rather dirty palm—but something happened to her in about '39 or '40—'

'Nearly twenty-five years ago! Imagine that!' Amy said breathlessly, as though the period of time had been aeons instead of merely decades, and Abby looked at her and bit her lip. Fifty-three was no age, dammit!

'And thereafter he remembered nothing. In spite of ample grease. However—'

150

'However, he did recall her name. She was—Lilith Lucas! Imagine *that*! Now, she could have had a son, could she not? I worked it out—according to my Papa's age, it could have been—'

'All this sounds very much a matter of surmise,' Abby's voice came sharply to cut across Amy's excitement. 'Really, my dear, you make too much of this, I suspect. You will need far more to show that this woman—whoever she was—had any connection with you. Lucas is, in all honesty, a common enough name. I daresay there are several brace of actors called Lucas in London alone—I would make no more of this, if I were you. Felix, my dear, do tell me. Have you seen Mrs. Braham lately? She tells me that she goes to meetings of a committee at the Middlesex Hospital, and I daresay that you will—'

'Oh, but it is not surmise, indeed it is not!' Amy said heatedly. 'I do assure you—'

Abby looked at her, one eyebrow slightly raised, and the chill could be felt by all of them and not just by Amy. But impulsively she jumped to her feet, and her face was red with excitement as she almost shouted the words.

'I am quite convinced of it! I really, really am, and you *cannot* say it is all surmise when you did not speak to the man or—'

'My dear child, you go too far!' Abby said icily and turned to Gideon who was looking very set about the jaw, and at once Martha moved forwards, her face wreathed in a bright smile.

'Now, my dear, we shall have a cosy little prose about this later, I am sure. But at present, will you not have some more tea and—'

'No—I will *not* have more tea! And I will not be treated as a child, as though I am imagining this. I tell you I am *sure*—quite, quite sure. This Lilith Lucas—she *must* have been a connection! I believe she must have been my grandmother and—'

'Lilith Lucas—' It was Oliver's voice which cut across now and Amy turned and looked at him eagerly.

'Do you remember her, Mr. Lackland? Do you? It was almost fifty years ago that she came to London first, and was the toast of the town, the man said, for many years—do you remember her? Can you tell me about her?'

Oliver reddened suddenly and took his glasses off to wipe them. 'I am not quite so old as you may think, Miss Amy,' he said stiffly, and the pain in his voice was plain to all of them except, perhaps, Amy. 'No, it was just that—' he looked at his sister, blinking a little without his spectacles. 'Do you know, Phoebe, I am wondering if that could be our Mamma's—'

'Nothing of the sort!' Abby said loudly. 'Really, Oliver, how absurd all this is! As if you could recall any such tiresome nonsense as the name of some cheap actress of all those years ago! Quite, quite absurd! Martha, my dear, I really *must* speak with you for a moment before we leave—about the meeting of your committee next Friday. I think that I could manage to—'

Once again Amy acted impulsively, and ran across the room to Oliver. 'I am sorry—of course you cannot remember—I did not mean to be so foolish—but you said that your Mamma—do you recall *her* speaking of Lilith Lucas when you were a child? Is that what you were going to say?'

'Oh, can we have an end of this!' Abby's voice came ringing across the room and Amy turned as though she had been struck. 'You go too far, Miss Lucas, indeed you do! None of us are in the least interested in this tiresome matter, none of us, do you understand? Do, for the sake of peace, hold your tongue! I am appalled that a young lady with any—with any pretensions to good manners should prattle on so and bore her company with—'

Everyone seemed to speak at once; Gideon stepped forwards and set his hand on his wife's arm with a low, 'My dear!' and Phoebe began to chatter loudly to her brother in an attempt to cover up her aunt's surprising outburst, while Freddy said urgently, 'Mamma—my dear—'

But it made no difference. Abby was now in a towering rage, and her face was suffused with it. She looked magnificent standing there with her head up and her tall handsome husband behind her, and Amy thought suddenly, 'I shall never forget this moment. It is an important one—a dreadfully important one—'

'I am sick and tired of it all!' Abby stormed. 'Do you hear me? Sick and tired! Lilith Lucas, Lilith Lucas, Lilith Lucas—that hateful woman has done more than enough damage to this family, more than enough! Leave it be, I tell you!'

'Abby, be quiet at once!' It was Martha who spoke then with her voice very low and it affected Abby as no other remonstrance had. She turned and looked at her sister, and after a moment shook her head and turned to stare up at Gideon who put his arm about her protectively, and lifted his chin imperiously to Sarah and Daniel who, silent and amazed and in some awe at this display of emotions by their elders, came to his side.

'We must go, Martha. Thank you for a most pleasant afternoon,' he said formally, and Amy could have laughed, staring at him, if she had not been so thunderstruck. Why had Abby spoken so? What was it about Lilith Lucas, whoever she had been, to cause this uproar in the usually placid and gentle Abby? It was all quite bewildering, and she turned to look for Felix for support and comfort, but he was now standing beside Martha as she made her polite farewells to her family, kissing the children and smiling with a forced bonhomie that was almost painful to watch.

'We, too, I think, Aunt Martha,' Phoebe murmured, and with much rustling and fussing with the three children the Caspar family left, Freddy casting one last worried look over his shoulder as he went after his mother, now downstairs in the hall.

And then only Oliver and Martha and Felix were left for Amy to stare at and there was a silence that seemed to Amy to ring in her ears with its intensity.

'I do not understand,' she said at last as the silence lengthened and became threatening, and she suddenly felt close to tears. 'I do not *understand*. Why was—why was Mrs. Henriques so distressed? I do not understand.'

'Then I had better explain, I suppose,' Martha said heavily, and sat down.

# CHAPTER FIFTEEN

At first, Martha's explanation was slow and faltering, even stilted, but as she warmed to her theme her words came more easily and, listening, Amy felt the weight of years of this family's history pressing down on her.

She heard the story of a small boy, a gutter boy who had dragged himself out of the horrors of the slums of Seven Dials almost seventy years ago and set out on the road that was to make him one of London's greatest surgeons. Martha's description of that ragged child tallied not at all with the memory Amy had of the old man she had seen in the casualty room at Queen Eleanor's Hospital on the day of Fenton's accident. He had been harsh, imperious, anything but pathetic. It seemed impossible that he could have started life as the sad child of whom Martha was talking. But that, it seemed, was how it had been, and Amy listened enthralled as Martha told her how the child had met a girl as ragged and poor as himself and loved her. How the girl had gone away. That there was some mystery there, about where she had gone and why she had gone, was obvious, but Martha was able to explain none of that. Instead she went on to tell how eventually the little girl, now full grown and very lovely, had come back into the ragged boy's life, a boy himself now full grown and filled with ambition. How the girl had become an actress, and succeeded in making herself a great draw, a superbly popular performer. And how the boy had loved her still.

At this point Martha stopped, sitting looking down at her hands on her lap, and Amy leaned forwards and said breathlessly, 'Yes? And then what happened?'

'Hmm?' Martha looked up, and her eyes seemed glazed, as though she were far away; and then they cleared and she shrugged and said, 'It is hard to know where to go on from here. Let me just say that this girl—and she was this Lilith Lucas of whom you have been told—refused my father. He was sadly hurt by this—and even many years later, long after he had married my Mamma, he refused to allow any of us to enter a theatre or to speak of matters theatrical. He had been so deeply hurt, you see. And so it has always been—the enmity has continued.'

Amy leaned back, her brow furrowed, staring at Martha in disbelief. 'But I do not understand! You are saying that Mrs. Henriques became so—so angry and distressed simply because I spoke about a lady who had refused her Papa's proposal so many years ago? Oh, come, Miss Lackland, that cannot be so! There must be more to it than that!'

Martha shrugged again, trying to look unconcerned, but her gaze slid away from Amy's direct stare. 'Oh, as to that, there were of course other—episodes. But they really do not need to concern us now, for they all happened so many years ago. It is all water under the bridge, surely! Can you not accept that for us this woman has been—that because of our father, we find it disagreeable to talk of her? After all, Miss Lucas, there is no reason why we should explain *more* than this to you! We offered you hospitality to a degree that I venture to suggest is beyond the ordinary! My nephew Freddy is a compassionate man, and he asked us to have a care of you and your brother. We have done so, I am sure you would agree, to the best of our ability—'

She looked over Amy's shoulder at Oliver, standing silent in his window embrasure. 'My nephew Oliver here has provided you with employment, Freddy I know sought out lodgings for you—is it so much to ask that you respect our wish—my sister's wish—that we should not be reminded of matters which cause us pain?'

Stubbornly Amy shook her head. 'But it cannot cause you pain—it cannot! It was not *you* or Mrs. Henriques who were refused! It was your father! How can you now think it reasonable of me to show no interest in my own grandmother when—'

'Amy, my dear, you have no proof that this lady was your grandmother,' Felix's voice came from behind her, all cool reasonableness, and Amy whirled on him, her face suddenly white and pinched.

'She is—she *is*! I know she is. I feel it—*here*,' and she clasped both her hands to her breasts with a gesture that was supremely theatrical and yet was quite unstudied and full of real feeling. Her eyes were bright now with unshed tears and she stared up at him and said in a tight little voice, 'You must understand—you must, Felix! You think me shallow and—and posturing—yes, you do, I know that is so, and with you I have learned to be more—more myself, to feel safe even when I am not acting. Well, I am not acting now! It is very important to me to find my family—my Papa's family. My mother's family are cold and dry and have no *muscle* in them. But me—I am full of, oh so much! I want so much, I need so much, and I have to know that this feeling that is in me is in other people as well. I have to know what made me as I am. That is why it is so important that I find my Papa's family! He was like me. He had this—this whatever it is—inside him, and I *have* to find others who belong to me who are the same. And I know, truly *know*, that this Lilith Lucas was one of them. Mine! You shall not say she is not, and you shall not stop me speaking of her or looking for her or—'

Felix was standing beside her now and he put one hand on her shoulder, looking down at her with his face very still and his gaze steady, and as the torrent of words faltered and at last stopped he said quietly, 'I think I do understand, you know. I too have feelings in me that derive from my forebears. I too know what it is like to miss a father. But all the same, Amy, you must not, you really must not, be so passionate about it all. You will distort the truth you are seeking. That is something *you* must understand.'

There was a brief silence and she turned back again to Martha who was staring at Felix with a sort of despair on her face. 'Tell me more,' she said tightly. 'Miss Lackland? You must tell me more. Please?'

Martha looked down at her hands again and shook her head. 'There is no more I can tell you,' she said dully. 'My father felt great enmity to this lady, and we do also.'

'All of you? Everyone of you? It is absurd—' Amy said and turned then to look at Oliver. 'You too? This—all this that your aunt speaks of. Is it so with you?'

Oliver was sitting now, looking out of the window and he did not turn his head to speak to her. 'Yes,' he said after a moment. 'It is so with me, also.'

He stood up then and came across the room, moving heavily. 'I think, Aunt Martha, that you should explain a little further.'

He came to stand between Martha and Amy and with his familiar mechanical gesture took off his spectacles to polish them, blinking down at his busy hands as he did so.

'Lilith Lucas was in fact a relation of mine, Miss Amy,' he said after a moment and she stared up at him with her mouth half open in surprise.

'A relation?' she said, and shook her head. 'I do not understand! You said—Miss Lackland, did you not say that she was a person your father had—how can your nephew be a *relation* in that case?'

Oliver spoke in a very precise voice, as coolly as though he were directing a rehearsal. 'It is not so difficult to understand. My father—Aunt Martha's older brother Jonah—was married to Lilith Lucas's daughter Celia.'

He turned and looked at Amy then, hooking his spectacles back over his ears. 'If you are right, Miss Lucas, and you derive your name and talent from this lady, we are first cousins. It is droll, is it not, how matters fall out?'

'Droll?' Amy said and shook her head again. 'Droll? I cannot—it is—I do not *understand*.'

Martha got up now and began to move about the room restlessly. 'It is not so difficult, for heaven's sake!' she said sharply. 'As Oliver says, there was a marriage which, much to my father's distress, linked our family with this Lucas woman. It caused much grief all round—and no, I will *not* tell you of it! It is none of your affair, Miss, and there's an end of it! I find this whole matter becoming very tedious. Let us talk of other things! I try to have agreeable Sunday afternoon family occasions, and here we are, all in a great turmoil and a pother over matters long since forgotten, and better so! Let us have an end of it, and speak of other things.

Oliver, my dear, give me news of the Supper Rooms. How are matters there? Are attendances good? Is the show pleasing you, or will there be any new numbers put in? I must come to see for myself—'

'Oh—oh, you are—you are too unkind to be borne!' Amy was on her feet, and her eyes were blazing with frustration and disappointment. 'I thought you were my friends. I really thought you were all my friends, and now when I find news of a person who means much to me all you can do is—is insult her and—'

Martha raised her brows at that. 'I am insulting nobody!' she said quietly. 'I have simply said I do not wish to talk more on a tedious matter. Now, Oliver—'

'Oh, Oliver, Oliver!' Amy mocked her cool voice with cruel accuracy. 'I know what it is! You are jealous! Thoroughly jealous! Lilith Lucas was a great actress, the greatest draw upon the London stage for years and years and *years*! And there you are with your silly Supper Rooms and your tinkling little shows—you are *jealous* and that is all about it!'

And she turned and ran to the door and snatched up her bonnet and tried to wrench the door open, but Felix was there beside her at once, his hand over hers, gently but firmly making her stand still.

'There is no need for all this high temper, Amy. You are upset, I know, and I can enter into your feelings. But you really must not fly off like this! It would be sad indeed if we were to part so, my family and you, for there could be much difficulty in healing the breach. And it is important to me that there be no breach. Amy?'

His voice was quiet but very firm, and she looked up at him and he looked back very directly and then, slowly, smiled. 'Come, my dear. All this is a little exaggerated, don't you agree? A storm in a teacup? You have heard about someone who may or may not be a connection of yours from long ago. This is not something that should cause a break between you and your friends of the present, is it?'

It was at this moment, in the middle of all the confused feelings that filled her, that Amy knew she was in love. She looked at the square face so near her own, felt the warmth of his

158

hand over hers and knew with complete certainty that this man was all her future. That without him there could be no real happiness, ever. And that he was tied to the two people who stood, shadowy but none the less real, behind them. If she behaved wrongly at this moment she could do irreparable damage to her own new-found love and to the feeling that she knew with equal certainty lay deep in him.

She closed her eyes and took a long breath and then, very slowly took her hand from the door knob.

'I am sorry, Miss Lackland, Mr. Lackland,' she said in a small flat voice. 'I allowed my feelings to have the better of me. I will not behave so again.'

'Of course, my dear,' Martha said at once with great cordiality in her voice. 'Of course. One is sometimes distressed and does not know what one is saying.' But behind her cordiality Amy felt a chill and looked at her, and saw the way her glance moved away from her own face to rest on Felix, and there was a deep sadness in her that Amy felt, and which, curiously, seemed to fill her with fear.

Again she shook her head. All seemed to be confusion and doubt, and she needed time to think, to decide what she would do. That she had found news of her grandmother she was certain; that she loved the man now standing close beside her was equally certain. But where she went from this point was shadowy, unimaginable.

'I think perhaps I had better return to Long Acre,' she said after a moment. 'No, thank you Felix, I think—I will be better for the walk, alone. Yes, I know—it is a long way. But I need time to think—'

Again she turned and this time opened the door, and Felix stood back, allowing her to go.

She hesitated in the doorway, and turned to look back at Martha.

'May I ask one more question before I go?'

There was a pause and then Oliver said unexpectedly, 'Of course. If I can help you in any way I am glad to.'

'Thank you.' She stopped then and looked at them consideringly and then said a little awkwardly, 'Is there anything else—any news you could give me that would be of help to me in finding my family? You see, if it is true, and I—this lady we spoke of is my grandmother, then I suppose I must be a connection of yours, must I not? I need time to think about that. But there must be others, too—other cousins? Perhaps aunts or uncles? I do not wish to distress you, Miss Lackland, but I do so need to know!'

There was a silence and then Martha said flatly, 'I can tell you of nothing more that will be of value to you, Miss Lucas. Nothing at all.'

Amy nodded. 'Thank you,' she said. 'Then I must rely upon the man at the stage door of the Haymarket for any further information. He said he would try. I will go now. And I thank you for—I mean, good-bye.'

'I shall see you to the door, if you will not allow me to accompany you further,' Felix said, and she opened her mouth to argue, but he ignored that and held the door wide for her and she bobbed her head at Martha and Oliver and went away down the stairs.

The silence they left behind thickened and lengthened and then Oliver said, 'Perhaps you should have told her of what happened in Constantinople.'

Martha shook her head, wearily. 'What would be the point? It would confuse it all still further. Oh, this is a wretched business! If we could ever have guessed that she and her brother were *those* Lucases, I tell you frankly, I would have consigned them both to perdition before raising a finger to aid them. But I did not think of it. I never think of the past if I can help it—Abby is right—that Lucas woman and her connections have brought us nothing but distress—oh, I am sorry, Oliver. I forget always that you and Phoebe—you see what happens? Whenever Lilith Lucas is ever mentioned, we have troubles! I can only pray we have no more!'

'I think we will,' Oliver said. 'I think we will.'

# CHAPTER SIXTEEN

'You cannot know, Mr. Wyndham, how grateful I am,' Amy said fervently and drank the rest of her chocolate, and put the cup down with a clatter. 'I swear it was guidance from above that I should seek you out in this affair—and that you have helped us so much. Really, you have been an *angel*, Mr. Wyndham!'

'I wish you would call me Charles—and as for being angelic—my dear, a very fallen angel am I! There is little in me of such icy virtue as you are likely to find on the other side of those Pearly Gates! Believe me, it was my pleasure to help you. I'm just delighted the management were so receptive, shall we say, to my suggestions!'

They were sitting in a coffee-house in Dean Street, just across the road from the Royalty Theatre; a raffish little place full of noisily chattering foreigners, some rather dingy men in shiny old coats who sat in a far corner with their heads together, whispering mysteriously, and some dubious-looking ladies whose complexions plainly owed more to artifice than nature. Not that Amy was at all put out by her surroundings; much as she enjoyed the finer things in life and revelled in rich clothes and elegant houses, she could be phlegmatic about tolerating lesser splendour when the need was there. And today it was there.

She had spent a wretched night in her little room in Long Acre, tossing from side to side and staring out of the small panes of the window at the scudding night sky above. The small hours had brought some fitful sleep and she had woken heavy and unrefreshed, but, at last, with her resolve firmly fixed.

She would have to find some other employment. It was inconceivable that she could, after all that had been said in Martha's drawing-room, continue to appear at Oliver Lackland's Supper Rooms. Somehow she had to find other work, and she lay staring at the early light creeping up the ceiling and listening to the dawn chorus of the sparrows outside her window, trying to work out a plan.

And then, suddenly remembering Charles Wyndham, had positively leapt from her bed and washed and dressed with great speed. She knew where his lodgings were, and if she could but get to him before he left for the hospital, surely he would be able to advise her where to find a part!

She left the house just after seven o'clock, holding her skirts high above the gutters left muddy and slippery by the previous day's showers. All round her was bustle and busyness as the manufactories opened their great doors and the workmen came trudging in to start their labours over the carcases of half-built carriages. She could smell the vinegary tang of new wood and the thick turpentine and paint reek of the yards as she hurried by them, and her spirits lifted as some of the workmen called cheerfully after her, and whistled and teased.

Yesterday had been a difficult day full of confusion and swooping feelings—and about her new-found feelings for Felix she steadfastly refused to think at all—and she needed action to help her climb above it all. She could and she would find a way to make her life fall out as she wished it; she *would* find her lost relations, and she *would* find her much wanted career—'and I shall find a way to love Felix too—' a secret little voice deep inside her whispered. But she would not listen to it, and hurried on through the morning streets, certain that all would be well and that Charles Wyndham would be able to help her.

She had been right. Once he was over the surprise of being called from his bed at so early an hour by such a caller and had heard her out he bubbled over with helpfulness and pleasure in being able to do so.

'This is uncommon fortuitous, Miss Lucas!' he had cried.

'Uncommonly so, for on Saturday—only the day before yesterday, I do assure you, I was offered a part in a new play to open at the Royalty in Dean Street! Not precisely a great drama, I cannot deny. In fact, it is a burlesque—by Burnand, you know. It is called "Black-Ey'd Susan," and is a merry romp indeed! I am to play Hackett, the leading man, and must dance. Indeed yes, dance! I, a legitimate actor! But I care not—I am so heartily sick of the reek of that hospital and I wish never to set eyes on another pill or potion or clyster. I have had my fill of the sick—from now on, it is the theatre and only the theatre for me! I feel it in my bones! And I feel it almost as strong that I can obtain an audition for you! The management was very obliging to me—very. I daresay if I present you as worthy of a part they will listen to me! Now, you wait here, and I shall dress with all speed, and arrange a little breakfast for us, and as soon as the theatre shows any sign of stirring, we shall be there!'

And so it had turned out. It was almost as though it had all been ordained by some higher power. Mr. Rourke, the manager, middling of age but very curly of hair, very long of cigar and excessively decorated of waistcoat, had greeted Wyndham as though he were his oldest friend—despite the fact that they had set eyes on each other for the very first time the previous Saturday—and agreed cheerfully to consider Miss Lucas for a part. Fortunately for Amy's peace of mind she did not see the leer with which Mr. Rourke treated Wyndham behind her back, for she had not thought of the possibility that anyone would assume his helpfulness was based on a less than respectable liaison between them; but then she had so much on her mind at the time that it was remarkable she was able to think logically at all.

The part, a small but showy one offering many opportunities to a clever actress—which Amy recognized and seized immediately—fell into her hands like a ripe plum. When she had completed her sketchy reading from a tattered script, Rourke beamed up at her from the front row of the stalls as she stood between the rather patched and shabby gold-coloured tableau curtains, chewing his cigar ferociously and nodding happily.

'A nice little performer, my dear, you're a very nice little performer! A bit of help with the pointing of the lines, a bit of attention to costume and I tell you, we're on to a winner. Glad to do you a favour any time, Wyndham, any time, but when it turns out I'm doin' m'self a favour into the bargain, then I'm your man, every time, I'm your man!'

Emboldened by her own success and flushing prettily Amy opened her eyes wide at the beaming Rourke and with her most beguiling smile asked if there were, by the remotest chance, a part for a most handsome and capable actor who could sing very well into the bargain. Anxiety about Fenton and how he would take her defection from the Supper Rooms had been haunting the back of her mind throughout and her delight when Rourke told her expansively that they were in the very early days of casting, and he'd gladly see anyone at all, and if her brother was half what she was, why, no question but he'd get a part, was huge.

And now she sat opposite Wyndham in a coffee-house drinking chocolate and bursting with all that had happened in the past couple of days. It seemed impossible that only last week she had been living so quiet a life with nightly performances at the Supper Rooms as her only occupation and weekly visits to the theatre with Felix as her only entertainment. Now, she was on the track of her lost relations, had a part in a real play in a real theatre, and the future seemed to shine with a different light.

Resolutely she pushed away the vision of Felix's face which was persistently trying to drift up into her consciousness, and leaned forwards with her elbows on the table.

'Mr. Wyndham, do you recall you told me the best way to find my Papa's relations was to talk to the stage doorkeepers at the theatres?'

Wyndham looked down at her eager little face with its wide eyes and thick lashes and smiled indulgently. It was a damned shame that Laurence had made it so abundantly clear to him that this lady was to be regarded as very much *his* friend, he thought. She is so very delicious a morsel that any man could be forgiven for finding her appetizing. But he remembered the steely glint in Felix's eyes when he had spoken to him of the high value he set on his friendship with Miss Lucas, of the faintly expressed but unmistakable warning that had been in his apparently casual words, and said in as avuncular a tone as he could, 'Indeed I do! Have you met with any success?'

'You cannot imagine!' Amy said, and plunged into an account of her conversation with the Haymarket stage doorkeeper with great relish, and Wyndham listened, enthralled. He was a man of the theatre through and through, and this story Amy was pouring out bore all the hallmarks of a great melodrama, and as he listened to her he clothed her words in his mind with images of long-dead people until he was as entranced with it all as though it had been his own family for whom he was searching.

'And now what will you do?' he asked eagerly when she had come to the end of the story—having with some prudence only touched upon the disagreement that there had been the day before in Bedford Row; there was no need to tell Wyndham *everything*, she told herself—and she shook her head.

'To tell you the truth, I am not sure there is much more I can do at present. The man said he would talk to me more, but—'

'Then let us waste no time!' Wyndham got to his feet and dropped a coin on the table with which to pay for their chocolate. 'Let us go and see him at once! I must know the end of this story—and you are in need of a companion to help you, I am sure. Not that I seek to—ah—replace Dr. Laurence as your guide, Miss Lucas. But he of course is at the hospital, and I am not—'

Amy stood up too, pulling her mantle about her with some speed. 'Oh, yes, do let us! I thought I would have to wait for Felix, but as you say, he *is* busy—and anyway, now I am not certain that he will wish—oh, yes, please, Mr. Wyndham, will you come with me? I am not shy, you know, nor am I incapable of prosecuting my own affairs, but it does help to have the company of a gentleman when one is dealing with such people—'

They sat in his little cubbyhole of a room, just behind the passageway which led from Orange Street through to the remoter fastnesses of the Haymarket Theatre stage, and let him talk. Amy was aching to hurry him, to make him concentrate on Lilith Lucas and such memories as he might have of her, but Wyndham had put his hand warningly upon her arm and shaken his head slightly, and she had subsided. And the old man chattered away, talking of people long since dead and plays long since forgotten, painting a picture of the almost fifty years he had spent backstage in this great building in a way that slowly gripped Amy's imagination, until she listened as eagerly as though he had indeed been talking of her own people.

He spoke of the days when the lights had been created by burning naked lime, so that the threat of fire had stalked the dusty corridors and crowded green-rooms as an ever-present fear; he told of the great pageants and pantomimes, the ballets that had seemed to make the whole building flutter with light-footed dancers and the wail of violins, when greedy audiences had demanded, and got, five or six hours of continuous spectacle in exchange for the few pennies they paid for their seats in the pit; of the great actors whose very names were enough to fill the house to capacity; of the delectable actresses whose entourages of adoring men had constantly hung about the stage door and the green-room.

At which point Amy sat up a little straighter and said breathlessly, 'Tell me of one of them—tell me of Lilith Lucas—'

The old man blinked at her in the dim light of the cubbyhole, his pale blue eyes with the milky rims around the pupils seeming to look far, far beyond her, down the receding corridors of the years.

'Lilith Lucas?' he said, and laughed, a surprisingly shrill little laugh that made Amy rear back in distaste. 'I told you about 'er yesterday, di'n't I? Can't remember much more 'bout 'er, not wiv me whistle that dry as I can't 'ardly let me tongue lay down to rest itself—'

'We shall send for some porter,' Wyndham said firmly, and put his hand in his pocket. 'You have a boy, I imagine?'

The old man laughed his shrill little cackle again, and whistled between his broken front teeth and after a moment a boy of some twelve years put his dirty face round the door and seized the money Wyndham gave him and bobbed his head at the old man's instructions and disappeared. And when he came back ten minutes later with a white jug brimming with froth the old man swallowed most of its contents in one long pull, and cocked his head at Amy and grinned and said in his thin old voice, 'Lilith Lucas, is it then? An' what does yer want to know abóut 'er?'

'All you can remember,' Amy said at once. 'Everything. Her plays, her successes—and her own life. Did she have any children? What happened to her? Where is she now?'

The old man drank again and grimaced above the hand he used to wipe his mouth.

'Lilith Lucas,' he said again, and now there was a reminiscent tone in his voice. 'I'll tell yer about Lilith Lucas. She was beyond any shadder o' any doubt the 'ardest, nastiest, cruellest ol' bat as ever set foot on any stage—'

Amy snapped her head back as though he had struck her, but before she could say a word the old man went on, 'But when she set foot on a stage, I tell yer, it was magic. That's what it was. Bleedin' magic. She must a' bin—oh, nigh on fifty when she did 'er last play 'ere—nigh on fifty. An' d'you know, she could walk aht there in one of her blue gowns—never wore nuffin' but blue, that one, not if she could 'elp it—walk out there she could, 'er curls all loose on 'er neck, and they looked at 'er, and what do yer think they saw, them 'alfwits aht there as'd paid their money to see 'er? Why, they saw a girl o' seventeen, I swears to you. She was nigh on fifty, and they saw a girl o' seventeen. If she'd wanted 'em to see a woman o' ninety, I tell yer, they'd a' seen that an' all. She was magic, she was, the old besom—'

And he drank again and then looked down into the depths of his jug and shook it suggestively and Wyndham thrust his hand into his pocket again and the old man whistled once more for the boy.

'How do you mean, a besom?' Wyndham said carefully after a while, and looked reassuringly at Amy, who was a little white.

''Ard, you see. Real 'ard she was,' the old man said, and shook his head in admiration. ''Ad to be, di'n't she? There wasn't no one as was was goin' to 'elp 'er when she was too old to confuse the payin' customers, was there? No one wants any of 'em, not the biggest of 'em, once they can't do the magic no more. So she was careful, and she made sure as she got 'old of every penny she could. Screwed the managers right down as 'ard as a coffin lid she did—oh, she was rich, real rich!'

The white jug returned and there was a further delay while the old man refreshed himself, and by this time Amy felt less shaken by his words, and better able to talk to him.

'Was she ever unkind to you?' she asked and the old man produced his cracked trill of laughter again.

'To me? Nah. I wasn't nobody, was I? Wasted nuthin' on me, she di'n't, not praise nor blame. But others—they 'ad bad times wiv 'er. 'Er daughter, like—she copped it over an' over—when she was a little 'un—'

'Daughter?' Amy sat up very straight.

'Aye. 'Er as was Lydia Mohun. Don't you remember 'er? Big draw she was, an' all, in 'er time, when it come.' He shook his head. 'Dearie me, but time does go. I s'pose it's been long enough since she was 'ere. Nigh on—let's see now—' He squinted up at the ceiling and its cobwebs. 'Must be—yes, ten years now. Oh, dearie me, 'ow the time do go! She an' 'er 'usband—a right one 'e was an' all—an' 'er children, they went off to foreign parts. Americky, so I'm told.' He shook his head. 'All this travellin'—don't 'old with it. Flyin' in the face o' Nature.'

'Was she her only child—Lilith's, I mean?' Amy said, her spirits at the lowest ebb she could ever remember. To have come so far to find her Papa and his family, and to discover that one of them—or one who might be one of them—had been in her own country for so long seemed the most cruel of ironies.

'Now, let me recall—' he squinted his eyes and stared at Amy and then shook his head. 'No, the Mohun wasn't the only one, bad a time though she 'ad of it wiv 'er Ma when she was a little 'un, as well I recall. No, there was others. There was—let me see. There was the girl what was so quiet and turned out to be so—well, never mind that one! An' then there was the very youngest one. 'E was a nasty piece, now, 'e was. Never took to 'im I didn't—what was 'is name? Oh, yes, I remembers—Jody, 'e was, Jody.'

And again he drank and laughed and drank again. He was

rapidly becoming fuddled, and Amy could recognize the fact and said urgently, 'And was that all? Three children? No others?'

The old man looked up at her blearily and tried to concentrate. 'I disremember—no, I don't. There was another. Just one more there was. All named after plays, you see, every one of 'em. There was Celia and Lydia an' Jody—that was from the play with Jonathan in it, but she always called 'im Jody—and there was another. Shakespeare, like the other one—Shakespeare—'

'Antonio! Sebastian!' Wyndham said suddenly and the old man shook his head in disgust and sighed deeply and drank again.

'It is no use,' Amy said almost despairingly. 'My Papa's name was never in any play by Shakespeare I knew of. He was called Ben—I suppose he was Benjamin, I never knew for sure, to be honest. He was just called Ben—'

'That's right,' the old man said, and yawned hugely, displaying unlovely yellowing remnants of teeth and a coated tongue. 'Benedict. That's 'oo it was. Benedict—'

Amy sat up, her face whitening with excitement. 'What did you say?'

' 'E was called Benjy—Benedict was all 'is name, but 'e was a right little limb, and 'e 'ated it. Wouldn't never answer to it, 'e wouldn't. Only if they called 'im Benjy or Ben. Nice little nipper 'e was—'

He yawned again and leaned back in his chair and closed his eyes, and Amy looked at him doubtfully and shook her head.

'I think we will not learn more now, do you?' she said crestfallen. 'There is so much more to know—so much more—'

The old man opened his eyes suddenly and sat upright. He stared up at Amy and said very loudly. 'She went away with 'im—Jody. Long time ago. Long after the accident 'appened. Went away to foreign parts and never came back. Left 'er 'ouse behind, all untouched, so I've 'eard. Grosvenor Square it was—main rich, was Lilith Lucas, and lived in Grosvenor Square. You try there—' and again he settled back in his chair and closed his eyes, leaving them both staring down at him.

There was a long silence and then, unmistakably, the old man snored and Wyndham put out his hand and gently tugged on Amy's sleeve, and bemused, she allowed him to lead her out of the stuffy little room into the passageway outside and eventually into the traffic-roaring street beyond.

She stood on the kerb, blinking up into the April sunshine, trying to absorb all she had heard, and after a moment Wyndham said, 'Well, you know, I think the next step is to take ourselves to your lodging, Miss Lucas, to tell Fenton of the plans made for his audition, and then, I suppose, to Grosvenor Square!'

She looked up at him and smiled tremulously. 'You have been very kind, Mr. Wyndham, and I have much appreciated it. But——' She hesitated, and he looked down at her with a slightly crooked smile.

'You wish to go alone?'

'Thank you for understanding,' she said. 'It is just that I am beginning to realize that all——that perhaps it is not a matter to be——oh, dear, it is so difficult——'

He nodded. 'You are beginning to realize that when family skeletons start to dance in their closets it is as well, perhaps, not to give them too large an audience.'

She put her hand out and touched him gratefully. 'Indeed, you do understand. But then, you are an actor. And actors can always enter into people's feelings so well. Thank you so much. You will never know how deep my gratitude runs, Mr. Wyndham.'

He bent and kissed her hand with all his usual flourish and smiled, his mouth curling agreeably. 'It is my pleasure, I promise you. Now, I shall go to Long Acre and speak to Fenton. You set about your visit to Grosvenor Square, and remember——we have a costume call for tomorrow! I shall be looking forward to seeing you, and I hope, Fenton, with great eagerness. There is a hansom now——I shall see you into it and then be on my way.'

He stood in Orange Street, watching the hansom clopping away towards Piccadilly, his hat in his hand and his dark curls lifting on his brow in the light breeze. An agreeable child, he thought. But more in need of help than perhaps she realizes. I think, after I have spoken to her brother, I will have a word with Laurence too. He will be the one to tell about this jaunt. And it would absolve me of any intentions towards the girl to which Laurence could take exception—

## CHAPTER SEVENTEEN

'Well, I don' know,' the old woman said again, and spat with remarkable accuracy over the railings into the street. 'Why should I? Tha's what I asks meself. Why should I?'

'To oblige me,' Amy said. 'Please?' and looked at the old woman with every atom of appeal she could. But the woman was impervious to her charm and merely hawked and spat again and repeated defiantly, 'Why should I? What's in it for me?' At which point Amy at last understood, and scrabbled in her reticule to find some money.

The old woman peered down shortsightedly at the coin Amy put into her grimy hand, bit it and then, apparently satisfied, turned and went on down the steps into the area towards the kitchen door.

Amy hesitated just for one moment at the top of the steps, looking round the Square. It sat quiet and elegant in the thin April sunshine, the trees in its central garden just beginning to blush greenly. Each of the tall handsome houses had its sweep of steps up to its porticoed front door, each had its wrought iron railings enclosing the sunken area that led to the servants' quarters, and each bore unmistakable signs of the wealth of its occupants. Except the one before which she was standing.

It was the only house in the Square which looked unoccupied, despite its curtained windows, for its window-frames were in need of paint, and its brass doorknob was green for want of polishing. Indeed, it had been this which had drawn her to it in the first place. She had tugged on the big rusty iron bell pull several times and had been about to give up in despair when the old woman in the dirt-streaked black stuff dress had appeared in the area below and peered up at her suspiciously.

And now Amy was about to enter the house, and she shivered slightly, a mixture of agreeable and disagreeable sensations filling her. It was very exciting to think that perhaps she was about to walk into the home of her own grandmother, someone she had never known but whose existence had been so important to her, but somewhat alarming to follow the smelly old woman in the rusty black gown down into her malodorous depths.

But then, as the old woman looked back at her over her shoulder Amy gave herself a mental shake, and lifted her chin and set her foot to the first of the area steps to follow her down. This was adventure, she told herself. Great adventure. She was the Brave Little Lady, facing up to fear and trembling with spirit and a high heart. She was the lovely heroine of a melodrama about to face up to untold terrors in a way that would ensure that all hearts would melt with love of her. She was the principal in this unique drama and she would justify her casting. So, acting with every atom of her being, she went down into the area and ducked her head to go into the big dark kitchen that lay beyond it.

She managed to keep her heart up with her acting for some time. The old woman led her over a stone-flagged floor past a vast wooden dresser and kitchen table and huge black iron cooking range, none of which, quite obviously, had seen water or scrubbing brush for many years, to the icy cold echoing corridors beyond. They had once had whitewashed walls and been floored with drugget, but now the whitewash was obscured with grime and cobwebs and the colour of the drugget could not be seen under the heavy layer of dust that shrouded it.

But once they left the kitchen quarters behind, ascending the back stairs to reach the green baize-covered door that led to the main part of the house, her performance deserted her. No longer was she the plucky little heroine; now she was her own frightened and saddened self, walking over black and white marble squares in a hall in which no one had set foot for years, going from drawing-room to boudoir to dining-room to library, each filled with furniture covered in great grey dust sheets.

That the house had once been sumptuously appointed, with rich brocaded curtains and lavishly upholstered furnishings, gilt embossing in all directions and the most exquisite of carvings and paintings and sculpture, was immediately apparent. And that it had been left suddenly was even more clear. In one of the big bedrooms there was still a bath and a row of now tarnished brass hot water cans beside it. Amy had no pretensions to any housewifely skills but even she knew that such impedimenta should have long ago been put away and the fact that they had not distressed her more than anything else she saw.

She stood in the middle of the big bedroom with its sheet-covered bed and chaise longue and stared at that long-forgotten bath and wondered who had used it last, and why it had been left so quickly. And the damp emptiness of the house seemed to seep into her bones, filling her with a deep melancholy.

'Well, seen enough?' The old woman's voice came harshly, making her jump.

'I—what did you say?'

' 'Ave you seen enough? Can't 'ang around up 'ere all day. Got other things ter do, I 'ave,' the old woman said and turned and walked stiffly away to the ornate door of the big bedroom.

'Who—whose house is this?' Amy said breathlessly, and stood still, refusing to be hurried away by the old woman's obvious impatience to be rid of her.

'I dunno!' the old woman said and sniffed horribly. 'Nuffin' ter do wiv me, is it? Nuffin' ter do wiv you, neither, come to that. Shouldn' 'a' let yer in in the first place, reelly—'

'You must know who employs you to be here,' Amy said. 'Are you the janitor?'

'The what?' The old woman peered at her with a huge sus-

173

picion. 'I ain't never 'eard o' no janitors. I'm the caretaker 'ere, tha's what I am, and don' you go callin' of me no janitors, or I'll have the peelers on to yer—'

'That's what I meant,' Amy said. 'The caretaker. If you are the caretaker here, how can you not know to whom the house belongs? You must know who employs you and pays your wages.'

'It ain't none o' your nevermind, missy! I lets you come an' look on account of you says yer interested, an' I thought, well, I thought, bin sent by Vivian an' Onions, that's why she's 'ere, an' now you go saying as you don't know whose 'ouse this is—'ere, you get aht of 'ere, d'you 'ear me? Aht you go, missy, and fast about it. Shouldn't never 'ave let yer in 'ere in the fust place—'

Grumbling furiously the old woman hustled her out, and perforce Amy went, coughing in the dust her footsteps sent up from the carpet.

'Vivian and Onions?' she said. 'Where are they? Who are they? You had better tell me, for I shall find out for myself, if you do not, and tell them that you let me in here when you should not, and—'

'Yer a wicked piece, tha's what you are!' The old woman went scuttling ahead of her as fast as she could, looking back malevolently over her shoulder. 'Wicked, gettin' an 'armless old woman into trouble. What'd I ever do to you, eh? No need to get like that, is there—' Her voice took on a wheedling note. 'You wouldn't make no trouble fer an old woman what never done no one any 'arm, would yer? Let yer in, di'n't I? Well then, why you want to go tellin' 'em as I ain't done my work right? I done all one old woman can do. Made sure no one comes an' steals nuthin'—'

'I'm sure you've done very well,' Amy said and drew back from the unpleasantness of the old woman's breath as she suddenly turned and peered closely into her face. 'All I wish to know is who owns the house. It really is only that. I will make no complaints about you, I do promise.'

The old woman looked at her with her rheumy old eyes swimming with doubt and anxiety and Amy felt a sudden stab of pity for her and put out one hand and said awkwardly, 'Truly, I will do you no harm. I just think—it is possible that this house belonged once to my grandmother. It is just that I wish to know if it is true. Will you tell me?'

There was a long pause and then the old woman said, 'Don't know 'oo owns it. All I can tell yer is the lawyers, them nasty ol' lawyers, they put me 'ere. Ten years ago it must a' bin, or more—I misremember 'ow the time goes on, an' there's no reason why I should care anyways. But ten years or more ago it was, they lawyers sent me 'ere. An' 'ere I bin on me tod ever since.'

'The lawyers are Vivian and Onions?' Amy said. 'Is that it?'

'You won't tell 'em nuthin?' the old woman said piteously and Amy shook her head with some vehemence.

'Of course I won't,' she said. 'Of course not. Just tell me where they may be found, and I shall go to them and say nothing about you.'

'Oh, damn yer eyes,' the old woman said and hobbled away to the kitchen door to throw it open. 'Lincoln's Inn, tha's where they 'angs aht. Lincoln's Inn. Now get aht of it, an' leave me in peace. An' don't never come back no more—'

The street outside seemed colder and crisper and cleaner than the open air had ever been, and Amy stood on the kerb breathing deeply, trying to blow the dust and the cobwebs out of her lungs, but, even more, the melancholy out of her spirits. Somewhere not too far away she heard the striking of a clock and automatically counted the chimes. Three strokes. Could it be so late? And yet so early? It seemed that an eternity had passed since she had left her little room in Long Acre that morning, and yet so much had happened so quickly; she had found—or Wyndham had found for her—new employment on a real stage, and it looked very likely that Fenton too would be accommodated in the same production, and she had found her grandmother's house. Of that she was quite sure. She had been in there but an hour or so, wandering about the rooms, but from the first instant she had been sure of it; this had been the house where the woman who had been her father's mother had lived. And lived with great passion. The very bricks had seemed to breathe familiarity to her, as though she herself had lived there once long, long ago, and had experienced passions and angers, happinesses and lovings

175

that had left their traces behind them in the fabric of the building.

She pulled herself together. Even for the fanciful Amy Lucas, this was going too far. The idea of ghosts had always appealed to her sense of the dramatic but she had never believed in them in any real way. They had been creatures to pretend to shiver at deliciously, or to be brave about, but never to take with any seriousness.

And yet now she stood on the pavement outside an abandoned house in Grosvenor Square in London and almost believed that some shadow of her own earlier self, some ghost who had gone before her and yet been part of her, had inhabited it. Too, too absurd. She set her bonnet straight and bent her head to look at the hem of her gown to see if streaks of dust marred its freshness. Practical, that was Amy Lucas's role today. She was searching out her own family connections, not out of any spirit of romance or gothic nonsense, but because it would be agreeable to find others like herself—and useful indeed to find connections who would be of help to her and her brother here in London, so far away from home in Boston. *Practical*. That was the key.

She turned then to walk briskly round the Square towards Brook Street where she might find a hansom plying for hire; she might not know precisely where in Lincoln's Inn Vivian and Onions were to be found but hansom cab jarveys, she knew, were knowledgeable men. One of them might well be able to help.

As she turned from the Square into the wide elegance of Brook Street, he almost cannoned into her, he was walking so quickly, and with such determination, and she gasped softly and said, 'Felix!'

He stopped and stared at her with his brow furrowed and his eyes almost blank, and for a moment she thought she had been mistaken. He seemed so different from his usual smiling friendliness and she said timidly, 'Felix?' and his face cleared and he smiled and was his own familiar self again.

'My dear Amy, what *do* you think you are doing?' he said and his voice was a little dry, and she frowned at the implied rebuke in his tone.

'I could as well ask you what *you* are doing here!' she said spiritedly. 'I have business in these parts, and am quite at liberty, I suppose, to prosecute my own affairs! You, on the other hand, are always at the hospital at this time, or so I have always understood. So why are *you* here asking me such questions?'

He tucked her hand into the crook of his elbow in his comfortable way, and smiled down at her.

'You are perfectly justified, of course. I have no right to quiz you. So I will be quite honest with you. Charles Wyndham came to me at the hospital perhaps half an hour ago and told me that you were to be found in the purlieus of Grosvenor Square. So, I thought I had best come and seek you out. I found a colleague to deal with my patients for me, and came to seek you. I was not sure you would be—well, I know your feelings are running high at present, and I did not wish you to be quite friendless and alone at a time when you might have need of comfort.'

She looked up at him standing there at the corner of Brook Street and Grosvenor Square, with passers-by jostling them and the clatter of traffic on all sides, at the way one errant lock of hair had escaped from beneath his hat to blow lightly on his forehead in the spring breeze, and felt her whole body fill with warmth and gratitude. And she spoke easily and freely without thinking for a moment of effect, or anything but the depth of her feelings.

'Dear Felix,' she said simply. 'Dear, dear Felix. I do love you.'

And he looked down at her, his hand set over her gloved one in the crook of his elbow and smiled his friendly smile and said unsteadily, 'And I you, my love, I you. And if you do not stop looking at me like that, I shall disgrace us both and kiss you here and now in the middle of the street and care not who looks at us.'

'I wish you would,' she said softly. 'Indeed, I wish you would—'

But he did not. They just stood and looked at each other, very close together and oblivious of anything but each other, their eyes seeming to speak torrents of words, until one particularly hurried man rushing past them on the way to some urgent business cannoned into them and swore and Felix pulled her closer to him and said, 'We cannot remain here, my love. Tell me—Wyndham said you had been told of some house in Grosvenor Square—did you find it?'

She nodded eagerly. 'I think so. Indeed I am sure of it. Please, Felix, can you take me to Lincoln's Inn? There are lawyers there who will be able to give me the news, I think. Will you?'

There was a long pause and then he nodded. 'If it matters so much to you, then of course I will. But I wish you would not pursue this matter further, Amy. You said you were searching because you needed to find the comfort of knowing to whom you belonged—but my love, you belong to me now. And to my family. Do you need more? There was such distress at Aunt Martha's yesterday. Must we perpetuate it? I would not try to dissuade you unless I felt it would do you more harm than good, but I would wish you would listen.'

'Let us take a cab, please, Felix. And then we can talk as we travel.'

He nodded, a trifle heavily, and turned his head to seek out a cab and hailed a passing growler, and directed him to Lincoln's Inn and then, when they were sitting comfortably side by side in its dusty leathery interior, he set his hand over hers and held it tightly.

'I meant all I said there on the pavement, Amy,' he said a little huskily. 'I love you, and see your future and mine as shared. I seek to marry you—do you understand that?'

'Of course,' she said and smiled up at him and even in the dimness of the cab the brilliance of that smile made his belly lurch and he bent his head and kissed her, gently at first and then with increasing urgency, and she clung to him and returned his ardour with a passion that startled him.

The cab lurched as it went round a corner and they were hurled against the window and she held on to him and laughed, and as the cab righted itself set her hands to her bonnet to straighten it.

'We really must behave ourselves, Felix,' she said primly, 'What would your family say if they thought so reputable a physician could behave so in a growler? They would be quite shocked!'

The mention of his family sobered them both and after a

moment he said, 'I was saying, Amy—is this search so important now? When you arrived here, friendless and alone, I can understand you had a need for connections. But now—must you?'

She nodded in the dimness. 'I must. It is the most absurd thing, Felix, but it seems to me that I have—that I *know* her. Was part of her. If I believed in theories of reincarnation as some do—why, I might even say—well, I do not, so let that be. But it has come to be important to me in a very strange way. Let me but find her, and discover for certain whether she was my grandmother—and I am convinced of it—and I will rest easy. I will never speak to your family of her again. I promise. But let me just find out. Will you?'

'Of course, if it matters so much. But let us do it quickly, our searching. There are so many other more important affairs upon which we must busy ourselves. Like where we shall live when we are married, and—'

'I cannot imagine it,' she said dreamily and drooped her head on to his shoulder. 'It will be so lovely! I shall go to the theatre each evening to perform, and then when I return you will—'

He stiffened. 'I cannot believe that you will go on performing at my cousin Oliver's after we are wed!'

She looked up at him. 'Oh, no! Not at Cousin Oliver's. Did not Charles Wyndham tell you? It is the most delightful thing, Felix! I have a part in a play at the Royalty! A *real* play, where I shall *act*. And they have said that Fenton may have a part too—well, he must audition, you know, but it is pretty sure they'll have him! Is it not capital? Charles Wyndham has a part as well—it will be so delightful! And then, when I am famous and we are wed, all the rich people in the town will wish to come to you because you are so splendid a physician and because they will hope to have a glimpse of me—oh, dear, dear Felix. We shall be so happy!'

The cab clattered and swayed on its way, and Felix looked down at her smiling face and lustrous eyes and sighed softly. Dear, dear Amy! He loved her dearly and knew he always would. But his task of changing some of her less attractive ways and more outrageous ideas was far from complete. But with the help of his aunt Martha, and possibly cousin Phoebe as well—for was she not an actress who had married a medical man?—he should be able to explain to this absurd but altogether adorable girl that her vision of the future was in need of considerable amendment.

He sighed softly, and set his arm about her waist and held her close, and as the cab made its final curving turn to stop at the old gatehouse to Lincoln's Inn at the top of Chancery Lane he bent his head and kissed her with great tenderness. Whatever else was to happen in the future this moment was a very special one, and he wanted nothing to mar it at all.

# CHAPTER EIGHTEEN

'I had thought to find lawyers' offices here like those we have at home,' Amy whispered to Felix. 'But these must be quite different from our attorneys who always seem to have very dusty ordinary offices. These must be very rich, I think.'

Felix smiled and squeezed her hand. 'There are no rules about how lawyers should appear, my love,' he said in a low voice. 'Some are dry and withered, like those in Boston you described to me, but others are like this—displaying their riches—in America as much as here, I daresay. Lawyers are like physicians and come in many guises.'

Amy shook her head doubtfully, and looked about her again. They were sitting in a large room well equipped with heavy pieces of polished mahogany furniture in the latest mode, with a rich blue Persian carpet upon the floor and the heaviest and most whispering of thick velvet curtains at the windows. They had been ushered in by a very proper young man wearing quite the highest of white collars that Amy had ever seen and a carefully brushed glossy black suit of clothes, and told loftily to 'wait for Mr. Onions who will be with you as shortly h'as 'e is able!'

Finding the lawyer has been far from difficult; clearly the partnership was one of great renown as well as affluence, and the first person they had asked for directions had sent them unerringly to this set of chambers; and now they sat in the splendour of the waiting-room, and duly waited.

But not for long. The young man returned and with a dignity that would have done justice to the major-demo of a prince led them along a carpeted corridor to the partners' room.

And there they sat, one on each side of a vast leather-covered desk, both round of face and lavishly whiskered, and both looking at their callers with stern expressions bearing more than a hint of let-us-waste-no-time-on-nonsensical-matters. Amy quailed, and looked up at Felix with alarm, very grateful to have him beside her, and she drew a little closer to him as he introduced her.

They were invited to sit down and Felix without any sign of discomfiture crossed his knees and set his hat upon them and said coolly, 'Miss Lucas is interested in the house in Grosvenor Square for which you are responsible.'

Mr. Vivian cast a swift look at his partner and said smoothly, 'Grosvenor Square? Now, which house would that be?'

'Oh, come, Mr. Vivian,' Felix said easily. 'You cannot tell me that you look after more than one there!'

Mr. Onions stirred and leaned forwards, his round face seeming to be full of bonhomie but still very watchful. 'I am exercised in my mind, sir, as to why you should be making any inquiries about this house. It is not for sale, and if you have been told so I am afraid you have been sorely misled.'

'It is Miss Lucas, not I, who makes inquiries, sir,' Felix said with great courtesy. 'Miss Lucas is seeking some information about her forebears. That is a search which I am sure you, as *family* lawyers, will well understand and will view with some sympathy. Miss Lucas believes that the house belongs—or belonged—to one Lilith Lucas. She thinks it is possible that this lady is her grandmother, and seeks some confirmation of her supposition. It is no more than that.'

Mr. Vivian and Mr. Onions looked at Amy and she reddened and then lifted her chin proudly and Mr. Onion's expression visibly softened. She looked exceedingly pretty in her new straw bonnet with its yellow flower trimmings and Mr. Onions was plainly a susceptible man. His partner, however, showed equally clearly that he was not and said crisply, 'We are not in any position to advise Miss Lucas on such a matter. We are not a firm which makes inquiries of this nature. I can recommend to you other lawyers who may be prepared to accept your young—er—friend—as a client.'

'I do not seek lawyers to make inquiries for me,' Amy said, on her mettle now. This man was looking at her in a way to which she was quite unused, with a sort of cool disdain, and her dislike of him edged her words. 'I am well able to make my own inquiries. So well able that I discovered that the house in Grosvenor Square which belongs—or as Felix said, perhaps it should be belonged—to Lilith Lucas, and that you are the people who set the caretaker there to look after it. I want only to know whether or not Lilith Lucas is still alive, and if so where she is. No more than that.'

'I cannot tell you,' Mr. Vivian said smoothly and looked at his partner. But he was still staring at Amy and showed no sign of awareness of the other's chill.

'That was enterprising of you, Miss Lucas! How did you manage to find out so much? Not that anyone is trying to hide anything, you understand, but after all, it is many years ago now since the lady was at all known on the London stage.'

'It was not too difficult,' Amy said, and bridled somewhat with pride at her own abilities, quite forgetting for a moment the aid that Charles Wyndham had given her. 'I did but ask the stage doorman at the Haymarket, you know, and he—'

'Oh, of course,' Mr. Onion's eyes seemed to become even softer in their expression. 'The Haymarket! Do you know, I remember so many years ago, when I was still a boy, being taken there to see the play as a special reward and I saw Lilith Lucas as Roxanna in *Cyrano*, you know, and she was so delectable, so very very—'

'This has little to do with the matter before us now, On-ions,' Vivian said sharply and looked again at Amy with the distinct air of scorn that had so irritated her. 'I am afraid there is not much that we can do to aid you, miss. So, if you will excuse us—'

Felix's brows snapped together. 'I do not think it necessary to be quite so cavalier, sir,' he said stiffly. 'We came to seek information about Miss Lucas's grandmother. I ask you now, do you act for that lady? If she is a client of yours then it is not unreasonable of us to ask that you convey a message to her if she is still alive, of course, or failing that, to her heirs and assigns. Indeed, sir, any refusal on your part to do so could be construed as some sort of—of dereliction of duty—'

The other man stared coldly at Felix. 'Are you threatening me, young man?'

'No, sir, I am not. I am merely pointing out to you that you have a duty to your client, if my companion *is* her grand-daughter, to enable them to meet. Miss Lucas is but recently come from America and—'

'I can tell you that Mrs. Lilith Lucas is not, nor ever has been, our client, sir. So that is the end of the matter.'

'She is not?' Amy jumped to her feet and clasped both her hands in front of her in her favourite gesture of appeal, di-recting the full flood of her imploring gaze at Mr. Onions. Despite Felix's dislike of her acting ways there were times when they could be very useful. And this she knew was one of them.

'Dear Mr. Onions, sir, you must tell me—is there no *way* you would be able to help me in my search for my family? I have no mother, sir, no aunts, no ladies of my own to whom I can turn in any distress, and to think that my own grand-mother may be somewhere and that I do not know of her whereabouts—it is very tragic, and makes me so sad! My Papa died when I was but a child, and so I cannot seek news of his mother or other connections from him—please, Mr. Onions, can you help me?'

Mr. Onions got to his feet and came round the heavy pol-ished desk to stand beside her and pat her shoulder in a very avuncular manner, and Amy bent her head and sniffed very delicately, and then, catching Felix's sardonic eye, subsided into her chair.

Mr. Onions, however, was now completely in her hands and he crouched beside her to look up into her face and say coaxingly, 'Now my dear Miss Lucas! You must not distress yourself so. No pretty little lady should ever disfigure herself with tears, and one with such a complexion as yours needs to be even more careful not to spoil the face she offers to the world! Now, cheer yourself up, do, and I will see what we can do to help you. No, Vivian—' for his partner was also on his feet now and showing signs of becoming very angry indeed. 'I daresay you are within the letter of the law in being so discreet, but really, there can be no harm in helping this young lady! She has clearly no intention of hurting anyone, and wishes only to find her connections. It is a most laudable aim—'

He got to his feet, stretching his stiff knees cautiously. 'You tell me why it is you think that you may be a descendant of Mrs. Lilith Lucas, and we will see what we can do. In the way of information, no more. Very well, then, Vivian,' as his partner scowled at him and began to remonstrate again. 'I shall see what *I* can do. You may leave us, Vivian, if you feel so strongly about it. But I have no doubt that Miss Lucas is worthy of our care. Besides, you have other work to do, have you not? Leave this to me—'

It took half an hour for Amy to explain all that had happened to her in her search for her English relations. She told her story smoothly and with some skill, explaining about Fenton, and how he had been injured in an accident. She said little about their meeting with Freddy Caspar, however, contenting herself with explaining that they had been befriended by a surgeon who had operated upon Fenton's injured leg and then helped them find lodgings.

'And then, you know, I became quite determined to seek even harder for my lost family,' she said, warming to her theme, 'and Mr. Wyndham helped me to make the discoveries I did and—'

'Mr. Wyndham?' Mr. Onions looked at Felix in some puzzlement. 'I thought, sir, that your—I do not perfectly recollect what it was, to tell the truth, since when you came in I was thinking of other matters—but I do not think it was Wyndham—'

'No, I am not Wyndham, Mr. Onions,' Felix said patiently. 'My name is—'

'Please, sir, is there anythin' else you'll be a'wantin', Mr. Bastable says, on account 'e wants to be on 'is way early tonight as you promised.' The young man with the high collar was standing by the door, looking rather less imposing than he had, and Mr. Onions looked up at him irritably.

'What's that? Bastable? Oh, the deuce take it—yes, I did say that he could—hmm. Well, now—'

He looked thoughtfully at Amy for a moment and then at his partner's empty chair, mutely accusing on the other side of the desk. 'Has Mr. Vivian gone yet?'

'Indeed, yes, sir. Went off in a right 'uff 'e did. Beggin' yer pardon sir, but he wasn't in the best o' moods, I oughta say. An' 'e was gone by 'alf past four—'

'Hmm. Wait outside a moment, Thornton. Then come back in when I call, and I will give you a message for Bastable.'

The young man went, and Mr. Onions looked seriously at Amy.

'My dear, as I am sure you realize, a lawyer's first responsibility is to his client. But we are humane men at heart, those of us who are best at our appointed tasks' (he threw a contemptuous glance at Vivian's empty chair) 'and must sometimes decide between what is most proper and what is most humane. Now, I must repeat what my partner told you—that Mrs. Lilith Lucas is *not* our client and never has been—'

He held up his hand as Amy opened her mouth to speak. 'No, do not look so dismayed! That does not mean I have no news for you. Indeed I have. You see, *through* a client of ours, it so falls out that I have news of this lady who, I must hasten to tell you, is no longer with us, having been gathered to her fathers, God rest her soul, in Constantinople in—let me see now—it must have been in 1854 or thereabouts. The second year of the affair in the Crimea, you know.'

'She is dead,' Amy said, and there was a note of tragedy in her voice. 'I had supposed she must be, but I had hoped, just a little, that—'

'My dear, please do not distress yourself,' Mr. Onions said

imploringly. 'I could not tell you all there is to explain if it is going to cause tears—'

At once Amy was still, her face displaying to a nicety her performance of Brave Little Lady, and Felix bit his lip. It would take many years and much effort, clearly, before he could teach his Amy to be always as sincere and direct as she might be. But even as he deplored her ability to sway others to her will by means of her posturings, he had to admire the skill she used. There was no question but that Mr. Onions would, if she were to ask it of him, go down on his knees and bite the carpet for her. But she made no such request, simply sitting there and looking at him with her eyes wide and her soft mouth drooping.

'I can tell you,' Mr. Onions said portentously after a long pause, 'that I have in my possession a copy of the Will made by Mrs. Lucas just before she died. I have it since the sole legatee is in fact our client. That is how I know. It is he who owns the house in Grosvenor Square, and all other property that the lady left.'

'Is he alive?' Amy said.

'Alive? But of course! As I said he *is* our client—not *was*,' Mr. Onions laughed merrily at his own joke. 'Why do you ask such a question?'

'Because of the state of the house,' Amy said. 'I saw it. I went all over it, and it is so neglected! Dust everywhere and falling into shocking disrepair, and yet so rich a house! It seems so strange that a man should own such a house and not live in it. Or sell it.'

Felix stirred in his chair. 'My dear, you cannot ask such questions, really you cannot! Mr. Onions has been exceedingly kind and told us what you wished to know. Can we not now leave the matter alone, and forget it all? You said you wished only to know whether your grandmother lived or died and—'

'But, Felix, I wish to know also if I have other connections! The stage doorkeeper said Lilith Lucas had four children, and one of them was called Benedict, who must have been my Papa who everyone called Ben. He is dead—but what of the others? And—' Her eyes glazed suddenly and she stopped. She had a sudden vision of Oliver standing there in the middle of Martha's drawing room and polishing his spectacles.

186

'My father,' he had said, 'was married to Lilith Lucas's daughter Celia—'

She turned back to Mr. Onions, 'I—it is possible that there are other connections,' she said awkwardly, and did not look at Felix. 'That is all I meant.'

Mr. Onions looked at her for a long moment, and then seemed suddenly to make up his mind. He got to his feet and went over to the door throwing it open suddenly and the young man in the high collar jumped away with his face red; clearly he had been listening very carefully indeed.

'Thornton! Tell Mr. Bastable to fetch for me the Lucas Will—he will know the one I mean—it is in the box that deals with the Grosvenor Square house—and then he may go.'

He came back to his desk and smiled at Amy with great good humour. 'Well, my dear, there is only one way to set your mind at rest, I think, and that is to tell you all we know of the lady. I have sent for the copy of her Will. It lists the names of some people to whom she deliberately *did not* wish to leave money, and so may be of some help to you. I will permit you to hear its contents. There! I can offer you no more than that—'

'It is uncommon kind of you to be so helpful to a lady who is not your client, Mr. Onions,' Felix said dryly and Mr. Onions reddened a little and shrugged.

'Well, as to that, she could see the Will soon enough if she went to the Registry so why not make it easier for her? M'partner is a stickler for the details of legal practice, but me, I am a humane man, sir, a humane man. I still have not quite caught your name?'

Even as Felix opened his mouth to reply the door opened and back came the tall-collared Thornton bearing a document in one hand, and Onions took it from his and nodded a dismissal, and the young man bobbed his head and went.

There was a long pause and Amy sat and stared at the document in Mr. Onion's hand. The afternoon sunshine was dwindling now and the room was dim, but she could see the glow of the heavy paper in the softer blur of Mr. Onions's hand, and for a brief moment tried to imagine the woman who had caused the document to be prepared, all those years ago. In 1854 Amy herself had been but eleven years old, a silly giddy schoolroom chit just beginning to discover her own abilities and to feel the urgent hunger of her ambitions moving within her, and she tried now to imagine the loneliness of a woman dying in a remote alien city and compare it with the life she herself had been living in Boston then. And could not.

Mr. Onions stirred and leaned forwards and with a match taken from a silver box he wore on his watch chain lit an oil lamp on his desk, and fussed with the wick for a moment or two before returning his attention to the document.

'It is an interesting Will,' he said at length. 'Such a long time since I saw it, but I recall it was interesting. But not as interesting as what happened when it was brought back to England from Constantinople.' He looked at Amy with his eyes bright in the lamplight. 'It was a large legacy, you see, a very large fortune indeed that the Will left. It mentioned only one beneficiary apart from my client—a servant of some sort, to whom she left all the property she died with there in Constantinople. The rest—the house, the various parcels of land about the city, the bank moneys, the jewellery—all of it left to my client. And he would have none of it. A strange affair.'

He seemed to be talking almost to himself now, and Amy watched him in silence, willing him to tell her more, to be more and more indiscreet. And he seemed to feel the compulsion coming from her and went on almost dreamily. 'All that money, all that property and he refused to even speak of it. So what could we do? We filed the Will and set a caretaker to the house, and did no more. But it seems so wasteful, so foolish. All that money and property lying idle. Such a *wicked* waste—'

'Why did he refuse?' Amy asked softly. Perhaps if she could encourage him to speak generally of the whole matter, he could be persuaded to tell who this mysterious legatee might be. It was none of her affair, she knew, but she was eaten with curiosity all the same. What sort of man could it be who could turn his back on a fortune, and leave a house like the one in Grosvenor Square to rot in neglect?

'I don't know—he refused to even speak of it. Oh, I tried.

It would have been a dereliction of my duty had I not tried. But he would have none of it. Consigned me to perdition, and told me to do as I wished. So what could I do? Nothing. Sad, sad—'

He sighed deeply then and looked down again at the document in his hand. 'I can tell you there is no mention here of any connection of Lilith Lucas, except for deliberate exclusion of her younger son, Jody—he was Jonathan, I believe, but she called him Jody—from any inheritance. The rest went to my client. And here are the witnesses' signatures affixed—' He turned the page and the document rustled softly in the lamplight like an autumn leaf. 'Quite clearly signed and dated. Alexander Laurence and Martha Lackland, in Constantinople on—'

'*Who?*'

Felix's voice seemed to crack across the dreamy quietness of the room, now almost dark except for the pool of lamplight in which Mr. Onions sat, and the lawyer started and peered at him.

'What did you say?' Felix's voice was quieter now but still very incisive, and Amy stared at him, puzzled, and trying also to sort out the confused feelings those two names had created in her. She too had been affected by the soft atmosphere of the room, and had not been thinking at all clearly, quite caught up in her fantasy of the lonely woman dying far away from her Grosvenor Square home, and it was only now that the import of what Mr. Onions had said began to sink in.

'The names of the witnesses,' Felix now said in a tight hard voice. 'Did you say Martha Lackland and Alexander Laurence?'

'Yes,' said Mr. Onions, and now the bonhomie had disappeared and he was watchful and sharp as he began to fold up the document almost protectively, as if he feared Felix would seize it from him. 'I cannot deny those are the names I said. Are they—ah—of significance?'

'They are,' Felix said very grimly. 'They are very significant. My father was Alexander Laurence, sir, and my—I was adopted after his death, by Miss Martha Lackland. Those names are indeed significant to me.'

# CHAPTER NINETEEN

'Who?' said Amy. 'Who did you say? How could that be? You told me that your father hated her—that he would never let you go to theatres because of her, that—'

'I know,' Martha said wearily. 'But who am I to explain the ways of such a woman? I know my father had come to hate her, bitterly. But that did not mean she felt so about *him*. And she left it, all of it, to him. I tried to tell her she should not, but Alex said—he said it was wrong to balk a dying woman. And of course it was. So she left it all to him. That is all I know.'

'Why did you not explain all this on Sunday?' Felix's voice came sharply out of the dimness of the window embrasure where he had been sitting throughout, and Martha turned her head and looked at his shadowed face, trying to see some expression on it, and felt an increase of the chill that had been in her ever since they had both come bursting in on her while she was doing her accounts; that Felix, her own loving gentle Felix, should sound so remote, so coldly angry, filled her with a curious sick fear that mixed ill with that icy coldness.

'Amy asked you then if there was anything else you could tell her. Yet you kept silent. I find this strange, I cannot deny.'

'I wanted no more fuss!' Martha cried and clasped her hands lightly in her lap. 'I abominate fuss and trouble above all things. You must surely know that, Felix, after all these years with me! I could not imagine that it would make any difference to you, Amy, so I kept quiet. That was the only reason—'

'I can understand that, Miss Lackland,' Amy said, but her voice came mechanically, as she tried to set all the new information she had been given into some sort of order.

There was a pause and then she said, 'I find it all so *confusing*. There is your father, Abel, and there is my grandmother, Lilith—and you do not deny now that she *is* my grandmother—and—'

'I have been certain ever since the suggestion was first made that it had to be so,' Martha said. 'I knew her only in her last hours, when she was ill and dying and tired, but she had about her much that you have—an inner quality—'

An ability to fill me with a jealousy that is sickening in its intensity, she thought, and looked again at Felix's shadowed face. I suffered jealousy of Alex when that woman looked at him and spoke to him, and now I feel the selfsame jealousy when my Felix looks at this one. It is wicked, wicked, and it should not hurt so much—

'I am glad of that,' Amy said. 'I wanted to know of my connections, to know if there were any like me, as I am now, and I am glad to know there were. That I had a grandmother who was so—so—well, everyone says she was exciting and—and dramatic and beautiful—all the things I want to be thought myself—'

'You do not need reassurance on that, Amy, do you? Not really,' Felix said, and once again jealousy slid into Martha at the tone of his voice; loving, bantering, above all vibrating with warmth. 'Watch yourself, my dear—'

Amy laughed, a little shamefaced. 'Yes, I daresay I was fishing for a compliment—well, let that be. It is confusion that now concerns me. How can it be that your family and mine are so *entwined*? You told me that they—Lilith and Abel—were once connected. And then Oliver said that his parents were one from each family, and now I hear that my grandmother's property is left to your family as well—all so *confusing*—'

'It has always been so,' Martha said, and turned her head to look at the dying embers of the fire in her grate and drew her shawl closer about her shoulders. The April evening was chilly, but she would not call a servant to tend the fire. This matter between them had to be sorted out in privacy, uninterrupted by even a parlourmaid. 'There have been other—episodes. Lydia. Your aunt Lydia—'

Amy looked up sharply. 'The one who went to America? What of her?'

'There was—a problem. With Phoebe. But it was all a long time ago, now, and all forgotten.'

'But she is my *aunt*—and I have a right to know about all that affects my family.'

'Indeed, you have not!' Martha said sharply. 'Only as much as they would wish you to know. If Phoebe wishes one day to tell you of her past experiences, then that will be her affair. You will be cross indeed if you *ask* her to do so, just as she would be cross to ask you to tell her every detail of your life, including those that you would rather not discuss.'

Amy face flamed. 'I have nothing to hide from anyone!'

'I did not for one moment suggest you had. But I daresay you, like all of us, have had thoughts and ideas and possibly experiences you would rather forget. We cannot all lead blameless lives. And it ill behoves any of us to display undue curiosity about our fellows, whether they be our relations or not.'

There was a silence for a while and the embers settled in the grate with a sharp crack that made them all jump, and then Amy said, 'Will you tell me more about Abel Lackland—about your father? Why does he not live in that house in Grosvenor Square? It is neglected shockingly, but it is a very beautiful house.'

Martha smiled thinly. 'He refused the legacy.'

Amy sat up very straight and stared at Martha, her mouth lax with amazement. '*Refused* it? How could he do so? The lawyer said—I do not understand—'

'There is much you do not understand, my child, nor ever will until you learn to listen to what you are told! I doubt the lawyer told you anything at all about my Papa. As I understand the matter from you, Felix, he told you only that a Will had been made, naming his client—but he did not tell you who the client was.'

'That is true,' Felix said and turned his head to look at the two women sitting primly beside the fireplace, for all the world like a pair of tea sippers enjoying no more than a harmless gossip.

'I am sorry,' Amy said almost impatiently. 'But of course I assumed—I mean, can a person refuse a legacy? When someone who is dead has decreed something, it is not possible to argue, is it?'

'You do not know my Papa,' Martha said, and for the first time since they had arrived in her drawing-room she smiled. A thin mirthless smile, but a smile none the less. 'If he decided he wanted no part of something then not so much as a tittle of it would he have! He refused to accept the legacy, refused to discuss it, and so the Will was set in the hands of the lawyers, who have dealt with it ever since. My father knows nothing of what has happened to this property and never will.'

'He must be very rich,' Amy said, a note of awe creeping into her voice. 'To refuse so *large* a benefit. The lawyers did not say precisely how much it was, but I believed from what Mr. Onions did say that it was a considerable amount.'

Now Martha laughed aloud. 'My dear child, you are so lacking in understanding that you quite frighten me! A man may be as poor as a church mouse and still refuse to accept money and property to which he does not feel entitled! Or because he bears ill feeling to the source of it.'

'She will learn,' Felix got to his feet. 'She will learn, will you not, my love?' He came and stood beside Amy now, and put one hand on her shoulder, and looked up at the older woman with a very straight gaze. 'Martha, I think it is right that I tell you now—that *we* tell you now—there is an understanding between us. We have not yet spoken of any details, but we will be wed. As soon as we may.'

There was a long silence as Martha stared back at him. All she could think was, '*He called me Martha, not Aunt, just Martha. He called me Martha. The happy years are over. He called me Martha.*' Then she swallowed and said carefully, 'I wish you joy, indeed I do.'

At once Felix smiled, a wide warm smile that brought back the boy she had watched over and loved for more than ten years, and he came over to her and bent and kissed her cheek.

'Thank you, Martha,' he said quietly. 'I knew I could trust you to be happy for me.' And this time the use of her name seemed friendly and not threatening and she drew a tremulous breath and looked over his shoulder at Amy, and held out a hand to her.

'It is strange, my dear, that you seem to be repeating history yet again, is it not? Once more our two families are— what was the word you used?—*entwined*. That is it— entwined. Lilith's granddaughter, and Abel's grandson— albeit an adopted grandson—to be wed. The family will be much amazed.'

'But will they be pleased?' Amy said and looked at her very directly. 'From all you have said so far, I am not sure that they will be so.'

'I hope they will,' Martha said cautiously. 'It will be more likely to be a happy acceptance if you will accept some advice from me.'

Amy looked up at Felix and he came back to stand beside her. 'Listen to Martha, Amy. She is a woman of more wisdom than I have in my little finger. And she has much love in her. Have you not, Martha?'

'I try,' Martha said. 'I can do no more,' but she was feeling better. That hateful river of jealousy that had threatened to engulf her earlier was dwindling, was little more than a cold trickle deep inside her. A trickle she could encompass, could live with, above all, could hide from Felix.

She leaned forwards now and spoke with great earnestness. 'Amy, my dear, if you would be a happy member of this family, you will forget all this matter of your forebears. You have identified your grandmother. You know now of two of your cousins—Oliver and Phoebe. There are others, of course. In America now, however, and unless you return there, which I imagine you will not now do, they need not concern you. You have found them, you know about them—and now forget them. Forget they are your cousins and forget your grandmother. Be one of *this* family, as Felix's wife, and they will learn to love you, I am sure, since Felix does. And let the sleeping dogs sleep on. Will you do this? Say nothing to anyone about it? Then I am sure we can all be happy and peaceful together—'

Amy smiled widely, and held out both hands to Martha. 'Of course I will. Now I know. It is all a great confusion, and I daresay I will go on feeling some curiosity for some time. But I will not speak of it to Mrs. Henriques or to Mr. Lackland and his sister. Truly I won't. Only Fenton, of course. I will have to tell Fenton, will I not?'

She had tried, Heaven knew, to get him alone for long enough to speak to him of all she had discovered, as well as her own private news, but she had quite failed. He had come home to Long Acre so late on Monday night that she had long since fallen asleep, in spite of her determination to remain awake to speak to him; and at breakfast next morning there had been Mrs. and Miss Miller fussing about them as usual, never leaving them alone for more than a moment or two as they hurried in and out with fresh coffee and hot muffins; and Amy knew that to speak of any private matter before them would be wildly indiscreet. Mrs. Miller was no more capable of keeping silent on any piece of news than she was of flying from her bedroom window to the street below; and Amy's news was much too portentous to be risked to those eager listening ears.

So, she had had to content herself all through breakfast with talk of the new play. She was delighted indeed to hear that Fenton had been given a part in 'Black Ey'd Susan' and he professed himself to be just as happy. But he was abstracted and ate his breakfast—and little enough of it—in silence except when prompted by his sister to respond; and even then did so only in monosyllables.

She had been able to contain herself, however, knowing that they had the journey to the Royalty for their first rehearsal, and that would give them time to talk. But as they reached the busy street Fenton said abruptly, 'Take a cab, will you, Amy? I will meet you there.'

'Fenton!' She almost wailed it. 'You must come with me—now! There is so much I have to tell you. It is very important. And it will be difficult there with all the people about! Please, do come with me—'

'I cannot—I—' He seemed uncharacteristically flustered and he took her shoulders between his gloved hands and looked down into her face and said urgently, 'Amy, my dear, there is much I have to tell you. So much—but not now. I—I am going to the Supper Rooms. To tell Lackland that we are leaving his show. We cannot just abandon it without a word, can we?'

Amy bit her lip. 'Oh dear, I had quite forgotten him, to tell the truth! So much has happened, you see, so very much I must tell you of and—'

'I know! I too, have news for you—but *later*.' He had let her go and thrust his hands deep into his coat pockets. 'Later, I will meet you at the Royalty. Don't argue, you silly creature—just go—' and he had gone hurrying away down Long Acre, weaving his way through the crowds at a remarkable speed, and she had perforce had to make her own way in the other direction, to seek a cab.

And so it had gone on all morning. Fenton had arrived breathless and late, and there had been no time at all to talk, for Mr. Rourke was already setting the stage for the first walkthrough rehearsal. And then they had started work, and as she read her way through her lines and was given her moves the magic the theatre always wrought in her began to take over. No longer was she on a dusty ill-lit cold stage on the first day of rehearsal. Instead she felt the audience that would be there for her moving into the shrouded seats in the auditorium like so many eager ghosts, felt the building excitement of a performance, felt the character she was playing grow inside her, pushing away the real Amy to make way for the greater reality of make-believe. And her own affairs dwindled away and lost their urgency.

But then they stopped for the luncheon interval, and after some raillery between Wyndham and Rourke, who were obviously all ready to become the closest of cronies, the company went off to the tavern across the road to take refreshment, leaving Amy and Fenton behind, for Amy said she was not hungry, having breakfasted very well, and Fenton said he wished to con his lines. And at last they were alone, and could talk.

Amy sat perched on the table that was in the centre of the stage, marking the Cottage Parlour which was the setting of the first scene of the play, hugging her knees and looking

more like an urchin than a young lady who was newly betrothed or a great actress about to make her London debut;
but for once she did not care about the appearance she presented to the world. Her own affairs were now once more in
the forefront of her mind, and she was bursting to tell Fenton
all about it.

But he did not give her a chance to do so. He started to
prowl up and down the stage, from one side to the other, with
a heavy measured step and Amy looked at him apprehensively; when Fenton marched so it boded ill. His uncertain
temper was something she had lived with long enough to treat
with respect, and she knew that he paced in this manner only
when he was deeply disturbed. This was not the time to blurt
out the news that she was to be wed; for all his offhand use
of her, for all his occasional scornfulness and unkindness,
Amy knew that she was important to Fenton, and that he
would take her love for another man very ill.

But perhaps, she thought, I can tell him of the matter of
Lilith Lucas; he will be as interested in that, surely, as I am,
and it may soothe his temper to talk of such things. And then
he will be able to tell me of what it is that is now making him
march up and down so miserably.

'Fenton,' she said tentatively, and he seemed not to hear
her, and she said again, 'Fenton!' And this time he stopped
and looked at her, and his eyes seemed to her to be filled with
misery, and alarmed, she scrambled down from the table and
ran to him.

'Fenton, whatever is the matter? You look so unhappy—
what is it, my dear? Tell your Sugar-Amy all about it, Fenton, my love—what is it?'

She was almost crooning to him, just as her mother had
been used to do when he was a little boy who had to be
coaxed out of his sulks, and she set her hands one on each side
of his face and looked up at him and smiled and said again,
'Tell your Amy all about it, my love. What is it that ails you?
Is your leg upsetting you again?'

He shook his head impatiently, pulling away from her.

'Damn it, Amy, don't treat me like a child! I am a man
grown, with a man's problems, and I can see no way out of
the tangle into which I have caught myself. What on earth I

am to do, I cannot imagine! I am so set about I can hardly think, and all you do is behave like some old nurse—you'll be offering me pap next—'

'Well, if that is the shape of it, perhaps you will tell me what it is that is making you look as though the world is sitting on your shoulders!' Amy said tartly, and stood in the middle of the stage, her fists balled on her hips, and her chin up. 'I have my own problems too, and my own news, but clearly you are too much of a *man grown* even to notice that! I told you this morning I had news for you, and all you can do is march about looking as though no one in the world has any concerns but you and—'

'Oh, Amy, do be quiet,' Fenton said wearily, and put his hands to his head. 'I am nigh exhausted, for I cannot sleep these nights. And if you start at me, I cannot be responsible for what will happen. I am worried, I tell you—*worried*—'

She looked at him for a long moment and then nodded and went and sat down at the table, her hands folded in her lap. 'Well, perhaps you had better tell me of it all,' she said quietly. 'I may be able to help.'

He looked at her miserably for a moment and then, moving heavily for one usually so lithe, came and sat down in the chair on the other side of the table.

'It is Isabel,' he said after a moment. 'Isabel Henriques.'

'What of her?'

'It is so *stupid*.' The words almost burst out of him and once again he got to his feet and resumed his pacing, throwing his words at her over his shoulder as he went. 'I will not deny that the prime attraction in her was her money. I saw her that night at the Caspars' and I thought—this is the one for me. If I can ingratiate myself with this one, there is a future aglow with money. Her father is as rich as Croesus, and so is her stepbrother—and I could see she liked me. So I made a beeline for her. It was not difficult.'

'So? Is that so terrible a thing? You aren't the first man who has found an heiress agreeable.'

'Oh, be your age, Amy,' Fenton said savagely. 'I am well aware of that! The problem is—damn it all to hell and back— my feelings are engaged now. I did not intend it to happen— indeed, I did not think it could! But here I am, as sick with love as any damned girl and not knowing which way to turn!'

She could have laughed aloud. He stood there staring at her, his face as woebegone as a child's who had seen his barley-sugar stick fall into the river, and did not seem to realize how absurd it all was. But she knew better than to give vent to her amusement, and said gravely, 'Are your affections returned?'

'That's the devil of it!' Fenton said, and resumed his pacing. 'I thought at first that they were. Indeed, I know they were. In the early days, when it was her money that most filled my thoughts, and I was exercised in my mind about how to ensnare her, there is no doubt she regarded me with great interest. Indeed, then, I know, she was quite thrown over in her mind by me. I could have—dammit, I could have seduced her then, I swear it! But now—'

'Now?'

He shrugged. 'It is so silly,' he said miserably. 'It came upon me by degrees that I did not care whether she had a cent to her name, that it was *she* who mattered. I could think of nothing but her face and her smile and the sound of her voice and the way she smelled of flowers, and I—oh, I did not at first know what had happened to me. I have never felt so about any woman ever. To be so confused by such feelings—well, I did not know what to *do*. And then I knew that I had to have her, that somehow we had to be wed, and I told her so, and—' again he shrugged and fell silent.

'And you were wrong? She did not return your feelings?'

'It was not precisely that—it was as though she—it seemed to me that she lost the feeling that she had. That it had been there, and she had loved me truly. Just like all the others. I have had experience enough, God knows, of lovesick girls. And I swear she was just like them—until I became lovesick myself—'

'Perhaps,' Amy said slowly, 'you stopped trying to please her? Perhaps you became so locked up in your own feelings that she did not find you the same person? It is a strange thing about us, Fenton, about both of us. We can be so different to different people. I can act the part that my companion wishes me to without having to think of it. But when I am not acting—then I suppose I am different. I am perhaps fortunate that Felix likes me better when I am not acting than when I am—but perhaps your Isabel prefers the acting you to the real you—'

'Felix? You mean Felix Laurence? What has he to do with it?' Fenton stared at her, frowning.

'I am to marry him, Fenton,' she said quietly, looking at him very directly. 'I too have found my feelings engaged, in a most surprising way. I—we agreed yesterday. We are to be wed—'

'Oh, God!' Fenton said, and flung himself into a chair, scowling. 'That is all I needed! The one woman I have ever wanted rejects me, and now my own sister will abandon me! How can such things happen to me when I have done no harm to anyone?'

'I had thought you would wish me happy, Fenton.' She tried not to let him see how hurt she was, and looked at him with her chin up.

'Oh, why the hell should I? Have I not miseries of my own enough? Why should I wish *you* happy when I am so miserable?'

'Perhaps if you could be more as you used to be she would love you as you wish her to,' Amy said after a moment. 'You made great efforts on her behalf as far as I could see. Perhaps the trouble now is that she can see that you care a great deal more for yourself—'

'And why shouldn't I?' Fenton shouted, glaring at her. 'No one else cares! *You* don't! If you did you would not be leaving me for that dull stick Laurence!'

'He is not dull, and if you dare to say one unkind word about him, Fenton, I swear to you I *will* abandon you! I love you dearly and always have, and always will, but Felix is— Felix is—he is *mine*, and you shall not sneer at him, you hear me? If you do, I promise you you will regret it! I shall—'

'Oh, do hush! So, he is yours and I must not slang him. Very well, I shall say nothing at all about him. Anyway, he is your affair, dammit—Amy, what am I to *do*? I want her so—' and he kicked the leg of the table viciously, for all the world like a child balked of a toy.

She stared at him for a long moment and then sighed softly. 'There is nothing you can do, my love, but swallow your feelings and forget her. For not only does she seem to have cooled towards you—even if she adored you, I doubt you would have much joy. Her Papa and Mamma, I am persuaded, are very careful of her. And as you say, they are very rich—you cannot imagine they would ever allow a penniless actor to wed her, can you? You had best forget her, truly you had—'

Fenton was staring at her, his eyes wide and very bright. 'What did you say? Her Papa and Mamma—oh, glory, glory, I did not think! What a fool I am, I did not think!' He almost crowed it and she stared at him in amazement.

'Don't you see, Amy? It is not *me* she has cooled towards. It is my poverty! Why, if I had the money to suit her parents, I have no doubt all would be well! It is because she knows I am *poor* that she tries to put me away. She knows I will suffer otherwise—oh, she is a dear girl, a dear dear girl, and I love her so much!'

'I think you are making too much of what I said, Fenton.' Amy said cautiously. His moods were so mercurial this morning she felt she did not know how to go on with him. 'I did not suggest she had cooled because you were poor—I only said her parents would reject you even if she had not—'

But he was now in tearing high spirits. He had seized on her words and clearly nothing she said would convince him otherwise and he began to dance about the stage, using the steps they had been shown that morning by Rourke. 'She loves me, she loves me, she does, she does, she *does*,' he carolled and she watched him, her lips quirking.

And then, as suddenly as he had soared to the heights he came plunging down again.

'But what am I to do, Amy?' He looked at her with his eyes huge with tragedy. 'What am I to do for money? How can I gain enough quickly enough, to show her she need not fear her parents' rejection of me? I must get rich, oh God, I must get rich *quickly*. Could this play launch me well enough, do you think? My part is small, but I can make something of it, I'm sure, and then, if another management sees it, and offers me a bigger chance, I would perhaps reach the heights fast enough to command good money—oh, how can I *do* it—'

Quite at what moment the idea came to her, she did not

know. She sat there and looked at him, her adored brother who had always needed and obtained the help of the people who loved him and now had only her to rely upon. Her brother who needed money and needed a lot of it.

And suddenly she thought of the house in Grosvenor Square and the empty sumptuous wasted luxury, and heard Martha's voice explaining why her father had refused his legacy. And the thought swirled and gained shape and substance in her mind and she leaned forwards and said earnestly, 'Fenton! There is perhaps a way. If you are convinced that it is money and only money that stands between you—there is a way that it might be obtained—listen. And listen carefully to all I have to tell you.'

## CHAPTER TWENTY

'So you see, Fenton?' she finished. 'If he does not want the legacy, and refuses to have any part of it, I should think he would be glad to get rid of it. And since we are Lilith's grandchildren, who better to give it to? I am sure if I explain it all to him in this way, he will agree. It is the only sensible thing to do! And then you will have the money you want, and perhaps Isabel will accept you. Though I think you must remember that there may be other reasons for her being as she is. Money alone may not be the answer—'

But he brushed that aside as quite irrelevant. He had listened to her in absorbed silence, once he had realized the import of what she was saying, his eyes opaque with thought, and now his jawline was set and his colour was high.

'If you think you can persuade the old man to agree, well enough. It will undoubtedly be the *easiest* way. But I recall him that day in the casualty ward at the hospital, when I was so ill. He was not very agreeable then, was he?'

'No,' Amy agreed. 'I remember that too. But that was different. It was a time of great anxiety, and it was in his hospital, and anyway all this is *different*. I go to him not as the sister of a patient he is looking after but as the granddaughter of his old friend—even though Martha says he came to hate her afterwards—it is a very romantic thought, that, is it not? He cannot, surely, fail still to have some feeling for his love of so long ago, and to see the justice of giving us her money!'

Her spirits were now nearly as high as his. The idea, now it was in her, seemed to her to be flawless. The old man did not need or want the money. They did. Nothing could be simpler or clearer than the plan she now had, and it seemed to her a matter only of explanation. She would but have to tell Abel Lackland the situation, and they would at last have their own money. Fenton would have most of it, of course; she expected that, for he was Fenton and anyway, his need was greater. She had her Felix and clearly he was not a poor man even though he was not as rich as some of his adopted relations. Not that riches seemed to matter so much any more, not with Felix. He was Felix and living with him would be exciting and safe enough, she was sure, without great quantities of money.

'I am sure he must agree,' she said. 'There can be no simpler way.'

'Well, even if he doesn't, there are ways to make sure he parts,' Fenton said cryptically and stood up as the company came trooping back into the theatre.

They were red of face and voluble, and Amy sighed. She had not infrequently suffered the discomfort of afternoon rehearsal with a company who were a trifle bosky after their luncheons; within an hour, during which they would be silly and noisy and make many mistakes, they would become sleepy and surly and it was all too likely the day would end with quarrels.

Thinking of that depressed her and thrust out of her mind her moment of doubt about Fenton's words: 'There are ways to make sure he parts.' What did that mean? She had no time to think of that now, and deliberately pushed her anxiety away. Wyndham came to stand beside her as the next scene was put into rehearsal. They were both off stage now for some ten minutes or so, and he asked her softly what she had discovered at Grosvenor Square.

She thought for a moment and then whispered back, 'I found that indeed she *was* my grandmother. Is that not interesting? But there are no other connections of hers in England—an aunt now gone to America—but that is all,' and then turned the subject to talk about the sort of costumes the play demanded and which she hoped to get; and Wyndham subsided. He knew when he was defeated and anyway his curiosity was only a little piqued. Suffice it that he had helped her to find her grandmother. Now the time had come to concentrate on the play, and above all to ingratiate himself well with her.

They had several scenes together and he had very quickly recognized the magic she could weave over an audience. If she were to remain his friend, then he had no fears; he could persuade her not to hog the scenes and to allow him sufficient leeway to impose his own considerable personality and talents. But if they were to be at loggerheads he had no doubt she could charm the audience right out of his hands, if she so wanted. So she was not to be allowed to want to.

He spent the afternoon, therefore, paying a great deal of attention to her, seeing to her comfort, sending out especially for a pot of hot chocolate for her because he was concerned to discover she had had no luncheon, and altogether behaving like a most affectionate uncle. And she relaxed and basked in his care of her and gave no more thought to the promise she had made her brother to beard the alarming Abel Lackland in his own den. She would worry about that when the time came.

It came that very evening. She had returned to Long Acre agreeably tired but not so tired that she could not look forward with lifting excitement to meeting Felix. They had so much to talk about, so many plans to make, and she felt a deep hunger for the comfort of his presence, a need for him that far from being irksome seemed to fill her with a sort of contentment.

But her happy anticipation rapidly dispersed. There was a letter awaiting her at the house when she reached it (alone because Fenton had gone off on some business of his own on the way home) and Mrs. Miller put it breathlessly into her hands as soon as she opened the front door to her knock.

'Come from the Middlesex 'ospital it did and when I saw the carriage outside and saw this 'ere porter a'wearin' of a uniform with the words Middlesex 'ospital writ right across the pocket, my heart turned over in my chest, it did, turned right over. Thought I was going to be took bad with one of my attacks, that I did, and so I said to Emma, but she said don't be so silly, she said, because she does like to tease of me, don't be so silly, Ma, it's just one o' they social messages, I'll be bound, seein' as they didn't say we was to send the letter on to wherever you are, Miss Amy, and I said, well, I daresay you're right, Emma, my duck, an' the man did say, takin' off his uniform hat as nice an' polite as you like, he did say as it was important you was to get it as soon as you got to the 'ouse but it wasn't a matter of such urgency as to alarm anyone an' so I said to him, I did—'

Amy managed to escape at last, clutching the letter close to her bosom, and ran up the stairs to collapse on to her bed and slit the envelope. And was filled with a sudden delight as she did it, for this was the first time, in all the months they had known each other, that he had written even the briefest of notes.

'My dear one,' he had begun in his neat square handwriting, quite free of any of the fashionable flourishes so many young men used in their private correspondence. 'I have not been able to think of anything or anyone but you all day. When I talk to one of my patients, it is your face I see superimposed upon his. When I set my stethoscope to a chest, it is your voice I hear above the sound of a thumping heart. When I touch a patient's hand it is you I feel under my fingertips. In other words, my dear, you are set fair to ruining my career as a physician! After I have written this letter to you I must return to the wards and with a great effort of will make sure it is my patients and their ills I think of. Miss Lucas may not, will not, *shall* not, set foot inside my head from now until I

205

take myself home to my bed. And then I shall dream of you. That will be my reward.

'These must seem strange words from me. But do not be too surprised at them. I may not have said much to you of my feelings; but they are there for all that. I have felt them growing in me and tried to give them some sort of voice but could not, until you unlocked the door to speech between us. And now you have, I find it easier to write my feelings for you than to speak them.

'Dearest Amy, I love you, I love you, I love you. I can think of no sweeter words, no greater offering to put at your feet. I love you, Even when I am criticizing you—and I know I do so with some frequency—never doubt that, will you? It is because I love you that I speak to you as I do, seeking to change aspects of you not to please myself, but because I truly believe that they will show you to the world as the wholly lovable and delightful person you are. Remember that always, will you? There will, I know, be hurdles for us to leap across in the coming months, not least that you wish to go on acting and I cannot imagine a life with you as my wife that does not see you safe in the home I will provide for you. But as I say, that is one of the hurdles that lies before us. Now I want to say only—I love you, I love you, I love you.

'And now I must come to the dismal part of this letter, and the reason why it had to be sent round to you in such a hugger-mugger fashion. I could not await the postal services, speedy though they are. My love, because I came to you yesterday afternoon, and abandoned my duties here, I must remain this evening on duty and so pay for my dereliction. I am sure you will understand this—though I hope you will miss me as much as I shall miss you. Although I have already promised, have I not, that from now on I must think of my patients, and only my patients. It will be very difficult, my dear one. Tomorrow, I shall contrive to come to see you in the evening. We have so much to talk about!

'My love goes with you always. Felix Laurence.'

She folded the letter carefully and tucked it deep into the front of her gown, feeling the paper scratch against her soft skin, and glorying in it. To be loved so dearly by one she loved herself was a revelation to her, and for a moment she felt a stab of compunction for the many men who, over the years, she had encouraged to love her and then laughed at and left behind with never a second thought. She had been very unkind, and had so much to feel ashamed about. And she sat there for a long time, luxuriating in her sense of guilt, allowing tears to trickle down her face, and enjoying it all immensely. So many feelings, so mixed up, and all so exciting and interesting. For Amy the experience of feeling was what mattered most; even disagreeable sensation was better than none at all.

She was restless and abstracted throughout dinner and so was Fenton and even Mrs. Miller realized that her chatter was not welcome and served them silently, only shaking her head and tutting softly over their half-eaten meals. And then left them alone beside the fire in her warm red room, hoping they would become less melancholy as the evening progressed.

It was Fenton who stirred first. 'When will you see him?' he said abruptly.

'See who?' Amy stared at him. She had been lost in a dream involving Felix watching her play Juliet and being so moved by the experience that he vowed he would never stand in the way of her lifelong career on the stage. 'Felix?'

'No, you fool,' Fenton kicked the fender irritably, making the fire flare suddenly and lift his face to a ruddy glow which belied the sulky expression on it. 'Him! Lackland! About that damned legacy—'

'I am not sure,' Amy said doubtfully. 'I will talk to him, of course. I said I would. Should I write him a letter, do you think, asking him when I should come to speak to him?'

'And have him tell you smartly to be about your business and never come near him? God, Amy but you're a fool! The only way is to catch him unawares, obviously.'

'I suppose so,' Amy said and looked at him with her eyes filled with worry. It had been her own idea and she had promised she would do it but now suddenly she remembered just how disagreeable the old man had been and her spirits sank beneath the weight of that memory.

'So, why not now?' Fenton looked up at the clock on the cluttered mantelpiece over the fire. 'It is but eight o'clock. You could be there in—oh, half an hour, no more.'

'Where? I am not altogether certain where he lives.'

'Gower Street—I have a note of it—' He scrabbled in his pocket and pulled out a notebook and began to riffle the leaves. 'Here you are—I have the full direction.'

She frowned sharply. 'How can that be? Why do you have it?'

He grinned then, a sharp, knowing little grin. 'I made it my business to find out,' he said. 'I went to Nellie's tonight, on the way home. Told 'em I had a friend who wanted to consult the old man in his own home, not at the hospital. So they gave me the directions. Will you go now?'

'Now?' she said heavily and wanted to sink deeper into her chair. The idea of actually facing the old man was assuming terrifying proportions. But Fenton was looking at her with his eyes glittering with eagerness, and she had promised, and putting it off would not make it easier, and Felix was not here and could not be seen tonight and—

'Now,' she said firmly and got to her feet.

The house felt very strange, sombre and watchful and full of long-forgotten emotion which had left behind a brooding silence which rang in her ears. She had been given entry by a soft-footed, elderly butler who had peered at her above the oil lamp he held in one hand and muttered dubiously, 'Well, I'll see if the master is available,' and then gone padding away into the dark fastnesses of the house, leaving her in the dim hallway, feeling her courage oozing out of every pore.

It was absurd to be here, absurd to think that this man would be as sensible as any other man, she must have been crazy to even suggest it to Fenton—

The butler came back and wordlessly led her to a small room to one side of the hallway and went round lighting candles from a taper held in one gnarled old hand, and the room lifted into tremulous light. She stood and looked about her as he went padding away again, and marvelled, for it seemed to her that it had not been changed in fifty years. The furniture was sparse and light in soft polished woods which seemed to be frail and spindly compared with the solid heaviness of the drawing-rooms she was used to. Martha's in Bedford Row was far from rich, but well enough furnished and seemed to Amy to offer a comfort that this room could never aspire to, with its delicately legged chairs and curly backed little sofas. And compared with Phoebe Caspar's exceedingly elegant drawing-room with its rich colours and heavy velvet drapes and padded stools and sofas, this pale-walled room with its touches of gilt seemed positively anaemic.

The door opened behind her and she whirled and stood staring. And saw there the old man she had last seen at the hospital, and felt all her fear return.

He was standing with his head thrust forwards and his jaw jutting out, but his back was as straight as that of a man half his age, and the muscles beneath his coat could be clearly seen as their contours shaped the cloth. This was no weedy desiccated tired old man. He was strong and still vigorous and it showed. Amy looked up into his narrow green eyes and quailed.

'Well?' the old man barked. 'My man said you had a matter of importance to discuss with me. What is it? If it is illness, then you would be better advised to seek one of the younger surgeons from Nellie's. I prefer not to go out to patients at night now—unless it is of some special import. What is the case, then, hey? Is it of special import?'

She swallowed and said carefully, 'No sir. It is not a case of illness at all.'

He frowned at that and came further into the room, peering at her more closely. And then stopped short and stared, his eyes narrowing even more.

He saw a girl in a yellow gown, with pretty shoulders rising from it seductively and with her bonnet fallen back from her head and caught across her slender throat by its ribbons. She had dark curly hair, coarse and springing, which lay on her forehead in tendrils that were very charming. She had wide grey eyes and a pointed face and there was about her expression a sparkling quality, a vivacity, that seemed to him to be infinitely familiar and infinitely lovely and yet full of threat—

He shivered suddenly, the way an elderly dog does, and said harshly, 'Not a case? Then what is it? I have better things to do with my time than waste it here with some chit of a girl! What is it you want? Tell me at once, or be about your business.'

There was a rustle at the door, and Amy looked up and beyond the old man, grateful for the interruption. He had alarmed her quite dreadfully, so much so that she had nearly taken to her heels and run past him to the safety of the dark street beyond the front door.

There was a small woman standing there, neat in a brown merino gown which was quite unadorned and with her hair set severely on each side of her head in a very outmoded fashion. Yet for all her dowdiness and apparent age she had dark lively eyes and a smooth round face and was looking at Amy with some concern.

'Abel, my dear, what *is* the matter? Jefferson told me there was someone to see you—but you know I cannot agree to your going out to a patient at this time of night. Someone from the hospital must go—'

'It is not a patient, ma'am,' Amy said breathlessly, and bobbed her head politely. 'You are Mrs. Lackland, ma'am? I have heard of you from Miss Martha Lackland, though we never met before. I am Amy Lucas of Boston—'

'What do you say?' The old man's voice came thinly and very sharply and Amy looked up at him, alarmed again. She should not have come. Martha had said that this man had hated her grandmother and now she was here the thought of telling him her errand made her feel very sick, filling her with a physical fear that was very hard to control.

She swallowed and managed to say huskily, 'Amy Lucas, sir. You—we have met before. My brother was at the hospital. He broke his leg and Freddy—Mr. Caspar operated upon it with the Lister method and—'

The old man's face seemed to clear. 'That is where I have seen you before, then. At Nellie's. I thought I knew your face—' He nodded again, and moved further into the room and sat down on one of the sofas, and thrust his legs out before him, staring at her sharply from beneath bushy eyebrows.

'Well? What is it you want of me now? You need not

stand and stare at me like that—you were free enough of speech when last we met, as I recall. Maria, do go away and drink your tea! There is not need to fear I am going out to a patient, as you can see. And this young woman is clearly put off her speech by your presence. I shall be with you shortly, I daresay—'

Amy looked over her shoulder at the little woman by the door who smiled and nodded her head. 'Well, my dear, if I can be sure you will not venture out, I will gladly go away. Goodnight, Miss Lucas. I daresay we shall meet again, if you have become a friend of some of our young people—' and she went rustling away, closing the door softly behind her, and Amy wanted to run after her, to cling to her and make her stay and help her talk to this terrifying old man.

But she stood her ground and turned back to Abel Lackland and looked at him. She was here, and would have to manage as best she might. She was a heroine of a tragedy, she told herself. A heroine set on seeking mercy for her Dear Brother from a Harsh and Cruel Villain who somehow had to be softened by the sight of a Piteous Maiden in all her innocence.

But somehow the fantasy would not take hold. She could not act herself into the right mood for the performance and stood there with her hands held tightly and nervously before her, very much herself facing a very real and very alarming situation.

She had meant to do it better. She did not mean to blurt it all out. She had planned, in that bumpy hansom ride from Long Acre, to tell him in a circuitous way of Fenton's need and her own, to tell him almost casually of the fact that she had discovered they were Lilith Lucas's grandchildren, and would like to lay claim to the legacy he had spurned. But it came out all wrong. Dreadfully wrong.

'My name, sir, is Amy Lucas,' she began.

'You've told me that. Now tell me what you are here for. I've said before—I've better things to do with my time than prose with a chit of a girl barely out of the schoolroom—'

Stung, Amy retorted, 'You were not always so!'

'Hey? What does that mean?'

'*She* must have been a schoolroom chit, as you are pleased to call me too—when she was my age—yet you talked to her and cared enough for her, didn't you? And she for you, or why else would she have left you all that property?'

He was sitting very upright now and staring at her, his eyes seeming to blaze, so concentrated was his gaze.

'What did you say?' His voice now was quiet and much more frightening than it had been when he had shouted at her.

She shrank back a little, but managed to gather her courage in both hands and lifted her chin and said loudly, 'My grandmother. That is of whom I speak.'

He stared at her for another long moment and then, moving very stiffly, got to his feet and walked across the room to the door. He opened it with what was to Amy agonizing slowness and then turned back to look at her, and his face seemed to be carved out of solid rock, so harsh were the creases on it, so deep the lines from nose to mouth.

'Get out.' His voice was softer than ever and now she began to shake, for her terror was mounting fast, but she could still speak and did so, letting the words tumble out of her in a deluge.

'Well, you *did* love her, did you not? Long long ago? They told me that—and that you had started to hate her too, but that is stupid, to hate someone you have loved, for love is too important for that, and then she died and left you all her property but you don't want it—do you? You don't want it. There is that beautiful house, left to spiders and mice and dirt, rotting away for want of living in, and money and jewels besides and Fenton *needs* it so! It means *nothing* to you, nothing at all, if you can ignore it as you have, and leave it lying there and no use made of it. And Fenton—if you knew him you would understand, surely you would! It is not that we ask any sacrifice of you, is it? Just to give to Fenton and to me—though I want little, I do promise you—it is *Fenton* who has the greatest need—give it to us and be rid of it and then you can forget all about it! It will make no difference to you, after all and—'

'Get *out*!' This time his voice was loud again, and the roar of it went echoing across the hallway and somewhere up the

212

dark stairs there was a rush of footsteps as a candle's flickering light appeared and Maria's voice came floating down, 'Abel? What is it? What is happening?'

'Get her out of here—out, out, *out*!' The old man flung himself out of the room and almost ran across the hall to stand at the foot of the stairs, and reached them just as Maria appeared there, holding her candle high. '*How absurd,*' thought Amy madly. '*How funny to use candles still. Have they no gaslight here? How absurd, like the furniture, quite quite absurd—*'

'There is no need to be so angry, Abel, whatever it is,' Maria Lackland said and her voice was cool and practical and she turned to Amy and smiled in a smooth polite hostess fashion that made Amy want to laugh suddenly even in the midst of her fear. 'I hope you can come to visit again, my dear, when my husband is feeling a little better. At present I am afraid he is somewhat put about, but I am sure that—'

'If that—that *creature* does not vacate this house instantly,' Abel said, and his voice now was flat and full of barely controlled rage, 'I will not be responsible for the consequences. You hear me? I will not be responsible—'

'Of course, dear,' Maria said, and moving smoothly tucked her hand into the crook of his arm and led him up the stairs. 'Come to the drawing-room now, and we will be comfortable again. Goodnight, Miss Lucas!'

And they were gone, leaving her there in the hall below, with the old butler, who had appeared noiselessly from nowhere, holding the front door wide open, and staring up after their retreating backs. There was a sour taste in her mouth and she was filled with a huge exhaustion and also a vast anxiety. How, oh, how was she to tell Fenton what a dreadful tangle she had made of his hopes for his future?

# CHAPTER TWENTY-ONE

'It really does not matter, Amy,' Fenton said and grinned at her. 'I told you—I have my own ideas on how to make him part. I should have known you'd make a hash of it anyway—'

'That is not fair!' she snapped. 'You would have made a worse hash of it, that is certain! He is a dreadful old man, quite quite dreadful! Grandmamma must have been clean out of her attic to have left him all her money, when he is so hateful!'

'Now, there you have the truth of it!' Fenton said softly and suddenly laughed and picked her up and swung her round so that her gown billowed over her ankles and she squealed.

He set her down on the stage again as one of the other actors looked up from his card game in the wings and shouted a ribaldry and she said urgently, 'What do you mean? You are so *tiresome*, Fenton—you confuse me so that I do not know whether I am on my head or my heels! You were so crazy keen I should go to the old man last night, yet when I came back and in dire need to tell you of all that had happened, you are gone out and did not come back till all hours, and now this morning when I tell you that the answer was no, you are in such a good humour that it makes no sense!'

She was still seething about it all. To have faced the old man alone and then come back to find Fenton absent had been maddening enough. But to have him sleep so late this morning that she had perforce to go ahead of him to rehearsals and tell some lie or other to cover up for him—that was the outside of enough.

And now this good humour! She stared at him with her lips set tight and then shrugged and turned away.

'I lose all interest in you, Fenton! If you want to behave in this stupid fashion it is no concern of mine! I have done all I can for you, and all I will for you. Now you can go to the devil!'

'Such intemperate language from so charming a lady!' Wyndham's voice, full of mock disapproval, came from behind her and she turned to face him and switched on a brilliant smile.

'Mr. Wyndham! Charles—how nice to see you! I missed you at the start of rehearsals this morning!'

'How delightful to be missed by so beautiful and talented a lady!' Wyndham said and bent his head with great style to kiss her hand. 'I had business to deal with, my dear young lady, and was not required until now—which reminds me—' He looked up at Fenton with his brows raised. 'Did you find those fellows of any help, Lucas? Willing to do the office?'

'Eh? Oh, yes—sure. Great, Charles, great. Very obliged to you—ah, I think Rourke wants me—' and Fenton turned hurriedly and went away across the stage and Amy stared after him, her brows furrowed.

'What fellows, Charles?'

'I beg your pardon, Miss Amy?'

'I asked—what fellows? When Fenton behaves so, I find I am very interested. What is happening?'

'Oh, I think you must ask him, Miss Amy—it is in no way my—'

'Charles!' She looked up at him very directly. 'Will you please tell me what it is that has made Fenton behave so alarmed! Rourke did not want him, and he was put about that you asked your question in my hearing. So, will you tell me or shall I go over there to him now and make a great scene and a fuss? For I shall—make no mistake about it!'

Charles looked over his shoulder at Fenton standing with the knot of people at the side of the stage, who were talking in a desultory fashion as the last few moments of their luncheon break in rehearsals passed, and the stage manager finished setting for Act Three, the Squire's Mansion, and Amy looked too. Fenton lifted his head and seemed to Amy to give

Charles an appealing look and she said again with greater sharpness, 'What *fellows*, Charles? What is my brother up to?'

'Oh dear, I find this very difficult!'

'I am sure you do—but you will find it less difficult if you answer my question.'

She was enjoying this now, playing the determined lady enforcing her will on the adoring hero, and in a way he seemed to play back to her, revelling in the performance as much as she was. He made a face of mock despair and said softly, 'Well, if he calls me out and shoots me in a dawn duel, on your head be my bleeding corpse, Miss Amy. But I can refuse you nothing, not even your brother's guilty secrets—'

He grinned and the performance seemed to come to an abrupt end. 'Not that it is so secret after all! I know nothing except that he asked me for the names of some lawyers who were not too nice to take on a case that might cause some fuss, and so I told him of the Wormold brothers. Henry and Horace Wormold. They are known by many actors as reliable enough in any—shall we say *complicated* legal case—and although they charge damned steep fees if they win their cases, they do not dun a man who loses.'

Amy frowned. 'Lawyers? That is very odd! Why should Fenton need lawyers?'

'That you must indeed ask him, for I know no more than I have told you. He went to see them last night, that I do know, for he called at my lodgings to ask me their direction and said he would go to their private house and not wait till they were in their chambers this morning—and he is a determined man, so I daresay he did just that! But no more do I know—'

'Then I shall ask him—and no, I will not make a scene!' she said, as he put his hand out to stop her. 'None that will involve you, that is—'

'Oh, then by all means.' He grinned again. 'A little display of temperament will add some spice to these rehearsals anyway, for they are becoming damned dull. Musical melodrama has its charm, no doubt, but it rapidly palls upon me—'

But even though she was determined to get from Fenton an explanation of his odd behaviour and his interest in not-too-

216

nice lawyers, she was also every inch a professional actress, and Rourke was calling the start. So start they did, and she spent the rest of the afternoon moving through her paces, speaking her lines and building little tricks of stage business into her rather insipidly written part with all the enthusiasm she had. But at the back of her mind all the time was her worry about Fenton and what his plan might be, and she watched him whenever she could.

But not closely enough. As she went through her last scene with Charles at the end of the afternoon she saw Fenton slip away through the auditorium door and tried to go after him. He should not go home without her! But Rourke, with considerable sharpness, called her to order and after one moment of hesitation she bit her lip and returned to her scene. But she was seething with fury at Fenton, and could do little more good work that evening, and Rourke, with a snort of irritation, called the end and told them all to be on stage at nine sharp next morning.

'For we open in a week, remember, and have no time to waste! 'Tis luxury enough to have ten days of rehearsals for such a play, and well you know it, or should if you're the professionals ye all tell me ye are! We've no time to waste with nonsenses! Tell that brother o' yours, Miss Lucas, that we expect him on the stage at nine, on the dot, d'you hear? Good as he is in his lines and in his part, I'll replace him if we've any troubles—'

'I'll tell him,' Amy said grimly, and pulled her shawl about her shoulders and went hurrying out to Dean Street, quite ignoring Charles Wyndham's attempt to stop her so that he could accompany her home, and he, prudently, let her go.

Outside in the late April sunshine the street was humming with activity. Many of the Italian and Greek restaurant owners who frequented the neighbourhood were out in front of their establishments in noisily chattering and gesticulating groups, and the traffic was thick, with horses, carts and hansom cabs in a melee of hooves and clatter and swearing drivers, and Amy stood there for a moment blinking to accustom herself to the brightness after the dimness of the theatre she had left.

Fenton had quite disappeared and she stared up one side of the street and then the other, trying to pick out of the passing crowds a glimpse of his rakishly angled hat; but with no success at all and she bit her lip.

'Miss Lucas!' She turned at the sound of her name, and at the sight of him standing there, his hat in his hand and staring at her owlishly through his round glasses she bit her lip even harder. 'Mr. Lackland!'

'I came to seek you, since you did not come to see me and tell me of your plans. I am sorry you did not, though I am not surprised you were unwilling to say you were leaving my show for this.'

He looked up at the front of the Royalty with a faint lift of his lip. And she, looking up too, had to admit it looked rather seedy, and much in need of a coat of paint, quite unlike the spanking pin-neat facade of the Celia Supper Rooms.

'It will be refurbished before the show opens, I daresay,' she said defensively. 'And one does not choose one's working-places merely for—for the look of them, you know.'

He nodded and the sun glinted on his glasses so that she could not see the expression in his eyes. 'Indeed no. One chooses one's work—or it chooses *you*—from necessity. At the time you came to me, you needed the work, as I understood.'

She reddened. 'Yes, we did. We were grateful to be able to earn our living. I do not deny that.'

'Then you will agree that you have behaved less than—well, shall we say you and your brother have shown little appreciation of that gratitude in leaving me so abruptly? It is not easy for a show to recover from the loss of two of its leading performers with so little notice. I did not think I had treated you so unkindly that I deserved such recompense.'

'Oh dear,' she said and looked at him miserably, quite filled with compunction. 'I did not think, I suppose—I was so angry, you see, with your family, and then—then this business of my grandmother, and Felix and all—I suppose I did not think.'

He smiled at her suddenly and his face lifted giving him that much more youthful look she had seen once before and his eyes behind his glasses were friendly and warm; and she felt worse than ever.

'Well, as long as there was no malice towards me and my establishment in your defection, I daresay I shall recover—'

'Oh, no malice, none at all,' she said hastily. 'How could there be? We are related, after all!'

He looked at her for a long moment and she stared back at him, standing there in the busy street with heedless passers-by pushing and eddying past them and now his eyes seemed to look bleak and lonely.

'Yes, I know. We are related. I am sorry about that.'

'Oh?' She was nonplussed.

'Sorry if it means I cannot speak to you as—in any other way than as a relation. I had entertained hopes that I might speak to you in different terms. One day!'

She felt it all suddenly. Felt the weight of his emotion and his distress and his yearning need for her. She had been loved by many men over the years, had had hearts and hands and fortunes piled at her feet, and had been able to laugh and walk away. But now, feeling as she did about Felix, she knew what pain love could be, and shook her head violently and said, 'No!—no, you must not speak so. You must not *feel* so! I did not ask for such emotion from you, and you shall not blame me for it!'

'I do not *blame* you,' he said mildly. 'How could I blame you for being as you are? How can anyone speak of blame in such a matter? You are beautiful and—and exciting in a way I have never known any woman to be. Can that be a fault in you? Or can it be a fault in me if I see you and feel attachment as a result?'

'But I did not ask it!' She almost wailed. 'I ask no more than that I do my work and have Felix and see Fenton happy—oh, dear, it is all so—such a *muddle*! I came out to seek Fenton and see what it is he is up to, and instead I see you standing here in the street about to make a declaration and—'

'You go faster than I, Miss Lucas. I was not aware I was about to make any declaration of any kind. I said only that I regretted that—'

'Oh, I know!' Her compunction was displaced now by irritation. He had a certain likableness about him, this solid sombre man, but he was so prosy and so precise and so dull

219

that being kind to him was very difficult. 'I *know* what you said. And what you were about to say. I am no schoolroom baby, you know! But that is not my fault! No, do not start again—let me just say that I am sorry you feel—whatever it is you feel, if it causes you pain. I am sorry we left your show so hugger-mugger, but there were reasons, you know and—well, I am *sorry*. It was wrong of us. But now I am much more anxious about Fenton and what he is doing and I cannot concentrate as I should on what it is I should say to you, so you must forgive me. I must find him, you see, before he does something that—well, I don't know what, but I feel anxious.'

' "But thou wouldst not think how ill all's here about my heart—" ' Oliver said and smiled again. 'You see? I can quote from the legitimate theatre with the best, despite my singing and dancing shows! But remember how it goes on—"we defy augury—" '

'Hamlet,' Amy said and then shook her head with some exasperation. 'I must look for Fenton! I cannot stand here prosing, Mr. Lackland, I really cannot! I must find Fenton and see what it is he is about—'

'Before you go—I must ask you how matters stand with you and my family.'

She had turned away from him but stopped now and turned her head to look at him again.

'I need to know,' he said, almost apologetically. 'I must not make any declarations, Miss Amy, and I know that now. I saw you with Felix—well, let be. But I should like to know that we—that I will see you again. See you a great deal, in fact. To call you cousin will be small recompense for the loss of my hopes, but it will better than nothing—'

She smiled then at his earnest face and blinking round eyes behind those absurd spectacles. For all his prosiness and dullness there was a charm about him. 'I hope, Mr. Lackland—Cousin Oliver—to be very much a part of your family. A happy part. I am to wed Felix, you see, and be a true cousin in every way! And I have promised Miss Lackland, your aunt, that I shall make no further problems regarding my grandmother by speaking of her. We shall forget all about her, and pretend that we have never heard of her! I know she lived

220

and was a great actress here in London, and that knowledge warms me. But now it is the future that matters and not the past and I shall speak of no more bygone sadnesses. There! Is that enough to please you? Can I be forgiven for behaving so badly as regards your show?'

'Of course you can,' he said huskily and coughed and took out a large white handkerchief and blew his nose loudly. 'Of course you can. I shall look forward to seeing you again soon, then. At Aunt Martha's perhaps, on Sunday?'

'Oh, yes! Yes—I am sure that will be most agreeable!' she said brightly and turned away again. 'And now I must seek Fenton! Do forgive me! But I am most concerned about him, truly I am!'

He watched her go away down the busy pavements of Dean Street and made no move to follow her. It seemed to him that she was taking with her in her billowing yellow skirts and bobbing flower-trimmed bonnet all hopes he had ever had of domestic felicity. She had been the first girl he had ever seen whom he had loved, and knowing his own nature as well as he did, he knew there would never be any other. And knew also that for all his prosaic surface appearance he was at his deepest depths a great romantic. If he could not wed for love, he would not wed at all. And as Amy Lucas's figure disappeared in the crowds he wrapped his bachelorhood about him, and put his hat on his head and turned and walked sedately back to his Supper Rooms.

And Amy hurried all the way back to Long Acre on foot, looking eagerly for Fenton's familiar figure all the way, and arrived breathless and somewhat irritable to find he wasn't there either. And tried to comfort herself with the thought that she had at least repaired matters as far as Oliver Lackland was concerned. She had repeated the promise made to Martha that there would be no more problems regarding Lilith Lucas, and that made her feel somehow better, as though she had paid for her own and Fenton's unprofessional behaviour in marching so insouciantly out of Oliver's show. Whatever it was that Fenton was up to now, she told herself, he could do no harm to this new family harmony. That was something to be glad of, at least.

'Well, there you have it in a nutshell, gentlemen!' Fenton leaned back in the rather rickety armchair and crossed his legs. 'Are you interested in taking on such a case?'

'Interested?' said Horace Wormold. 'I'd say we were interested, wouldn't you agree, Henry?'

'Indeed I would—' Henry nodded and beamed, his round cheerful face seeming to shine with soap and good fellowship and virtue. 'I will tell you the truth, Mr. Lucas. We are interested in any case that looks to bring with it sufficient to bring us plenty of *solid* interest!' and he laughed heartily at his own joke. 'Solid interest, yes. Solid in sovereigns, eh?'

'This one could. If you can bring it off,' Fenton said. 'Have you adequate experience in such cases?'

Again Henry Wormold laughed his fat happy laugh. 'Experience? Plenty. Believe me, Mr. Lucas, this Will is as good as upset already! If we don't get it on insanity, then we get it on undue influence! Either way, believe me, either way.'

'You'll remember our share, Mr. Lucas,' Horace said sharply. 'A forty-sixty division exclusive of costs. Those are the terms.'

Fenton stood up. 'On the grounds that I'd rather have sixty per cent of something than a hundred per cent of nothing, you're on, gentlemen. But make damned sure you bring in a winner first past the post, on account of I tell you not a penny piece do I have to fly with if you lose.'

'We won't,' Henry Wormold said and laughed again. 'Can't afford to! Good afternoon, Mr. Lucas! We'll talk again in two weeks. We'll have got our hands on the documents by then. And done a bit of ground-laying too, I daresay. Good afternoon!'

# CHAPTER TWENTY-TWO

'And when does your new play start, Amy? I had heard, on the grapevine, you know, that the first night has been delayed.'

Amy looked up at Oliver absently. 'What? Oh—yes. Indeed it has. Mr. Rourke has been able to obtain greater backing money, and now wishes to improve the scenery and curtains.' She smiled then, a little maliciously. 'And to repaint the front of the house as well.'

'Then he is very wise,' Oliver said. 'A theatre which looks in the least shabby deters patrons from entering, however well-spoken of the performances may be. Will you take more tea?'

'Thank you—I should indeed like some more.' Amy was watching the door as covertly as she could. She had been there for an hour and a half already and the entire family had gathered, and yet still there was no sign of him. And she took her tea from Oliver's careful hand and sighed softly and looked resolutely about the room, refusing to allow herself to look at the door any more.

Across the drawing-room beside the fire where sea coal burned cheerfully, even on this May afternoon, Felix was sitting beside Abby who was talking to him very earnestly indeed over her plateful of sandwiches, and he caught Amy's eye and gave her the ghost of a smile, and it was as though he had reached across the room and touched her hand warmly and comfortingly. 'He will come,' his glance seemed to say. 'Do not worry—he will come, and if he does not, then I will deal with him for you.'

'Has the play been changed very much since it went into rehearsal, Amy?' It was Phoebe who was speaking now, and Amy turned her attention back to the company amongst whom she was sitting. *It was quite absurd, she thought somewhere deep in her mind, that I should sit here so willingly among dull relations. In Boston when they tried to make me behave so I did all I could to escape. Yet here I sit, even enjoying it in a way and wanting only Fenton here to complete my happiness. It is very strange.*

'A good deal, indeed, Cousin Phoebe,' she said, and shook her head smilingly as small James offered her a plate of maids-of-honour cakes. The child had developed a distinct tendre for this pretty newcomer to his family's Sunday afternoons, and attended her assiduously and offered her food continually. But her patience had not been exhausted yet, and James watched her unwaveringly, his nine-year-old eyes wide and worshipping.

'The play is not precisely a work of great literature, you must understand,' Amy said. 'Indeed it is a sorry melodrama! But with some imagination in the direction and some songs and dances added, it is becoming more and more entertaining. Mr. Rourke has a very rich imagination and Charles Wyndham is turning out to be a remarkably fine dancer.'

Phoebe raised her eyebrows a trifle, watching the girl beside her over the rim of her teacup. 'Songs and dances, Amy? Dear me! And I thought that was what you objected to in my brother's show, and was the reason for your departure!'

Amy reddened. 'I am sorry about that. I have already said—'

'Cousin Phoebe, are you well?' Felix's voice came from behind them in a lazy drawl and Amy looked up at him with huge gratitude. 'I have not spoken to you all afternoon—tell me all your news. How are Cecily's pianoforte lessons progressing? And Young James here—can he construe his Latin Verbs as he should?'

Phoebe was diverted at once. For all her interest in the theatre and her enjoyment of a little malice there was nothing she liked more than talking of her children and their prowess at everything they did, and she launched herself into an account of her trio's doings and sayings while Felix listened with his face looking as friendly as it always did, though Amy knew that behind that facade his thoughts were quite elsewhere.

As were her own, and almost against her will she let her gaze drift back to the door. It stood there solid and uncompromisingly shut against the dark-papered wall, its velvet curtain looped across it, and she willed it to open and allow Fenton to come in. And then grimaced at her own silliness, and let her gaze drift further.

On the sofa in one of the window embrasures Isabel Henriques was sitting with her head bent as Freddy rumbled on and on about something, and looking at her Amy felt a sudden twinge of emotion she could not quite recognize. It was disagreeable and she frowned for a moment, trying to place it, and then stood up in a rustle of silk—for she was wearing her new turquoise blue gown and knew how delightful she looked in it—and moved away, after a brief smile at Felix and Phoebe, towards the sofa. To be jealous of this girl was absurd; she would not wish to stand in the way of Fenton's happiness, ever, and if this was the girl he cared for and had chosen to be his own, then it was proper for Amy to know her and understand her, not to resent her. And she moved slowly and apparently casually towards the other girl.

Freddy was on his feet by the time she got there. 'Good afternoon, Amy! It is good to see you! I am sorry not to have spoken to you more this afternoon, but there—you know how it is here at Aunt Martha's on Sundays!'

'I am beginning to,' Amy said and smiled at Isabel with her eyes wide and friendly. 'Good afternoon, Isabel! I do like your gown—that shade of green suits you perfectly! Do tell me—did you go to one of the town modistes or have you a private dressmaker of your own?'

'If you girls are going to talk clothes, I shall go and talk sense with your Felix, Amy. Fripperies make no sort of conversation for a surgeon!'

'They are talking about your children, cousin,' Amy said. 'James's Latin and Cecily's pianoforte, you know! Almost as dull for you as fripperies, I imagine.'

Freddy laughed. 'Far from it! I am every inch the paterfamilias, Amy, as you will discover when you are even longer in this family. I like nothing better than to hear my children praised—even by their besotted Mamma!'

As he moved away Amy hesitated, for Isabel was looking down at her hands clasped on her lap and seemed to be offering no sort of welcome, but after a moment she sat down anyway, settling her blue flounces neatly beside the rich green ones of her companion.

There was a brief silence and then Amy said softly, 'May I speak to you of personal matters, Isabel?'

The other girl looked up at her, her eyes dark and lustrous but seeming somehow to be flat and dead in their depths.

'Your own personal matters, Amy? But of course! We all know you are to wed Felix and wish you much joy.'

'That is kind of you. But no, I did not mean that. Although talking of Felix gives me great delight, naturally.'

'I am sure it does,' Isabel said politely and Amy looked at her consideringly. There seemed to be a guardedness about this girl that did not match her pleasant expression and she gave a small sigh and tried to think what she should do. To plunge directly into talk of Fenton could be disastrous, if in fact Isabel had complicated feelings about him. Amy would not for the world do anything that might upset the balance of her brother's relationship with this handsome but quiet girl; and there was also a healthy selfishness in her tenderness for Fenton's interests, for she knew better than anyone how painful Fenton's rage could be when he was crossed. So she sat and thought for a moment and then said carefully, 'It is very delightful, Isabel, to know that one has found the man with whom one knows the rest of a happy life will be spent.'

'I am sure it is.' Isabel looked up at her, her eyes wide and limpid and quite uncommunicative, and feeling some exasperation, Amy tried again, keeping her voice as easy and light as she could. 'Have you never wished to be in such a situation, Isabel?'

'What a strange question! Why should I?'

'Oh, not strange at all!' said Amy. 'I ask only because I used to feel such a yearning to be in the position in which I now find myself that I assumed it was one shared by other young ladies—' Amy was most amused at her own mendacity; she who had sailed so insouciantly through so many male conquests and who would have hated above all things the idea that she had met the one man she ever wished to love, to speak so! It was absurd.

'As for other young ladies, I cannot say,' Isabel said. 'I know only of my own desires and interests. Will you take some more tea, Amy?'

'No thank you—do tell me then—of what it is that you most dream when you think of the future and what it may hold?'

Isabel smiled sweetly. 'I do not dream at all, Amy. I have much too busy a life to permit it, and any way Papa and Mamma would, I am sure, be most put out by a daughter who wasted time dreaming! It is not in their style of living at all!'

Amy stared at her, baffled. Such verbal fencing was the last thing she had expected from this quiet girl, and for a moment she wanted to shake her and shout at her and make her lose that infuriatingly calm exterior. Inside somewhere there were great fires of some sort burning, of that she was certain. This was no insipid English girl with an empty head and an emptier heart. This was a woman with real emotion in her, but clearly it was so battened down and so controlled that no hint of any of it would ever get out without her full intent. No wonder Fenton was finding life so difficult, having fallen in love with this sphinx-like creature.

And for a moment, Amy could have laughed aloud, trying to imagine her mercurial, selfish Fenton, so responsive to his own least whim, coping with the quiet steeliness that Isabel was now presenting. And then sighed and said, 'Perhaps I will have some more tea, after all.'

At which for the first time Isabel smiled widely and seemed to melt and said almost merrily, 'Talking is thirsty work, indeed! I shall bring you some myself?' and stood up and went rustling away to the fireside where Martha sat ensconced before her handsome silver tea equipment.

And Amy watched her go, a puzzled line between her brows, and wished heartily that she did not love her brother so dearly, nor care so much for his welfare. Life would be so agreeable just at present if she did not; there was Felix and the love they shared, and the happy way in which the family had seemed to accept the announcement of their betrothal (although Phoebe had produced one or two waspish comments, on the whole Amy had felt a genuine warmth in her welcome by them all) and her play was going well. Felix had agreed to say no more at present about whether or not she should go on with a career as an actress now she was to be his wife, and seemed as interested as she was herself in gossip about the day's rehearsals and chatter about scene design and music and dance arrangements. With all that to fill her thoughts, she had no need of Fenton and his tiresome mysteriousness, for he had flatly refused to tell her who 'those fellows' of whom Wyndham had spoken might be, and what he was doing with them, only laughing at her questions and footstamping anger; and she had had to settle at that.

But she had indeed been anxious, for he was behaving so strangely. His mood of gloom, which had been so apparent when he first spoke of his love for Isabel, was quite gone, and he seemed filled with a sort of bouncing anticipation which at first she had put down to his excitement over the play, but now knew came from other sources, for he showed less and less real interest in rehearsals, playing entirely on technique and with no real emotional involvement. He was clearly 'up to something' as their mother had been used to saying, Amy told herself—but quite what, she did not know. And worry about it lay deep beneath her happy daily busyness like a cold stream.

It was as Isabel came back to her with a cup of tea that at last the door opened and Fenton came in, and there was a small rustle in the room as people looked up and conversations faltered, and he stood there framed in the doorway, his hat in one hand, the other hand thrust negligently into his trouser pocket, smiling lazily around at them. And his eyes were so flaming with mischief and laughter that he looked even more exquisitely handsome than he usually did, and Amy's heart sank. She knew that look, and it spelled trouble.

She looked up at Isabel then, who was still standing beside her, and tried to see some expression in her eyes, but the other girl's face remained as smooth and as bland and as uncommunicative as ever. If only, Amy thought savagely, other people had speaking countenances—it was so *unfair* that some people could be so reserved and secretive.

228

'Well, it is good to see you, Fenton!' Felix said just in time to prevent the silence that had greeted the opening of the door from becoming embarrassing. 'We missed you—'

'I am so sorry to arrive so late, Felix—and Miss Lackland—' and he sketched a bow in Martha's general direction. 'But I had business to deal with. Urgent business.'

'On a Sunday?' Phoebe said artlessly, but with an edge to her voice. 'How strange! I know of no urgent business that is ever transacted on Sundays!'

'Medical business sometimes, my dear,' Freddy murmured and Amy looked at him sharply, recognizing that he, like her, was feeling uneasy. There was a disturbance in the room which seemed to be eddying about them all, and she opened her mouth to say something cheerful and amusing to break the strain. But she was too late, for Fenton was saying smoothly, 'And legal business. Sometimes!'

'Legal business? What is legal business?' It was small James who was speaking now, standing in front of Fenton and staring up at him, and his treble tones seemed to go through the room like a bell. 'Please to tell me what is legal business?'

Fenton looked down at him and smiled and tossed his hat nonchalantly on to a chair and bent and picked the child up, swinging him high. 'Legal business, my child, is interesting business! It is to do with money and Wills and that sort of thing!'

Amy felt rather than saw Martha stiffen and turned her own head awkwardly to look appealingly at Fenton, who caught her glance but let his own eyes slide away. He was still tossing James in the air, who was squealing with delight.

'Money and Wills and legatees! Money and Wills and legatees!' he chanted and the child laughed again, as the room sank into an expectant silence.

'Fenton!' Amy was on her feet now and staring at him. 'Fenton, I *will* be told! I will not have this—this—what are you talking about?'

'Why, Amy, my little love, how are *you* this afternoon?' Fenton set James on his feet and smiled easily at Amy. 'I did not see you there—'

'Fenton!' She almost shouted it. 'What are you talking

229

about? Why are you so—so sleek and self-satisfied? You look like the cat that stole the cream!'

'Oh, I have stolen nothing! Nothing at all!' He opened his eyes wide with mock innocence. 'Quite the reverse, I promise you. I have been stolen *from*. And you, my dear, and you!'

'I? Stolen from?' Her lips felt stiff suddenly. The premonition of trouble which had so filled her a couple of weeks ago when Wyndham had first spoken of 'those fellows' and which had since become fainter, suddenly flared up so that she felt sick for a moment. 'No one has stolen anything from me!'

'Oh, indeed they have, indeed they have,' Fenton drawled. 'But your loving brother is going to put it all right, every bit—'

'I really don't know what all this is about,' Gideon Henriques said suddenly. He had been sitting in a deep chair on the other side of the fireplace dozing, and now got to his feet and stood, tall and thin, straddling the hearth-rug. 'Am I being stupid? I am not usually so. I do not understand this conversation yet everyone else appears to be listening to it. Will someone explain? I think perhaps I fell asleep—' and he smiled so that his cheeks cut themselves into long crevasses.

'I will explain, Mr. Henriques!' Fenton said and his voice was now silky and yet full of cold anger. 'I will tell you! I have discovered that my sister and I have been sorely misused. And by whom, you may ask? That is the question *I* had to ask, and the answer I have obtained has made me very, very sad. It will make you sad too, Mr. Henriques, because, you see, the people who have taken from my sister and from me our rightful dues are members of your own family.'

Gideon stared at him for a moment and then shook his head. 'I must have been asleep for longer than I realized,' he said petulantly. 'I don't understand a word of it. Will someone explain?'

'I think Mr. Lucas had best explain his own words, Gideon,' Freddy said in a quiet voice and stepped forwards, his hand on Phoebe's shoulder and his eyes fixed watchfully on Fenton's face. 'Immediately!'

Fenton was still beside the door, and now leaned against the jamb with both hands set insolently in his pockets. His chin was up and his hair flopped on his brow in a most beguiling way, and again Amy looked up at Isabel. But she stood there silent and very still, showing no hint of emotion of any kind.

'Well, gentlemen, and of course, ladies, I guess I'd better tell you all I've discovered. It'll come as no news to *you* of course, though it will to my poor sister, I think.'

Again his eyes flicked over Amy, refusing to lock into her direct gaze. 'The facts are, little sister, that while we are living in penury, scratching our living as best we can, a large fortune which is ours by right has been filched from us. It is not too strong a word I think, filched—'

'You had best watch your tongue, Lucas,' Freddy said sharply, but Fenton just smiled at him and went on cheerfully as though he were talking of nothing more interesting than the weather.

'Well, we discovered all this by accident. It seems that our grandmamma, Lilith Lucas, died exceedingly rich in strange circumstances, sad to say, in the middle of a war. She was in Constantinople. Imagine that—so far away from home and family, and dying! A piteous state to be in, indeed! And then what happens? Why, along come two people to *help* her make her Will—and who should benefit most by the terms of that will? Why, a close relation of one of the helpers. Who, mark you, later on increased her involvement with the whole affair by adopting the son of the other helper, after he died. I find it all a *very* strange circumstance—'

There was an icy silence and Amy tried to turn her head to look at Martha, wanted to run to her, to tell her that she had indeed meant to keep her promise never to mention Lilith Lucas again, that she did not know why Fenton was being so dreadful and making such hateful—

'Well, there you are!' Fenton said and his tone was all sweet reasonableness. 'What would *you* do in my shoes if you discovered such a thing? Why, exactly what I did do, I am sure! I went to my lawyers. Splendid people they are, splendid. Quite indignant about the injustice that has been perpetrated, and ready to fight in every court in the land for justice to be done!'

'Fenton,' Amy's voice seemed to croak in her own ears. 'Fenton, what have you done?'

'What have I done, my dear? Why, set out to improve your

future comfort, dear sister! I have filed a case which will be heard at Doctors' Commons in Westminster Hall. I am contesting the Will made by Lilith Lucas on the grounds of undue influence by the witnesses. I have every hope that there will not be too great a delay before the matter comes before the judge.'

His glance slipped easily about the room, from Felix's white face to Martha's rigid stillness and from the expression of cold horror on Phoebe's face to Gideon's blank amazement. But not once did he look at Amy. Or at Isabel.

## CHAPTER TWENTY-THREE

'She is a bad girl, Felix! You cannot make me believe that she did not know perfectly well what her brother was about, and indeed egged him on with his plan! That you should be so—so beguiled by such a one—it is that which causes me most distress, not this nonsense about the Lucas woman's Will!'

Martha was standing with her back to the dying fire, staring across the room at Felix with her head up and her face very white. Even as the words came tumbling out of her she regretted them; she was not even sure she believed what she was saying. But still they came, words full of rage and hurt and misery.

'She is a fortune-hunter—came here from nowhere, from some gutter or other, and set out to captivate you by what means she could, and all to get her hands on whatever she could by any means she found. She has no conscience, no morals, no feeling, no—'

'Martha! I know you are upset, and I make allowances for

it.' Felix too looked tight and strained and there was a white line round his mouth, but his control was absolute and his words came as quietly clipped as they ever did. 'You have suffered considerable embarrassment because of Fenton's inexcusable behaviour. I share your anger with him, and I will be doing all I can to deal with him. But however you or I may feel about Fenton, that does not excuse your hurling such unjust accusations at Amy. She did not know what he was planning, of that I am certain, and the promise she made to you about not speaking of her grandmother was one she had every intention of keeping. Indeed, has kept. It is her *brother*, not she, who has caused all this brouhaha.'

'So you say! But how can you *know*? Who is she? What is she? Where does she come from? How can you be so certain of her veracity? You have seen the misery she and this brother of hers have caused to this family. They must be cut from the same piece of cloth—how could it be otherwise? Yet you defend her against me, against us—'

'I will tell you who she is, and what she is and where she comes from,' Felix's voice was quieter than ever but the ice in it crackled in her ears. 'She is Miss Amy Lucas of Boston. In due course she will be Mrs. Felix Laurence of London, the wife of my choice, the woman I love above all others. As for *what* she is—she is at heart good and loving and full of intelligence and kindness. Yes, she has faults. So have I and so have you. Her faults may seem large to you since she has an exotic quality about her, coming as she does from another country. But none of that gives you licence to so abuse her. I love her and know her and I tell you from my love and knowledge that she is *good*. She has *not* brought this distress on your head. And if you cannot believe me and trust what I say about the woman I love then the years we have spent together have been a lie. I thought you loved me and cared for me as your son. If you truly did, then you could not give voice to such ideas as you have here this evening. I said before and I say again, I make allowances for your distress. But stop now and think—and take back what you said about Amy. You must.'

'Must? Why must I? Why *should* I?'

There was a silence and then he said with a note of real

sadness in his voice, 'Because of me. Because of the love you say you have always borne me. For if you do not take back your words, I must reject you, as you have rejected her. There is nothing else I could do—'

'You are asking me to choose? Between you and her?'

'No! I am asking you to allow your own good sense and loving nature to have sway over your present natural distress. Oh, Martha, you are usually a kind and good woman! Do not behave like—like some *ordinary* female who cannot think, but always allows her stronger, baser feelings to rule her life! Use your common sense. Amy is not to blame for this debâcle— her brother is!'

Again there was a silence as she tried, very hard, to allow the wisdom of his words to enter into the maelstrom of feeling which now filled her. At a deep level she knew he was right. Amy had been as distressed as anyone else at Fenton's announcement. In the stormy quarter-hour which had followed it, in which many cruel and abusive words had been spoken by everyone in the Bedford Row drawing-room, her voice had been as loud in condemnation as anyone's. Fenton had stood there, laughing at them all, even mocking them a little, and Amy had made it clear that she stood on the side of her betrothed's family. She had wept and been almost inconsolable, and Felix had had to take her back to Long Acre in a cab as the afternoon had broken up in a tangle of tears and loud words and children crying at the unexpectedness of all this adult emotion.

But all the time he had been away from her, while she tried to restore some semblance of order to her thinking, the feeling had been there, rising and simmering and eventually boiling up into the tide of furious words with which she had greeted him on his return. Jealousy. The hateful emotion with which she had been plagued all her life, and yet which she usually managed to control, took hold of her and washed over her in great sickening waves.

And even now, as she stood there staring at him and trying to push the feelings away, even now though she knew how much she had to lose in giving way, she could not succeed.

'You *are* asking me to choose! You are telling me that unless I do take her and her hateful brother, unless I believe her

234

and trust her as you do, that you will reject me! Well, if I must make such a choice then I must—and I tell you she is wicked and cruel and—and *bad*. She set out to ensnare you and steal you away from me, and she has done it, and I hate her, I hate her—'

He shook his head and his face seemed to be infinitely sad rather than angry; but his tones were clipped and cold.

'If that is your decision, Martha, then there is no more I can say. I hope you will think better of it, eventually. You know where to find me if you wish to. Good-bye.' He took his hat and coat from the chair upon which he had thrown them on his return and went to the door.

'What do you mean—I know where to find you? You live here!'

He shook his head. 'No. I cannot live here any longer. I shall move into the hospital. They will find a set of chambers for me, I daresay. I regret that our—happy years should end like this, Martha. But you know how to mend matters.' He paused again, his hand on the doorknob, and looked at her very directly.

'I must tell you that it will be you who will do the mending. I will never step towards you again, until you make the move towards me. And Amy. We are now an indissoluble pair. Somehow you must learn to understand that.'

And he was gone, leaving her alone in her quiet drawing-room staring at a closed door.


'Oliver! Have you taken leave of your senses altogether? How can you possibly think that—'

'It is very easy, Phoebe, and if you will stop speaking and start listening then perhaps you will understand.'

'I understand well enough!' Phoebe said vigorously. 'That wretched female has addled your brains, that is what I understand. I saw the way you ogled her the first time you saw her at my house—and bitterly do I regret the day I agreed to entertain such a scapegrace pair of ne'er-do-wells—and I need little more to—'

'If you cannot contain your tongue better than that, Phoebe, then there is no more to be said. And anyway, keep your voice down. Do remember that we are among my servants here and I would not wish them to hear one jot of business that does not concern them! They are avid enough with curiosity as it is.'

Phoebe looked up and saw an alert waiter ostensibly cleaning silver at a table on the far side of the big room in readiness for the customers who would come when the Supper Rooms opened its doors in a couple of hours' time and obediently dropped her voice. 'Well, why ask me to come here to talk to you if it is all so private? You could have come to my house, for heaven's sake, and—'

'I have no time to pay visits like that. I wished to speak to you, yes, and since you, I believe, have far more leisure than I enjoy, I saw no harm in asking you to come to me. After all, Phoebe, allow me to remind you that although you enjoy a half share in the profits of the Supper Rooms, I do all the work here! It is little enough I ask of you, after all. And anyway, it is the end of the month and the books are ready for your perusal.'

'Oh, as to that, pooh!' Phoebe said, but her voice was less sharp and she smoothed her gloves carefully on her brown silk taffeta lap with an air of great nonchalance. She was looking particularly fetching this afternoon in her newest gown and summer pelisse, trimmed with feathers, and well she knew it. She had come to the Supper Rooms from a visit to her milliner, where she had been quite shocked by the size of the bill she had allowed to run up; indeed she had considered, as the carriage had brought her from the elegance of Belgravia to the bustle of Covent Garden, the possibility of asking Oliver for some extra money; Freddy was a loving, even uxorious husband, but he was also a careful one as far as money was concerned and could be very acid when she exceeded her allowance. And money at the moment was tight in her purse, and it would be agreeable to have access to more. But even so—she shook her head again, quite determinedly.

'No, Oliver. You are wrong. I cannot see that there is any sense in espousing this nonsensical cause. Just think what it will do to the family! There will be such trouble and such—well! Look at what happened at Aunt Martha's yesterday! Was that not enough?'

Oliver was leaning back in his chair, staring down at his

fingers tapping on the table. Ever since last night his mind had been in a turmoil, and even now he was not sure quite where his thinking was leading him. So he spoke slowly, trying to organize his mind as he went along.

'I can quite see that the family is annoyed. Grandfather Abel's family that is—'

Phoebe stared at him. 'How do you mean, Grandfather Abel's? That is us—all of us—'

'Indeed it is—but we, you and I, we are different, are we not? We had another grandparent. In addition to Abel. The same one as Amy and her brother. We too, remember, are the grandchildren of Lilith Lucas.'

'And from all accounts that is not something we need to be especially proud of!'

'Aye, indeed, so we have heard, when the matter has been broached at all, from Aunt Abby and Aunt Martha. But you must remember that they are Abel's daughters. Are they not? They would not be likely to be sympathetic towards anyone he—disapproved of.'

He stopped and looked up at her and took off his glasses with that familiar gesture of his and began to polish the lenses as he peered at her and he looked naked and very vulnerable suddenly. 'Phoebe, do you remember your mother?'

She frowned and then shook her head. 'I do not know,' she said shortly. 'I recall only living with Aunt Abby and Uncle Gideon. They gave us a good and happy home and—'

'I know all that. I asked only if you had any memory of—before.' His eyes seemed shadowed suddenly. 'I am but two years your senior, Phoebe, but I seem to recall so much more. I remember Papa—'

'Yes,' Phoebe said quietly. 'I remember Papa. Of course. Poor dear Papa—'

'And Mamma.'

Phoebe stiffened and then shook her head.

'She was very beautiful,' Oliver said. 'She had dark hair, curly, you know, and grey eyes. She was not unlike Amy to look at—'

'There you go again! I tell you, that girl is trouble! You create nothing but misery if you allow her to beguile you any more than she has already! Isn't it bad enough she has ensnared poor Felix? Aunt Martha must be—well, I can only imagine how distressed she must be, poor dear! And now you—'

'Mamma was Lilith Lucas's daughter, Phoebe. That is the point I am trying to make—'

'I know you are. And I do not wish to pay any attention to you. I am not interested in any part of it. We have enough money, surely! You are making a good income from the Supper Rooms, and—'

'Indeed I am. But are you? I daresay you will be seeking more money from me soon enough—you usually do at this point of the month! Freddy is a careful man, for all his wealth and—'

She stood up in a sussuration of taffeta and with great determination drew on her gloves.

'No! I will not hear of it! If this Fenton Lucas wishes to create such a scandal by suing over this Will, that is his affair. But if you attempt to join in on his side, why, Oliver, you will be mad! And alone, for I will never speak to you again, and that I promise you! And nor would anyone else in the family.'

'Would they not?' Oliver said and blinked up at her. 'Well that is possible. But our other cousins would. Amy and Fenton—'

'You're a fool!' Phoebe said and her voice was so scathing that the waiter looked up, unable to hide his curiosity any longer, and Oliver frowned sharply. 'Yes, you are. A *fool*. Do you think that—that *female* will be interested in you any more than she is simply because you join in their squalid grubbing for money to which they have no right? No, do not argue with me! Money to which they have no right! Any more than you or I have. Grandmother she may have been but we did not know her, and she left her money elsewhere. It is not any concern of ours!'

He smiled then, a thin little smile which looked odd on his stolid features. 'Of course, it is all right for *you*, is it not, Phoebe? When Abel dies no doubt his money will come down in due course to his favourite grandson, Freddy. Your husband. It is all right for you—'

She shook her head at him, speechless with rage, and then

turned and swiftly wove her way through the tables towards the curtained door which led out into King Street. 'I have told you my views, Oliver!' she said in ringing tones. 'I have no more to add to them. You ally yourself with these—these *creatures* and I for one will never ever speak to you again! It is in your own hands!'

'Oh, Isabel, do not be so stuffy! You know quite well what I mean! Connections of the family, then.'

'I will not talk about it further. Have you the music for the new Strauss waltz? If we practise it now we may have it ready in time for next week's party at the Montefiores—'

'Oh, I do not want to practise silly waltzes! I want to talk about Fenton and—Isabel—where are you going? Isabel!—oh, Isabel, you are tiresome!—do come back!'

'I can only tell you what he has told me to tell you, Freddy. Come, you know better than to expect more!'

Maria smiled at him with great tranquillity and bent her head again to her needlework. She was making a drawn-thread firescreen for Phoebe and quite obviously considered this of much greater importance than any fuss about a Will. Freddy sighed a little impatiently.

'Dearest Grandmamma Maria—I do not wish to fuss you, nor do I wish you to make any troubles with my grand-father—but something has to be done! He cannot go on pretending that this is none of his business and refuse to admit he is involved. It is quite absurd.'

Patiently Maria put down her sewing again. 'I have tried to explain to you, Freddy. This is a subject upon which he will not be drawn. If it were merely that he lost his temper and shouted and stamped when I tried to discuss the matter, that would not perturb me in the least. I am accustomed to behaviour such as that—' Her lips curled reminiscently. 'In—the twenty-seven years we have been wed, my dear boy, I can promise you there have been many occasions when I have had such set-to's with him. And usually won my point, if it was a good one. If it was not, then of course—however, the case here is quite different. He will not talk at all about anything to do with Lilith Lucas or her Will. He becomes like—like an oyster if I even mention the matter. It is as much use talking to him about it as talking to the wall. This is why I tell you there is nothing to be done. He told me only to bid you to mind your own affairs, and pay no heed to any of his. And that is the start, the finish and the whole of his message. And now, my love, talk to me of other matters. The children—'

'Oh, they are very well—' He stopped and stared at her, pulling at his lower lip in a way he had when anxious. 'I suppose I could talk to his lawyers—Vivian and Onions—'

'I suppose you could, dear,' Maria said equably and bent her head once more over her sewing. 'I daresay that will make you feel a little better. It will not make any difference, however. Tell me, do you like this stitch? Just here? It is a new one I have invented and venture to congratulate myself upon its intricacy. Do you think Phoebe will admire it? I do hope so—'

It had been a long time since the Caspars and the Lacklands and the Henriques had been so disturbed. And so remote from each other. For the first time in many years, Martha took her tea alone on Sunday afternoon.

# CHAPTER TWENTY-FOUR

'Black-Ey'd Susan' opened on 9th June 1867 at nine in the evening.

It had been raining heavily all day, much to Rourke's chagrin though not to his surprise, for the summer had been wet throughout and bade fair to remain so. At first he and the entire company had been afraid that the rain would badly affect business. If the weather were too inclement then the audience would prefer to remain dryshod at home, and in a business which relied more heavily on word of mouth recommendation than on puffs in the daily newspapers a sparsely attended first night could be disastrous.

But the rain cleared for an hour or so after eight o'clock, and the audience came. They filled the newly painted Royalty with a hubbub of chatter and new clothes and bibulous laughter, and their good humour seeped from the auditorium through the heavy red rep curtains to the stage beyond.

Amy, sitting in her tiny dressing-room which she shared in great discomfort with the leading character lady who was stout in person as well as in voice and appetite, and who smelled rather strongly of her favourite cheese and onion and ale suppers, felt the stirrings of excitement and let her spirits rise for the first time in many days.

The past few weeks had been wretchedly miserable; Felix had tried hard not to allow her to know how distressed he was at the way matters had fallen out, and made no complaints or comments; but she knew he was unhappy about his rift with Martha, and felt keenly for him. But there was nothing she could do and anyway, was deeply hurt herself by her own rift with Fenton.

He had been obdurate. She had tried all the ploys she could, tears and temper, even feigned illness, begging him to desist from this absurd case and to call off his hounds, the disagreeable Wormold brothers (whom she had not met but heartily disliked) but it made no difference. There was a hard glittering determination about him that was new to her. He was so unlike the Fenton she had known all her life and loved so dearly. The weak petulance that was so much a part of him and which had always been within her ability to soothe was quite gone. Now he just smiled thinly and remotely when she tried to talk to him, and refused.

And so for the past weeks they had been on silent terms. They spoke to each other no more than they had to, and sometimes not even then, and poor Mrs. Miller was almost in tears as they sat on each side of her table in Long Acre eating her food in total silence. In her bumbling well-meaning way she did try, one day, to persuade Fenton to 'stop your sulks, there's a dear boy, and be your own loving self again—' and was treated to such a blistering response that she burst into

241

tears and remained red-nosed and sniffing for several days thereafter.

At rehearsals it had been little better; Wyndham had done all he could to help, being cheerful and friendly to both of them, whether they responded to him or not, and acting very much as a plaster laid over the fracture between them. All of which made it possible for the play to go on rehearsing smoothly and successfully.

But until tonight there had been for Amy none of the lifting excitement that rehearsals ought to have meant. The smell of glue size as the scenery was put together, the sudden blazing of the lights on to newly painted flats which had once made her feel she was likely to float into the air with the joy of it all—none of that helped. Until now, feeling the lift of an audience beyond the stage, hearing the low roaring buzz of their voices and the tinny sounds as the strings and reeds of the little orchestra tuned up, when the theatre gave back its magic to her.

She hurried out to the wings, her costume carefully covered with a woollen shawl, and stood there peering out through the little peephole cut into the curtain. There below her in the pit she could see the more raucous section of the audience, the street loungers and young men of the town, the dubious women and the out-of-work actors coming to stare belligerently and critically at other more fortunate companions of their craft. They would take a lot of pleasing, she thought, and felt her resolve hardening in her. Please them she would. That was for sure!

Beyond them she could see the more respectable seats, with family parties and well-upholstered female bosoms and gold chain-embellished male bellies full of good living and success and she smiled a little into the folds of her shawl. They were never hard to please; she had no fears about *them*.

And then she saw him, Felix, sitting with his legs crossed in an aisle seat with his head bent over a playbill, and she felt her belly contract and then seem to lift at the sight of him. That so ordinary a young man, so square and undistinguished a young man, so *serious* a young man as this physician should have become so dear to her was quite, quite absurd. She, who had always been determined that she would grace the stage with her presence till the day she died, who had never intended to live the sort of dismal dull life her poor mother had, who was sure that all the glitter of success and riches were lying out there waiting for her, to feel so—it was madness. But it was a madness she needed and she smiled in the darkness behind the curtain, reaching out towards him with her love for him. And as though he felt it he lifted his head and seemed to look directly at her beyond the curtain and her eyes blurred with a sudden rush of emotion.

In the past she had needed spurious feeling to carry her through a performance. She would spend some hours before each appearance thinking herself into a part, feeling herself into the person she was pretending to be. And the method had always helped her, and given her the audience to hold in the palm of her hand.

But tonight her emotion was real. Out there in the darkness of the auditorium, for now the house lights had been lowered and the orchestra was rippling tinnily into its overture, was Felix. And the way she felt for Felix was the bedrock of her performance.

As the curtain rose to show the sparkling newly painted colours of a Cottage Interior and she felt the heat of the audience come pouring onto the stage, she took a deep breath and shed her woollen shawl and tweaked at the white muslin of her costume and then, as the sound of the music altered to give her her cue, she stepped out into the blaze of light that awaited her. She was Black-Ey'd Susan, as real and as important and as fascinating as any person who ever lived. The play was not tawdry silly melodrama tricked out with songs and dances, but a slice of reality, cut fresh from the life-pattern of a living person. That audience must feel every atom of it, she told herself.

And feel it they did. Long before the end of the first act Rourke knew he had a huge success. Wyndham, infected somehow by Amy's wide-eyed breathless sheer excitement, gave a performance of such virtuosity that even the stagehands looked up from their cribbage boards to applaud him. The actors with lesser parts caught the excitement too and slid into their roles with a zest that carried the indifferent lines over the absurdities of the plot with such panache that the audience thought it all exquisitely funny rather than foolishly banal.

And Fenton—he seemed to be a new person. He was as responsive to an audience and the feel of a living piece of theatre as was his sister, and he gave to his audience a picture of himself that they revelled in. He was funny, he was tender, he was stern, and he was kind. He was exciting and soothing and romantic and sombre; whatever any woman in that audience wanted to see in a hero figure she saw in him as he moved from one mood to another as smoothly as butter sliding over a hot plate.

The applause that ended the play was tumultuous. They shouted and stamped and clapped and even, Rourke swore afterwards, threw their hats in the air, though no one else could be certain they had seen anything quite so remarkable. But hats or not, the audience had clearly thoroughly enjoyed the scrap of nonsense which was 'Black Ey'd Susan' and next day tickets sold as fast as Rourke could hand them out. And Fenton and Amy, as well as Wyndham, found they were successes, were being talked of all over theatrical London, and were clearly set for a long run.

All of which, Amy thought, would heal the breach between them. She had tried to talk to Fenton after the curtain had come down on their splendid first night success, but so crowded was the green-room and the dressing-rooms with well-wishers and friends that she could not get near him. And by the time she got home to Long Acre, so weary that Felix had almost to carry her up the stairs, she was unable to wait up to talk to him. And next morning he was sleeping when she left the house to be fitted for additional costumes (for, Rourke said, with such an obvious success on their hands, the spending of some money on extras was more than justified) and it was not until evening when he arrived at the Royalty that she could get near him.

And even then she could not. Somehow he contrived to be always surrounded by other people, often women, who chattered to him and sometimes positively fawned over him in a way that made Wyndham laugh and Amy herself thoroughly irritable. He would nod and smile at her for clearly he thought it worth while to keep up a semblance of brotherly affection in public, but it was just not possible for her to get a moment alone with him to talk.

The first week slid into the second and then into the third, and still she had not been able to talk to him, and frustration rose in her, and even threatened to interfere with her performances, although now the play was carried along by its own success-inspired momentum, and she brooded over the situation a great deal.

She felt she could not talk to Felix about it; he had suffered enough, she told herself, because of her. After all, if she had not offered to go to Abel on Fenton's behalf, would he ever have thought of this mad scheme? She turned that thought round and round in her head, and at last decided that somehow Fenton must be made to see how absurd he was being, and how essential it was that he call off his case.

There was one point during the play when Fenton came on stage from the prompt side, shortly before she herself had to make an entrance from the opposite side. If only they could be together in the wings there for a few moments, she thought one evening, standing there watching him across the intervening brightly lit stage, would it not be possible to talk? In whispers, admittedly, but there would be no one there but themselves, and nowhere he could get away from her, for he would have to await his cue. If only she could change her entrance—

It was almost as though fate were conspiring with her. The next evening, as she came down from her dressing-room, she saw Rourke leading a large and handsome if overdressed young woman to a seat in the wings so that she could watch from there, and Amy, recognizing her as a regular visitor to the tavern across Dean Street where the company took its luncheon break during rehearsals, said smoothly to Rourke as he came back, 'It will be easier, I think, if I change the business slightly tonight, Mr. Rourke. I shall make my Act Two entrance from the prompt side, shall I? Then your friend will see clearly, and I will not be impeded in my movements,' and she smiled sweetly at him.

'Hmph—oh, well—no need for that at all, no need, for I'm sure ye'll do as well comin' on in the usual—'

'I will prefer it, Mr. Rourke,' she said still very sweetly.

'*Much* prefer it. All I need to do is change my line a little, about having come in from the dairy rather than from the barn. The audience will take it well enough.'

And she went, slipping away behind the rear flats leaving him embarrassed and muttering on the opposite prompt side. She was no prude, but she had made it clear from the very start of rehearsals that she was not one of the easy women of the theatre either; the whole company had early learned to treat her as a lady, and her insistence on this made her behaviour now fully understandable. Not that she would really have minded standing next to Rourke's bit of muslin—but it suited her now to play the superior lady. And as one of the most successful cast members of his successful play, she knew Rourke would not risk upsetting her.

And so she found herself standing in the wings waiting for her brother. It was an absurd way in which to have to seek a discussion with him, and well she knew it. In a way, had she been honest with herself, she would have seen it as a piece of play-acting in itself, for determined as Fenton was to avoid her, had she really been equally determined not to be avoided then talk to him she would. But there was a piquancy in arranging matters as she had, a theatricality that suited her well and she stood there in the wings, hugging herself tightly and shivering in the myriad backstage draughts as she waited for him.

He stopped and stared at her as he came round the edge of the flat, his stage gun in his hand, for this was the scene in which he did his extremely funny dance with a gun in one hand and a dead rabbit in the other, and glowered.

'What are you doing here? You enter from the other side,' he whispered harshly.

'I cannot. He has a female there,' she hissed back, and looked over her shoulder at the stage where Charles Wyndham was dancing with great energy to a jig tune, and Rourke's lady friend, her hat bobbing with green and crimson feathers, could just be seen in the shadows beyond. 'Do you see? So I'm entering from this side tonight.'

'Stupid—' Fenton said in a low growl and moved into position on the far side of her against the spare Squire's Castle flat waiting to be set for the next act.

'No, it isn't,' she said, still keeping her voice low. 'I wanted to talk to you.'

'Not now, idiot! This is no time or place for gossip. Be quiet.'

'I will not! If you refuse to listen to me, then I shall shout—yes I shall! I am determined you shall hear me!'

'You're play-acting,' he said scornfully and turned his back on her. 'I have no patience with you.'

'I am not play-acting! I'm telling you I will make a great noise and pother if you don't listen to me—and I can, you know—'

Unwillingly he turned and looked at her, and his eyes seemed to gleam a little in the dimness. 'Well?' he said after a moment.

'Fenton! We have a great success here, you know! I have no doubt that we will be offered bigger and better parts after this, and make a great deal of money!'

'I'm sure we shall,' he said. 'Is that all you wanted to say? Such a fuss to make to say just that!'

'You know it is not,' she hissed, furiously. 'I want to say— to tell you—oh, Fenton, please to forget this mad Will business! It is nonsense, you know it is! They will not give you that money so easily—'

'That is not what you said when you first suggested talking to old Lackland about it,' Fenton said and grinned sharply at her and from the stage beyond there was a clatter as Wyndham whirled into the fastest part of his jig. 'You thought it made sense *then*. So, does it not still make sense?'

'Of course it does not. Not going to court, and making such a scandal and—'

'Oh, scandal, scandal' he mocked, and even in his whispers she could hear the venom in this tone. 'Have you become so mealy-mouthed and virtuous that you care about scandals?. You were sharp enough about the Cabot uncles at home, and cared not a whit for *their* nice feelings, but these damned Lacklands and Caspars have but to beckon and you go running like some squirming lap-dog! They have robbed us—and I will not give in so easy, even if you will.'

'They have not robbed us, you fool! Lilith Lucas did not even know we existed when she made that Will! How could there have been any—any malice in it? She meant no harm to us, and nor did they. She left her money as she chose and it is wicked of you to upset everyone so, and to upset me and Felix and—'

Suddenly his eyes seemed to her to blaze there in the darkness, at the same time as the music coming from the stage changed its rhythm and became a heavy stamping that seemed to fill her with fear, and she took a step backwards as Fenton moved towards her, his hands held out as though he wanted to seize her and shake her.

The gun, which had been held loosely under his arm, shifted as he moved, and toppled forwards and she stepped even further back as it came towards her in the dimness, looking much larger than it was because of its foreshortening. Quite what happened then she was never to know. Whether the gun actually slid to the floor and tripped her up, or whether Fenton actually pushed her against the flat before which she was standing or whether her own emotion so overcame her that she stumbled and fell was a total mystery.

But fall she did. She seemed to herself to be falling a long way, down and down, and she heard rather than felt the sick crunch as the base of her skull hit the curling metal loop of a stage brace, one of the great metal hooks which held the flats safely upright with coils of rope pulled tautly around them.

The last thing she was to remember was staring upwards at Fenton's blank stare as first his face and then his body seemed to dwindle and shrink away to nothingness, until he was no more than a dot in the blackness. And then even the blackness was gone.

# CHAPTER TWENTY-FIVE

Had Amy set out to create the theatrical furore of the season she could not have had a greater success. Within minutes the theatre was in an uproar, for Wyndham finished his dance and after taking his well-earned applause gave the line that was Fenton's cue and which should have brought him leaping on stage waving his dead rabbit about his head. The delay in his entrance alerted the audience and a ripple of unrest moved across them and made Wyndham nervous. He repeated his line and looked sidelong into the wings of the prompt side.

And then quite lost his professional aplomb, for he could clearly see the white huddle on the floor that was Amy, with Fenton bending over her, and fear filled him in a great rush. He knew more than anyone of the animosity that lay between them and for one dreadful moment he thought Fenton had killed his sister, and he ran off stage to the wings as the audience, now thoroughly excited by the strange goings-on, began to mutter and some people got to their feet and craned their necks in an attempt to see more of what was happening.

The curtain dipped, rose again and then finally came down with a rush, and an agitated head appeared round it on the OP side and hissed something at the orchestra leader who at once lifted his arms and led his musicians into a spirited if ragged reprise of Wyndham's jig. But the damage was done. The audience knew perfectly well that trouble was afoot and their voices were raised harshly and someone started a slow handclap which swiftly spread through the entire theatre. The noise was tremendous.

Backstage there was no less of an uproar. Fenton was still

249

beside Amy but no longer staring at her. He was standing with his eyes screwed tightly closed and his face immobile, an expression Amy herself would have recognized but which thoroughly amazed everyone as they came running and looked at him and then down at the white-faced huddle on the floor.

It was Wyndham who knelt down beside her and with some trepidation began to examine her. Doctor though he had been trained to be his heart had never been in the profession and consequently his ability was limited, and well he knew it; but even he could see that Amy was badly hurt. Her eyes were only partly closed, so that a rim of white could be seen beneath her thick lashes, and her face was almost as pale as the muslin dress she wore. At the back of her head there was a soft spongy area and blood was matting her thick curls, and as his fingers moved gingerly across it his face became very still and his expression tight.

'What the devil is going on here?' Rourke came pushing his way through the cluster of actors and stage-hands standing staring all agog at the tableau before them. 'Christ take ye all to hell an' back, we're givin' a performance here! What d'ye think ye're all about? I'm over there on the OP side mindin' me own affairs and then I hear an uproar that's fit to—God in heaven!' He stopped and stared down at Amy. 'What's happened to her? Is she—oh, my God—'

'She's badly hurt,' Wyndham said curtly. 'We'd better get a surgeon to her, fast.'

'You're a surgeon, ain't ye?' Rourke said, and bent down beside Amy and awkwardly touched her cheek with his forefinger. 'Can't ye bring her round? We've a performance goin' on, and she's got another Act to get through. Get some brandy, someone. And some cold water—'

'You fool!' Wyndham said sharply and pushed him away, for now he was trying to shake Amy into consciousness. 'I'm a physician, not a surgeon, as well you know. The girl's badly injured, and needs operating upon. If she doesn't get help from a good surgeon fast, she could die! She's broken her head, damn it—'

From beyond them there came a faint keening sound and Rourke looked up and saw Fenton standing there, and now

250

his eyes were wide open and he was staring down at Amy with his face white and his eyes wide with terror.

'What happened, Lucas?' Rourke shouted, and he straightened up and took Fenton by the shoulders, shaking him, seeming to find some comfort in being able to be rough with him. 'What the devil happened to her?'

'They were alone rahnd 'ere,' the leading character lady said shrilly. 'Come rahnd 'ere she did, to make 'er entrance—'eard 'er wiv me own ears sayin' to you as 'ow she didn't want to wait there wiv your fancy piece and was goin' to come to this side to take 'er cue, an' there was just the two o' them 'ere on their own. 'E must 'ave—' she stopped as Rourke again shook Fenton and shouted, 'What happened, man? Tell me what had happened or I'll bloody well shake it out of you!'

'Will you listen to me, Rourke!' Wyndham roared. 'If this girl doesn't get help soon I can't be responsible for what happens to her! To hell with *how* it happened—we've time and enough for that—it's her care now that matters. Send at once for a surgeon, d'you hear me?'

'We could carry her to the hospital,' one of the actors volunteered and pushed his way through the knot of watching people. 'We could use one of the flats and with four or five of us we'd have her there in no time—'

'She's not fit to be moved,' Wyndham said curtly. 'We can get her as far as her dressing-room but that's as far as is safe. If we carry her through the streets in this condition—look at her, damn it!'

She was looking even worse now they could see her more clearly, for someone had brought a light into the little space there between the flats, and it was all too clear how white her face was and how unevenly she breathed and a silence fell on them which was underlined by the uproar and slow clapping still coming from beyond the curtain.

'I'll have to deal with them,' Rourke said distractedly. 'Oh, Christ, what did I ever do to deserve this? What did I ever do—move her then, Wyndham, and someone fetch the bloody surgeon and the devil take ye all for the useless gowks y'are!' and he went hurrying onto the stage and pushed his way through the curtain to make what soothing speeches he could at his now thoroughly enraged audience.

It took Wyndham more than fifteen minutes to get Amy lifted carefully on to a stage flat, carried to her tiny dressing-room and then transferred to the couch there, for he would not allow the smallest jar to disturb her. 'For,' he said portentously to the sweating actors who were doing the work, 'I believe she is bleeding within her skull and that could be the death of her. The least jolt and the bleeding could be greater than it is, and that would be fatal—fatal—'

Amy herself would have much enjoyed the whole affair, for they all threw themselves into her transport with an alacrity and an exaggeration that was very theatrical, carrying her to her dressing-room with such measured steps that they looked as though they were supers in the last act of *Hamlet*, bearing the Prince to his last sleep, and with an expression of such dolour on their faces that onlookers would have been forgiven for thinking their small burden was already long past any help.

All of which took time, and when Rourke at last came rushing backstage, having—much to his chagrin—been forced to promise his disgruntled audience a full repayment of their ticket prices, more than half an hour had passed since Amy had crumpled at Fenton's feet. And still she lay white and silent and breathing in an erratic and very alarming way.

'Well?' said Rourke. 'Where's this bloody surgeon ye was on about, Wyndham? What does he say has to be done?'

'Eh? I told *you* to send for someone!' Wyndham looked up from Amy's side where he was kneeling with his fingers on her wrist, checking her pulse rate. 'Do you mean you've not done aught about it?'

'I? *You're* the one who said she needs a surgeon—'

'But I told you—'

'I'll go.' One of the actors who had carried Amy to her room began to pull a coat on over his costume. 'I'd have gone sooner if you'd only told me—I'll go. Where to?'

'What?' Wyndham looked up at him, worriedly. Amy's pulse was fast and thready and anxiety rose higher in him. 'The Middlesex is nearest—no! No, not there. Laurence—he'll—oh, God, this is a sorry tangle!' He looked at Fenton sitting slumped in a corner of the dressing room where someone had led him and then pushed him into a rickety old chair.

'I'll send word there separately. Better go to Nellie's. She has friends there—ask for Caspar. He's a surgeon. Tell 'em you want Mr. Frederick Caspar. Tell him Miss Amy Lucas is the patient and to come fast, for she has a head injury which much alarms us. D'you understand?'

The man nodded and went, and the dressing-room slid into an uneasy silence, as Rourke and Wyndham stood beside the terrifyingly still figure of Amy and the leading character actress stood watchfully beside Fenton, staring down at him with an expression of great ferocity on her face.

Once or twice Wyndham looked up at her and then at Fenton with his brow creased. Clearly she was thinking as he was; had Fenton been the direct cause of Amy's injury? He was a short-tempered, self-indulgent man, as Wyndham well knew, and self-control had never been one of his qualities. And they had been at odds with each other, the brother and sister, as everyone knew. Could this be a matter for the law as well as for surgical aid?

It was a sobering thought, and Wyndham looked down at Amy and sighed softly. To have this happen in the middle of a successful run was heartbreaking; though, he thought optimistically, if she was well again soon and could return to the play, it could mean a better run as a result of the publicity. Especially if it turned out that her brother had been the origin of her misfortune.

He tried to push the thought away as ignoble, but it was not easy, any more than it was for Rourke who was chewing his large cigar very lugubriously and with a slightly glazed expression in his eyes as he tried to compute the cost of returning the money to tonight's audience as well as the cost of losing the next few performances, until either Miss Lucas was fit to return or a replacement had been found, for the understudy could not carry the part for more than a day or two at the outside.

All of which filled the little room with an atmosphere of gloom and tension which was almost palpable to Freddy when he arrived an hour and a half later. He had already left the hospital when the messenger seeking him had arrived, and he, since he had been so firmly told to seek Mr. Caspar, refused to tell the surgeon who was on duty what was amiss and went toiling away to Tavistock Square to find the man he had been told to seek. And since he was wearing his stage costume under his borrowed topcoat he had no money with him, and could not hire a cab (although he had tried, but was refused by the very suspicious jarveys who would not dream of taking up such a disreputable character, especially one who admitted he had no cash) he had had to walk all the way.

But Freddy Caspar had responded immediately to his breathless explanation and had come running out of the house imperiously to wave down a passing hack and swept himself and the messenger back to Dean Street with great expedition.

Now he pushed his way past Rourke, who glared at him, and knelt beside Amy, his fingers moving gently over her head as Wyndham explained as best he could what had happened.

'She has some neck rigidity—' Freddy murmured after a moment. 'Was there any when you first examined her?'

'I—I did not seek for it,' Wyndham said wretchedly. 'Damn it, I may have trained as a physician, but I am an *actor* by profession—I told them to fetch a surgeon at once, but—'

'How long ago did this happen?' Freddy asked curtly.

'About—when was it? Rourke?'

'Middle of Act Two,' Rourke growled, looking at his watch which he swung from his waistcoat pocket with his usual exaggerated gesture. 'That would have been about—oh, nine o'clock, give or take a few minutes—'

'It's gone eleven now—why have you waited so long?' Freddy snapped and glared at Wyndham.

'We thought word had been sent,' Rourke said. 'But it hadn't. Still, you're here now, so that's all right. Will ye get on and deal with the matter, damn it? Can't stay here all night like this—'

Freddy shook his head. 'I can't,' he said quietly. 'Perhaps, a couple of hours ago, as soon as it happened—perhaps—I could have found a way to stem the bleeding. But as it is—look.' He lifted Amy's hand, and the wrist instead of flopping as they all expected remained rigid and the fingers were set in a clutching stiff posture that looked very strange and alarming. 'There is pressure on the brain. She needs burr holes—'

'Oh God,' Wyndham said softly.

'Burr holes—what's burr holes?'

Freddy looked up at Rourke. 'An operation that makes small holes in the skull to release the blood that is being lost by the injury. It is essential if her life is to be saved.'

There was another sound from Fenton now, who was sitting bolt upright, at last showing some signs of animation.

'No—' he said and shook his head violently. 'No. You are wrong.' His voice was hoarse and again he shook his head as Freddy frowned and said abruptly, 'What do you mean, no?'

'No operations. Not by you. You hate her. You hate me. All of you—you all hate us. You shall not touch her—'

'Be quiet, Lucas!' Wyndham said and got to his feet and at the same time Fenton stood up and Rourke moved forwards as if to stand between the two men.

At which point there was a sound outside the door, voices raised in some expostulation and sharply the door opened and a sweating stage hand put his head round and said apologetically, 'I keep tellin' 'im as 'e can't come in, but 'e won't take no for an answer—'

And then the door opened even wider and Felix came in, softly but with a determination that was unmistakable.

'What is happening?' he said quietly. 'I went to Long Acre to meet Miss Lucas after the play as we had arranged and found Mrs. Miller in a great pother because neither of them have returned. What is happening? Will someone please—'

He stopped sharply and his face seemed to freeze as he saw beyond Wyndham and Freddy to the couch upon which Amy lay, and after a long moment he shifted his gaze to Freddy's face and said, 'What is it, Freddy?'

'Fractured skull,' Freddy said after a momentary pause, and turned his head to look down at Amy. 'I've only just arrived. It happened close on two hours ago, apparently.'

'Two hours—why did you not send for help sooner?' Felix's eyes shifted and his gaze rested on Wyndham's face. 'Charles?'

'The confusion—we each thought the other—dammit, Laurence, don't look at me like that! We did our best, but it was the middle of the performance! I was on stage, looked up, saw her lying there with Fenton beside her and didn't know what was amiss—I thought he had hit her and—well, never

255

mind that. But there was the noise and the audience. I did my best, believe me—'

'He shan't set a finger on her, Laurence, you hear me? Not a finger! They will kill her out of spite, those people, you know they will—' Fenton's voice was rising now and his eyes were glittering excitedly. 'If they lay a finger on her it will be *they* who hurt her, not me, they, you hear me? I did not hurt her—it is *they*. They hate her because they've robbed us and they'll try to hurt her—don't let them—'

'What is he talking about?' Felix said, and his cold clipped voice cut across Fenton's shrillness like a knife and he flicked his eyes over the rumpled costume and the painted face of the other man with a contempt that was unmistakable. 'Charles? Freddy?'

'She needs burr holes,' Freddy said shortly. 'To reduce the pressure. I said as much and that—he launched into that nonsense. Felix, I cannot do this operation. I am sorry, but I cannot. It has never been my field of endeavour. We must find another surgeon, quickly, who has experience of the brain.'

'Who would you suggest?' Felix was still standing in the middle of the room, making no attempt to come to Amy's side, but they could all feel the tension in him and the control he was maintaining as powerfully as though they were exercising it themselves.

'Well, there is Grandfather,' Freddy said. 'He was a pupil of Charles Bell, you know. He gained much knowledge of brain and nerve afflictions from him. Especially when my grandmother had her illness—the one of which she died. She had suffered a similar injury you see. He has gained much experience in this work over the years—'

'No!' Again Fenton's voice rose above theirs and now he sounded hysterical. 'That man shall never touch my sister! He will kill her as well as rob her, he will get his own back on me by injuring her, and it shall not be allowed and—'

Felix turned now, his square stocky body making one swift movement.

'Lucas, be quiet. You have done enough damage already. I do not know what happened here tonight but I have heard enough to make me suspect you are at the heart of it all. Make no more mischief and keep your mouth shut. You hear me?'

'He'll kill her, you fool, that Lackland man will kill her—he hates us and me especially and—'

It seemed to Freddy that Felix moved slowly, almost lazily, as he raised his arm and with one smooth movement bunched his hand and brought it round towards Fenton's face. It was not until he heard the crunch as Felix's fist made contact with the other man's jaw, and saw the way his head snapped back and his mouth fell open with shock that he realized just how much power Felix had put behind that blow; and Fenton crumpled and sat down and began to whimper softly, holding both hands to his face and rocking his body a little, like a frightened child.

Felix turned his head and looked at Freddy. 'Is she fit to be moved?'

'No. I am sorry, but I think no. It is a matter of—urgency now.'

Felix nodded, his face as inscrutable as ever. 'Then we had better send a messenger at once to Gower Street, to bring the old man. I will be glad if you will go, Freddy. He will come for you. Tell him—'

For the first time his voice cracked and he looked down at the silent Amy on her couch. 'Tell him it is important, please, Freddy. Dreadfully important—'

# CHAPTER TWENTY-SIX

Abel had been feeling less than well all day. It had been damp heavy weather, with the sun seeming to steam sullenly behind the clouds which filled the May skies, and this, he told himself, was the cause of the way he felt. Certainly the day had been effortful, seeming to drag on his feet as he made his way from ward to ward and from operating theatre to outpatient waiting-rooms. His accompanying students and nurses had seemed aware of his lassitude and been solicitous and helpful and this had infuriated him, making him so irascible that he shouted at students and snarled at nurses and made them sullen and slow. All of which was added to the effortful feeling with which he was filled; and so the afternoon had crept miserably to its end.

Altogether a disagreeable day and now he stretched his legs across the red turkey carpet before the drawing-room fire and glowered at his slippered feet. Across the hearth Maria smiled at him and he scowled back, but it did not matter. She had, with that brief smile, reaffirmed her care for him, told him that whatever happened at Nellie's, here in Gower Street all was peaceful and happy and always would be, while he with his scowl had told her that he knew of her care and needed it and was grateful for it and loved her too, in his fashion.

In the fashion of these years, that was. He stared down at his feet again, his face set in hard lines. Damn that chit of a girl and her unpleasant brother! Until she had arrived in this house, had stood there with her bonnet hanging about her slender throat by its strings, had smiled at him with those long-lashed eyes of hers, and bounced those coarse curls at him, he had managed not to think of Lilith Lucas for a long time. Not really think of her with any clarity, that is, for there were few days when some whisper of a memory of his first and most violent love did not come creeping tendril-like into his mind. But after seeing that girl the memories had been sharper, more urgent and much more painful. He had been able to see Lilith's face, to see it clearly with all its vivacity and loveliness as well as all its hidden cruelty and its casual glances full of invitation and laughter, but no love or real feeling.

He moved awkwardly in his chair and felt the heaviness that had been in his chest all day thicken and press outwards, making his left shoulder ache, and he tried to take a deep breath and muttered irritably as a pain shot through him.

Maria looked up, apparently as tranquil as she always was, but with watchful eyes. 'Are you well, my dear? Perhaps you should go to bed and I will bring you some hot—'

'Maria, you are behaving like a governess again! I do not want any of your pap and well you know it—'

'Well, old habits die hard. I was a governess long enough, after all. If you do not wish to take anything, well enough. But you look tired, my dear, and I think are less well than you will admit. And even Abel Lackland is a man, like others, and in need of care sometimes.' She bent her head again over her sewing and he looked at her smooth dark hair and thought confusedly, 'Good soul—best of all of them. Good soul—' And then moved awkwardly again, angrily wondering what megrim had entered into him tonight for, just for one fraction of a second, a brief memory of Dorothea, his first wife, had come swimming into his mind, and he had not thought about her for years. He must be reaching his dotage to slide into such ancient memories so fast. He was much too young for that—he knew men ten years older than he, at eighty-seven, who were not so mawkish.

Seventy-seven. It was odd to be seventy-seven, he thought, and looked into the fire. It seemed so short a time since he had been brought to this house, a scrawny hungry scrap of a creature, thick with dirt and stinking of the gutters, to stand here in this very room before this very fireplace and be stared at by the assembled company of well-dressed men and women, and that horse-faced hateful Charlotte and her timid stupid daughter, Dorothea—

Again he stirred and looked across at Maria. 'Am I wrong?' he asked her sharply. 'You would not say, one way or the other, on this issue. Am I wrong?'

She looked up at him and after a moment set her work down on her lap.

'The Will, you mean? I wondered when you would agree to speak of it. Are you wrong? I cannot say, Abel. I do not know why you decided as you did, you see. If you can explain that to me, then perhaps I can help.'

He stared back at her, and frowned. Even after twenty-seven years as his wife there were things about him she did not know, could never know. How could he ever tell her, with her smooth dark head and her serene round face and capable hands, of Lilith who had danced and laughed and made him love her so agonizingly and then derided him and hurt him so? How could he ever explain to her how sick he had been made at the money she had and the way she had obtained it? How could she ever help him deal with the pain of that?

'It does not matter, after all,' he said after a moment and returned his attention to the fire. And she looked at him with her eyes quite clear of any expression and then nodded her head and returned to her sewing; and if she was hurt or offended by his brusqueness she did not show it, any more than she ever showed any of her feelings.

The silence sank into them again, interrupted by the faint crackle of the fire and the distant sound of clopping hooves from the dark street below; so that when the cab came rattling to a halt outside their door and someone ran up the steps in great haste they were both very aware of the fact and lifted their heads to listen. And then, the doorbell pealed, and a few moments later Freddy appeared at the drawing-room door.

'My dear boy,' Maria said equably. 'I collect this is not a social call, but it is good to see you none the less.'

'Thank you, Grandmamma Maria.' Freddy was clearly very abstracted and his eyes were fixed on Abel. 'Grandpapa, I would not disturb you for the world, as well you know. I have refused to call you many times when you were needed. But this is important.'

'Well?' The old man looked up at him and would have smiled had it been in his nature to display such warmth, for he had a great affection for this square red-headed man who was so unlike him to look at, yet so very much a man of his own stamp.

'A fractured skull. There is clearly pressure building up, so there must be continued bleeding. The neck is rigid and there is spasm of the right arm and hand. The eyes show the signs, also, with a fixed unresponsive pupil.'

Abel was getting to his feet, slowly, for every movement seemed hampered by the heaviness of his chest. 'Where is the fracture?'

'The surface injury is at the occtiput. However, I suspect some movement of blood to the left hemisphere—'

'Aye. The right hand you say. Yes. Well, we had best get

there at once. Is the cab waiting? Good. Don't wait up Maria. I daresay I shall sleep at the hospital when all is done—'

'Not at the hospital, Grandpapa.'

'Eh? Not the hospital? Where then?'

There was a short pause, and then Freddy said deliberately, 'The Royalty Theatre in Dean Street. The patient is in her dressing-room there. She is Amy Lucas.'

Abel stood at the door of the dressing-room with his hands thrust deeply into his coat pockets and stared at them all, and they stared back. They saw a tall spare man with a face as hard and brown as a rock and cut into deep crevasses from nose to mouth; and he saw a tatterdemalion group of actors, clustering round a couch upon which lay a girl in a white dress, her dark hair curling on the pillow and her face white and expressionless above her hardly moving breasts as she took shallow jerky little breaths.

Again time seemed to slip sideways and backwards, and he was a boy again, a frightened apothecary's apprentice seeing a girl on a couch in a green-room, writhing in pain and crying; but this one was still, and now he remembered other dressing-rooms and other green-rooms, and he pushed the thought away and moved forwards, very deliberately. When he moved so the heaviness in his chest seemed to be less, and no one noticed that he was awkward in his movements. Deep in his surgeon's mind he knew he was far from well; that he ought to be a patient in another doctor's care—Freddy's for choice—rather than working over someone else at this time of night.

Someone else. He was beside her now and looking down and the face on the pillow was so young and vulnerable and so very delicate that for a moment he wanted to reach out and touch the softness of the cheeks. But he only turned his head and said harshly, 'Freddy!'

'Yes, sir,' Freddy said, and came to stand beside him, jerking his head at one of the actors as he did so. He at once brought a table close to the head of the couch and stood there waiting.

'This is Charles Wyndham, sir,' Freddy said softly. 'A physician as well as an actor. He too will help us. He will handle any anaesthetic that is required.'

'Hmmph.' Abel was examining the girl now, his hands with their square spatulate fingers moving slowly across her skull. 'None to commence. We shall need her responses to assess our progress.'

'You will operate without any painkiller, sir?' Wyndham said, and looked over his shoulder a little fearfully. But Fenton was gone, of course, and he breathed again. As long as the others could keep that fool out of the way until Amy was all right, things might work out well enough. But if she were to cry out in any sort of pain, was there not a risk that Fenton would break away from the two tired actors looking after him, and push Rourke, guarding the door of the dressing-room, out of the way, and come storming in? It was a daunting thought. 'No painkiller, sir?' he said again.

Abel merely scowled, but Freddy said softly, 'You need not worry, Charles. I too was alarmed when I first saw a skull opened without benefit of chloroform or ether but the patient in this state feels no pain, and will not until the pressure is released. And as soon as there is any response, we can let you give chloroform. So be ready. Don't worry—I'll guide you. Where is Felix? Did he not wait?'

Wyndham shook his head. He was watching Abel, who was with great deliberation taking instruments from his bag and arranging them on the cloth-covered table at the head of the couch. 'He said there was nothing he could do here, and trusted to you and your grandfather to take best care of her. He said she would need special nursing after, and went to arrange for that.' He shook his head then, a little puzzled. 'He's a cool man that one. I thought he was to wed Miss Lucas?'

'He is,' Freddy said shortly, as he too began to help arrange the instruments and dressings on the table. 'His care is of the wise kind. He works. He does not stand and weep. Felix is a good man, and never think otherwise.'

'If you have nothing better to do than talk, then do it elsewhere,' Abel said harshly. 'Where is a razor? I did not bring one—have any of you one about you?'

The little group of actors in the corner shivered and broke

up and the big woman who shared the dressing-room with Amy pulled out a drawer from her dressing-table and after some rummaging brought out a wide-bladed razor.

'If you're goin' to cut 'er up wi' that, I'm goin', she said loudly and her gin-thickened voice filled the room with truculence. 'I said as 'ow I'd 'elp but there's some things as mortal eyes shouldn't 'ave to look upon, let alone suffer, whatever you surgeons may say. If she's marked to die, well, let 'er die. All this cutting about—don't 'old with it, I don't—'

'Get out,' Abel said, without raising his voice at all, but it was icy enough to hit home, for the big woman reddened and opened her mouth to speak, but as she caught the sharpness of his glare she closed it again and shrugged her shoulders and went lumpishly to the door.

' 'Oo'd want to stay, as was a *normal* 'uman Christian? Poor little soul—she'll need prayin' for with you at 'er poor 'ead,' and she was gone, with the other actors following her, throwing scared glances over their shoulders.

And then there were just the four of them. Charles and Freddy, standing watchful and waiting at each side, and in the middle the silent figure of Amy. And looking down at her, very still and quiet, Abel Lackland.

'This is the girl who is seeking to take me to court?' he said suddenly and Freddy shook his head.

'No, sir, not she,' he said quietly. 'Her brother. He is a very different matter entirely. This girl is not like him. A little—well, flighty perhaps. And somewhat given to performing all the time, so that one can never be sure when she is being strictly honest. But then—' he smiled a trifle crookedly. 'My own dear Phoebe has been known, when very young, to be much the same. But like my Phoebe this girl is good and loving at heart, however captious she may seem at times. And Felix loves her dearly and is to wed her. But then, you know that.'

Abel nodded, never taking his eyes from Amy's face. 'Yes, I know. It is no affair of mine. Felix is Martha's concern and no blood of mine, after all. Not that I do not find the boy well enough—well enough—'

He looked up again and there seemed to be a faint air of appeal about him and Freddy looked back at him, puzzled.

He had never seen his grandfather anything but his own implacable self before tonight. And now he seemed to be somehow softer, more concerned about others and their feelings than he had ever been—

Almost as he thought it, Abel seemed to change. He pushed the heel of his hand briefly against his chest and arched his back and said harshly, 'Well, to work. I have not all night to waste here. Whoever the girl is and whoever is to wed her she needs treatment and she needs it very soon if she is to live. So—the razor.'

'I shall shave her, sir,' Freddy said and did so, as Charles held her head gently with a hand on each side of her face, and Freddy, with great care not to remove more than was strictly necessary, shaved away the coarse dark curls, moving smoothly and very delicately, until at last the extent of the injury could be seen.

It was big—an area of some two inches across—and the soft white skin was bruised and swollen. In the centre there seemed to be a depressed area, and gingerly, Abel touched it.

'Hmph. A splinter of bone there needs to come out, I suspect. Well, let's evacuate what clots we can and then we shall see better what's to do—'

The room sank into a silence as Abel started work. Charles stood ready at one side with a green chloroform bottle in one hand and a piece of soft gauze in the other, ready to administer his soothing anaesthetic at the first sign of need, and Freddy stood on Abel's other side, his cuffs pushed back up his arms, and with a small carbolic spray in his hand.

As Abel worked, he made swift darting movements which never impeded the older man's actions in any way, but which kept the area clean for him, removing the blood which oozed out steadily as the incision Abel was making was enlarged, and wiping a film of red pungent carbolic acid on all the parts the instruments touched.

The knife moved smoothly and easily, making a gently curving red line in the white skin, which opened and spread like a wave lazily breaking on a beach, and the little bleeding points sprang up in the depths of the incision, waiting for Freddy's darting touch with a swab of gauze to remove the blood so that they could start their steady ooze again.

As Abel worked on the curved cut became the edge of a flap, and widened and lengthened until he could fold it back upon itself and they could all see the bone beneath, pearly white and glistening, as softly pretty as the inside of a shell. Except for the centre of the revealed part, where the bone was displaced, curving down into a shallow well of damage.

'That is how an eggshell looks when it has been tapped with a spoon,' Charles said suddenly, and his voice cut across the quietness like a whipcrack, and Abel grunted and said, 'No doubt such poetical similes have a place in a physician's dictionary, sir—especially that of a physician who is also an actor. They have, however, no place at all in my language. That is a depressed fracture. No more and no less—Freddy, the spatula.'

Freddy reached for the instrument, a tongue of gleaming flattened silver, and moving with great precision Abel took it and very gently inserted the fine edge at its tip under the edge of one of the fragments of bone that could be clearly seen to be at the rim of the broken part.

Until now, Amy had not moved at all, or shown any sign of life, apart from her barely moving chest, and Charles looked down at her white face and lax mouth and tried to see the laughing wide-eyed creature who had so beguiled him with her 'speaking countenance' and could not, for this countenance spoke of nothing. It was as blank and as empty as the window high in the dressing-room wall against which the black night sky was pressing from outside.

But then, all at once, there was a change. As Abel eased the spatula upwards and forwards, so that the bony splinter was displaced enough for it to be grasped, Freddy leaned forwards and with a delicacy to match Abel's seized the tip of the bony scrap in a pair of forceps and eased it out; and at once a veritable tide of blood rose in the wound, a deep red swelling that for a moment seemed to mesmerize them all with its gleaming beauty.

And then, she moved. The head that had been so still seemed to jerk slightly, and the right arm twitched and Abel said urgently, 'Good man—now, a ligature. That is a big vein and if I can but find it, we may—that's it—the silk—aye—

no, I will use an aneurysm needle—the long tortoise-shell-handled one—well done—hold that head tightly in case it moves again—'

Freddy as well as Charles held her head, and Abel took a deep breath, and with one hand mopped away the blood which was now covering the whole exposed area. The heaviness in his chest seemed to be increasing, and he was finding it difficult to breathe as he should. 'Damned theatres,' he muttered, so thickly that even Freddy could not hear him properly. 'Never a breath of air—' and as he wiped the blood away once more, his eyes narrowed as he peered deep into the wound, searching for the source of the blood.

And then his hands seemed to him to work of their own accord. No longer was he directing operations; it was as though he was there just as an observer, lazily and comfortably watching those long flat-fingered hands moving so surely about their business. They passed the curved end of the aneurysm needle round and down into the wound and bore the thread triumphantly back again, and the other hand delicately took hold of the loose end of thread and seized the first with one curving finger and tied the two together, pushing the knot inwards and downwards with one smooth movement and then cutting the ends of the thread with the scissors those self-assured hands took from the table beside the couch. Then again threading and rethreading the long-handled needle, passing it down and into the dull pink brain beneath that translucent bone, and tying the same elegant little knots. The blood seemed to ooze less and less and finally stopped, and the hands stopped too and waited. And after a moment the girl on the couch moved and the right hand rose with a sort of beckoning movement and the white face seemed to crumple a little and take on a new expression.

'That has released some of the pressure, sir—oh, well done—' Freddy said breathlessly and Charles laughed suddenly, a silly little sound born of the tension that filled him.

'Not yet,' Abel said, and his voice now seemed to come from a long way away in his own ears and he shook his head irritably to bring himself back to his normal senses. But still everything seemed to be remote and dreamlike, and he stopped trying and let his hands do what they wanted to, and his head think as it wanted to. His concentration seemed to him to be fixed on his own chest, which was feeling heavier than ever, and more starved of air than ever.

'There is a clot to be removed.' The remote voice that he knew was his own seemed to clip out the syllables. 'That will complete the business satisfactorily, I hope—there will be no need for burr holes after all. If I can get it all out—be ready with the chloroform.'

His hands moved again, this time bearing a swab of gauze, and one finger slipped in under the edge of bone, again, moving slowly and delicately, and looped itself and emerged to show, nestling in the white gauze, the rich red fabric of blood which had tied itself together into a clot; and the figure on the couch moved and Abel heard his own voice say, 'Now. Chloroform now. She is emerging—the pressure is lessened and she will be conscious any moment—'

It seemed to go on and on and on. The gauze mask over the face swallowed up the chloroform and the erratic movements stopped as the breathing sounds that filled the room became loud and regular. Tirelessly the fingers that Abel knew were his but somehow seemed to have a personality of their own worked on, removing piece after piece of the clotted blood. Until at last there was no more, and the bleeding was quite stopped, and all there was to look at was pearly bone under a flap of skin.

'I think those ligatures will hold—but we must remove a little more bone to ensure her safety.' He listened to his voice with interest. It sounded very normal, he thought briefly. Yet I feel so very strange—so very strange. 'She will have a sizeable section of unprotected brain there, but she is young and hardy, and her scalp will heal well. If she learns always to wear her hair thick there, and to make sure she has no further blows, she will survive, I think. And if she bleeds again in the coming days, the skin will take the pressure and show us then the need for any further intervention—'

The voice stopped and as its conversational tones died away the hands began again, smoothing, replacing, sewing, until all was neat again. Until the girl on the couch lay with her eyes closed fully instead of showing a line of exposed white, and her cheeks had a faint flush of life on them. On the back of her head there remained only a neat curving scar covered with a white bandage which itself was almost hidden under the tangle of curls that fell over it.

Abel stood and stared down at her, and his face seemed to Freddy to be as it always was. Until he looked up and stared at him and opened his mouth to speak, and then shook his head. Alarmed, Freddy put out his hand to hold him, unheeding of the smear of blood his movement left on the older man's coat.

'Grandpapa, are you well? What ails you? You are very tired—'

Moving heavily, allowing himself to be led to the rickety chair at the other side of the small room, Abel shook his head.

'Not tired,' he said, and closed his eyes. 'Not tired—ill.'

'Grandpapa!' Freddy knelt down beside the old man, and reached for his wrist, looking urgently for his pulse. 'What— oh, my God—Charles!' And he managed to catch the tall spare figure as it slid sideways into his arms.

# CHAPTER TWENTY-SEVEN

She was swimming. Deep in the dark water of the pond in the Uncles' garden, down among the black and green of the weeds with little fishes touching her cheeks and stroking the hair from her forehead. Swimming upwards as the light behind her closed eyelids thinned, became a deep red and then a rich pink until at last she broke the surface and took a deep breath, and moved her body luxuriously among the weeds.

But she was not swimming among weeds. She was lying on a soft bed and a hand was stroking her hair from her forehead, and her limbs felt warm and floppy and deliciously relaxed. She was dreaming, not swimming, and as though to reassure herself that this was so, she made herself say it aloud, 'Dreaming,' she murmured. 'Dreaming. Dreaming, dreaming, dreaming.'

'Amy, dear child, do not agitate yourself. Just be still and all will be well.' Now her dream had changed and she was ill. She had the measles and was lying hot and miserable in a tangle of blankets, rolling her head from side to side on her pillow until the back of her scalp hurt quite dreadfully and gave her the headache and it was Mamma who was stroking her forehead and telling her to be still.

'Amy, keep still,' a voice said firmly, and, surprised, she remained still. That was not Mamma. Not that deep strong voice. That could not be Mamma.

'Mamma?' she said experimentally and opened her eyes. But the blaze of light was too much for her and she closed them again. 'Mamma?'

'Poor child—she remains delirious yet,' someone said. Someone she knew well, and she tried to recognize the voice but could not. Yet her own mouth opened and as the word came out she knew at last that she was neither swimming nor sleeping.

'Martha,' said Amy and again opened her eyes, and looked up. And this time she could see, for the light seemed less bright and she saw above her two faces—but it was at only one of them she looked directly. A square steady sort of face surmounted by short cut curling hair, and she felt her own face relax into a smile.

'Felix. Oh, Felix. I do have such a headache,' she said.

'Not delirious at all, Martha, not at all,' Felix said. 'A little confused, no more. She will sleep now and when she wakes all will be well. Sleep, my love, your headache will soon be gone, I promise you. Sleep now—'

And she did, turning her head obediently on her pillow and slipping luxuriously into slumber.

'Are you sure he left no message, Felix? Quite, quite sure?'

'Quite sure, my love. I am sorry, and I would have kept it from you if I could, but it was just not possible.'

She closed her eyes and leaned back against her chair, and tried to collect her thoughts. It was now almost three days since she had first woken in Martha's bedroom in the house in Bedford Row, three days during which she had recovered slowly from the two days of unconsciousness which had preceded them, three days during which she had slept a lot and eaten a little and felt her headache slowly recede until now it was only a faint heaviness above her brows. Three days of Felix coming to sit with her and hold her hand and talk desultorily of their future and how happy they would be. Three days of living only for the moment.

Until this morning when she had begun to remember some of what had happened and begun to ask questions. First, and most important, her injury. How had that happened?

Felix had looked sombre and then said quietly, 'No one is quite sure. You were waiting in the wings to make your entrance at the end of Act Two and Fenton was with you. He missed his cue, and when Wyndham looked to see where he was, he saw you on the floor with Fenton standing beside you. That is all anyone knows.'

'Fenton,' she had said and frowned, trying to disentangle her memories. She could see herself standing there in the wings, wanting to talk to Fenton, feeling the urgency of it; but that was all. At first. But then, as she tried, more and more came back to her, and she saw him come threateningly towards her and saw the gun slipping in his grasp, and frowned again.

'I think—I cannot be sure, but I think it was a silly accident with that gun—it is all so hazy. I tried to say something and he came towards me and he had the gun—the one he danced with—and it slipped and seemed—I cannot remember. Let us ask him, Felix. He will explain all, I am sure. Let him come to me, will you? I know he hates sickbeds and sick people especially since he broke his leg and was in the hospital but if you tell him I am almost well now, he will come to see me, I know he will. And then he will explain all.'

There had been a pause and then Felix had taken her hand

in his and held it warmly and tightly. 'I am afraid I cannot do that, Amy, my love,' he said carefully, 'for he has gone away.'

Her head had whipped round at that, making her wound hurt so that she winced. 'Gone away? Where? When? How do you mean? When will he return?'

Felix had shaken his head. 'I mean really gone away, my love! That night—while Abel Lackland operated on you, he went away—'

'Abel Lackland?' she said wonderingly. 'I do not understand. He did an operation upon me?'

'It was he who saved your life, Amy. There was bleeding in your brain, and he stopped it. He—he is a very remarkable surgeon.'

'Will he come to see me so that I may thank him? I surely should do that—'

Felix bit his lip and then shook his head. 'Later perhaps. There is much I have to tell you regarding him, but later. Let me tell you now about Fenton. He was left in a dressing-room with two actors to watch him, and—'

Again she had turned her head to stare at him. 'To watch him? But why?'

'Because it was believed by the people at the theatre that he had—well, that he was a problem. He was behaving very strangely and could not be trusted not to interfere with the care that was being taken of you. He tried to prevent your operation—and without it, my dear one, you would have died. So, with my—aid—he was put to wait in a dressing-room until you were taken care of. But—' he shrugged. 'It had been a long and exhausting time for the actors, I suppose. Anyway, they fell asleep, and Fenton walked out of the theatre, and went back to Long Acre—'

Her face cleared. 'Oh, well then, Mrs. Miller will know where he is and all about what is happening, for she took great care of us, especially of him and—'

'No, Amy. She cannot help.' He looked down at her hand held so closely in his, and with his other forefinger traced the shape of her thumb. 'I am sorry, Amy, but you must know the truth about this brother of yours. He is very—he is not a good person. He packed all his clothes, and he took all the money from Mrs. Miller's cash box in her little shop, and also some of her better trinkets. She had been awakened by the sound of his arrival there very early in the morning, she told me, but went back to sleep, and when she rose in the morning she found what had happened. She was—very distressed.'

Amy's eyes had filled with tears. 'Oh, no! Not Mrs. Miller! She is so kind, and so—she truly loves Fenton, I think. He could not have taken from her!'

'I am afraid he did.'

'And he left no message for me? No letter or—'

'No message at all.'

She had sat there with her head resting against the soft pillow at the back of her chair, trying to understand, trying to see Fenton rifling the cash box among Mrs. Miller's pots of paints and sacks of colours, trying to see him slipping out of the house in Long Acre with his valise in his hand, out into the dawn light without looking back, and all too easily the vision was there. And the tears spilled over onto her cheeks and she let Felix wipe them away tenderly.

Her weeping ceased after a while and she said weakly, 'I am sure he will come back.'

There was a silence and then Felix said a little harshly, 'The best way to get him back is for us to lay a complaint against him. Then the police will seek him and—'

'A complaint? Because of Mrs. Miller? Oh, Felix, please do not! Tell Mrs. Miller I will give her back all her money, but do not treat Fenton like a common thief!'

'But that is what he is, Amy. You cannot pretend otherwise. But no—not because of Mrs. Miller. Anyway, I have already dealt with that matter. She is not out of pocket, I do promise you. It is because of you that I think we should lay a complaint—'

'Because of me?' She opened her eyes wide. 'How can you mean?'

'If he was the direct cause of your injury, Amy,' Felix said carefully, 'then it is surely—'

'But how can the police be interested in that?' She was genuinely mystified. 'I cannot remember, exactly, I know, but whatever happened it was a silly accident and how can the police care about that?'

'If it was an accident.'

'But what else could it have been? You are being very strange, Felix!'

'I think not, Amy. It was well known about the theatre that he and you were—angry with each other. That there was some issue between you. I must tell you that Charles Wyndham believes that Fenton deliberately attacked you, and so do others who saw you there. And the fact that he has run away in this fashion confirms such suspicions, you must agree. It was feared that night that you would die. And I am afraid that Fenton, knowing himself to be the cause of your condition, did not wait to find out. He left you to save his own skin. That, I think, is the truth of the matter.'

Her face had become very white and she sat and stared at him with her eyes so fixed that he put out a hand to touch her cheek and said sharply, 'Amy? Amy—'

Slowly she shook her head. 'No. It is an infamous suggestion! Fenton, to deliberately—oh, it is impossible that anyone should think so! He is my *brother*! He loves me! He may be wild sometimes and selfish and so forth, but to do such a thing as to—oh, it is cruel in you to think it!' And again the ready tears of the convalescent filled her eyes.

He took her face between his hands and kissed her very gently. 'No more distress, Amy. I did not for a moment think you would agree with me—and do not really care that you do not. Whatever happened, I am not a vengeful man and care only that you are alive and well. It could have been—oh, it does not bear thinking of. I could have lost you, but I did not, and now I do not care a whit about Fenton. Only inasmuch as you do. You will be sad for a little while, dear one, but I hope you will forget him and not fret for him. For love him though I know you do, I have to say he is a ne'er-do-well, and is best as far away from us as possible. I will help you remember only the good things about him, and forget the rest. We will speak of him no more—no more at all! And we shall be happy, and think only of the future and not of the past.'

There was a long silence as she sat there and tried to take it all in, tried to imagine life without Fenton being there to worry about and look after and sometimes be happy with. But she could not, and shook her head a little in weariness and Felix kissed her again and repeated softly, 'We shall think only of the future and not of the past.'

And she nodded and tried not to think of Fenton. But it was not easy. It was not easy at all.

It was the next day before she could arouse herself from her preoccupation with Fenton and consider other matters, but by mid-morning she was feeling much stronger. She had woken to find Martha as usual at her bedside, ready to wash her and dress her wound and brush her hair and give her some breakfast, and she had enjoyed her ministrations and eaten a better breakfast than she had since she had been ill. And afterwards, when Martha came back to make sure she was comfortable she watched her moving quietly about the big bedroom with its rich mahogany furniture and rose-patterned wallpaper, tidying the marble-topped wash stand and rearranging the bowl of roses which were set upon a tallboy in the corner, and felt relaxed and comfortable and aware that she was mending fast. And smiled at Martha and said warmly, 'I do want to thank you, Aunt Martha. May I call you that? I feel that it is—well, right! We are to be related after all, are we not, and—'

Suddenly she went very red and stared at Martha who was standing now at the foot of the bed, her hands folded against her brown merino gown and her face very composed.

'I—I think I am being very foolish,' Amy managed after a moment. 'I keep forgetting things. Before—before this happened and I was hurt—I thought that all was well about Felix and me and—but it is not, is it? Or did I dream it? I suddenly thought—Felix had gone away from here, to live at the hospital, and you and he—oh, *did* I dream it? Is it my stupid head that is making me say all the wrong things? I felt so good seeing you there and was so grateful and wanted to say it and now I do not know what I should say—' and again tears threatened to overtake her.

Martha moved round the bed and came and sat down beside her, and put one hand out to rest it on Amy's.

'No, my dear, you are not mistaken. Before you were ill,

Felix and I *were* in disagreement. It was my fault. Entirely my fault. And I much regret it.'

'Is it no longer so now?' Amy said timidly. 'I cannot quite remember why—what the trouble was. It seems as though things before I was ill are floating in my mind and when I try to hold on to them I lose them or they melt away. It is very strange. But if the trouble is gone, I am glad—'

'It is gone,' Martha said soberly. 'As far as Felix and you and I are concerned, that is. I know now that the matter of this case at Doctors' Commons was not your doing. It was entirely your brother's—'

'My brother—' Amy said and her face crumpled.

'No, please, do not distress yourself. It is sad enough that there have been these past troubles. Let us now forget as much as we can of them—'

'Doctors' Commons,' Amy said after a moment, and her eyes glazed as she tried to remember. 'Doctors' Commons. I cannot—'

And then she remembered. In one great rush she remembered it all. The case that Fenton was bringing, the split in the family, the argument that Martha and Felix had had about her, all of it came back in a great sickening flood of knowledge and she turned her head towards Martha and said impulsively, 'Oh, I am so sorry—so dreadfully, dreadfully sorry! If I had ever dreamed Fenton would cause such—well, I would not have started the searches at all. But I did so want to know about who I was, and where I started from, and to know about my grandmother was so very important to me! And that it should have caused all this misery—oh, it is all so dreadful!'

'Not so dreadful,' Martha said soothingly. 'Not entirely! It is sad of course that you are ill, but you are mending well, and that is what matters. And Felix and I have made our peace, I am happy to say, and will never again quarrel so bitterly, I am sure.'

She bent then and kissed Amy's forehead. 'And we shall be friends. I must tell you, my dear, that my besetting weakness is jealousy, and when I saw how dearly Felix loves you, I think I was overtaken for a while with it, for I care so deeply for him. He is very precious to me. For his father's sake as well as his own.'

'His father's sake?' Amy said and blinked. Her memory was hazing again. She knew she had heard something of Felix's father, but she could not remember what. Something to do with the war in the Crimea. She shook her head. 'I cannot remember.'

'I will tell you all about it. One day. When you are well.' Martha smiled a little crookedly. 'After all, when you and Felix have children he will be their grandfather, will he not? It will be important to you to know of your children's grandfather, just as it was important for you to know all about your own—'

Amy blushed rosily and smiled, and Martha smiled too and they sat in a companionable silence for a long moment. Then Amy stirred and said doubtfully, 'That silly Will business— the case. Now that Fenton has gone away, will all that end?'

Martha's face clouded. 'I cannot say, my dear. I wish I knew. Felix has today gone to see what can be done—but I fear that the wheels of these things, once set in motion, are like the juggernaut and cannot be stopped.'

'Oh, I hope it can,' Amy said fervently. 'It would be *so* dreadful if all this were to go on upsetting everybody—so dreadful.' She paused and then went on tentatively, 'I wonder—Aunt Martha, now that Fenton has gone and I do not wish this hateful case to continue, cannot the matter be settled by your father? It is he who encouraged Fenton, I fear, by refusing to defend the case. It—I think it made him believe there was some justice on his side. Cannot you ask your Papa to settle the matter with his lawyers? I am sure he can, if he so wishes, and if *you* ask him—'

There was a long silence as Martha sat with her head bent and Amy bore it as long as she could and then said more firmly, 'Aunt Martha? Did you hear what I said? Could you not ask—'

'I heard you. I was wondering whether to tell you. But I think—well, you are almost one of the family now, and have a right to know. He is ill, Amy. My father is very ill and we are not sure if he will live. I go there to be with him every

276

afternoon, and Abby and Phoebe are·there every morning—but he does not seem to know us. It is all very—'

Amy was sitting bolt upright in bed. 'Ill?' she said and her voice showed her amazement. 'But how can that be? Felix said that it was he who saved my life. He operated upon my head—' and gingerly she raised her hand and touched the bandage that covered the scar '—and stopped the bleeding that would have ended my life. How can he be ill?'

'He collapsed after he had completed your care, Amy. Freddy was there, fortunately, and he took him at once to Nellie's, but—' She shrugged. 'They do all they can. He is suffering they say from angina pectoris and fear that another such attack as he had the night of your injury might be the last. It—I believe there must be more than that however, for he behaves differently to the people I have known with that affliction.' Her eyes shadowed suddenly. 'Felix's father died of that. And my father seems to be so different. But there is no physician we can find who can help. They have all come to his bedside, for he is a much respected man, my father.'

She lifted her head with a sudden childlike gesture of pride. 'He started as a gutter boy, and now every great physician in London comes hurrying to care for him. He is a very remarkable man—Amy, what are you doing?'

'I am getting up.' Amy had turned and was sitting now with her feet out of the covers and edging her way to the far side of the bed, and Martha jumped to her feet and ran round to the other side to stop her.

'Are you quite demented, you foolish child? You must stay there for at least another week! You may sit in a chair in the afternoons, but you may not go walking about until—'

'Aunt Martha!' Amy sat with her hands clenched into fists which were thrust deep into the mattress to support her, and she was holding herself very straight. In her white lace-trimmed nightgown and with her crumpled hair she looked about five years old. 'I am going to see him. I cannot sit here being looked after by you when he who saved me lies on a sick-bed himself!'

'Well, now, my dear, that sounds very interesting and indeed dramatic,' Martha said mildly. 'But it is not very commonsensical, is it? You will find if you set your foot to the ground that you are unable to support your own weight. So what use will you be if you do get up? None at all.'

Amy reddened. 'I know I am sometimes dramatic, Aunt Martha,' she said with great dignity. 'But you will find that I mean what I say, however contrived it may appear to your eyes on occasion. I am quite serious now and I would wish you to believe that I am. I know that I am weak, but I am not so very large, after all. Is there not a footman who could carry me to a carriage once I am dressed? And carry me to your father's bedside when we arrive there? It is my request that such arrangements be made.'

Martha shook her head and opened her mouth to speak but Amy stopped her.

'Aunt Martha,' she said quietly. 'You said he is not expected to live. I would wish to say farewell to him, as well as to thank him. You cannot deprive either him or me of that. Can you?'

Martha looked at her for a long moment and then, slowly, turned and moved to the fireplace and lifted her hand to ring the bell.

'I will send for Edward to come and carry you down,' she said quietly. 'In half an hour, then? We should be able to have you ready by then.'


# CHAPTER TWENTY-EIGHT


The night-time sounds of the hospital seemed to wrap them round, acting as a distant barrier beyond the circle of light in which his bed lay. Amy could hear the clatter of dishes from a kitchen not too far away, and a rattle of wheels as someone pushed a trolley along the stone-floored corridors. There was a sound of voices, too, subdued but busy, and she turned her head to see if she could see any of the other men in the ward, but she could not. There were screens drawn up to each side of his bed, and the light that came from the gas bracket above deepened the shadows beyond. But she could feel their presence even if she could not see them, those other men. They were anxious and concerned and talked softly to each other of their worry about their fellow-patient and in so doing shared it with her.

At first she had been horrified to discover that the old man was lying in a bed in the middle of a ward full of other patients, and had said as much to Martha who walked beside the tall footman who was carrying her, but Martha had merely smiled gently.

'He made Nellie's, my dear. He *is* Nellie's. When he became ill it was to Freddy's mind the only place to bring him. My father would himself wish it so.' She smiled then. 'I can imagine his rage if anyone ever dreamed that he should be anywhere but in one of his own wards. To be among the patients he cared for—that would be all he would ever require.'

They had sat there, between Maria and Abby, all afternoon. Others had come and gone, Oliver and Phoebe and young Cecily and then Freddy, and after they had gone Isabel and Sarah had come with Gideon. Amy had looked hard at Isabel, trying to see beyond the marble smoothness of her face to what deeper store of feeling might be there, to see if she showed any regrets about Fenton, for it was clear to Amy now that the whole family knew of his defection. But Isabel just looked back at her gravely and showed no hint of any expression other than natural concern for her grandfather, and made no special move towards her, and Amy sighed, and looked away. Poor Fenton, she thought confusedly. Poor darling Fenton, to have chosen so chill a creature. Perhaps all of it is in part her fault—poor Fenton.

At six in the afternoon, as the sunlight lengthened across the ward floor and the men sat up in their beds wrapped in red blankets to drink their hot soup and eat their supper bread, Abel seemed to rouse himself for a little while.

He had been lying still and remote, little more than a vague hump amid the bedclothes, his chin and nose jutting up to the ceiling and his eyes beneath his heavy white brows tight closed. But at six o'clock his eyes opened and his head turned as though he were seeking someone, and Abby rose to her feet and came to one side of him, and Martha to the other while Maria remained in her chair beside his pillow, never taking her eyes from his face. Amy sat and looked at them all, feeling suddenly very much an interloper and wishing she had not come. She was tired now and the back of her head was aching; but then Abel spoke and she forgot her own feelings as she leaned forwards to listen to him.

'Where is she?' he whispered. 'Where has she gone?' and he looked up at Abby with an appeal in his eyes which seemed so foreign to the man that Amy suddenly felt her eyes prickle. It was as though a child inhabited the spare body of the dying man, an eager hungry child searching for someone or something very important.

'Who, Papa?' Abby said quietly. 'Who is it you want to see? We are here, Martha and I. And Maria, of course. Who is it you want to talk to?'

He turned his head on his pillow and now Amy could see how changed a man he was from the one she had seen in all his imperious command in the casualty room that long ago day of Fenton's injury, and in his own home just a few short weeks ago. His temples had become sunken now, and his nose looked as sharp as if it had been cut out with a razor. The crevasses in his cheeks which had seemed so hard looked soft and papery, mere hollows between the high cheekbones, and that jutting narrow nose. He had lost so much of his essential energy that now the true state of the man beneath could be seen, and it was painfully, heartbreakingly clear. He was old and very very tired.

'I wish she would not hide away so,' he said fretfully and stared at Maria as though he had never seen her before, and she sat there and looked at him with her eyes opaque and her face a mask of misery and said nothing. 'Tell her she should come back to me,' he said and then closed his eyes and Martha leaned forwards and with her handkerchief wiped his forehead, which had become damp with sweat.

He opened his eyes again and reared up a little, and moving

with all the smoothness of the experienced nurse Martha again leaned forwards and slipped a hand beneath his head and with a lift of her chin indicated to Abby that together they should pull up his pillows so that he could sit more upright.

They settled him back again, gently, and now he could see more clearly and his eyes seemed to fix on Amy, still sitting quietly at the foot of his bed, in an armchair specially brought for her from Freddy's office.

'Why did you not tell me you were there?' he said fretfully after staring at her for a long moment, and closed his eyes. 'I knew you would come. But you should have said you were there.'

Martha and Abby turned to look at her at the same time, and suddenly Amy wanted to laugh, for they looked so absurd, so very much alike with their jerky movements and their concerned faces, but even as the bubble of laughter reached her lips it changed itself into a sob and she found her eyes had once more filled with those silly weak tears and she shook her head and put her hands to her face.

Abel was now lying as still and quiet as he had been all afternoon and after a moment Martha came and sat beside her and patted her hand comfortingly.

'Don't fret, my dear. He is very ill and his mind is wandering. I daresay he thought you were someone else. It happens often when people are dying. Don't be alarmed. He means no harm.'

Amy tried to speak but could not, and sat there with her face still in her hands trying to control her tears and after a while she felt Martha move away from her side and wept harder, needing so much to feel the touch of a warm and comforting hand on hers. And then Felix was there. He did not have to touch her nor speak to her; she felt him come round the screen and lifted her tearstained face towards him and managed to smile tremulously.

His brows cracked down into a frown. 'I did not believe it when they told me at Bedford Row that you were here. How comes this, Martha?'

'I wish to say my thanks and farewells, Felix,' Amy said, and looked at Martha for confirmation. 'That is so, Aunt Martha, is it not? You tried to prevent me, but I wanted to show him that I—that I am not like my brother.' And she lifted her chin at Felix and looked at him challengingly.

There was a short pause as he looked at her and then at the figure in the bed, and then he came and crouched beside her chair and looked searchingly into her face, until, as if satisfied with what he saw, he nodded and smiled at her and set his hands on each side of her head and kissed her brow, and it was as though the atmosphere lifted for all of them, for Abby and Martha smiled indulgently at them both and Maria too raised her head and smiled gravely. And once more they settled themselves into a watchful group about the bed and silence slid among them again as they sat and waited.

As the evening thickened into night Amy dozed fitfully, her head against Felix's arm as he sat perched on the side of her chair, waking occasionally as other members of the family came to join them, and then sleeping again.

At midnight Felix insisted that she should go to lie down and sleep properly. 'For,' he said, 'nothing, I think, will happen for some time yet. If there seems any sign of his sinking further, or rallying, I promise you I will call you. But now you must rest. And so must you, Aunt Martha. I shall arrange it.'

And so he did, finding a room with two small beds in it upon which each of them curled up fully dressed and slept as soundly as if they had been in beds as familiar as their own. Until five in the morning, when Amy woke abruptly to find Felix sitting on the side of her bed, his hand on hers.

'I promised to call you, so I have,' he said quietly. 'He is sinking rapidly, my love, but is conscious now, I think, if you wish to speak to him—'

'I'll come now,' she said, and struggled to get to her feet, but he shook his head and with one smooth movement slipped one arm beneath her knees and the other behind her shoulders and lifted her as easily as if she had been an infant, and carried her, following Martha who had woken as he came in, back to the ward.

She was never to forget that jolting little journey. Up a staircase carpeted with calico over drugget, past closed mahogany doors to the main men's ward, and then down the centre of the long room passing beds in which patients slept, some noisily and some silently, on each side; the smell of his jacket against her cheek, the strength of his arms about her—it was all unreal and yet so vivid that it imprinted itself upon her mind indelibly.

He was sitting bolt upright in bed when they arrived, and Felix set her down gently into the armchair which had remained there waiting for her return. They had propped him up on pillows and in the soft gaslight his eyes glittered and his hollow cheeks seemed to be as dark in their depths as the eyes themselves. But in spite of his obvious difficulty in breathing, in spite of the clear evidence of his failing life he was somehow filled with an energy that flowed out to encompass them all. There lingered behind the shell of the old creature who sat against the pillows the figure of the vigorous powerful man he had been in his prime, and also the handsome green-eyed boy who had worked and sweated and struggled to build himself and his hospital out of the same unpromising gutter materials.

And further back still there stood another boy, the child who had been born in the filth and stench of Seven Dials, who had been pickpocket, burglar, liar and thief before he was ten years old, yet had had the wit and the strength and the sheer granite will to create from such beginnings the life he wanted for himself.

Amy looked at him and saw it all, even though she had never known him in those days. She saw the young heart that had been there and her own lifted in acknowledgement of it and she raised her chin and smiled at him, a brilliant glittering happy smile and she said softly, 'I wanted to thank you. I wanted to thank you for all you did for me, and to tell you how sorry I am for all that went wrong—I never meant to hurt you, I truly did not. Please, can you believe that?'

The old eyes looked back at her, green and narrow and very cold and slowly and tremulously the dry lips lifted and parted and the chin came up and he said in a clear, thin voice, 'Of course I do! Of course I do. I always knew you loved me best. I always knew.'

He closed his eyes and lifted his chin once more almost as

though he was triumphing over some secret doubt that once had filled him, and again his lips quirked and moved into a smile.

'Dear Lilith,' he whispered. 'I always knew—I always did—'

He did not open his eyes again, but died an hour later with his wife and his daughters and some of his grandchildren clustered round him. They were weeping, but he was not. He was still smiling.

On June 30th 1867 the case of Lucas Versus Lackland was brought before Judge The Right Honourable Sir James Plaisted Wilde at Doctors' Commons in Westminster Hall, Dr. Bayford being the Registrar and George Thomas Billings the Crier. It was immediately discharged, on the grounds that the plaintiff had disappeared and the defendant had died, so there was no case to argue or answer. Costs were awarded against the absent plaintiff, for which his solicitors, Henry and Horace Wormold, were held responsible.

And on July 22nd 1867, the day that Probate was granted to the Will of Abel Lackland, Apothecary and Surgeon of London, deceased—a Will that left the considerable property of which he died possessed to his widow, Maria Lackland— Miss Amy Lucas of Boston was married to Mr. Felix Laurence, physician of London, at All Souls' Church, Langham Place.

As Mr. Laurence and Miss Lucas both agreed, it seemed a fitting day.

# THE RUNNING YEARS

## Claire Rayner

She was born in 1893, in the slums of London. The daughter of immigrants, the descendants of exiles, she was part of a people doomed to wander, forever strangers in the lands they had chosen as home.

But Hannah Lazar was different. She was born and bred a Londoner, and London was where she belonged. As Strong-willed as she was beautiful, Hannah would uproot herself from the gloomy poverty of her parents' lives to enter a world of elegance and wealth. As her ancestors had journeyed from land to land, with only their own resilience and determination to help them survive, Hannah would move from the slums of the East End to the salons of Mayfair, to a life that she could call her own.

*The Running Years* is Claire Rayner's most powerful and spectacular novel to date, a breathtaking testament to the human spirit – a richly dramatic and intricately woven story that traces the fortunes of two Jewish families from the razing of Jerusalem in 70 AD through two thousand years of violence, love and change.

'A huge canvas, this, with powerful characters and a gripping story' *Woman's own*

'A feast' *Yorkshire Post*

# HESTER DARK

## Emma Blair

Even to a girl from the slums of Bristol, the streets of Glasgow were inhospitable and grey; the wealth and splendour of its mansions cold and heartless. But for Hester there could be no turning back – she would make this cruel city the home of her dreams.

Everyone said that Hester was lucky. Lucky to have a wealthy uncle in Scotland who was willing to take her in. Lucky to have all the advantages that his money could buy. But Hester's new, bright world held dark secrets, jealousies and fears. And no one had spoken of the woman who would despise her for her beauty and her independence – and the men who would buy her soul and call it love.

# BESTSELLING FICTION FROM ARROW

All these books are available from your bookshop or news-agent or you can order them direct. Just tick the titles you want and complete the form below.

| | | | |
|---|---|---|---|
| ☐ | THE COMPANY OF SAINTS | Evelyn Anthony | £1.95 |
| ☐ | HESTER DARK | Emma Blair | £1.95 |
| ☐ | 1985 | Anthony Burgess | £1.75 |
| ☐ | 2001: A SPACE ODYSSEY | Arthur C. Clarke | £1.75 |
| ☐ | NILE | Laurie Devine | £2.75 |
| ☐ | THE BILLION DOLLAR KILLING | Paul Erdman | £1.75 |
| ☐ | THE YEAR OF THE FRENCH | Thomas Flanagan | £2.50 |
| ☐ | LISA LOGAN | Marie Joseph | £1.95 |
| ☐ | SCORPION | Andrew Kaplan | £2.50 |
| ☐ | SUCCESS TO THE BRAVE | Alexander Kent | £1.95 |
| ☐ | STRUMPET CITY | James Plunkett | £2.95 |
| ☐ | FAMILY CHORUS | Claire Rayner | £2.50 |
| ☐ | BADGE OF GLORY | Douglas Reeman | £1.95 |
| ☐ | THE KILLING DOLL | Ruth Rendell | £1.95 |
| ☐ | SCENT OF FEAR | Margaret Yorke | £1.75 |

Postage _____

Total _____

ARROW BOOKS, BOOKSERVICE BY POST, PO BOX 29, DOUGLAS, ISLE OF MAN, BRITISH ISLES

Please enclose a cheque or postal order made out to Arrow Books Limited for the amount due including 15p per book for postage and packing both for orders within the UK and for overseas orders.

*Please print clearly*

NAME................................................................................

ADDRESS...........................................................................

..........................................................................................

Whilst every effort is made to keep prices down and to keep popular books in print, Arrow Books cannot guarantee that prices will be the same as those advertised here or that the books will be available.